Angels of Bastogne

Angels of Bastogne

A Remembrance of World War II

Glenn H. Ivers

A PEACE CORPS WRITERS BOOK
2022

Angels of Bastogne
A Remembrance of World War II

Copyright © 2022 Glenn H. Ivers and Glenn Ivers, Jr.
All rights reserved.

Printed in the United States of America by Peace Corps Writers of Oakland, California. No part of this book may be used or reproduced in any manner whatsoever without written permission except in the case of brief quotations contained in critical articles or reviews.

For more information, contact peacecorpsworldwide@gmail.com. Peace Corps Writers and the Peace Corps Writers colophon are trademarks of PeaceCorpsWorldwide.org.

Registered, Writers Guild of America
Author's website: angelsofbastogne.com

Illustrations © Glenn Ivers Jr.
Situation Maps courtesy of U.S. Army
Cover design Glenn Ivers Jr.
Back cover photo Glenn H. Ivers

ISBN-13: 978-1-950444-39-7

Library of Congress Control Number: 2022900277

First Peace Corps Writers Edition, January 2022

I dedicate this book to Laura,
the best wife and mother in the known universe.

Contents

Illustrations

Acknowledgments

Many thanks to family members and friends, too numerous to list here, who critiqued multiple drafts of the book. I hope that all our efforts bring honor to Jack Prior, Renee Lemaire, Augusta Chiwy and the soldiers and civilians described in Angels of Bastogne.

Angels of Bastogne

The Ardennes

To Antwerp

Brussels Leuven

The Netherlands

Aachen

To Flanders

Liège

Hurtgen Forest

River Meuse

Henri Chapelle Cemetery

Germany

Belgium

Namur

Werbomont

Wereth

Saint Vith

Dinant

Marche

The Ardennes

Houffalize

Clervaux

Bastogne

Hosingen Bitburg

Hamiville

River Our

Neufchateau

The Ardennes

Luxembourg

River Meuse

Sedan

Arlon

Luxembourg City

North

Merl

France

Thionville

Reims
Mourmelon

Remeling

Metz

Late Winter 1994

As another harsh Central New York winter loosens its grip, fog saturates a stand of pine trees. With the midnight hour approaching, a light from an attic window nearby pierces the darkness.

Inside, an elderly man stoops amid rafters and searches among covered furniture and dusty boxes for his old army trunk. Finding it, he drags it to a chair and sits down heavily.

While he catches his breath, Jack Prior reflects upon the tumultuous winter fifty years before when he served as a battalion surgeon with the 10th Armored Division in Patton's Third Army in 1944, during what became known as the Battle of the Bulge. The events that led up to the battle are well documented: the Allied invasion of Europe at Normandy on June 6th of that year; the rout of German forces across France, Belgium, and Luxembourg during the summer and autumn of 1944; and the unexpected German attack through the heavily-forested Ardennes in Luxembourg and Belgium in December that caused a vast bulge in the Allied lines and lent the battle its name. The counteroffensive was Hitler's all-out gamble to break through thinly-held American lines; capture transportation hubs and fuel depots to accelerate his heavily armored forces; cross the River Meuse; retake the vital seaport of Antwerp; split the Allied armies in the field; and sue for peace on the Western Front. Had he achieved those objectives, he could have turned his full attention to the Russian bear clawing at the Third Reich from the east, and the war might have had a very different ending.

Even fifty years on, Jack marvels at how a campaign so overwhelming in scope and impact could continue to feel as personal as the blood of dying men in his care during the heat of the battle. He involuntarily wipes his hands on his pantlegs as he gazes beyond the attic into the distant past.

The town of Bastogne, Belgium, is offering a year-long commemoration on the 50th anniversary of the Battle of the Bulge. Though some of the veterans will visit on the actual dates marking the battle's beginnings during December, Jack has opted to attend the June events. A professional life spent in America's snowiest city and the prospect of gathering in shirtsleeve weather tipped the scale for him.

With his plans finalized, Jack was drawn upstairs to the battered case stuffed with World War II memorabilia. Though the hinges protest, Jack coaxes the rusty lid open. Straight off, he finds a roll of documents and flattens them on his lap. They turn out to be time-yellowed maps showing the disposition of both hostile and friendly forces in the Bastogne area from December 20-26, 1944, when the Germans gained a stranglehold on the town. Since he was an officer, Jack received the maps daily. But as a physician, he was powerless to act on the information other than to prepare his aid station and scant medical staff for the inevitable, daily flood of wounded.

Jack studies the maps in sequence and tracks German forces in overwhelming numbers and armament attacking from the east and flowing north and south of Bastogne as far fewer American forces contract into a tight defensive perimeter on the outskirts of town. Jack is struck by how clear and simple it all seems from a birds-eye view. Little symbols representing German and American armored, infantry or paratroop divisions, each with roughly ten thousand men, maneuver in and around Bastogne. War must have seemed like a board game to the generals calling the shots from far behind the front lines. But what of the experiences of the ordinary foot soldier and, for that matter, the civilians caught up in the struggle? For them all was chaos and confusion.

Jack reaches the map labeled "Situation 24 Dec 1944" and lingers long over it as his eyes begin to water. Though it was Christmas Eve, it was anything but a silent night as destruction rained down upon Bastogne. A deep breath and slow release betray Jack's continuing amazement, even after fifty years, that he survived that fateful night.

Outside the attic, the temperature is plummeting, just as it did in Bastogne during that holiday season so long ago, when fog, rain, and mud gave way to snow, bitter cold, and misery. As if on cue, a few snowflakes fall gently into view outside in the light cast by the attic bulb.

Jack sets the maps aside and rummages in the chest until he finds the large manila envelope that is the object of his quest. After a moment of contemplation, he pulls out a dozen yellowed papers, each covered with handwritten names and notations he made to record the casualties he treated during the siege of Bastogne. Each page has four columns: Name, Serial Number, Diagnosis, and Outcome. The Diagnosis column is crowded with Jack's tiniest script, since many of the soldiers suffered from multiple wounds and maladies.

When he leafs through the papers, their strong musty scent triggers a cascade of memories. Jack swears he hears the murmur of low conversation among wounded men. When he comes across the name "Pearson," the soldier's face comes to him, then his voice. Fifty years whisk away, and he is once again kneeling by that critically wounded soldier whose chance of survival was all but gone. A soldier nearby moans, and another man cries out in pain, and Jack is fully transported back to the dank, foul-smelling basement where he treated the wounded. He closes his eyes but cannot escape the dozens of agonized voices tumbling into his consciousness, contorting his face in a painful grimace. They reach a crescendo as a strong gust of wind rattles the attic window and blows snowflakes chaotically about outside. When the wind dies down, the voices fade away.

It was all so long ago. Yet even now, at times, it is still so present, so vivid.

As Jack handles the flimsy pages, he has a moment of clarity. Someday they will all be dust. Who will remember? What will be lost? Can anything be done about it? Nothing comes to him at the moment, so he slides the pages back into the envelope and sets it aside. When Jack reaches for the lid to close the trunk and return the rest of the contents to the limbo of unrecovered memories, something catches his eye. He pulls out his World War II jacket, stands, and slips his arms into the sleeves. Try as he might, he can't manage a reunion of the buttons and their mates across his girth, and he removes it with a sigh.

He sits downs and spreads the jacket on his lap.

While his hands smooth the wrinkles in the fabric, he recovers a small measure of whimsy as he checks the seams. It occurs to him that if he could shed a few pounds, it might fit with a bit of tailoring. But what chance of that? Smiling to himself, Jack resolves to dry-clean the jacket whether it can be forced to fit him or not. As is his habit, he checks all the pockets. In one he detects a triangular shape and fishes out his 10th Armored Division patch, resplendent in red, blue, and gold. Jack places it on the jacket sleeve where he tore it off 50 years ago.

Jack checks the other pockets and finds a bit of fabric in the left chest pocket. He unfolds it to reveal a square of white silk cut with pinking shears. There is a dark stain on the edge. What is this? As he gently kneads the smooth material, another voice comes to him. A woman's, just above a whisper.

"Remember."

With a look of puzzlement on his face, Jack tries to place the voice. It returns.

"Remember."

Christmas Eve 1944

It is bitter cold. The moon is rising and casting deep shadows in the blacked-out town of Bastogne. Gusting winds shove accumulated snow into drifts over the rubble of broken buildings that German artillery shells have spilled into narrow streets.

Yet, in this battered town, on this miserable night, the strains of a popular tune can be heard faintly in the town's market square, and louder still just down the hill on Rue de Neufchâteau. There, outside an abandoned, three-story residence, a knot of well-bundled soldiers is listening intently to a melody coming from inside the building. As they talk quietly, several swing ever so slightly to the irresistible tempo of "In the Mood" by the Glenn Miller Orchestra, as if trying to recapture the warmth of dancehalls and sweethearts left behind.

An officer leaves the shuttered storefront next-door, pulls up his collar, and steps quickly through the blowing snow over to the residence, where the soldiers materialize in the deep shadow on the porch of the building.

"Where're you men supposed to be?"

"We just came off the line, sir, and..."

"Yeah, and we're waitin' for word."

"Our buddy's in there."

The soldier throws a thumb over his shoulder toward the red cross over the door of the residence, indicating the location of the medical aid station of the 20th Armored Infantry Battalion, 10th Armored Division.

"Can't you step inside?"

"Nah, ya gotta have reservations."

The officer wishes the men a Merry Christmas, receives assorted grunts in return, and enters the building. As he descends into the dark basement, powerful odors of mud, blood, human waste, infection, and disinfectant mingle and rise to meet him. He stops short on the last step as the floor is covered from wall to wall with wounded men lying on straw mats and blankets. While he adjusts to the low light of lanterns, he scans the room. Here and there he sees a toe or finger tapping along with the ever-popular swing number playing loudly on a radio in the basement. From their midst, Captain Jack Prior, a 28-year-old doctor fresh out of medical school, stands and steps carefully through the wounded over to the foot of the stairs.

"Anything, Hank?"

"No. Sorry, Jack."

The rumor has circulated among the troops for several days that General Patton sent an armored column to relieve and reinforce Bastogne. But there has been no word of a breakthrough. Too tired to be discouraged, Jack simply thanks his friend and returns his full attention to the wounded men sprawled at his feet. When Hank heads up and out, Jack makes his way over to Augusta Chiwy, a lively young African-Belgian nurse who appears perpetually on the verge of a smile. Once she finishes changing the bandages on a youthful soldier, Chiwy stands and almost cheerfully reports to Jack.

"I'm finished, Doctor. What can I do?"

Jack acknowledges her good work and looks around the room at a situation fairly well in hand, for the moment. Another Belgian nurse, Renee Lemaire, perhaps a year or two older than Jack, is gathering soiled and blood-stained sheets and blankets in a large basket. Renee is an uplifting presence among the soldiers, though her lovely dark eyes are edged with sadness. Jack frequently thanks his lucky stars that the two nurses volunteered to serve with him when his aid station was dangerously shorthanded and running low on medical supplies.

Three comrades lying below the radio are among the wounded enjoying the music from Berlin. Frank, heavily bandaged around the shoulder, is trying unsuccessfully to get some shuteye. Sal and Slim, each with a severely damaged leg, are quietly playing cards. The sultry voice of Axis Sally, the American-born traitor who serves Hitler's propaganda machine, is a sudden, unwelcome interruption.

"Do you remember when you danced with your gal cheek to cheek? Who dances with her now?"

As if to stem the rising grumbles among the wounded, she lets the tune play out before departing from her usual, provocative script.

"Thanks for the memories, Glenn Miller. All of Germany mourns your loss."

For Frank, Axis Sally has dropped a bombshell that snaps his muddled head to attention. He turns to Sal.

"Wha... what'd she say?"

"Yeah, I heard about it. Someone said Miller's plane went down in the channel."

Her crocodile tears shed, Axis Sally moves briskly on.

"This next song goes out to all of you Americans in Belgium suffering the worst winter of the century. Are you cold? Are you lonely?"

Many in the room go silent, reminded of their solitude even as they lie in the midst of a sea of humanity. Frank, a grouch even at the best of times, is now fully awake and incensed. He can barely contain himself as he loads up a tirade of insults to fire at the sweet-talking turncoat. But she beats him to the punch.

"It's Christmas Eve and you aren't home. Why? Because the generals are sacrificing you, especially you young men in Bastogne. You are surrounded with no hope for survival unless you surrender."

"Play the goddamn song, you Nazi bitch!"

As if on command, the orchestra strikes up the tune, and Sal attempts to pacify his friend.

"Gee, Frank. You sure have a way with women."

"I'll be home for Christmas
You can count on me
Please have snow and mistletoe
And presents on the tree"

While Bing Crosby croons and calms the room, Sal turns to Slim. Together, they look on the bright side.

"You know it's not so bad being surrounded."

"Yeah, now we can attack in any direction. We got 'em right where we want 'em."

It's anyone's guess as to how they are so upbeat, since each faces the prospect of losing a limb if he is not soon evacuated to a fully staffed and stocked field hospital. Perhaps it is because they are still drawing breath and they have each other. Oh, and the cognac.

As the Germans tightened the noose around Bastogne, painkilling medicines dwindled to desperate lows. The chance discovery of a cache of cognac in a boarded-up warehouse saved the day. And though some medical supplies were finally being airdropped into Bastogne, cognac remained the analgesic of choice among the men. Another warehouse gave up a dozen pallets of flour, just when rations were running low. Yet, with eggs and milk hard to come by, it took all the ingenuity the cooks could summon to come up with a passable, almost edible pancake. But they did, to the endless gripes of the men on the line. Many swore that if they survived the war, they would never eat another pancake.

As if taunting Frank from afar, Axis Sally throws another stinging jab.

"Home sweet home and you're not there. Don't you hear your sweetheart calling you? Come home, come home."

Before Frank can sputter out a single invective, a soldier with a critical chest wound languishing nearby suddenly cries out in reaction to something familiar in Axis Sally's voice.

"Caroline!"

With great effort, the soldier raises his head to look with bloodshot eyes at Frank, Sal and Slim whose attention he has captured.

"My Caroline."

He adds meekly, weakly to Frank.

"Her voice."

Frank's not buying it.

"Yeah, sure. Nice voice. But she probably has the face of a goat!"

"Hey!"

The confused soldier is ready to defend his Caroline's honor. Slim lays a gentle hand on the soldier's shoulder.

"Hey, take it easy."

The soldier's head drops like a rock as he succumbs to exhaustion.

A spray of snow chases Corporal Wallington and an orderly he calls Beagle into the building as they carefully stretcher another wounded man in. The two have been Jack's indispensable aides ever since he landed at Cherbourg and the corporal and orderly, Private Begala, were assigned to him. Wallington was quick to give his subordinate a nickname, and it stuck.

Chiwy clears a space as Jack's aides carefully carry the wounded man through the congestion of bruised and broken bodies. Working together, Jack and Chiwy remove the soldier's bloodied field dressing and clean and redress his wound. When Jack offers the soldier reassuring words, the valiant defender of Caroline's honor recognizes the doctor's voice and perks up.

"Doc! Hey, Doc!"

Jack steps over to the grievously wounded soldier and instinctively palms the young man's forehead. He is alarmed at the heat the soldier is generating and calls out to Renee who is carefully picking her way to the washroom carrying her basket full of soiled laundry.

"Nurse! Renee! Get a cold pack for this man!"

Renee sets down her basket, makes her way carefully across the crowded floor, and rushes up the stairs and out the door. She quickly returns with a rag packed full of snow. This time the wounded see her coming and make way for their favorite Belgian as best they can. With a practiced smile for her admirers, she reaches the feverish soldier and holds the pack against his burning forehead as Jack takes his blood pressure. Momentarily revived, the soldier musters all the energy he can.

"Doc! I gotta write a letter... to my Caroline."

"OK, soldier."

"She's... she's really swell. I got her picture right here."

The soldier pats the chest pocket of a jacket he no longer wears. It was cut away and set aside when Jack did what he could to stem the man's bleeding and ease his suffering. Jack unfolds the wadded jacket and locates the photograph. It is ruined by mud and blood. The image is completely obscured.

"Say, she's a real catch."

Renee leans in with curiosity to see Caroline's photo and gives Jack a puzzled, questioning look. When she understands what Jack has done and quickly brightens at his kindness, Jack nods to her in acknowledgment. He returns the photo to the jacket pocket then gently pats the soldier's chest.

"Here you go. You're a lucky guy."

"Doc! I gotta let her know... that I'm coming home for Christmas."

He shows the soldier nothing but encouragement, but Jack is in turmoil. Trained as a generalist, he was accelerated through medical school and rushed to France, then on to Belgium where he is standing in for a surgeon down with pneumonia. He is acutely aware that he lacks the skills needed to treat the most severe head, chest, and abdominal wounds. With the 101st Airborne Division's field hospital west of Bastogne destroyed and all evacuation routes out of Bastogne blocked, Jack is face to face with his worst fears. No one is going anywhere. Many of these boys aren't going to make it. It is a painful reality punctuated by occasional moans and cries of distress throughout the dank, darkened basement.

Together, Jack and his nurses can plug holes, stop hemorrhages, restore fluids, set simple fractures, debride and irrigate wounds, fight infection, alleviate pain, perform some simple surgeries, and do several other things they didn't know they could do. But the most serious cases, like the young soldier prone before him, must wait for the hands of more experienced surgeons. And mangled limbs like Sal's and Slim's must remain, for now, stubbornly attached, unless gangrene sets in and Jack is compelled to amputate.

Jack's only hope is to prolong as many lives as possible as they await Patton's breakthrough to Bastogne. Once that occurs, the evacuation of the wounded to surgical hospitals in France will be possible and more of them will survive their wounds, retain their limbs, and see their families once again. In the meantime, Jack is alone with dark thoughts as he kneels by the feverish soldier. He feels he is failing these men and this soldier, in particular, who will be lucky to survive the night. The soldier's blood pressure is dangerously low and his pulse is weakening. Jack looks up at Renee with resignation. Her tender expression in return speaks volumes and, in an almost electric moment, Jack suddenly understands Renee's extraordinary compassion. Yes, this soldier may be dying. But he is alive now. Jack watches with wonder as Renee continues to gently stroke the soldier's forehead. Uplifted, Jack is moved to learn the young man's name and turns the soldier's dog tag toward the light of a nearby lantern.

"OK... Pearson. We'll write your letter."

Cockpit of a German Bomber

A Junkers JU88 medium bomber with a crew of four begins the long run in toward Bastogne. Having set the course to target, the navigator fiddles with a shortwave receiver he stowed aboard, skips over Bing Crosby singing, and continues further along the dial. The pilot and copilot recognize the singer's voice and protest.

"Joachie!"

"Halt! Er ist der Bingle!"

The navigator spins the dial back to Radio Berlin.

"I'll be home for Christmas
If only in my dreams"

With the song ended and Axis Sally blathering anew, the search down the radio dial continues until the navigator lands on the BBC. Furtive glances are exchanged all around, knowing that Goebbels, the Minister of Public Enlightenment and Propaganda, deems it treason to listen to foreign broadcasts, especially the BBC. Yet each of the men aboard knows it is the only place to hear the truth about the war. After several moments of hesitation, allegiance prevails and he continues to spin the dial, grows tired of finding nothing of interest, and switches it off. All that is heard now is the droning of the twin engines of their plane heavily laden with more than two tons of high explosives.

In this moment, on this special eve, the copilot contemplates the meaning of Christmas in his life. Many happy memories come to him. Smiling to himself, he turns to the pilot and breaks the silence.

"What does your family do on the holy day?"

"We burn the Yule log and sing. Uncle Dieter plays the piano... very badly."

The copilot chuckles in response. He stops short when a darkened mass appears on the horizon far ahead in contrast to the fields of snow illuminated by the moon. It must be Bastogne. Confirmation is immediate as the string of bombers makes a slight adjustment to new bearings, aiming the lethal formation at the heart of Bastogne. He announces that the target is in sight. Though they may be very young men, they are veterans of multiple bombing missions and show no outward signs of anxiety. But fear is an implacable foe, and the four friends steel themselves for battle. This time, the bombardier ventures a thought.

"Is it just me? Or does anyone else wonder?"

"Go ahead, Karl."

Encouraged by the pilot, Karl offers a cautious query.

"Well, sir. Why are we bombing Bastogne?"

"Ya, it's just a little town."

With the navigator chiming in, and the copilot turning toward him, the pilot weighs his response.

"I can only tell you that it comes from the top."

"Göring?"

In spite of his reluctance to reveal orders meant for his ears alone, the pilot cannot contain the strained expression on his face. The copilot presses his luck.

"Der Führer?"

The pilot considers his options. All aboard are close friends and comrades with whom he can speak openly. Yet, as a professional in the *Luftwaffe*, he is tugged by the call of duty to maintain discipline. But, at this point in a war, it is not enough. He nearly spits out his response in frustration.

"He is furious that Bastogne still holds. He wants it crushed like a nut!"

"But it makes no sense."

Emboldened by the bombardier's sentiments, the navigator chimes in.

"Ya, especially on the eve of Christmas."

"Joachie, you didn't hear perhaps? The *Amis* bombed Bitburg today! Bombed it down to the ground! Don't you have family there?"

Having said it, the pilot immediately regrets it as the navigator sits in stunned silence. Seeing that he has caused his friend pain, the pilot surrenders to a tangle of emotions. He is tired of war, tired of the senseless death and destruction. He believes the cause is lost, but he also believes in his crew. They are all hardened warriors who count on each other. So, he tightens his grip on the control wheel and keeps the bomber on track for its deadly mission.

Instinctively, the co-pilot reaches out to clasp the pilot's shoulder, wordlessly acknowledging a struggle that they all share. Then he offers a clumsy parody of party doctrine to the bombardier.

"Come Karl, a good Nazi always does his duty."

"Heinz! You! Of all people! You know that I hate the Nazis. That is shit from a pig!"

After several moments of uncomfortable silence, the pilot tries his hand at easing the tension in the cramped cockpit.

"Speaking of swine, let's get this over with and get back before Klaus drinks all the beer!"

Jack's Aid Station

After Chiwy checks the IVs on several wounded soldiers, she catches her breath as she scans the basement. Her gaze falls upon Renee, who continues to comfort Pearson. Responding to her touch, Pearson rasps out his gal's name as he grips Renee's hand. Chiwy watches transfixed as Renee bends to whisper in his ear, causing the dying soldier to release a single sustained breath, smile contentedly, and close his eyes in repose. For several moments, Renee listens to Pearson breathing evenly and placidly. When she rises to take on her next task, a competition for her attention begins.

"Renee. Hey, Renee! I got a fever too!"

"Yeah, how 'bout me? I'm burning up over here!"

Renee puts on a cheerful face and goes to the soldiers who called out to her in jest. Her presence immediately lifts their spirits, along with those of a dozen other men nearby who shift their damaged bodies with great effort to admire Renee. Chiwy takes it all in, shakes her head, and smiles knowingly. When they first started working together in the aid station, she had pangs of jealousy when Renee drew all the attention. Now, she scolds herself for such frivolity. After several days thrown together in the crucible of conflict, the nurses have connected on the deepest levels of trust and understanding. She picks up Renee's basket and heads to the washroom.

With things under control for the most part, Jack decides to head next door. At the top of the steps, he has a few words with Wallington, takes a last look around the basement, opens the door, and ventures out into the blowing snow.

Just outside the door, Jack finds Beagle having a smoke. As they exchange brief words, Jack cocks his ear toward the east where he hears a deep, droning sound ever so faintly. As he does so he is struck by the stark beauty of the night as the moon trims the rooftops of Bastogne with silver and casts the streets of Bastogne into deepening shadows.

The soldiers huddled on the porch see the red cross on Jack's helmet.

"Hey, Doc! How's Andrews?"

Off the cuff, Jack can't match a name with a face. The men help him out.

"The guy with his arm all torn up."

"Yeah, and that burnin' thing."

Jack replays an unpleasant scene of a soldier thrashing in agony with a white phosphorus wound, who nonetheless expressed the vilest of sentiments while being given lifesaving care. He quickly banishes the vision with a mental snapshot of Chiwy, the nurse who treated Andrews.

"He's in very good hands. Lost a lot of blood, but he's stable now."

Jack is hesitant to offer more since there is no guarantee of full recovery or even survival in these conditions. It turns out the men are satisfied. Their murmurs of encouragement to each other fade as Jack follows Hank's footprints over to the office next door.

"Hello, sir? Come take a look at our Christmas tree."

Though he is preoccupied with matters of life and death, Jack cannot decline such a heart-gladdening offer. As he heads toward the voice, he discerns two men in the shadows, one tall and one short, standing by a scrub tree festooned with empty C-Ration cans. Jack steps toward the shorter man and is met by a spray of snow blowing around the corner of the building. But it would take a blizzard to dim Jack's suddenly elevated spirits.

"Well, soldier. I think you're in line for a medal. You found some positive use for C-Rations."

"How 'bout that. Who says Team SNAFU is good for nuthin'! Here, hang one on, will ya? For luck."

"Glad to. We need all the luck we can get."

As Jack accepts and hangs the can, the thrumming of heavy bombers approaching from the east is unmistakable now. Reminded of his promise to Pearson, Jack takes his leave and mounts the steps to his office. He pauses on the landing and turns toward the sharp reports of anti-aircraft fire rending the night air. Jack concludes that he'd better shake a leg and get back to the aid station as soon as he can.

The smaller of the two soldiers draws a similar conclusion. He turns to prod his oversized friend but finds him unmoved by the growing threat from the skies. The big ox of a man gazes silently at his handiwork, as if imagining the scraggly Christmas tree to be something grand. Finally, calmly, the little guy prevails.

"OK, Joey, ya got your tree. Can we go in now?"

Rattling the night with urgency, the bell of Église Saint-Pierre begins to ring vigorously at the north end of town, pleading with the populace to take heed and take cover.

Inside the office, Jack stamps the snow from his boots and exchanges nods with Hank who is intently watching a radioman working his dial, checking all known frequencies for Patton's Third Army. The young technician pays little notice to the gathering tempest in the east or the gusts of wind rippling the blackout curtains hung inside the large, drafty windows he faces. He is intensely focused on his job.

Jack tosses a chunk of wood onto glowing embers in a potbelly stove and settles at his desk. He finds writing paper and a pen in the top drawer and continues digging through the other drawers. Momentarily stymied, he pauses and ponders his casualty records that are secured to a clipboard. He looks up as an officer enters the building, bringing a blast of frigid air. The officer greets Jack and Hank and turns to query the radioman.

"Anything?"

"Nothing yet, sir. A lot of noise."

The officer heads over to the far corner of the room to fetch something from his desk. All heads turn as the radioman rolls the dial past, then quickly returns to a distorted voice. Jack looks up as Hank bends closer to the set and awaits an explanation from the radioman.

"Hard to fix a direction, sir. But... it could be Patton."

When the garbled transmission is consumed by static, Jack returns to his task. He unclips his casualty records and weighs the loose papers down with a handful of dog tags. He affixes his writing paper and pen to the clipboard and stands, ready to depart. Hank steps over to Jack's desk and nods toward the officer who is now holding a bottle of champagne and three glasses aloft.

"Jack, we're just about to toast... Hey! What gives with the parachute?"

With an expression that speaks to its significance, Jack ponders the white parachute wadded up on the end of his desk, but only manages a cryptic response.

"It's a gift."

His soft words go unheard, as Hank's attention has been yanked back to the radio when the distorted voice breaks through the static once again. Though anxious to return to his aid station, Jack takes a moment to wrap the parachute in brown paper. He writes a few words on the paper and sets the large package aside. He steps over to Hank and the officer who are equal parts hopeful and sardonic.

"That's gotta be Patton. Come to rescue us!"

"Old Blood and Guts himself."

"Yeah, our blood, his guts."

"He'll be the hero of Bastogne, just you wait and see."

Jack heads toward the door to complete his mission for the dying soldier. But now the distinctive crumping thud of bombs landing can be heard out on the perimeter of Bastogne, where grizzled American paratroopers hug the muck at the bottom of their foxholes. He stops and turns to Hank and the officer as the three of them suppress expressions of anxiety. The Germans have not yet bombed the town proper, but there is always a first time. As the clock ticks on toward midnight, the officer searches for safe harbor and solace in the spirit of the season.

"C'mon, Jack. It's Christmas Eve!"

Jack wavers. Encouraged, the officer makes a request of the radioman.

"See if you can find some Christmas music."

After plugging in a headset to continue monitoring the field radio, the young soldier switches on a shortwave radio and quickly locates the US Armed Forces broadcast.

> *"It came upon a midnight clear*
> *That glorious song of old"*

Hank catches his friend's eye.

"What do you say, Jack? What difference can a couple of minutes make?"

> *"From angels bending near the earth*
> *To touch their harps of gold"*

"OK. Better make it a quick one."

> *"Peace on the earth, goodwill to men"*

The officer fills the glasses and pauses to consider, but can't think of a better toast.

"To peace on earth."

Hank responds, smiling.

"And goodwill to men."

Having renewed mankind's ever-tenuous hopes and dreams, the three men drink. Suddenly, the searing light of a German phosphorus flare pierces the gaps in the blackout curtains, followed by the whistle of a falling bomb. An earth-shaking explosion knocks them to the floor and blasts shards of glass in on the hapless radioman. Dazed and deafened, Jack comes to with a ringing in his ears and a disorienting swirl of distant voices rising and falling in his head, some shouting out, some singing. Slowly, Jack realizes the radio somehow escaped the blast unscathed.

> *"And man, at war with man, hears not*
> *The love song which they bring*
> *O hush the noise, ye men of strife*
> *And hear the angels sing"*

Once he regains clarity, Jack gets up from the floor and takes tentative steps to find his balance. He helps Hank and the officer to seated positions. Jack presses a cloth against Hank's forehead, where a gash is bleeding profusely, and guides his friend's hand it.

"Keep some pressure on it."

When the officer indicates he is all right, Jack turns to the radioman lying motionless on the floor in a rapidly spreading pool of blood. He checks for vital signs but finds none.

"He's gone."

Realizing he has done all he can for his office mates, Jack wrestles the heavily damaged door open and steps outside. He is horrified to see that the aid station has taken a direct hit. Half the building has collapsed, while the other half leans precariously. The night is filled with agonized cries from the wounded men within the wreckage, while the bell of Saint Pierre continues to toll at the far end of town.

Bastogne 1994

Of the many American soldiers who survived the battle, some attend the 50th reunion events in Bastogne in 1994. Of those who opted for the June gathering, a few were acquainted during the war. Most are meeting for the first time, including several who are spilling over from the D-Day commemoration in Normandy and making their first visit to Bastogne. All find the town thickly populated by ghosts, an experience both exhilarating and exhausting. Though Bastogne bustles and teems with friendly people, more than a few veterans feel a profound sense of isolation as they remember buddies made and buddies lost during the war.

A lucky double handful of them find refuge in each other in the warm and friendly confines of a public house in the heart of Bastogne.

Le Nut's Tavern

It is late in the day and light fog is giving way to misty rain over the central town square, renamed Place Général McAuliffe after the American general who commanded the American forces in Bastogne during the battle. On the square sits Le Nut's, the watering hole that honors the concise declaration that McAuliffe uttered at a pivotal moment of the battle. Inside, the veterans all have glasses of beer before them at various stages of consumption, except for Jack Prior, whose glass of red wine is untouched. The room is subdued as Maurice Ravel's melancholy masterpiece "Pavane for a Dead Princess" plays on the tavern radio. It weaves a contemplative spell that would spare only men made of wood.

Several of the veterans are talking quietly with those sitting nearest to them. Jack seems to be in deep dialogue with himself, while staring intently at his hands clasped tightly before him on the table. Though he has relived many times the events of that Christmas Eve fifty years ago, he is surprised at how potent the memories have become here in Bastogne. Now, just a block away from the site of the wrecked aid station, the swirling sounds of grievously wounded men come to him. He makes no effort to suppress them, knowing they will not easily be silenced. Instead, over time, he has learned to embrace them, to comfort them. Once again, the cries of pain are soothed by Jack's healing touch and slowly fade away.

"So long ago, but can I still hear them."

As he relaxes and his fingers uncoil, Jack looks up and into the eyes of men who served in or near Bastogne when he did. Their conversations had stopped with Jack's soft utterance, and he smiles at them weakly, almost contritely. When he finally takes a sip of his wine, all gratefully take a pull on their beers and murmur support and understanding for Jack. They have all heard more than their share of voices over the years.

One veteran who goes by the nickname of Sarge, an infantryman Jack treated during the battle, puts a brotherly hand on his shoulder.

"Who can you hear, Doc?"

"Oh, just some of the boys who were in my care... mostly the ones..."

A couple of the men assembled know about Jack's harrowing experiences during the battle.

"... the ones who didn't make it."

But none of them can truly fathom the anguish and agony Jack felt when, day in and day out, he was immersed in blood and pain and suffering as he grappled with the dark angel of death.

As Jack looks from face to face, he becomes concerned that he is suppressing the mood of the gathering.

"You didn't come all this way to hear my sad story."

"Well, sure we did, Doc. That's why we're all here."

Sarge speaks for all of them, evidenced by the nodding of heads in the affirmative around the table.

Each of the men present spent decades sparing his family members and friends from the horrors of war. How could one describe the indescribable? Better to not talk about it at all. Oh, sure, from time to time they deflected attention by sharing the good times. And there were some, though they were few and far between. But for years they steadfastly kept the darkness from their loved ones. At the same time, they rebuffed any efforts to put them on pedestals. They saw themselves as survivors of the war, not heroes. They just did their jobs in the army and were lucky enough to dodge bullets. So, for the longest time, they kept their war stories to themselves and tried, with limited success, to forget about the whole damn thing.

But now, surrounding Jack at the table are men who not only survived the war. They survived the peace. Some they knew died later of their wounds. Others surrendered to booze. A few succumbed to madness. Somehow, these men endured. Here they all stand in Bastogne. They have come a long way on their lifelong quests to finally feel at home in the world. So, they are sure as hell ready to talk and listen.

Yet still, Jack stalls. Sarge picks him up.

"It was Doc's aid station that got hit on Christmas Eve."

Two veterans of the of the 82nd Airborne chip in.

"That's news to me."

"Yeah, we were up in Werbomont."

Their division was known as the All-Americans since it boasted members from all forty-eight states when it was formed in 1917. During the battle, Simpson and Brown were deployed well to the north of Bastogne to block the northern thrust of the *Wehrmacht's* surprise counteroffensive through the Ardennes. Fifty years later, the two old men are always together, seemingly inseparable, but often engaged in petty arguments. Having tossed their two cents in, they return to a low-level debate that they have been having about the piece of music on the radio and quickly ramp up their intensity.

"Yeah, yeah, sure. It's Ravel, but it's about a dead prince."

"I'm tellin' you, it's princess!"

"And I'm tellin' you... you're a jackass!"

Sarge is quick to mediate.

"Whatever it's called, it sure is a sad melody."

"Sad, but beautiful. Kind of like... well, like a dead princess."

Colleti, a military policeman during the war, has drawn the only conclusion one can from Ravel's haunting ceremonial dance. When Jack turns to find the former MP looking his way, the two men lock eyes for the briefest of moments and then nod affirmation. Jack's aid station on Rue de Neufchâteau in Bastogne was on Colleti's beat, and they share indelible memories of the darkest days and nights during the siege of Bastogne.

Sitting beside Colleti and humming along in appreciation of the Renaissance revival melody is Jaworski, who served on General McAuliffe's headquarters staff. Across the table are McEvoy and Turner, two veterans of the 101st Airborne Division, the Screaming Eagles, who were dug in on the northern perimeter of Bastogne with their mates in the 506th regiment during the desperate defense of the town.

Sitting quietly at the end of the table is Will, a survivor of the 28th Infantry Division that was shattered on the first day of the battle. He is the same soldier of small stature who hung C-Ration cans on a scrub tree outside Jack's aid station. But neither Jack nor Will recalls the other. Their brief encounter on a dark night was soon forgotten in a jumble of chaotic events. Jack, ever the healer in search of a wound, is drawn to the somber man who is gazing out the window as misty rain surrenders to a steady downpour. Perhaps a story might reel Will back to the group, so Jack gives an abbreviated version of his saga, right up to Christmas Eve and the moment when the bomb fell, then he falters.

The pub goes silent save for the rattle of rain falling outside, until the All-Americans insist on hearing more.

"So, what happened to the nurses?"

"The one they called the Angel of Bastogne."

"Renee... Renee..."

"Lemaire. Renee Lemaire."

Jack's response is like poetry to their ears.

"Yeah, and the other one."

"Augusta Chiwy."

Jack's soft, almost reverential recitation of the nurses' names moves Sarge to chime in.

"There were two, two Angels of Bastogne."

When Jack fails to pick up the thread of his story, Sarge is quick to take the measure of his old comrade, read his reluctance to continue, and offer a reprieve.

"Look, fellas. It was a terrible night."

Colleti follows suit.

"Yeah, it sure was."

But Jack feels compelled to carry on, as if in confession.

"I lost a lot of lives."

Once again, the table goes silent as several surrender to fleeting glimpses of buddies who perished in the war: their names, their faces, what they said, what they did, how they laughed and cried together, how they lived, how they died. But Sarge is steadfast and sees no reason for Jack to apologize for things that were beyond his control. On the contrary.

"But Doc, you saved a whole lot more."

The door at the back end of the pub swings open, and the bar matron enters with baguettes and a block of cheese for the veterans. As she doffs her raincoat and hat, she sees at a glance that Ravel's slow dance has subdued the mood of the gathering. She shakes her head in gentle admonishment of the youthful bartender, who is completely entranced by the music. Sarge, ever observant, takes the cue.

"This is supposed to be a reunion, not a funeral."

He has the bar matron's attention.

"Say, Madame? Can you play us some of the old songs? You know, from the war."

A clap of thunder shakes the building, inspiring Sarge to test his rusty singing voice.

"Don't know why there's no sun up in the sky"

All of the veterans, save for Jack and Will, get a kick out of joining Sarge in song with a cacophony of sharps and flats.

"Stormy weather!"

Then they prove once again that laughter is the best medicine. Delighted by the ebullience of the old men, the matron comes to the table with a generous smile and a bounce in her step gained from decades of waiting tables.

"You must forgive Sergio. He is *romantique.*"

She has a motherly attitude toward the recent graduate of the Royal Conservatory of Liège, having hired him after he found few outlets for his musical gifts. Several of the veterans turn to the young man behind the bar who is still glued to the radio, mesmerized.

After clearing empty glasses and taking orders, the matron returns to the bar and speaks softly to the sensitive young man. He looks around her at the veterans, gets the picture, and begins what will ultimately be a fruitless scan of the radio dial in search of the old songs. Sarge is undeterred as he seeks to maintain the elevated atmosphere at the table. He zeroes in on McEvoy and Turner.

"So, what about you fellas? Where were you that Christmas Eve?"

"In a foxhole."

"Yeah, freezin' our nuts off!"

"I trust it didn't inhibit your procreativity."

Turner turns to Jack, who has reentered the conversation with a weak smile. The old trooper processes the doctor's light-hearted comment and brightens.

"Say, I'm glad you mentioned that. Four children, eleven grandchildren, and three... no, let's see... four great-grandchildren. Would you like to see them?"

"With pleasure."

Turner checks his pockets and produces a small photo album. Jack studies the smiling faces of Turner's kith and kin as he listens to anecdotes of a veteran's life fully lived. Tuning out the world for a spell, the two are like old friends on a park bench, snug in their overcoats and woolen hats, oblivious to the chill of the late autumn of their years.

McEvoy, on the other hand, can't get those miserable days and nights out of his mind, and he feigns annoyance as he centers Sarge in his crosshairs.

"Anyway, I blame you guys, 10th Armored. If you hadn't blocked the Krauts, we never would've gotten to Bastogne in time to dig into that goddamn frozen ground! Thanks, but no thanks!"

Having pulled Sarge's leg and rendered him speechless, a rare event, McEvoy finally cracks a smile and meets him halfway to keep the discussion alive.

"But... I guess it wasn't a picnic for you either."

Sarge rallies.

"Well sure. We had it tough. But, what about all the others who took it on the chin when they hit us on that first day? You know, 7th and 9th Armored and, up on the line, the 99th, the 106th, and..."

He pauses as he turns to Will, who hasn't even been half listening as he sits just beyond the glow of the single light fixture hanging over the table.

"... the 28th... you Pennsylvania guys. What'd they call you?"

Will turns toward the voice directed his way but is unable to form a response. Colleti steps up to the plate to pinch-hit for him and points to the red insignia on Will's nametag.

"The Bloody Bucket."

Seeing that Will is still working his way back from wherever his thoughts had strayed, Colleti takes a swing for him.

"I guess you guys got hammered... "

It's a foul ball, but he quickly recovers.

"... but you gave as good as you got."

Encouraged by the other veterans, Colleti knocks the next pitch out of the park.

"Hell, the 28th held up the whole German army for two days!"

All second Colleti's statement enthusiastically. Though they were pummeled during the first days of the battle, the 28th Infantry Division bought just enough time for reinforcements to swing in behind them. Once the history was written, it was clear that the Battle of the Bulge could have been lost without their sacrifice. Jaworski takes a closer look at Will's nametag and unit identification.

"110th Infantry Regiment. If I recall, you boys put up a hell-of-a fight at Clervaux!"

All are attentive as Will seems on the verge of joining in. He responds with a somber expression and shake of the head.

"Yeah, but no. We got separated... and lost."

Without words, all the men around the table give him a warm welcome as he takes the final steps on the long journey that brought him to this place, this moment. Will pulls his chair closer into the light and shows a face with readiness etched upon it.

"OK. It was me and Joey. He was brand new, a replacement, see?"

"One of those 'repple depple' wonders, huh?"

Sarge uses the slang term for the replacement depots that, often with ill effect, plugged fresh troops from the States directly into hardened combat units up on the front line. It draws a guffaw or two around the table, but falls flat with Will, who continues.

"And he was slow, kinda slow. You know what I mean?"

All at the table sit in rapt attention. What can they say?

"Yeah, Joey... Ha!"

Somehow, Will manages a smile.

"He was my buddy."

These last words move all of the veterans to reminisce. Each had a pal, or two or three, in the service.

"We were up on the line that morning, spittin' distance from the German border. You couldn't hear nothin' and you couldn't see nothin' with fog like that."

Will turns to gaze out the tavern window. The rain has slackened, and the fog is rolling back in as he continues his story.

"Some of the guys were sayin' the Krauts were licked and we'd be home for Christmas. Me? I was just tryin' to get some sleep."

16 December 1944

Since landing in Normandy on June 6th and breaking out of hedgerow country, the American Army and its allies had pushed the *Wehrmacht* across France, Holland, Belgium, and Luxembourg. Now, with the Germans presumably licking their wounds behind the fortifications of the Siegfried Line in the German Fatherland, the Allies are dug-in to weather the winter.

It is the opinion of General Eisenhower and his staff at SHAEF (Supreme Headquarters Allied Expeditionary Force) that German forces are so decimated and discouraged that they pose no threat until spring, when the Allies will beat them to the punch with a final thrust into the heartland of the Third Reich.

Little intelligence is available about the disposition of German forces, since the eyes and ears of the Resistance stop at the border. The German code word for the strategic posture of their forces is *Wacht am Rhein* (Watch on the Rhine), indicating an entirely defensive attitude and vindicating SHAEF's wishful thinking.

As such, it is a time for rotating weary soldiers to the rear for rest and refitting, including the 101st Airborne Division, which is settled into winter quarters near Reims in northeastern France. However, a significant portion of their number is sleeping off a night of revelry ninety miles away in Paris.

The 28th Infantry Division, which also needs rest and reinforcement after brutal fighting in the Hurtgen Forest near the Dutch-German border, is thinly spread along a frontline in Luxembourg in what top brass figures will be the quietest sector on the Western Front. Dead center in this weak defensive position sits the 110th Infantry Regiment, with manpower at only a third of the strength recommended by army doctrine for the ground they are defending. From time to time, they swear they can hear heavy vehicular traffic from the German side of the border, but their concerns are discounted. Not much goes up the chain of command, but every foot soldier will tell you that a lot sure does come down it. Like shit down a chute.

In the pre-dawn darkness of December 16, 1944, the German army lies in wait. They have assembled infantry and armored forces far in excess of anything the Allies thought possible. While German officers watch the time tick toward dawn, all is deceptively quiet as heavy fog continues to muffle the rugged, heavily forested Ardennes.

Will and Joey

Blissfully unaware of the storm brewing in the east, two members of the 110th Infantry Regiment lie sleeping side by side in a foxhole just outside the town of Hosingen, Luxembourg. The temperature dipped below freezing during the night, turning heavy dew into a pool of slush on the oilskin that covers them. The larger of the two stirs and drags the tarp with him as he rolls over, spilling the ice-cold mixture onto the other's face.

"Christ! Joey!"

"Uh... oh... sorry, Will."

Assuaged as always by his meek friend, Will's startled anger gives way to a series of diminishing grumbles and, finally, head-shaking affection.

"Ya big lug."

As he rearranges the tarp to his satisfaction, Will hears the morning's first crow of a rooster in the distance.

Beethoven's Birthday

Down in the valley below the ridgeline that the Americans are holding, a solitary farmhouse stands on the German side of the River Our. There, a second rooster takes up the challenge tendered by the first. Soon the two chanticleers are competing for a dominance that only their minuscule brains can appreciate. Their owner, rudely stirred from his slumber inside, cannot.

Though he has been early riser all his life, the farmer grumbles, sits up in bed, and stares blankly before him. As he checks the clock and ponders what could possibly have stirred those blasted birds so early, an awakened thought suddenly energizes him. He pulls on his robe with some difficulty, having lost an arm above the elbow in World War I, and works his feet into his slippers. He shuffles into the next room, ignores a portrait of Adolf Hitler, and sleepily salutes a portrait of Kaiser Wilhelm II, Germany's last emperor and the King of Prussia during the Great War. He stops to straighten a bust of Beethoven on the mantle and then steps over to his horn gramophone. With practiced dexterity, he manages to put on a record, crank the handle, and cue the needle. He bends to hear the barely audible sound of Beethoven's "Fifth Symphony." Satisfied, he starts the record over and turns the volume all the way up.

His face brightens with a mischievous smile as he hears his daughter and grandson stir in adjoining rooms. Several moments later, the young woman drifts into the room, well bundled in an oversized housecoat.

"What's happening, Papa?"

"You know, of course. Come along, Kurt!"

His call brings only a groggy groan from the boy. His mother slowly registers the symphony and the situation.

"Must we do this every year?"

"Yes, yes. Beethoven's birthday comes every year!"

With gentle resignation, the daughter pads softly into the kitchen where she throws a log into the stove and stirs the embers from the previous night's fire. She checks the teapot by swirling its contents and sets it upon the stove to heat what passes for coffee during this time of austerity. Then she steps over to the windowsill and gazes at a small, framed photo of her husband, handsome in spite of a distinctive L-shaped scar on his chin, in his *Wehrmacht* dress uniform. It is rumored that his unit is stationed nearby. If only she could see him. Desire and loneliness surge through her, but there is nothing she can do. She kisses her fingertips and touches the glass protecting the pocket-sized image. She turns to see eight-year-old Kurt drag himself to the kitchen table wearing several layers of clothing, and she is uplifted, as always, by his uncanny resemblance to his father. The moment passes quickly when the boy hides his drowsy face within folded arms on the table.

"Happy Beethoven's birthday, grandson!"

The man's enthusiasm is now boundless as he takes up a wooden spoon and conducts the orchestra. He is rewarded with yet another incoherent moan from the boy, prompting the daughter to take her son's side as she has for eight years running.

"But Papa. Why so early?"

"It is Beethoven's birthday all day. And look! The day is nearly five-and-one-half hours old already!"

The man thrusts the spoon like a saber at a clock that reads just shy of 5:30. Unmoved, the daughter begins to putter about, assembling plates and cups, bread and jam. While Kurt manages to fall asleep at the table, his grandfather vigorously conducts the symphony. He splits the air with swift strokes at its three-chord, percussion-heavy crescendo, but is stunned as the house shakes with the simultaneous pounding of massive bass drums thundering down from the hills above the river. Dumbfounded, the man stares at his spoon, then toward the east where a barrage from a thousand artillery pieces has begun. When the house begins to shake, his daughter scrambles to catch cups and crockery as they tumble, then watches in horror as her husband's portrait falls, shattering the glass in the frame.

While the needle jumps around on the record, blurting out bits and pieces of the symphony, the bust of Beethoven rattles to the edge of the mantle. With the agility of a much younger man, Kurt's grandfather flings aside his wooden spoon, lunges for the bust, and saves it as it tumbles. He takes two halting steps while he listens carefully to the shells hurtling like freight trains over the farmhouse from east to west.

"What is it, Papa?"

"Artillery! Firing at the *Amis*. Go down to the cellar! Hurry!"

Acting through terrified instinct, Kurt's mother runs to the boy, yanks him to his feet, hastens him to the cellar door and sends him down the stairs. Yet, oblivious to her father's exasperation, she reverses course to the kitchen, works her husband's photograph free of the frame, and slips it into the pocket of her housecoat. When his daughter vanishes down the steps, the man follows, clutching his beloved bust of Beethoven to his chest.

A Field of Poppies

A little dark-eyed girl steps softly through a field of dazzling red poppies. As she does so, she hums a melody passed down by Belgian mothers and grandmothers who lost loved ones in the Great War. When the wind picks up and blows the blossoms about, she adds words to the melody.

> *"Dans les champs de Flandre*
> *Les coquelicots soufflent"*

Darkening clouds billow above the horizon but where she stands the sun is shining and nothing troubles her. She pauses and considers, perhaps searching for the words of the song. Finally, as she resumes her stroll through delicate blossoms swinging on sturdy stems, she takes up humming the melody once again.

Renee

Renee Lemaire, RN

In the Lemaire household near the center of Bastogne, Renee stirs uncomfortably in her sleep as a pleasant, sunlit dream gives way to rolling thunder. The thunder turns out to be the thudding sound of heavy boots as her father tromps down the staircase outside Renee's bedroom. In the stillness, the sounds are amplified and shake Renee's sleepy, hazy grasp on reality.

"No. No! Josef!"

Her cry of anguish beckons her mother, Berta, who hurries in to find Renee illuminated by the light from the hallway, disoriented, sitting bolt upright in her bed.

"Renee! What is it?"

"They... they are coming."

"Who? Who is coming?"

Heavy thudding is heard again on the stairs as her father dashes back up the stairs. It calls to mind the jackboots of Nazis parading across Europe.

"The *Boche!*"

Renee turns slowly to the sound, unseeing and unknowing. Her mother takes her hands.

Having retrieved a forgotten item, Gustave Lemaire hurtles loudly down the stairs again. Berta makes sense of Renee's response and is sympathetic, but ready to scold her husband in almost the same breath.

"Ah, that's just your father rushing off to work..."

Louder, but not quite loud enough for Gustave to hear.

"... wearing those dirty boots in the house again!"

Nazis marching! Josef in trouble! Renee is in a muddle as the night terror recedes and her mother comes into focus. She shudders and shakes off her confusion to find herself at home, safe in her own bed. It is as if a veil is lifted.

"Oh. Oh! I need to get up!"

Renee slips out of bed and bustles about the room gathering her clothes for the day.

"I promised to help Papa at the store."

Berta looks on with concern carved on her face.

"But you are home for the holidays. You deserve your rest. And... who will come to the hardware store so early in the morning?"

Renee is clearly undeterred. Her mother, silenced by Renee's resolve, turns to the sound of stirring in the bedroom where Renee's younger sisters Gisele and Marguerite are sleeping.

"Mama? I heard a scream."

"Go to sleep, Gisele. It was just Renee."

"Again?"

"Go to sleep, girls."

When the heavy front door opens and closes, Berta goes to the window to watch her husband, weighed down by his work sack, tramp heavily down the street into the fog. She turns to see that Renee is fully dressed for the day.

"Well, if you must go, there is still coffee and some bread and butter."

With that, Berta leaves the room muttering to herself about Renee's stubbornness, so like her husband's. Renee pauses at her dresser to quickly brush her hair. She stops when she hears what sounds ever so faintly like rolling thunder in the distant east. Unconsciously, she draws a pendant from within her blouse and caresses it tenderly as she whispers to herself.

"I can't let him down."

Jack

Jack Prior, MD

Light is slowly filtering through an early morning fog. Several sets of footprints chew up the muddy ground outside a large tent marked with a red cross. Inside is Doctor Jack Prior's aid station with the 10th Armored Division, now bivouacked in eastern France. It is the calm after the storm of a long and bloody battle that ended when Patton's Third Army subdued German forces in the city of Metz. The flow of casualties has abated as Patton rests, reinforces, and retools his forces for an armored thrust into Germany, giving Jack time he needs to catch his breath. It has only been a matter of days since he was rushed to the front from a field hospital thirty miles behind the fighting. It has taken some getting used to. Fortunately, he brought along his two closest aides who work comfortably and efficiently with him. While Wallington and Beagle busy themselves with stocking the aid station, Jack takes advantage of the lull in the action to mark this last leg of his journey across France on a map of the country he has hanging in the tent. Somehow, knowing where he is gives him comfort.

As a soldier limps in pain into the tent with the help of a comrade, Wallington exits the tent and mucks over to a truck to retrieve medical supplies. When the corporal reenters the aid station heavily laden, Beagle heads out. Once outside, the orderly stops abruptly and turns toward a rumble at the very edge of audibility in the distant north. As he listens carefully, he is rejoined by Wallington.

"Hey, Wally. There it is again. Ya heard it this time, right?"

"Ah, you're hearing things."

But impressed by a look of absolute certainty on the younger man's face, the corporal turns to the north, where the rumble has faded, while

Beagle scans the horizon as if looking for evidence of a sound that can no longer be heard. Shaking his head, the corporal gets back to work. When he returns from the truck with another box, Wallington gently admonishes his buddy.

"C'mon, get to work. There'll be no fightin' today."

"Maybe it was thunder."

Inside the tent, the corporal places his box onto a stack of supplies and fetches his clipboard to tally up the inventory. A sudden shout of agony snaps his head around to the soldier Jack is treating for trench foot. As he carefully removes the soldier's boots and socks, Jack winces involuntarily with each gasp of pain. When Beagle enters the room with the last of the boxes, Wallington makes a final check mark.

"That's everything, Doc. Uh... I mean, Captain, sir."

"OK, take ten, men."

After Jack spreads topical pain killer liberally on the exposed feet, the patient enjoys a respite from the agony, as does the physician. Smiling weakly with relief, Jack turns to his aide.

"And... you can call me Doc."

The corporal shares a knowing look with Beagle, who nods in return. There is something special about this guy, this Doc Prior. He's a regular guy, unlike every other high and mighty officer they have reported to. As a result, they find themselves working twice as hard as they might have otherwise. Nevertheless, when the opportunity arises, Beagle is happy to knock off. He finds a sturdy crate, sits down heavily and ponders what seems like a mountain of supplies they've stacked in the tent.

"Gimme a buck for every time we've moved this stuff."

Jack is sympathetic.

"Well, hopefully we'll hold here for a while."

Wallington hears their chatter and ponders Jack's wishful thinking as he turns his attention to a 1935 Smith Corona Silent typewriter, his most prized possession. Once he uncovers it, he sets about dusting and cleaning and testing the action of each key. His ritual ends with a soft cloth to raise the sheen of the burgundy finish on the body. Then, and only then, does he respond to Jack.

"Say, Doc? I heard what you said. But Patton don't believe in sittin' tight. None of that ready, aim stuff."

"*Semper en hostes.*"

By the look on the corporal's face, he is not a student of classical languages. Jack translates.

"Always into the enemy. From the Latin."

"Yeah, yeah sure. So, he ain't gonna stop now. He's got his reputation."

Jack applies fresh wraps on the soldier's feet and carefully covers them with a pair of dry socks, perhaps the most valuable commodity on the entire front. As he helps the soldier pull on a dry pair of boots ever so gingerly, Jack is impressed and relieved by the soldier's teeth-gritting stoicism. An ambulance driver enters the tent with evacuation forms for the soldier with trench foot. Jack signs in triplicate. The driver gives Jack a copy that Jack peruses and hands off to Wallington. Once Jack's patient is helped out of the tent by his buddy and the driver, Hank enters with two tin cups of steaming coffee. Jack's new friend has gone out of his way continuously to make Jack feel at home in his new assignment.

"Hey, Jack. How 'bout a cuppa joe?"

"Thanks, Hank. You're a one-man welcome committee."

As the smell of strong, fresh coffee fills the tent, Jack's aides appear to have ants in their pants.

"Go ahead, men. Coffee's up."

The words are barely out of his mouth before his aides are through the flap and out of the tent. Jack and Hank soon follow. Stepping outside, the two officers carefully sip their hot brew as they peer through fog that is quickly thinning in the face of a rising breeze. Before them, sprawled across the field, they see tents, trucks, and tanks that represent a fraction of an entire armored division. As the driver starts up the ambulance, the soldier with trench foot waves gratefully to Jack from the back end of the vehicle. Jack returns the gesture and watches as the driver guns his engine through the mud of the heavily rutted field and out onto the road beyond. Only then does Jack become aware of a low rumbling sound in the distant north. Could it be?

Apparently, Hank hasn't heard it.

"So, Jack, how are you adjusting to life in the field?"

"Hard to believe I was at a field hospital on Thursday."

Jack takes another sip as he reflects on the whirlwind of the last 48 hours. By the time the wounded reached his previous post, they had been through several levels of treatment and medication. Once he reached the Metz area, Jack had to hit the ground running. Here, so close to the fighting, the injuries are fresh and the pain is excruciating. Fortunately, with the lull in the action after the taking of Metz, Jack has only seen the tail end of a flow of men wounded by shrapnel and small arms fire. He has improved their field dressings, administered pain medication, and passed them along to the clearing station down the road. Nevertheless, he has treated a steady stream of soldiers suffering from infection and exposure.

"I'm seeing a lot of immersion foot out here."

That's a new one on Hank, so Jack uses the more common term for the condition.

"Trench foot. Damned painful."

"Yeah, it's rough. But cheer up, Jack. It's almost Christmas!"

Jack marvels at how easily Hank reads his mood, and he thanks his lucky stars for making a friend like Hank. It has made his sudden transition manageable. As the two sip their coffee, Jack spies an officer chatting amiably with several soldiers who are warming themselves with a fire in a 55-gallon drum. Their laughter rises while embers leap, swirl and dance around them.

"Who's that?"

"That's our new CO. Christ, he looks green."

"Seems to have a very good rapport with the men."

"Yeah, sure. But can he lead in battle? Patton is champing at the bit to strike into the heart of Germany, and you can bet dollars to doughnuts 10th Armored will be the tip of the spear."

As if his ears are burning, the battalion's new commanding officer, Major William Desobry, leaves the soldiers by the fire laughing and heads over to Jack and Hank. Jack is struck by his height, long lanky strides and youthful appearance. They exchange salutes, and the major smiles at Jack.

"Captain Prior?"

"Yes, sir."

"Sorry to drag you up to the front line. You heard our surgeon is down for the count?"

"Yes, sir. I'll try to fill his shoes."

"Just do the best you can, Doctor. I'm sure it'll be more than enough."

The major's warm smile gives Jack a reassurance he had not yet found within himself. As Hank and Desobry talk quietly, Jack takes stock. His last year of medical school was accelerated to rush him to Cherbourg, France, where he landed in September. Once on the continent, his unit had raced across France to catch up with Patton at Metz, hard by the German border, where the Third Army was the first to take the heavily fortified city by force in 500 years. It had all happened so fast. And now, Jack is taking the place of a sick surgeon. Trained as a general physician, he has little experience in major surgical procedures. For the life of him, he can't get the image of a square peg and a round hole out of his head.

If the past two days have been a test, Jack passed. Still, the doubts tease and trouble him. If the division spearheads a thrust into Germany, 10th Armored will be in for a desperate, bloody fight. Jack wonders how well he might hold up under fire? And what kinds of wounds might he have to contend with?

The doctor takes a restorative sip of hot coffee and finds a measure of equanimity. Perhaps the offensive will be delayed, or even called off. Perhaps Jack's aid station will remain behind as a clearing station. And, he ponders wishfully, perhaps the surgeon has already made a swift recovery and is on his way back to the front.

As if to mock his musings, the wind picks up and blows in his face with the first bite of a cold front coming in. And a low rumble tumbles out of the distant north once again.

Renee and Jaquin

Renee stops short on the sidewalk of a narrow street and looks eastward toward an unfamiliar sound. Perhaps it is a delivery truck making an early round on the outskirts of town or a heavy overhead door opening and closing. She cannot place it and quickens her pace toward her father's hardware store. On her way she comes upon old friend Jaquin, the village pharmacist, whose business has been in his family for generations. Jaquin is standing before the pharmacy door fumbling with a dozen keys on a chain. When he sees Renee, he breaks out the warmest of smiles and limps over to her, favoring his right leg. It was injured and bent out of shape in World War I, the war to end all wars. But he pays it no mind.

"Ah, good morning, Renee."

"Good morning, Monsieur Jaquin."

He kisses both cheeks of the lovely daughter of his good friend Gustave Lemaire, an exercise that clearly makes his day. Energized, the pharmacist resumes his search for his shop key with fingers that lack dexterity, almost rejoicing when he inserts the correct one. As he swings the door open with a jangling of jingle bells, he beckons Renee to enter.

"Can you visit with me for a while? Come in, come in."

Renee cannot refuse this dear man, her jovial surrogate uncle, and follows him in. He signals that he needs just a moment to complete a pressing task lest he forget it. The pharmacist switches on an overhead light and gets right to work on a prescription. Comforted by the smells of the old store, Renee glances around at crowded shelves and wooden floors worn down by nearly a century of customers. Once Jaquin bags and places the medicine on the counter, he gives Renee his full attention. A keen observer, he sees the darkness of many sleepless nights under her eyes.

"So, you are an early riser. Just like your father."

"I'm used to it. I have the morning shift at the hospital."

"But you're on holiday. Why not sleep in? Ah! You are helping your father at the store?"

"Yes, he needs me. Why are you here so early?"

"Madame Peyroux is out of her stomach medicine. I need to get it to her straight away."

Renee knows that the old lady lives a good distance from the pharmacy and that delivering her medicine would normally fall to the orphan who sleeps in the back and assists Jaquin.

"But where is the boy who helps you?"

"Etienne? He stays at the barracks now. They have reformed the 5th Belgian Fusiliers. He wants to fight the *Boche*."

"But he is just a boy!"

"He is of age now. All the young men are joining."

"Let me take that for you."

They both look at the package on the counter.

"Your father is expecting you, and Madame Peyroux will want you to visit with her."

"I will tell her... that I will come again this evening after I finish with Papa."

Jaquin wavers and Renee presses her case.

"She is on my way."

Though they both know that this is an exaggeration, Jaquin weighs his options and acquiesces. He cannot deny this charming young woman who is so eager to help him, and he cannot defy his body, impaired as it is.

"Let me help you while I am home. I can be your Etienne."

"But you will be doing too much. You won't have time to enjoy yourself."

Even as he prevaricates, Jaquin assembles two more packets for patients who live quite near to Madame. He is unprepared for the tone of resignation in Renee's response.

"Yes, perhaps."

Since it is Jaquin's nature to sort through the puzzle pieces that people offer unwittingly, he finds himself posing questions. What is she saying about herself? Is there something else there? He seeks out the honesty of her eyes, but she has turned away. He buys a moment to think over her offer by turning to his bulletin board and leafing through a dozen scripts that are pinned there. Renee is quick to capitalize on his reticence.

"Monsieur, there are so many. They are sick and lonely. Perhaps I can lift their spirits."

"Oh, well..."

He gives in completely.

"... I'm sure you will."

As he hands over the three packets, Renee receives them as a matter of course and nestles them in her shoulder bag.

Whatever Renee might be shielding from Jaquin, it is obvious that she has a burning need to stay busy. But at what cost? On the other hand, why fight it? Give the dear girl all the room she needs. She is a nurse, a healer. She just wants to help. But no, there is something else. At this point in his inner debate, he almost regrets his ability to read people and thus become entangled in the cares and woes of so many others. He surrenders and returns to the moment but resolves to consider Renee's situation further when the time is right.

After a brief exchange of pleasantries, Jaquin limps over to the door with her. When they step outside Renee lingers, looking into the heavy fog as if straining to see what cannot be seen. Try as he might, Jaquin finds that he cannot suppress his inquisitive nature, though he lands upon the most innocuous of queries.

"So, you are happy there? In Brussels?"

"I love my work at the hospital."

Her matter-of-fact answer only raises questions and eyebrows further for Jaquin. What about the rest of her life?

Renee is also very intuitive, but with a default setting to give aid and comfort. She reads between the lines and opts to calm her old friend with a smile.

"But... it's good to be home for Christmas."

"Especially this Christmas! With the *Boche* gone, we are free again!"

Every time he thinks of the liberation, Jaquin is tickled. With Belgium emancipated and the holiday coming on, smiles have returned to the faces he meets. To their delight, Renee and Jaquin watch a workman climb a ladder to string Christmas lights on a lamppost. The magic of the season cradles them for a few precious moments more.

Once again, a rumbling sound rolls in from over the hills and through the forests of the Ardennes. This time, it occurs to Renee that it might be a train on the Bourcy rail line.

Chiwy

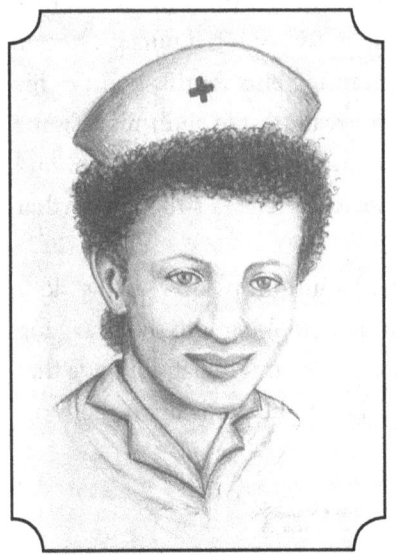
Augusta Chiwy, RN

Augusta Chiwy steps out onto the platform at the train station in Brussels, looking very trim and proud in her warm, woolen St. Elizabeth Hospital uniform. She turns to the cabin boy who hands down her suitcase and gives him a generous tip. With a loud huff of steam and smoke, the train begins to pull away. She is in transit and soon finds herself alone on the platform. All the other passengers who descended have reached their destination and quickly departed.

She walks to the big board to confirm her connection and finds the 7:20 train for Bastogne and Luxembourg. She made it just in time, but is puzzled to see no other train in the yard getting up steam for departure. As a station worker walks to the board and climbs his ladder to update the schedule, Chiwy makes her way over to the ticket office. There she finds the station master listening intently to the radio and sharing a look of consternation with an elderly office clerk.

"Pardon, Monsieur. Which is the Bastogne train?"

"All passengers for Bastogne are changing to the 7:45 train for Namur. It is delayed, but it will soon be here."

"But the schedule?"

As she turns to point to the big board, she sees the station worker removing the letters and numbers for the Bastogne train and dropping them into a box below.

"I'm sorry, Mademoiselle. All trains to Bastogne and points south are cancelled. In Namur, you can get transport to Marche and there... with luck... find a ride into Bastogne."

"But the trains have been running so well since the liberation. What could be the reason?"

"You have not heard perhaps? There is fighting in the Ardennes."

"Oh! But are you sure it is the only way?"

"Yes, Mademoiselle. Everything is shutting down."

Will and Joey

Though the artillery barrage ended some time before, Will and Joey are still rattled by the earth-shaking explosions that seem to echo forever in the hills and forests of the Ardennes. Now the even more ominous sound of heavy armor grinding up the hill into Luxembourg can be heard just to the north and south of their position. Joey is wide-eyed with dread.

"Wha... what's that?"

"Sounds like armor. If it's the Krauts, they're flankin' us."

Joey twitches and turns about as though shot through with a jolt of electricity, settles on a direction, and tries to climb out of the foxhole. Will lunges to grasp Joey's jacket, yanks him back into the hole and wraps him tightly in a bear hug. But Joey is the bear and Will struggles to hold him as he goes nose to nose with him, hissing with anger and alarm.

"Goddamn it, Joey! Keep your head down! You're gonna give us away."

They are locked in this desperate embrace for several moments, until Joey seems to recognize Will. As Joey's coiled body unwinds, Will loosens his grip and rocks back on his knees, breathing hard from the effort expended. Joey falls against the back of the hole, reaches his thumb inside his collar, and appears to gently knead the fabric. Will notices the nervous tic but thinks nothing of it. Soon Joey is back to himself, simple and oblivious.

"I'm sorry Will. But... I'm scared."

"Hey, me too. But don't worry. Guys like you got a guardian angel."

As if caught with his hand in the cookie jar, Joey releases his collar and snaps his hand back to his lap.

A heavy vehicle crests the hill up from the River Our, shifts gears, and accelerates on the level ground perhaps a quarter mile away. Joey looks into the fog with growing alarm. From the sounds of it, it is a German Tiger II, a 70-ton behemoth. It comes to a stop and cuts loose with an ear-splitting volley from its 88mm cannon. Will quickly grasps Joey's arm and holds on tight to short-circuit Joey's renewed cycle of terror. Then he speaks as calmly as he can.

"Listen, Joey. You gotta get your mind off it. Think about something else."

"But... but there is nuthin' else!"

"Well sure there is. There always is. For instance, I like to remember when I was a kid and used to hike around the battlefield. When I was sad, or lonely, or something, I'd go up Little Round Top and pretend I was one of Chamberlain's boys."

"Chamberlain?"

"Yeah! C'mon, Joey. You're in the Pennsylvania National Guard! Every Keystoner knows about Chamberlain... at Gettysburg."

"I never been there."

"OK. Anyway, listen."

Will pictures himself as a young boy, kneeling in the dirt. His face is grim as he listens to Chamberlain summarize their desperate situation, which calls for desperate measures.

"Chamberlain's boys from Maine were just about out of ammo, so he ordered a bayonet charge down the hill to catch them Rebs flat-footed. I used to run down that hill, hollerin' to beat the devil!"

"Will?"

"What?"

"I can't see it."

"Jeez, Joey. It would help if it was one of your own memories."

"But I like your story, Will. I just can't see it."

"Remind me when we get home to send you a picture postcard. Would that help?"

"It sure would. Thanks, Will."

Seven Roads to Bastogne

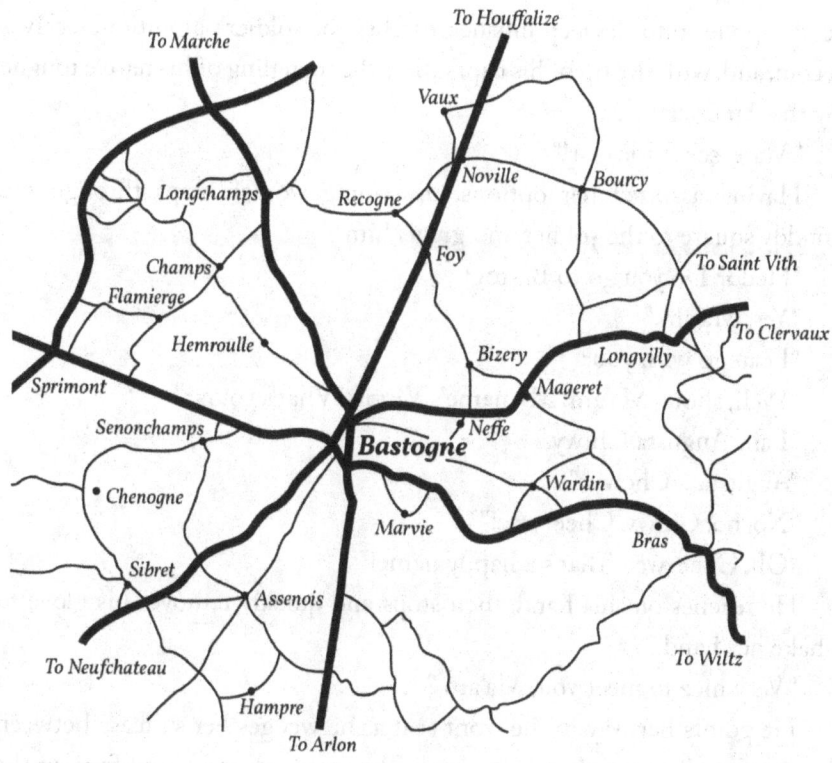

Chiwy

The market square in the center of Marche, Belgium, slowly sheds the last of its customers, and a few local farmers and tradesmen stand by their near-empty barrows sipping coffee and chatting about the latest news from the front. Several turn when a tractor pulling a large, open wagon full of hay bales rumbles into the square from the Namur Road. A burly man jumps down from the tractor and sets a box down to assist his lone passenger as she steps down from the wagon. Conversations around the square pause at the sight of a petite woman of mixed lineage and then resume as it seems that, at this point in the war, these men have seen it all. But one pair of eyes continues to stare with evident fascination. An American soldier who has been loading his jeep, which is marked prominently with a red cross, stops to take in the sight of the young lady. Her bright countenance is, to him, the only light in the square. A young Belgian man who has been helping to load supplies into the jeep finishes, catches the soldier's attention, receives a coin, and, with the tip of his cap, suffers the mangling of his native tongue by the American.

"Mare-see, Mon-sur!"

Having assessed her options, the young woman steps through the muddy square to the soldier and greets him.

"Hello? Do you go to Bastogne?"

"Yes, Ma'am."

"I can go with you?"

"Well, shore, Ma'am. My name's Virgil. What's yours?"

"I am Augusta Chiwy."

"Augusta... Chewy?"

"No, no. Chiwy, Chee-wee!"

"Oh, Chee-wee. That's a happy name!"

He reaches out his hand, then stops and quickly removes his glove to shake her hand.

"Very nice to meet you, Ma'am."

He points her way to the front seat as he wedges her suitcase between boxes of medical supplies in the back. They settle in and Virgil fires up the engine. He takes in her St. Elizabeth uniform.

"You a nurse, Ma'am?"

"Yes, yes. A nurse. We go?"

"We go."

Virgil releases the hand brake, pumps roughly on the worn clutch, forces the gears into first, then starts off with a lurch. He offers a sheepish look of apology, to which she returns a gracious smile. As they pull out of the square and onto the Bastogne road, Virgil cannot resist stealing a sidelong glance or two at Chiwy.

"Begging your pardon, Ma'am, but... are you a Negro?"

Chiwy bristles at the sound of the word, with equal measures of surprise and resentment. She has never thought of herself this way.

"I am *Belge!*"

There is an awkward pause as Chiwy scrutinizes Virgil. The mistreatment of the black race in America is well known to every European schoolgirl. Many of Hitler's early policies toward the Jews were modeled after the Jim Crow laws in the southern states, and his brown-shirted goons were inspired by the Ku Klux Klan. She proceeds cautiously.

"My father is *Belge!* And my mother is *Congolais... Africaine!*"

"Please be forgiving me, Ma'am. It's just that you look different."

"I am different! You are different! We are all different!"

"Heck no, I'm just a country boy. My Pa's from Kentucky and..."

The engine lugs as the jeep struggles to mount a hill. Virgil grinds the gears badly before settling on one. Finally, he turns to Chiwy to finish his thought which he evidently thinks is of little consequence to anyone.

"... and my Ma's from Kentucky. So, no Ma'am, I'm as same as I can be."

Chiwy suddenly realizes that Virgil is completely innocent and feels her momentarily stiffened pride washed away by her natural upbeat charm. She turns to Virgil, who appears chastened, and offers a last word to him, gently.

"Even so, to me, you are different."

After several miles of silence, Chiwy attempts to draw the reserved soldier out.

"Tell me about yourself."

"Gosh, there's not much to tell."

"Please, tell me something. Something different about you."

"Well... there is one thing. My family loves strawberry rhubarb pie. But me? I can't get enough blueberry!"

"Ah, yes. The blue berry. We have these. But I mean... tell me something important."

"Now that you mention it, I like to take in animals that are hurt and try to fix 'em up. All the fellas tease me 'cause they just wanna shoot the critters!"

"Ah! Just like my father. He is a doctor for the animals, a *veterinaire.* You are a medical man?"

"No, Ma'am. Just a driver and..."

The jeep hits a rough patch of road, catching all the worst holes. As Virgil and Chiwy are jostled about, he turns to Chiwy with a sheepish look.

"... and a bad one at that!"

Chiwy cannot contain her mirth. Though so often stung whenever people laugh at him, it finally dawns on Virgil that she is laughing with him. In a welcome release, they burst out together and roll along happily on smoother roads for several miles.

It has been quite a day so far for them both. Chiwy had to hitch several rides along the way from Namur to Marche, with the last short leg accomplished in the plodding wagon. Virgil had a solitary run out to Marche to pick up supplies and did not relish the lonely ride back in the cold and thickening fog. Little did he know that he would have such delightful company during the run back to Bastogne. He feels lighter than he has in weeks and cannot suppress a song rising up inside him.

"Mairzy doats and dozy doats"

He stops short when Chiwy turns to him with a searching look. He heard the nonsense song a couple of times before shipping out and cannot get it out of his head.

"What is that you are singing?"

"Aw, shucks... it ain't nothing. Just somethin' I heard on the radio back home."

"Please sing it for me."

He is reluctant. She adds.

"You have a very nice voice."

It tips the balance. Virgil has learned that in times of war, people can come and go quickly. One could have just moments to share with another. It forces one to judge a person's character, to suspect or trust, quickly. For Virgil, it is usually the latter. Besides, he is absolutely charmed, and cannot deny this spirited young woman.

"Well, OK."

"Mairzy doats and dozy doats and liddle lamzy divey
A kiddley divey too, wouldn't you?"

"What does it mean? Mairzy doats?"

"Well... I don't rightly know."

Virgil finds it too hard to puzzle out, so he keeps his peace for a spell. Chiwy joins him as she surrenders to the droning engine. A smile creases her lips as she contemplates the warm embrace of her father's family. It will be so good to be home for Christmas.

A military truck appears in the fog parked on their side of the road. Virgil brakes to pass it carefully. American infantrymen have dismounted to stretch and urinate. A few are laughing as they watch the jeep pass. Virgil is sure they are mocking him and hunches down in his seat. Chiwy puts two and two together and turns questioning eyes to him. Virgil responds sheepishly.

"What I really want to be is a rifleman, like my Pa and his Pa. But the army says I'm too soft."

"Too soft? But this is a good thing for a man. It means you are gentle."

"It does?"

"Yes, yes! And women love a gentle man."

In spite of herself, Chiwy offers just a hint of flirtation. It leaves Virgil blushing and stumbling over his words.

"Gosh... well... I mean... nobody ever called me a gentleman before. I'll be thanking you for that."

The harmony they forge sustains them as the afternoon wears on. Once they pass the Sprimont crossroad they meet sporadic civilian traffic coming toward them. As they slow to a crawl, a motley parade of motorized and horse-drawn vehicles trudges past them in the thickening fog. Faster vehicles overtaking slower ones fill the road, forcing Virgil to pull over. He steps out behind the jeep to warn following vehicles but finds nothing coming on. When the traffic clears, Chiwy's attention is drawn to a man across the road checking his horse's hoof while his wife, children, a goat, and a variety of belongings fill the back of his horse-drawn cart. Chiwy steps out to stretch her legs. In the hope of making sense of the stream of refugees headed away from Bastogne, she calls out to the man.

"Pardon, Monsieur. What is happening?"

"The old boy is limping."

Chiwy stands by patiently until the man finds a stone wedged in the horse's hoof, pries it out, and looks Chiwy's way. He quickly gathers that she is referring to the exodus underway.

"Oh! The *Boche* are coming again."

"To Bastogne? But why?"

"They must, Mademoiselle. They need our seven roads in and out of town in every direction, like the spokes of a wheel."

He taps the cartwheel with his hand tool and steps to the back of the wagon where he offers his wife a few words of encouragement. She responds by pulling her three young children closer to her and tucking blankets tighter around them and under their legs. With the fog shifting to their advantage, Virgil returns to the jeep and encourages Chiwy to join him. As she steps back to the jeep, the man mounts to his cart seat, takes his reins in hand, and calls out his last words of explanation.

"It was the same in 1914 and in 1940. People want to forget, but the *Boche* always come through the Ardennes. Always."

"When will they be here?"

"Tomorrow, maybe. Listen."

While the horse and cart clatter away, Chiwy turns to the rumble of artillery in the east and tries to place it beyond the horizon. With the muffling effect of the fog, it is impossible to gauge direction and distance, but Virgil is suitably alarmed. He turns to Chiwy as they settle back into the jeep and prepare to get underway again.

"Are you sure you want to go on in?"

"Yes, of course. I am always home for the holidays."

When the fog thins, they move easily through Senonchamps and follow the road signs for Bastogne. At the edge of town an American military policeman is monitoring traffic in and out of Bastogne on the Marche Road. Few citizens are entering, and all those who are leaving are silenced by the gloomy weather and the extreme discomfort of dislocation.

Here and there, elderly men and women wear hollow expressions of foreboding, having been forced from their homes by German aggression twice already this century. As the MP waves Virgil and Chiwy through and into Bastogne, artillery blasts are still heard in the distance, but clearer and closer. Virgil turns to Chiwy to offer a final word of warning. To his surprise, he reads in her face perfect serenity, the kind of composure that comes from great resolve and purpose.

"Well... it's a good thing you're a nurse. There's bound to be a heap of trouble around here."

"There! Stop there. My father's house is behind. I will go to him first, then I will see how I can help."

"That's mighty Christian of you, Ma'am. You shore are different. And... and a very pretty lady."

"And you are different too. And a very handsome man."

"Shucks, I don't know about that."

Virgil steps out to unload and hand Chiwy her suitcase. Chiwy thanks him and offers her hand.

"Thank you, Virgil."

Virgil takes her hand like a gentle man and scares up the courage to look her square in the eye. What he sees, he swears, is a hint of mischief. What the heck? In just a few hours she has completely captivated Virgil and befuddled his emotions. This gal is one in a million, and he searches for the right parting words to say.

"Uh... you're welcome. Any time Ma'am, I mean Augusta. I mean, I wanna say... "

Chiwy heartens him with a smile, and he happily stumbles on.

"... we sure may be different, but... vee-vah the dif-fer-ence!"

"Oui! Vive la différence!"

Virgil's day is made. He jumps into the jeep, guns the engine, and grinds the gears again. He turns to share one more laugh with Chiwy before the jeep surges forward. As she watches it pull away, Chiwy marvels at how well her long day ended, in such pleasant company. But when the jeep rounds the corner, her thoughts turn to her father, who would have been expecting her arrival from midday on. He must be worried sick. Chiwy grasps her suitcase and quickly walks down an alleyway that opens up to a sequestered side street.

As she scurries down the foggy street, a solitary figure materializes leaning against a streetlight pole. She slows as she passes an American soldier, not much taller than she, who is staring transfixed at the second floor of a building across the narrow street. He seems unaware of Chiwy's presence. She follows his gaze to the source of his wonder. Someone is playing the piano with feeling. It is a romantic melody speaking of love, loss, and longing that has mesmerized the soldier and offered him respite on this ominous day. As always, Chiwy takes things as they come, shrugs it off, and resumes her quick pace homeward.

Madame Peyroux's Apartment

Renee is seated on a bench before an old upright piano, but her thoughts are far, far away as she plays "Air in G," an arrangement for piano of a well-known Bach masterpiece. Tiny, frail Madame Peyroux sits heavily bundled and nearly invisible within several cushions and blankets she has arranged on an overstuffed chair. Her withered legs are raised on a hassock, and her hands and feet are covered by heavy woolen socks. Beside her sits a tray holding a cup of peppermint tea and the package from the pharmacy. Now that her digestive tract is under control, this is as good as it gets for the lonely, housebound widow. With eyes closed, she drifts along with the lilting melody.

With a tricky part coming, Renee concentrates on her right hand, then evidently makes a mistake and softly scolds herself. She repeats the passage correctly, with Madame none the wiser, and carries on flawlessly to the end. As the last chord fades away, Renee turns to face Madame and wonders if she has fallen asleep. As though reading Renee's thoughts, Madame Peyroux opens her eyes and offers Renee a great sigh of gratitude.

"That was lovely. Thank you, my dear. It takes me back to the early days with my Johannes."

Renee is similarly moved by the melody and the memories it stirs of a special time in her life. Yet she turns away from Madame toward the window. As she dabs at her eyes discreetly, a single streetlight shines faintly through the fog. She finds its solitude almost overwhelming. A clock chimes. Renee suddenly becomes aware of the lateness of the hour and rises from the bench. Madame is quick to respond.

"Won't you stay a little longer?"

Renee composes herself and turns to Madame with a sympathetic smile.

"I'm sorry, Madame. I have two more stops to make."

The time they spent together has been a comfort for the two women. But now Renee must make haste to complete Monsieur Jaquin's deliveries and hurry home, where Mama will be expecting her to help with the evening meal.

While Renee gathers her coat and shoulder bag, Madame begins to prepare herself for another evening alone. Her only company will be the ticking clock that patiently marks the passing of another sleepless night. As dawn approaches, she often dozes for an hour or two. It is then that Johannes comes to her. He beckons her, and she responds that she will soon join him. How soon? She doesn't know. Perhaps she will be given yet another day among the living and, if she is lucky, another visit from Renee.

"Will you come tomorrow? Tell Monsieur Jaquin the pain in my neck has returned."

While she rubs her neck, Madame betrays herself by suppressing a smile. Renee shakes her head affectionately as they share a tender moment. It is as though they are children again, without a care in the world, keeping and sharing secrets, and playing little tricks on each other.

"It comes and goes."

"Well, either way, I will try to come by."

Renee goes to the door and turns to breathe in Madame's simple life one more time. A part of her wants to stay on in Madame's cocoon, where it is safe and warm and no one can find her, no one can hurt her.

At the same time, Madame is watching Renee thoughtfully, as if a part of her wants to leave with Renee and be young again. Wouldn't Johannes be pleased? He was just about Renee's age, and she much younger, when they met and fell in love. They had many wonderful years together before

Johannes was taken from her in The Great War. There were no children. She is utterly alone with her memories.

Renee closes the door gently behind her, descends the stairs, and steps out of the building into the gathering darkness. She looks up and down the deserted street and is startled when an American soldier comes up to her out of the fog. She is quickly disarmed by the fresh-faced young man who is perhaps half a head shorter than her.

"Oh, I'm sorry I gave you a fright. I was passing by and… was that you playin' the piano?"

"Yes."

"It was beautiful."

"Thank you."

Having screwed up the courage to say his piece, he ventures to look into Renee's eyes. He finds them to be so dark and deep that he feels like he is drowning. As he shifts uncomfortably on his feet, he struggles to regain his senses. He is at a complete loss for words before such unexpected beauty. Renee responds with patience and the hint of a smile at the corners of her mouth. The soldier suddenly snatches his woolen cap from his head and crushes it nervously in his hands.

"Well, look at me, will ya? Where're my manners? My name's Ruben."

"Roo-been."

"No, Ruben, like the sandwich."

"I am Renee."

He reaches out and formally shakes Renee's hand and grins from ear to ear. At that moment, he must be the happiest man in Bastogne. Renee returns the smile.

"Can I come tomorrow to hear you play?"

"Oh. This is not my house."

"Well… do you have a piano at your house? Can I come there?"

"Yes, I do. But…"

"Then it's a date!"

What should she say? Before she can form a response, Ruben expresses his manhood, his duty.

"Say, I'd better walk you home."

If he learned anything from his father, it is how to treat a lady. No self-respecting man would let a woman walk down a darkened, foggy street alone. Renee sizes up Ruben, who is little more than a boy with fuzz on his lip. It occurs to her that he could be her little brother, deserving of her protection. But, after all, he is a soldier who is putting his life on the line for Belgium. To deny him would be inhospitable and a pointless wound to his pride. Besides, she finds him amusing, the perfect antidote for a heavy heart. So, what is the harm? Renee acquiesces and they disappear together walking into the fog.

Will and Joey

At the front, the sounds of battle have receded as German armor has punched through American lines and rumbled westward into the Ardennes. Here and there elements of the 28th stand and fight, others fall back, and still others have been bypassed and are nervously sitting tight, awaiting orders. In this exhausting state of tension and uncertainty, it is a comfort to have someone beside you. Knowing that Will is watching over him, Joey doses off under their heavy tarp for a late afternoon nap. Will keeps a silent vigil with the fog while wondering how the hell Joey can just nod off like that and sleep like a lamb. The slumbering giant only stirs when snow starts to fall and tickle his nose, awakening him with a goofy grin on his face. Now what?

"Hey, Will?"

"Yeah?"

"Remember your story about runnin' down that hill? Well, I remembered something too."

"Gee, that's nice. Why don't you tell me about it?"

"OK. So, we wuz down at the old quarry."

Joey was much younger than the other boys that day at the quarry, but almost as tall as them and skinny as a rail. They teased him mercilessly and called him chicken bone as they held a rope out to him. Joey looked up the rope's length to where it was attached to the massive limb that hung out over the void of the abandoned mine. He declined, shaking with fear, while the boys continued to pelt him with taunts and insults. Somehow, that day was different, and Joey found courage he never knew he had. He took the rope firmly in his hands and propelled his gangly body over the edge. He let go of the rope and tumbled out of control and out of sight, so frightened he could not even scream. The older boys were stunned silent and rushed to the edge to see only disturbed water below. Anxious moments passed and at least one boy ran for home. He knew that if Joey was hurt or drowned, he was sure to get a whipping. Just as the older boys began to look at each other, ready to blame the meanest among them, Joey flailed to the surface gasping for air. His look of terror changed quickly to surprise, then to triumph.

"Yeah!"

"Jeez, Joey. Keep it down."

"Oh, sorry, Will. I didn't mean to shout."

Now whispering.

"That... that was the last time I was really scared... 'til now."

"Yeah, well. You just gotta, you know, come up for air again."

Will nearly jumps out of his skin at the sound of a harsh, whispering voice, way too close for comfort.

"Hey, Bloody Bucket."

As though electricity courses through him, Will frantically grabs his rifle, dives to the edge of the hole, and levels his weapon in the direction of the intruder. The voice sounds again, suitably alarmed.

"Hold your fire."

Will's thoughts trip over each other: Sounds like one of our guys. He knows about the bucket. But these Krauts are clever sons-of-bitches. Better make sure. He manages to spit out a challenge.

"Ty?"

"Cobb. Best hitter ever."

Kraut or no Kraut, he doesn't know what he's talking about.

"Like hell he was!"

"Lifetime batting average of three sixty-six. Who you got that beats that?"

The stranger seems to have a southern accent and a god-awful smell that seems familiar to Will. He lowers his guard.

"Gotta go with the Iron Horse."

"Gehrig?"

"Yeah."

"Ah, he was a bum."

Scared out of his wits just moments ago, Will feels a surge of temper. Nobody bad-mouths his Yankees, especially his hero, who isn't around anymore to defend himself.

"Them's fightin' words, buddy."

"Hey, take it easy."

Keeping himself at arm's length just in case, the intruder shows himself as he kneels by the foxhole. Oh, oh. It's that bullet-headed sergeant from Baker Company, the one who's always chewing on a sodden, stinking cigar, and he means business.

"Listen up! We're holding tonight, but we're falling back at oh-six-hundred."

Will ducks away, not wanting to be recognized and get on the bastard's list. He attempts a civil tone.

"Where we headed?"

"Eighth Corps."

"Where are they?"

"Bastogne."

Clearly ill-advised, Will vents just a bit of frustration with the Yankee-hating yokel.

"Never heard of it."

"OK, smart aleck. Sleep tight, and don't let the frost bite!"

For some cock-eyed reason, Will is emboldened.

"We got a comedian over here!"

"Just be ready, dogface."

When the sergeant disappears into the fog, Will turns to Joey and detects a question forming on the face of the gentle giant. Out it comes.

"Hey, Will? Did he say we're going to Boston?"

The Typewriter

Jack is grateful that it has been a manageable day at the aid station, with nothing he couldn't handle. Now, with 10th Armored in the process of bedding down, he enjoys a bit of respite. He studies a map of France on which he has marked his trek across the country. He runs his finger north of Metz to try to locate Remeling, purportedly the nearest town. It doesn't appear to be on the map. Where the hell are they?

Meanwhile, Wallington is bent over his beloved typewriter rattling away at his paperwork. He finishes his reports and busies himself placing carbon copies in various files, which he then tucks away in a couple of boxes. There is evident satisfaction in a day's work finally done, and done well, as he calls out to Jack.

"All set, Doc."

Outside, the relative quiet of the encampment is broken by nearby shouts. Beagle bursts into the tent, sending the flaps flying. He rushes over to Jack, almost breathless with excitement.

"We're movin' out!"

"OK, catch your breath. Now... what's the score?"

"I don't know, sir."

Hank steps into the tent to confirm Jack's orders formally.

Wallington is quick to respond and channels the orderly's frenetic energy into the task of moving equipment and several dozen boxes of medical supplies once again. The two captains stand aside as Beagle rushes by fully loaded on the way out to the truck. Meanwhile, Wallington covers his typewriter, sets it carefully down inside a box labeled "Admin," closes the lid, and stacks the box atop two other boxes of administrative records. With "job one" taken care of, he grabs a couple of cases of ether and rushes out of the tent.

Jack and Hank take their conversation outside, where they are momentarily struck dumb as tanks and trucks roar to life all around them, and headlights probe the fog. Jack turns to Hank.

"Any idea where we're headed?"

"All I know so far is we're supposed to fall in line behind Cherry's boys at twenty-three hundred."

Hank recognizes another officer nearby and jogs over to quiz him about the move. Jack watches after him in anticipation, then stands aside as Beagle comes up with a hand cart and rushes by him into the tent. He prepares to follow the young man in and steps aside again as Wallington rushes out of the tent with his arms full. Once inside, Jack dodges the orderly yet again as his aide heads out to the truck with administrative records stacked on the cart.

With MPs not yet in position to direct traffic, vehicles start to move out in disorderly fashion. As they bounce up and down across the rutted fields, their headlights shift wildly in the fog. Wallington waits for a break in the flow of traffic before crossing back to the tent, then watches, to his horror, as Beagle pushes his hand cart directly into the path of an oncoming truck.

"Hey! Look out!"

The orderly stops in the nick of time, but his momentum tips the top box over and spills the typewriter out. The truck promptly crushes it under its front wheel and again, for good measure, under its rear wheels. Beagle is stunned speechless, and the best buddy he ever had is frozen in place staring at his mangled, mortally wounded machine. Having heard the corporal call out in alarm, Jack rushes out of the tent and quickly sizes up the situation. Finding no one hurt, he is relieved, until he spies the crushed typewriter.

"Damn! Those are hard to come by."

Jack quickly reverts to the instincts of a healer when he takes in the corporal's anguish and the orderly's distress at being the cause.

"It's OK, men. We'll pick up another one along the way."

Wallington retrieves his typewriter, examines it and solemnly marches it over and into a trash barrel, where he mourns for a moment as though putting a cherished pet out of its misery. While he walks listlessly back toward the tent with a dazed look on his face, Beagle follows him at a safe distance, with his tail between his legs. Jack takes the initiative and enters the tent ahead of them. He stacks a couple of boxes and heads back out to the truck. His aides follow his lead and shift into a higher gear. Hank catches up to Jack on his way back to the tent.

"What's it look like, Hank?"

"They're saying the Krauts have counterattacked and broken through somewhere up the line, and the scuttlebutt is we'll be heading to cut 'em off."

He studies Jack's response, as anxiety plays briefly across the doctor's features. Are they headed directly into battle? Who will die? Who will survive? Will he be able to handle it? It is uncharted territory for Jack, with so much that is unknown. Thankfully, Hank changes the subject for him.

"Oh, by the way. I know how you love your maps, so I got this for you."

Hank hands Jack a map which the latter unfolds to reveal two nations nestled side by side.

"Luxembourg... and Belgium?"

"They always come through the Ardennes. You'd think we'd wise up."

While he studies the map, momentarily losing himself while he traces the roads snaking through the hilly, heavily forested region straddling the two countries, Jack's anxiety slips away. He thanks Hank for his thoughtfulness and folds the map into his jacket pocket. Jack follows his friend's gaze to a couple of soldiers painting over the 10th Armored Division identification on their truck. Others are doing the same on a tank. Once they are done, they quickly move on to other vehicles. Jack is puzzled.

"What're they doing?"

"It's right from the top, from Patton. He doesn't want the Krauts to know 10th Armored is on the move. And look, they're burning arm patches. We better get to it."

Jack and Hank step over to a roaring fire in a 55-gallon drum and watch a group of soldiers rip their patches off and throw them into the fire. Hank follows suit. Jack tears his off, but takes a moment to study the red, blue, and gold insignia he has worn with pride. It'd be a shame to burn it. With only the slightest twinge of conscience, he unobtrusively slips the patch into the right chest pocket of his field jacket.

Le Nut's Tavern 1994

While the bar matron decorates the tavern in red, white, and blue, the veterans discuss their recollections of the first day of the Battle of the Bulge. At the next table a new arrival, wearing a nametag that marks him as a veteran from the United Kingdom, listens in with keen interest. Meanwhile, Sergio has set up a turntable and is going through a stack of record albums he borrowed from the town library. He selects one and cues up "And the Angels Sing."

> *We meet, and the angels sing*
> *The angels sing the sweetest song I ever heard*

Sarge turns to listen to the music, and his eyebrows rise along with his spirits.

"Now, that's more like it!"

Several veterans nod in agreement as they tap their toes and strain to remember the last time they danced to the upbeat tune. As is their habit, Simpson and Brown listen intently as they try to identify the singer.

With a break in the conversation, some wet their whistles, while others pick at snacks in baskets on the table. The veteran from the UK detects an opportunity. He rises with some difficulty, straightens his sore back, and steps over to the Americans.

"I beg your pardon, gentlemen. May I join in?"

Sarge pulls out a chair for the newcomer, who drops into the seat with all the grace of a sack of barley. He shakes his head in resignation and receives warm and knowing smiles from men who understand the physical price of living for so long.

"I heard your remarks just then. I recall the first day of the battle as clearly as a highland stream. I was Monty's man on Patton's staff. We knew something was afoot that morning when we heard the old man cursing, as you say on your side of the pond, a blue streak. With words to the effect of how he does all the hard fighting while Monty sits on his royal arse!"

The veterans' warmth turns to mirth as they are tickled by their new friend's irreverence. Sarge leans in to study his nametag.

"51st Highlanders. No wonder you've no love lost for Montgomery. You're Scotch."

"Scotch is a drink. I am a Scot."

Sarge nods respectfully in acknowledgment of the common error he made. He beckons the Scot to continue his story and listens with rapt attention.

"As you well know, Eisenhower ordered Patton to send reinforcements to the Ardennes, dividing his forces in the face of the enemy, something Patton was loath to do. Reluctantly, Patton sent 9th Armored right square into the breach to block Jerry at Saint Vith. Then he sent you fellows..."

When the Scot turns to Sarge and Jack, he pauses while a low-level argument between Simpson and Brown overheats.

"No, it's Doris Day and the Harry James Orchestra."

"For the last time, it's Martha Tilton and Benny Goodman!"

Several heads turn to the argumentative pair. The two old troopers realize they are being disruptive again and defer to the Scot. Sarge is eager for him to continue his story.

"Go ahead, professor. You're coming to the good part!"

"Patton sent you fellows as well, 10th Armored..."

"Yeah! He threw us on a long, left hook to hit 'em right in the kisser!"

"We kiss and the angels sing
And leave their music ringing in my heart"

Martha Tilton has chimed in to finish the song with one of those coincidences that roll around now and then as the dice of life are thrown.

"Like I said, right in the kisser!"

This gets a chuckle from several veterans. They marvel at Sarge's energy and exuberance, something they apparently forgot to pack for this long trip back in time to Bastogne.

"Right you are. He sent you here..."

The Scot adds punctuation with a rap of his knuckles on the table.

"... to Bastogne!"

17 December 1944

Little daylight penetrates the cloud cover and heavy fog that saturates the forests of Luxembourg. As Will and Joey trudge up a long, low hill, wet snow begins to fall and accumulate. It makes it easier for Joey to follow the treads of soldiers who fell back before them. While they hike, they are propelled by the staccato of small arms fire and the thud of artillery from every direction but before them. Though strong as an ox, even Joey slackens his pace under the burden of his heavy pack, rifle and the tarp rolled up on his back.

"C'mon, Joey, pick it up."

"OK, Will. But... I'm hungry."

They reach the top of the hill and take five. Will fishes out a packet of crackers and hands several over to Joey.

"Listen, this is the last of the rations."

"Thanks, Will."

"It ain't much, so chew slowly. It'll seem like more."

As always, Joey takes Will's advice to heart. He nibbles on the crackers at first, but soon fills his mouth with a viscous mass that's difficult to swallow. He shakes his empty canteen and turns to Will, who rattles his canteen in response. When they stand to resume their journey, Joey has a bright idea and scoops a handful of slush to swallow. It does the trick with one big gulp, but for twenty paces his mouth is shocked by the cold, and his countenance is comically contorted. At the bottom of the hill, the snow-covered ground ends, and they enter a pine forest where branches reach out to scratch at the two weary men. Joey realizes Will was right about the crackers. It wasn't much. The gentle giant's hunger returns with a vengeance. He refrains from complaining, but his mind wanders as he contemplates hot meals of yore: wheat cakes, sausage, fried potatoes, and onions stacked high on a plate; Mama standing by with seconds and thirds for her growing boy; all washed down with the freshest, creamiest milk.

Joey stops abruptly.

"Hey, Will. I think we're lost."

"Nah, just keep followin' the footprints."

When Will reaches Joey's side, he finds the soggy pine needle carpet lying before them undisturbed.

"What the hell? Joey!"

"Sorry, Will."

"Ah, forget about it. I ain't been payin' attention either."

Will turns to confirm only their two sets of imprints marring the ground behind them.

"They must've turned off and dug in somewhere."

Mumbling to himself, Will consults his compass and confirms their westerly orientation. At least they haven't been going in circles. No sense in picking on the big guy. He's got a heart of gold, even if he isn't the sharpest knife in the drawer. As he returns the compass to his pocket, Will studies his giant, gentle friend. Joey is standing still and expressionless like a statue, pinching his collar between thumb and forefinger.

"What're you doin' there? Let's go."

Joey, still stinging from letting his best buddy down, drops his arm like a dead weight. Will shakes it all off and waves his hand with a flourish as if to say "after you." With a deep breath, Joey puts one foot in front of the other, and lets the weight of his load give him sustaining momentum forward. At the edge of the forest, they step through weeds onto fallow farmland. Uncomfortable out in the open, Will steers them toward a copse of trees materializing ahead of them. Upon entering the sequestered area within, Joey stops abruptly, spooked by something he sees.

"Will! Wha... what's that?"

Will levels his rifle and takes a menacing step forward. The fog shifts ever so slightly to reveal a moss-covered statue of an angel standing guard over what appears to be an ancient family burial plot.

"That?"

"Yeah."

"Jeez, Joey. You're gonna give me a heart attack."

Will shakes his head, shoulders his rifle, and trudges out of the cemetery. Joey lingers by the angel, the only monument of stature among a half-dozen smaller headstones in various stages of collapse and degradation. He carefully maneuvers to a spot where her downcast eyes seem to look directly into his own. Though the eyes are cold and opaque, he almost feels her sorrow. Who does she mourn? The names on the stones have weathered away. Beyond exhausted, his mind plays tricks on him. She is looking at him, but she cannot speak. If she could, what would she say? He turns to comment to Will and finds himself alone. When Will calls back to him, Joey jogs to catch up.

"Hey! Wait for me!"

10th Armored Convoy

With fog so thick, morning is not much of an improvement over the long, dark night as the convoy of the 10th Armored Division rolls slowly, methodically, up and down the hills of Luxembourg.

"Doc, this is the worst goddamn fog I ever did see."

"Just try to keep in line."

The toll of twelve hours of non-stop driving shows in the corporal's hands, as he grasps the steering wheel in a death grip, and in his eyes that strain to see twenty yards into the fog, even with the headlights on. It concentrates Jack's mind as well, yet he is startled when Wallington slams on the brakes. They fall just short of the vehicle that suddenly stopped in front of them, to the relief of the soldiers packed in the troop carrier.

The thud of a body tumbling off a bench in the back of Jack's truck is the prelude to a concert of colorful curses.

"Hey, Beagle. You all right back there?"

Wallington's genuine concern serves to lower the orderly's volume to the level of a grumble, which soon subsides. He returns his attention to the truck in his headlights and holds out his hands in apology. The soldiers respond by hunkering down once again to fight the tedium and cold discomfort of the long drive. When the convoy begins to inch forward, Wallington follows at a safe distance. He finds that he can't help feeling sorry for the boys in the truck.

"They must be freezing. Why don't they have winter gear?"

Jack weighs his response.

"I don't know. But if I had to guess, top brass expected the war to be over by Christmas."

As the shockwaves from the surprise attack by the *Wehrmacht* reach down through the rank and file, Jack ponders the plight of the ordinary foot soldier who must pay the piper for the overconfidence that infected the Allied high command. While he watches the young men bounce along in the truck ahead of them, Jack acknowledges that they have every right to grouse and gripe. Indeed, he sees it as a healthy outlet for their grievances.

When the convoy slows to a stop again, Wallington vents his frustration.

"Hurry up and wait! That's the army for you. Hurry up and wait."

A rumble of heavy cannon fire sounds in the north and captures their attention. Try as he might, Jack can't determine the direction, but it sounds like the battlefield is shifting westward, a worrisome sign in the age of *blitzkrieg*. Finally, the convoy starts to move again and ascends a long hill into thinning fog. As the corporal cranes his neck to look skyward, he becomes increasingly concerned about the improved visibility.

"Doc, I still don't get it."

"What's that?"

"They wanna get us there in a hurry, wherever there is. So, we're runnin' with our lights on. But it doesn't help much in this soup and... and what if Fritz spots us? We'd be sittin' ducks."

Jack has no good answer for his agitated aide. Orders are orders.

As they approach the crest of the hill, Jack becomes aware of the truck's radio, which is giving off a low level of static. Perhaps some music would pacify his driver. He turns up the sound and rolls the dial, only to find Axis Sally trying to sow her usual seeds of discontent among the Allies.

"Why are we fighting each other? We should join together to fight the Russians, our common enemy. They are Communists! They don't even believe in Christmas!"

Jack dispatches the smooth-talking traitor and spins the dial to the upper end of the scale, then rolls it back and bypasses Radio Berlin to find melodious French spoken at the bottom end.

"Ici Radio Luxembourg. Eh maintenant
pour nos amis Americains."

When the familiar voice of America's sweetheart Judy Garland fills the cab, tension is swept away like fallen leaves in a windstorm. Beagle yells for them to turn the music up, and his buddy obliges.

"Have yourself a merry little Christmas, let your heart be light
Next year all our troubles will be out of sight"

Explosive flashes appear dimly on a horizon now visible from the higher elevation. Their troubles are no longer out of sight as they inch closer and closer to the fighting, to Wallington's dismay.

"Damn."

"Have yourself a merry little Christmas, make the Yuletide gay
Next year all our troubles will be miles away"

A massive fireball appears on the horizon, not miles away, but closer, and is soon followed by the sustained roar of an enormous conflagration. Now he is alarmed.

"Shit and damn, Doc! They must've hit a fuel depot!"

Jack does his best to subdue his own surge of anxiety, modulating his response to calm his driver.

"Or we blew it to keep it out of German hands. Either way, not a good sign"

"Once again as in olden days, happy golden days of yore
Faithful friends who were dear to us will be near to us once more"

The station comes in clear as a bell at the crest of the hill, then slowly gives way to the crackle of static as the convoy gathers speed down the slope and disappears into the dense, dark forests of the Ardennes.

Dusk in Bastogne

The streetlamps in Bastogne are already shining as the last of the day's light is gradually absorbed into the fog. Gisele is skipping along carrying just a baguette, as Rene and Marguerite lug bags full of groceries and produce. The two older sisters are talking about the grim turn of events in the Ardennes in hushed tones. They are only interrupted when Marguerite catches Gisele breaking off bits of bread to nibble.

"Gisele! No wonder Mama thinks we have mice!"

"Oh, look! Can we stop?"

Gisele is captivated by a pair of dolls in a window display of a little department store. Judy Garland can be heard faintly singing within, adding another layer of allure to the brightly lit shop. But as much as she would like to stop, Renee is weary from a long day of toil at the hardware store, topped off by a walking tour of Bastogne with a shoulder bag full of Jaquin's deliveries. She admonishes her little sister as she bends under the weight of her load.

"Mama is expecting us."

"Just for a minute?"

With Gisele on the verge of pouting, Marguerite reads Renee's impatience. But she also notes her big sister's growing interest in the hats, blouses, cosmetics, and fine linen showcased in the window.

"Renee, why don't you stop with Gisele? You're on holiday!"

Renee impassively allows Marguerite to coax her bag off her shoulder. But she smiles when Marguerite, though now burdened with two heavy sacks, snatches the baguette from Gisele. As Marguerite heads home, Renee slowly follows Gisele, who fairly bounds up the steps and into the shop.

> *"Someday soon we all will be together if the fates allow*
> *Until then we'll have to muddle through somehow*
> *So have yourself a merry little Christmas now"*

The old man who keeps the store is sitting very close to his radio, as though warmed by the words of the song. When the melody ends, he turns to the sisters with misty eyes and wishes them Merry Christmas. As Renee returns the sentiment, Gisele dashes to a larger display of dolls in the aisle.

"Where did you get these, Monsieur?"

"From Paris, my dear. Just in time for Christmas. And we have soap now too."

Renee picks up a bar of soap and draws in its fragrance, while Gisele selects a bridegroom doll for a dance partner and twirls around with it.

"Look Renee! Isn't he handsome?"

"Yes, very nice, but... aren't you a bit old for dolls?"

The romance is brief as Gisele carelessly discards the doll in favor of a sparkling, winged angel, all in white. When Renee stoops to pick up the jilted groom that had tumbled to the floor, her necklace slips out from her blouse. In the bright lights of the shop, the pendant's colorful depiction of an angel holding an infant is clear. Gisele is almost breathless.

"Oh! What a beautiful angel!"

Unaware that her pendant is visible, Renee nods as she admires the doll Gisele is holding.

"Yes, Gisele. Very nice."

"No, no. Around your neck."

"Oh, this?"

Renee considers whether to share the origin of the jewelry and the love story behind it, but quickly rejects the idea. Gisele is too gabby and too much the butterfly, flitting here and there. True to form, her little sister spies the next shiny object and dashes over to a display of lipsticks on the counter. She selects one and looks through her little change purse for coins.

When she spreads them on the counter, the old man counts them in his head, smiles, and nods. Gisele is ecstatic. Renee is at the other end of the emotional spectrum. As she gently tucks the pendant back into her blouse her eyes water. She is almost grateful for Gisele's flighty behavior at the moment. It gives her room to breathe and serves as a welcome distraction from her own cares and woes. But when Gisele rushes to a mirror to apply the lipstick, Renee decides that this is one antic too far.

"Aren't you a bit young for lipstick?"

Gisele contorts her features into a childish scowl, ready to say something cruel to her sister, who is nearly thirty and unmarried. She is cut short by a sudden commotion in the street that draws the shopkeeper to the window, then through the door and outside. He listens to an American military policeman who is standing tall in the midst of a cluster of townspeople down at the corner. Peering out over his shoulder, inquisitive Gisele becomes a chatterbox of questions, until the shopkeeper holds up his hand to still her. With considerable effort, the old man overhears and pieces together just enough of the English to decipher the soldier's message.

"He is saying... a curfew! Tonight, at six o'clock! And... and a black... uh... a blackout! Effective immediately!"

"But what about Christmas?"

The shopkeeper turns to comfort Gisele but is unable to find words to say. He has seen too much of war in his long life to believe that this Christmas will be merry. To survive it will be enough. When artillery sounds in the distance, citizens up and down the street scramble to their shops and homes to meet the MP's requirements.

While others are in motion, Renee remains in place suffering a sudden, startling dread. With great effort, she beats it back and joins Gisele at the door where they watch several men get to work disconnecting the town's decorations. To their chagrin, strings of lights in the street blink into darkness one by one. Pained by the disappointment he sees on the faces of the sisters the old man struggles to find his voice.

"I'm sorry, my dears. But everything is going dark."

Lost in the Ardennes

With darkness upon the two lost soldiers and no prospect of shelter, their exhaustion, hunger, thirst, and low spirits make for a brutal combination. Will is wary of coming unexpectedly upon German soldiers in the impenetrable fog. While his load has been lighter than Joey's, his hair-trigger tension has fully drained him.

"Hey, Will?"

"Shhhh!"

"Come here."

Though anticipating another false alarm, Will detects the slightest hint of hope in Joey's voice. The big man is invisible in the fog, but Will is guided by his buddy's labored breathing. Soon they are feeling along the exterior of a building. Will stubs his toe on a step, suppresses a curse with great effort, and feels a door frame, then a door handle. He finds the door unlocked and slowly pulls it open. To his alarm, the hinges seem to announce their presence to anyone within shouting distance. He stops to listen but hears no one. Perhaps it is an evacuated area. Will grasps Joey's sleeve and whispers as he pulls him in.

"C'mon. Watch your step."

Joey stumbles anyway and teeters dangerously under his top-heavy load, but, with Will's sure grip, he manages to keep his balance. He steps into the pitch-dark building where Will is standing still, with all of his senses on high alert. Satisfied that they are alone, he sniffs the air and wonders aloud.

"Thought it might be a barn, but..."

A flash of light behind him startles Will.

"Joey!"

He is harsh and immediately regrets it as he steps quickly to blow out the flame on Joey's lighter. Joey is contrite.

"Sorry, Will."

"It's OK, Joey. There's nobody here."

They edge along the inside wall and find an open space. Will speaks for both of them.

"Let's get some shut-eye."

Joey drops everything with a thud and the heaviest of sighs, then joins Will as they kneel against a waist-high wooden wall and fix their packs for pillows. Joey uses his last ounce of energy to spread the tarp over them in the chilly building and settles in. As he does every night, Joey mumbles to himself. His voice trails off as fatigue invades him from head to toe. Will's curiosity finally gets the better of him.

"Hey, Joey. I gotta ask ya. What's that you say every night?"

"Well... it's my prayer."

"Lemme hear it."

Joey hesitates.

"C'mon. We're buddies, ain't we?"

"Well... OK. Angel of God, my guardian dear, to whom God's love commits me here. Ever this day, be at my side, to light, to guard, to rule and guide."

"That's real nice, Joey."

Joey is beaming. Will is just about the best pal a guy could ever have. He trusts Will with his prayer, his feelings, even his life. For Will, his fondness for Joey mingles with bemusement.

"But most guys pray in their heads, you know?"

"Mama told me to *say* it every night."

"Ha! If I ever get the chance, I'll let her know you did!"

"Oh, yeah. And God bless Will."

"Gee, thanks Joey. Now go to sleep, ya lug nut."

Merl, Luxembourg

Jack's convoy slows to a crawl as they pass a sign that reads "Merl." Jack flicks on his flashlight and unfolds his map. He traces a northerly route from Metz as he runs his finger from town to town.

"Let's see, we passed Thionville heading due north, I believe. Ah! Here we go, Merl. We're just outside Luxembourg City."

An MP stands clear in the truck's headlights, signaling a turn and calling out. Wallington rolls down his window and gestures that he hasn't heard and is met by a terse riposte.

"You heard me! Bivouac!"

Jack's driver, giddy with tension and fatigue, breaks into his favorite verse from the cadence count song.

> *"I don't mind a bivouac*
> *If I take along a WAC!"*

Not amused by the bawdy reference to the Women's Army Corps, the MP narrows his eyes at the insolent soldier and makes a mental note before he carries on with his duties. Wallington gets a kick out of taunting the bull, until he catches Jack's puzzled expression. He cranks up his window, follows the MP's directions, and takes a hard right into an open field. When they reach their designated spot, Jack and the corporal step down from the cab and are met by Beagle, who is working out the kinks of the long, rough ride. Jack surveys the ground and makes quick decisions.

"OK, men. Pitch our aid tent here, and our quarters there."

Jack spots Hank in consultation with other officers and waves hello. Hank steps over to Jack to catch him up.

"Don't get too comfortable. We're moving out at the crack of dawn."

"Have you heard where to?"

"No, just more rumors. But I heard Arlon mentioned. That's in Belgium, so I stand by my hunch."

While the column of deuce-and-a-half-ton trucks pulls into line and parks, tanks and half-tracks maneuver into place along a tree line. Weary men dismount and turn as one toward artillery sounding in the north. With the fog thinned, explosions faintly light the sky. Anxiety is written on their faces as they realize they are headed directly into combat.

18 December 1944

With the Ardennes still socked in by fog, a diluted light marks the dawn and filters into an ancient stone chapel. Bone weary, Will and Joey are sound asleep against the waist-high wall fronting the pew at the foot of an altar. Will stirs and snorts a prodigious, guttural snore, startling the sleeping giant beside him.

"Wha... who's there?"

Will returns to the depths of slumber, leaving the chapel as still as a crypt. Joey's eyelids flutter and drop like a curtain but are soon cinched up again as he hears a whispering voice. He slowly begins to focus on his surroundings. Looking up and to the right of a wall-mounted crucifix, Joey discovers an angel that seems to float in the air. An electric pulse raises the hairs on the back of Joey's neck when the angel makes eye contact and deigns to speak to him. Again, the whisper!

"Are they *Boche*?"

The angel is answered by another just like it that hovers on the other side of the cross. She also makes eye contact with Joey.

"Or English?"

Joey shakes off his confusion and, to his astonishment, looks up into the searching eyes of two women. One is middle-aged and the other is quite elderly. While they peer down at him, the older woman's wiry, gnarled fingers grip the wall that separates them from the two soldiers.

"Will. Hey, Will!"

"Huh?"

Will stirs, catches sight of the women, and sits up abruptly. He scrambles to make sense of the situation. A place of worship. The crack of dawn. Two ladies in their church-going finery. Clearly, they have come for morning prayers and were surprised by what they found at the foot of the altar. He also reads apprehension. The younger of the two grasps her friend's hands to offer comfort, and to receive it as well. Will doffs his woolen cap and puts them at ease.

"Good morning, ladies. We're Americans."

He indicates the flag on his sleeve, bringing nods of approval from the ladies.

"Ah, *les Amis*."

Just then Joey's stomach rumbles, and he shrugs apologetically. The elder of the two women searches in her bag, unwraps a biscuit, divides it, and hands the pieces to the soldiers. The morsels are dry as a bone, and Will and Joey labor to chew and swallow them. The younger woman points to Will's canteen with a questioning look. He shakes the empty container. She steps out from the pew, takes Will's canteen in hand, and softly pads to the base of the altar. She crosses herself and steps behind the lectern and returns with the vessel full of holy water. Her old friend is alarmed.

"Madeleine!"

"Oh, Marie. What is the harm?"

Madeleine has always had a measure of mischief in her, yet she crosses herself several times as if to make amends. She repeats the exercise with Joey's canteen. As the two soldiers drink their fill, Madeleine's transgression is quickly forgotten by Marie, who seems to be studying Will very closely, as if, even with her failing vision in the dim light, he seems familiar to her. Madeleine is puzzled.

"What is it, Marie?"

"It's just that he favors Antonin."

As Marie wanders silently down a path of remembrance, Madeleine offers an explanation to Will.

"Antonin is her grandson. He is missing in the war. She prays for him every morning."

When heavy explosions thud in the distance, a hint of dismay on Will's face brings a tear to Marie's eye. Madeleine also turns from the angry sounds to the vulnerable young men. Will reads their thoughts and tries on a cloak of bravado.

"Ah, it ain't nuthin."

Convincing no one, he looks from Madeleine to Marie, and then looks away. He cannot bear to look into the old woman's watering eyes, the same eyes that must search the street outside her window, day after day, hoping to see Antonin come marching home. While Joey stands to take a closer look at the wooden angels by the cross that so captivated him before, Will endures several moments of awkward silence. He casts about for something to say and finally holds up his canteen in gratitude toward Madeleine.

"Thank you, Madame. So... where are we?"

"Here? It is Saint Nicholas."

"No, I mean..."

Will spreads his arms around indicating the wider location, beyond the church.

"Ah! This is Hamiville. Where do you go?"

Joey jumps in. Since he repeated the town's name a couple dozen times as they hiked, he can't possibly get it wrong. He does anyway.

"Boston."

"That's Bastogne, ya lug wrench!"

The town is known to Madeleine.

"Ah, Bastogne. It is far from here."

This is not the best of news at the start of another day in full retreat, but Will and Joey suck it up and pull their gear together. They stand and face the ladies. Marie searches for words to say. Seeing young men off to war is a painful experience. How will she remember them?

"What are your names?"

"I'm Will and this here's Joey. And your names?"

"She is Madeleine, and I am Marie."

"*Enchanté*, Marie."

Will reflexively takes Marie's hand and, to everyone's surprise, including his own, bows to kiss it. Marie lights up with the spark of a coquette, in spite of carrying the weight of more than eighty years of life and loss. This morning has brought a roller coaster of emotions for her!

"Oh, *chéri*."

Will is so delighted by Marie's affectionate response that he reaches for Madeleine's hand. She shakes Will's hand very formally and quickly snatches hers back. With this, Will turns back to Marie who is all aglow, spreading a blanket of warmth and caring over him. In the giving, she becomes neither old nor young, but timeless. Madeleine studies her old friend as if with new eyes.

Joey is simply flabbergasted by the whole scene.

After farewells are exchanged, the two men step out into the cold. When the door latches into place behind them, Marie makes her way to the window to watch through irregular panes of glass as the two young men tramp across the yard. Madeleine comes to her side, ready to chide.

"Marie! At your age!"

"I know, I know. But sometimes, even now when I look in the mirror, into my eyes..."

For the briefest of moments, with the distortion of her reflection in the windowpane and the random surfacing of a distant memory, Marie sees something in the glass that creases her thin, dry lips with a smile.

"... I see the young woman I once was."

Madeleine is taken aback, but then her curiosity overcomes her, and she looks into a windowpane and sees only her own skeptical face staring back. She steps over to Marie's pane and watches Will and Joey disappear into the fog.

Those Who Left Bastogne

Bastogne is spending another day muffled in a heavy overcoat of low-lying clouds. While Chiwy ambles along the street, she passes family after family loading their possessions onto trucks and horse-drawn carts. As the German counteroffensive picks up steam and the pace of abandonment in Bastogne quickens, all westerly roads out of town are clogged.

She arrives at a doctor's office, hopeful that she can pitch in at his practice. The aging physician alone would not be equal to the medical emergency Chiwy believes is descending upon the town. She finds the door locked and the shades drawn. There is no answer to her knocks. She turns to look up and down the street. Her eyes come to rest on an old woman holding the railing knob at the base of a set of stairs. Her labored breathing alarms Chiwy, and she rushes to assist her. The old woman brightens at the sight of the young woman's smiling eyes, smart nursing outfit and professional demeanor. As she catches her breath, some color returns to her pale features. Chiwy is relieved and asks after her neighbor.

"Pardon, Madame. Have you seen Doctor Deschamps?"

"He left this morning, my dear. He has family in Marche."

"Where will his patients go?"

"I don't know. But you are a nurse. Perhaps they can come to you."

"Yes, of course. You will leave Bastogne?"

"Ah, no. I will stay here."

Chiwy follows her glance up the stairs.

"I have no place to go."

Energized by Chiwy's positive spirit, the old woman attempts the steps up to her dwelling, with Chiwy holding her arm firmly with one hand and bracing the small of the elderly lady's back with the other. When they reach the landing, she finds her key, unlocks the door, and turns to see concern etched on Chiwy's face. Drawing on a long life well-lived, she settles on words she hopes will give the young woman peace. After all, she is reconciled with her fate.

"I was born here, my dear. And I will die here."

Destination Unknown

Late afternoon light is fading as Jack's convoy slows to pass pedestrians and several cartloads of refugees leaving town. Wallington is impatient but sobered by the sight of American soldiers in retreat, many on foot, several disarmed, intermingled with the passing locals. One soldier shuffles by close to the driver's window.

"Did you see that guy? I've heard of a thousand-yard stare. But that was a two-thousand-yard stare!"

"Dissociation."

The word is not familiar to his aide, so Jack explains.

"Severe physical and emotional detachment from his surroundings."

"He's detached all right."

Jack ponders the shock that must have caused such a level of disorientation and cannot suppress foreboding about what might lie ahead of them. Eventually, the convoy starts up again, only to snarl to a halt at a crossroads where a familiar MP is positioned to direct the convoy through the outskirts of a town. When Jack rolls down his window, the MP steps over to salute the captain and to explain, with some frustration, that cattle have wandered onto the road, and the farmer is having a hell-of-a time clearing the way.

"His dog damn near bit me!"

Jack attempts to calm the agitated soldier.

"Thanks for the update, Sergeant... ?"

"Colleti, sir."

"Keep up the good work, Colleti."

Across the cab, Wallington exchanges fisheyes with the policeman and makes a mental note of the sergeant's name.

Underway again, the corporal calls Jack's attention to signage that materializes in the fog. As they pass darkened houses at the edge of a town, Jack pulls out his map, turns on his flashlight, and searches in a sector where he thinks they might be.

"Say, Doc, this place looks deserted."

"So it would seem. Perhaps there's a curfew in effect."

They come to a stop, and Beagle shouts from the back of the truck.

"Hey, Wally! Where the hell are we?"

Wallington turns to Jack before replying to his buddy.

"How would you say it, Doc?"

"Bastogne, I believe."

Wallington turns and shouts.

"Bastogne!"

It doesn't ring a bell for Beagle.

"Oh. What country are we in?"

"Doc?"

"Belgium."

"Belgium!"

Beagle quickly lands upon the one thing he knows about Belgium.

"Hey! Can we stop for some chocolates?"

Jack and Wallington share a smile before Jack offers his own wish.

"I'm thinking waffles."

"And I'm thinkin' beer, Doc. Off duty of course."

"Of course."

The convoy inches forward, only to come to a full stop once again. The corporal shakes his head and turns to Jack with a comment on his lips. Jack, oddly in remarkably good spirits, beats him to the punch.

"Hurry up and wait."

Bastogne Puts on Armor

In Bastogne's central square, Colonel William Roberts, commander of the 10th Armored Division, is working up a sweat. He is waving through town his entire division of tanks, half-tracks, tank destroyers, trucks, and infantry, along with assorted reconnaissance, engineering, ordnance, signal, and medical personnel.

When his convoy won the race to Bastogne earlier in the evening, he found the town devoid of defenders, except for remnants of the Eighth Corps headquarters staff and an unknown number of rearguard troops. The latest intelligence on the German juggernaut approaching the town was daunting, with positive identification of at least ten hostile armored or infantry divisions in the vicinity. But how many would bear directly on Bastogne, and by which of the three all-weather roads arriving from the east and north of town? After consulting with departing Eighth Corps staff, the decision was made to divide 10th Armored to cover them all, on the double.

While he watches the convoy roll by, Roberts thanks his lucky stars that his division is organized into three coequal teams, making such a rapid deployment possible.

A couple of middle-aged Belgian men on their way home from work stop to watch the convoy grind and rumble through town. After a long day of labor, the fellows have consumed enough of the hops to wax poetic. The mason describes the drab vehicles bristling with weapons as a train from hell. The machinist conjures up the image of a long, coiled snake ready to strike. Eventually, they conclude that it would be proper to have one more beer to toast *"bon courage, bonne vitesse"* to the Americans.

As they reverse course back toward their favored taproom, the machinist wishes "good evening" to a dark-eyed woman witnessing the passing spectacle from her doorway. Once safely beyond her, and thankfully far from the sharp hearing and tongue of his wife, the mason turns to his mate and indulges his aging pride.

"If I were a younger man, I would…"

"Sure, sure. In a pig's eye."

The dark-eyed beauty pays them no mind. She looks beyond the parade of heavy armor to see what appear to be mere boys posing as men as they roll by in the night.

Word is flying from street to street, house to house. The Americans are here in great strength. But what does this portend for Bastogne? Will our streets become a battleground? Will the Germans capture the town once again? Will there be retribution against the citizens? To their private shame, a few dig out the German flags they tore down during the liberation. Just in case.

With his first team under the command of Lieutenant Colonel O'Hara well on its way east on the Wiltz Road and his second team led by Lieutenant Colonel Cherry rolling slowly by and heading out the Mageret

Road, Roberts takes a bit of a breather. On the advice of his adjutant, he scans the nondescript Hotel LeBrun with a discerning eye. He notes its sturdy structure and location hard by the square, just a stone's throw from the confluence of several main roads. He makes a snap decision to establish the hotel as his command post. Within minutes a flurry of activity is underway, as a dozen soldiers carry office equipment and supplies into the lobby.

Roberts' break is brief but rewarding. Somehow, the cook got some coffee brewing. With cup in hand, the colonel takes a moment to reflect. He is proud of his men. Their forced march landed them in a strategic town before it could fall into enemy hands. With his CP rapidly becoming operational, Roberts has cracked yet another nut. However, as Team Cherry picks up steam, hastening an encounter with their destiny, Roberts is reminded that everything pales beside the task of sending young men into battle. He must manage the difficult balancing act of having the greatest possible impact while, hopefully, sustaining an acceptable level of casualties. He hates playing God but is trained to do so when he must. Several soldiers in an open half-track recognize Roberts and wave, salute, or offer a combination of the two. He observes, for no one in particular.

"Christ, some of them look like teenagers. But damned if they aren't spoiling for a fight!"

Out of the fog, a jeep maneuvers past the tail end of Team Cherry and catches Roberts in its headlights. The colonel immediately recognizes the lanky form that steps out of the vehicle. Major William Desobry lopes up to him and salutes. Roberts returns the salute, steps over to the jeep, and opens a map on the hood. He pauses to connect eye-to-eye with his subordinate.

"Major, we are tasked with blocking the Germans on the main roads into Bastogne from the east and north. All accounts say we'll be outnumbered and outgunned, but we may have the element of surprise. If we are stout at key points, we will be a formidable shield."

Roberts shines his flashlight on the map.

"I've posted Team O'Hara here... at Bras. I'm sending Cherry's boys to Longvilly... up here. I need you to get north to Noville... up this road. Set up your roadblocks east and north of the town, here and here."

The colonel carefully folds his map and inserts it into his jacket, then takes the measure of the man once again. He always likes what he sees in Desobry.

"Major... Bill, you've got to buy time so the 101st can get to Bastogne and dig in behind you. I'm not gonna sugarcoat it. It could get pretty hot up there, but I need you to hold that town as long as you can."

"Understood, sir."

With its vanguard now at the square, Team Desobry is waiting for the last of Team Cherry to clear away. In the relative quietude of his truck's cab, Jack is studying his map of Belgium by the glow of a flashlight. He notes the seven main roads that have carried traffic in and out of the ancient market town for centuries. When he wipes the fogged windshield and scans the buildings surrounding the large central square, he imagines farmers, traders, and townspeople mingling there on weekends buying, selling, and socializing through the ages.

Wallington is killing time talking to a half-dozen other drivers who have stepped out of their vehicles. When his favorite MP shouts orders to move out, Jack's driver is sure they are directed at him, personally.

"Damn! This son-of-a-bitch is everywhere."

When several drivers turn to him in puzzlement, a couple of wisecracks occur to Wallington. But the last thing the corporal needs right now is a hassle from an oversized oaf in a white helmet, especially this guy. So, he beats a hasty retreat back to the truck. When he jumps into the cab and revs up the motor, Jack gives him a questioning look. The corporal blurts out the news.

"They're sayin' Eighth Corps skedaddled... and the 101st ain't here yet 'cause they can't jump in this goddamn fog. So... they're coming by land."

"Where are they coming from?"

"Uh... Reims! That's in France!"

Jack studies the portion of France bordering Belgium.

"Hmm, it's off this map. That's got to be over a hundred miles away. It could take them quite a while."

"Yeah, and until they get here, we're it!"

When the convoy begins to move, Wallington muscles the truck into gear and lurches forward. At the corner of the square, Colleti is waving and shouting repeatedly for the convoy to skirt the square and head down the hill. Against all common sense, Jack's driver can't resist one last dig. He rolls down his window as the truck slowly passes the MP.

"I heard ya twice the first time!"

"OK, wise guy!"

Wallington mutters mostly to himself.

"OK, Colleti spaghetti."

Wallington suddenly realizes he was overheard and that the pot has started to boil. When Colleti takes several angry strides toward the truck, the corporal quickly cranks up his window and punches the truck beyond the MP. He takes a sidelong glance at Jack, expecting disapproval, but finds the doctor peering intently through the windshield. Whatever opprobrium Jack may have offered is forgotten when the truck's headlights illuminate a doorway where the dark-eyed woman is still standing and watching the column pass. Jack sees her very clearly, vividly, and is struck by her beauty, all within the briefest of moments. She vanishes when the truck turns and follows the convoy down the road.

Renee takes a deep breath and prepares to enter her family residence but lingers a moment longer when a jeep with an officer seeking more details on the route pulls up to the MP.

"Take the left fork at the bottom of the hill past Saint Pierre. You can't miss the church. It's as old as the hills. Then north on the Houffalize road through Foy about five miles, to Noville."

Renee repeats the name of the little farming village.

"Noville."

She can't help wondering why they've chosen Noville. To Renee it is just a sleepy hamlet that she passes through now and again. Whenever she does, men who stop at her father's store smile and wave to her. No one could mistake Lemaire's lovely daughter.

Though she can't appreciate the town's strategic importance, sitting as it does on a vital crossroads a short crow's flight from Bastogne, she can calculate the value of human lives. As heavy armor clanks and rattles by, all she sees are the tired, solemn faces of young men who will soon be in harm's way. She is unprepared for how emotional she becomes and only recovers when she offers a silent prayer for them. Oblivious to the chill in the air, Renee resolves to stay in her doorway until the last vehicle passes.

Those Who Stayed Behind

When the convoy is finally swallowed by the shadows of night, Renee descends the stairs into the basement of her home. By the light of a single lantern, she makes out her sisters, mother, and father setting up temporary living quarters. Gisele is in rare form, whining while her father's patience is quickly eroding.

"Why can't we leave? All of my friends are leaving!"

"I will not discuss it again! We stay!"

Having shouted down his youngest daughter and released his frustration, Lemaire sees that his words have only incited Gisele's ire as she flings pillows wildly about. His wife catches Lemaire's eye with a subtle admonition, and he softens. He looks around the cellar at the solid stone foundation and the heavy overhead joists.

"We will be safe here. Anyway, I have to keep the store open."

"Gustave, all your customers are leaving."

"Well, what about the Americans?"

Surely the soldiers who have arrived in force will need hardware. He can almost hear his cash register ringing. His wife knows that it is useless to debate her husband further once his mind is made up, so she busies herself laying out blankets on the cots.

Away from all the fuss, Renee is talking quietly with her other sister at the base of the stairs. Marguerite is the middle daughter, the steady one. Renee feels she can tell her most anything, especially when it is in confidence. She cannot keep secrets from her family forever and must start somewhere. She shows Marguerite her pendant and whispers.

"Josef gave it to me."

Marguerite reads her sister's restraint and admires the jewelry discreetly.

For some time, the family has known that there is a young man in the picture, but little more than that. Renee's letters from Brussels have not exactly lit a fire. Now Renee is torn. How much should she tell them? About Josef? About her dreams, her fears, her loneliness? More to the point, how much could father handle?

Lemaire calls across the room with the kind of casual question that is asking so much more.

"Renee, what news from Brussels?"

As his first-born, Renee resides in a special place in her father's heart. But now that she is nearing thirty, he is cleaved between a desire to never let her go and a hope that she will soon wed and give him grandchildren. More and more, Lemaire is succumbing to the latter sentiment.

"So... your young man. You must tell us all about him."

Renee takes a short, sharp breath which only Marguerite hears and reads as extreme discomfort. She speaks to Renee in the lowest possible voice.

"Is it about Josef?"

Renee nods discreetly. A church bell rings in the distance and, almost as one, Renee and her father turn to the sound. Taking it as a cue, he decides that, in matters of his family, patience is not always a virtue.

"Ah, Saint Pierre. While you are home, we should plan for your wedding."

Lemaire, content that the topic has been broached, turns to Berta and is met by an ambiguous expression. He doesn't give it a second thought while he exerts himself in moving a heavy table into place. Marguerite stays focused on Renee, who is beside herself. She suspects that there is something that stands between Renee and their father. Something that weighs heavily on her big sister. Something, perhaps, that Renee may want to confide in her.

"From the north? Is he Protestant?"

Renee knits her brow and gives a quick shake of her head. Marguerite looks into Renee's glistening eyes and is puzzled for a moment. Suddenly, she seems to understand.

"Oh!"

Renee peers over Marguerite's shoulder to see that both her mother and father are turned her way, then back to her sister's sympathetic eyes. Much as she trusts her sister with her private thoughts and feelings, Renee suddenly feels overwhelmed. The basement is stifling and hot. She glances around searching for an excuse to escape.

"I need to get my bedding."

As Renee hurries up the stairs, Lemaire watches her flight closely, then turns to Marguerite, who looks away. Finally, he seeks out his wife, who simply shrugs her shoulders.

Upstairs, Renee steps carefully through the darkened sitting room, feels her way to the upright piano, and orients herself toward her bedroom. She gathers her bedding, but instead of returning to the stairs she is drawn to the bench by the window. She parts the blackout curtains and stares out into the night and the silence. Why does life have to be so hard?

Though she appears to have led a charmed life, fanned by the fervor of her father's pride, it has not always been easy for Renee. Love had been so elusive she began to believe she would never find it. Once she finally did, it felt so easy and light that it could blow away in the slightest of breezes. Now that the world has been caught up in a hurricane of hate and violence, she fears the worst, and her love has taken on the weight of a burden. Each day, when she rises, the conflicting feelings are there, love and fear, silently vying for supremacy.

In the darkness of her family's sitting room, she reflects upon the passage of troops in the night and upon the battle that is sure to come. Who will die? Who will survive? What of families torn asunder and lovers forever parted? Josef, are you there? It is all so painful. When will it end? She seeks and finds the smooth surface of her pendant, and rambles through her memories in search of relief in another time and place.

A Field of Poppies

The little dark-eyed girl is picking the biggest and brightest of the poppy blooms and collecting them in a basket she carries lightly on her forearm. The thunder on the horizon has abated. Perhaps the storm will pass her by. As the breeze freshens in her face, she continues her lilting song.

"Entre les croix, rang par rang
Qui marquent notre place"

Brussels, Belgium

The 6th of June 1944 dawns like all the days since Brussels fell to the Germans. There is no joy or laughter among the citizens, only grim day-to-day survival amid growing hunger and deprivation. No greetings are offered to Renee as she passes people on the street. There is no light in their eyes. As is the case so often these days, the only peace she finds is in the company of the man she loves.

In a garret in an old apartment building, a frail old man is nearly buried in blankets in an oversized easy chair. He stirs as if in fitful sleep, though the slightest of smiles seems to quiver on his lips.

The old man wakes to see Renee and Josef studying him from the piano bench where they sit side by side. Their knitted brows speak volumes of their concern for Josef's father, who is ailing, feeble, and who, for all they know, could die at any moment. He stills their anxiety when he recognizes Renee.

"Hello, my dear."

At that, the old man turns away, settles back into his armchair, and pulls his blanket up to his chin.

"I was dreaming."

He closes his eyes to try to bring back the vision.

"There was a little girl. She was singing. And, just for a moment, I thought it might be you, Renee, bringing flowers."

Josef betrays his impatience while indicating a vase full of fresh-cut, red poppies on the top of the upright piano.

"Of course it was Renee. She is always bringing us flowers."

His father soon dozes off again. With Renee's encouragement, Josef starts anew on the piece he had been playing before his father woke. She watches with great admiration as Josef works on his arrangement for piano of Bach's "Air in G," pausing now and again to correct his handwritten transcription of the piece. While he does so, he explains the origin of the melancholy masterpiece just as a teacher might for a pupil.

"It comes from the Second Movement of Bach's Orchestral Suite Number 3 in D Major. It was rearranged in the 19th century by August Wilhelmj, who found that he could play the entire melody on the G string of his violin."

But Renee is only half listening as the melody reaches her on a spiritual level. As he plays, they are touching at the hip, setting off the special spark that flashes at the intersection of the spiritual and the sexual. When he finishes, it is like she emerges from a dream of perfect love. She slowly turns to look into his eyes, which are brimming with pride and waiting for a response from her.

"So, you worked out the whole piece. It is wonderful. Play it again."

He starts the piece again, playing this time with even greater feeling, while Renee focuses on his right hand. His father stirs again.

"Did I ever tell you that his mother, may she rest in peace, loved this melody more than any other?"

Josef interjects, with the slightest hint of frustration in his voice.

"Yes, Papa. Many times."

Josef's facial expression matches his impatience, which is quickly eclipsed by alarm and concern as the old man falls into a violent fit of coughing. When Josef's nimble fingers fall limply on the keyboard, Renee takes his hands firmly in her own to give him strength as they wait, hopefully, for the storm to pass. It does. The old man wipes his mouth with a handkerchief and composes himself. Renee's grip on Josef's hand eases, and she encourages him to begin the piece again. After several measures, Renee offers to take over the right hand and Josef yields. When

Renee reaches a tricky part, she makes a minor mistake and scolds herself. He begins the measure over and she corrects the mistake, giving them a special moment of lightness and shared joy. The music leads the old man's thoughts elsewhere.

"Your mother would have loved the piece to be your wedding march. In that way she would be present."

He turns to the couple, as if expecting a response. Renee is puzzled by this and whispers to Josef.

"But... Bach was German... and a Lutheran."

Josef whispers back.

"Ah, but do you know what Bach said?"

She does not but matches Josef's faint smile with one of her own as she listens in anticipation.

"He said: I play the notes as they were written. It is God who made the music."

Still on his own private track, Josef's father falls back on an old ploy.

"Naturally, it is your decision and..."

Josef and Renee wait patiently as another of the old man's coughing fits comes and goes.

"... and I probably won't live long enough to be there."

"Nonsense!"

His son won't hear of it, not on this day or any other. But Renee is quick to take his hand again. Josef warms to her touch and reminds his father.

"You are my only family. Who else will stand with me?"

The old man nods in approval at this response and enjoys a rare moment of foresight and fervor.

"The *Boche* will be gone and the synagogue will be rebuilt. It will be so beautiful."

Spent by the effort, the old man settles deeper into his armchair and seems to drift off again. Nevertheless, Renee still feels a need to whisper.

"What about my faith? Have you spoken to him?"

"Why trouble him with that now?"

They turn as one to the old man, so small and weak and so near the end of his days. Renee sighs, knowing what it is like to put off a difficult discussion, knowing that whenever you have it, it will cause pain. It is as if Josef reads her mind.

"Have you told your family yet?"

"Well, I... it's just that... Oh, Josef! My family will love you, but... my father is very traditional."

"If only I could go home with you. He would see how devoted I am. But I can't."

Nearly all the Jews who did not flee the country have been forcibly removed from Belgium. Renee has heard the rumors about work camps where they are sent, never to return. Those few who remain are in hiding. But somehow, Josef walks the tightrope. He continues to work while taking pains not to draw attention to himself. And his father has not left their tiny loft apartment since the Germans rolled over Belgium and locked down the city.

Will they endure?

Renee tries not to think about it, but when she does, she searches for assurance that they will survive She remembers that there was something about Josef's late mother, some ambiguity about her origins perhaps. And was she not, after all, a celebrated pianist? Is that it? Or is Josef's liberty simply a bureaucratic mistake? Each time Renee tries to make sense of it all, she is drawn into the endless carousel of possibilities and perils that is Josef's life, and she finds no comfort. As she studies Josef's handsome face in profile, Renee brightens as she suddenly recalls the rumor that flew around the hospital that morning.

"Oh, I meant to tell you! They said that the *Amis* landed in France today. The war will soon be over!"

Renee's exuberance is all the greater for having lurched from depressing thoughts to joyful news. It stirs the old man from his slumber and seems to breathe life back into Josef, who warms to her optimism.

"Yes, soon. Someday soon and until that day, I want you to wear this."

Josef produces a beautiful necklace and pendant depicting a winged angel holding an infant. Delicately, Renee takes it into her hands. Josef defers to his father to share the significance of the gift.

"It belonged to Josef's mother, and her mother before her."

When the two men lock watering eyes, they each find the peace that comes with giving. It is in moments like these that Josef's dear mother, the love of the old man's life, is most alive for them.

Renee tries to put her feelings into words.

"It... it is..."

When she falters, Josef steps in.

"It is Raphael. The angel of healing."

Archangel Raphael

With the passing on of the pendant, a burden is lifted from the old man, who has no daughter. There was no one to inherit the treasured heirloom until Renee came into their lives. As the old man beams at her, Renee reflects on how appropriate the gift is. She wants nothing more in this life, in this world torn by war and unimaginable suffering, than to be a healer. Gently, Josef takes the necklace from her and holds the ends of the chain up. She pulls back her hair and offers her bare neck. Josef attaches the clasp, surrenders to temptation and kisses her neck, then her ear, and whispers.

"Ani met alaih", Renee. I love you."

A surge of warmth and weakness overcomes Renee, and she falls gently against him. Lost in ardor, his lips find the soft hairs on the back of her neck and his hand finds her breast. Renee closes her eyes and submits, then suddenly becomes aware of the moment. She blushes and affectionately takes Josef's hand away from her breast. She holds both his hands in her own and transfers their passion into the sensuous intertwining of their hungry fingers. The old man coughs ambiguously, perhaps knowingly. With laughing eyes, Renee grips Josef's hands firmly.

"We'd better give these hands something to do. Why not the stardust song?"

Josef playfully assumes the attitude of a concert pianist. He sweeps back the tail of an imaginary tuxedo and poises his hands above the keyboard as the audience in the Royal Conservatory of Brussels holds its breath. Unable to contain his mirth, Josef bursts out laughing and launches into a rousing rendition of the Hoagy Carmichael composition, their shared favorite at the time.

It is all too much for the old man.

"Ack! I don't care a fig for your new music!"

Stardust Memories

The warmth of Josef's touch and the words whispered in her ear linger, then dissipate. Renee is once again fully present in her father's home. She lets the blackout curtains fall and sits in the stillness. Only the calming cadence of the grandfather clock reaches her, and she recovers the song that was on their lips on that special day in June.

"Sometimes I wonder why I spend
The lonely night dreaming of a song
The melody haunts my reverie
And I am once again with you

When our love was new
And each kiss an inspiration
Oh, but that was long ago
Now my consolation is in the stardust of a song"

Was it so long ago? It has just been a matter of months. But it already feels like forever. She wonders if he will ever hold her in his arms again. The answer comes when tears gather in Renee's eyes and begin to freely fall. There is little consolation for an aching heart.

"Renee?"

Renee is startled as her father pads up the stairs swinging a kerosene lantern. She quickly wipes her eyes as Lemaire stands at the landing trying to adjust his eyesight while light and shadow dance around the room. He makes out her form sitting by the window and goes to her.

"Are you all right?"

"Yes, Papa. Papa?"

She pauses to consider her words as he sits down heavily beside her and dims the lantern. He assumes a posture of readiness and openness to his inquisitive daughter. Theirs is a special relationship that began the moment she was born and changed his life forever. His little dark-eyed girl would ask question after question, and he would explain the world to her. She was always quick with a smile and a puzzle of some kind for him to solve. Even as the years passed while she was away working in Brussels, they remained close. But now?

Renee wants to open up to him, to tell him about Josef and their big plans for a life together. But now the future is as uncertain as the past is immutable. She searches for the words to begin but loses her way.

"Papa... you seem so tired. You should rest."

"Yes, my princess."

He leans against the wall and exhales another long day of work in one sustained breath. He listens to the silent house, the silent street outside, the world which is mercifully silent at that moment. But he also wonders what is in store for Bastogne in the coming days, and for the Americans who have arrived in force.

"Did you see any markings? On the trucks?"

"No, I just saw their faces. Some of them are just boys."

The silence is broken by the faint thuds of explosions in the distance. When Lemaire turns to the sounds, Renee tries to follow his sightline, and wonders.

"Is it Noville?"

"No, farther away... and to the east. Come, let's go down."

Renee is relieved that the young men who passed by that evening have been spared, for now. Lemaire stands, gathers Renee's bedding under an arm and starts to lose his balance. Renee rises quickly, catching his other arm to steady him. It has a strengthening effect on her.

"Papa, I want to talk to you."

"Yes, yes, but downstairs. We will be safe there and have plenty of time to talk. We have so much to catch up on."

"Yes, Papa."

She would have told him. She is sure of it. But perhaps her father is right. There must be a better time, a better place. It can wait.

19 December 1944

The morning brings a sober assessment of a rapidly shifting battlefield. The German counteroffensive, which had been underestimated at first by Allied brass, is now seen for the well-organized threat it has become. Powerful German forces have advanced across a broad front with ambitions well beyond the Ardennes. But it is not a complete rout thanks to Americans who stood their ground at Clervaux, Trois Verges, and Saint Vith, or who engaged in delaying actions in dozens of small towns and crossroads across Luxembourg and southern Belgium.

As a result, concern is growing among the German high command about the likelihood of crossing the Meuse River within their timetable. They must reach the river before the bridges are blown so they can press on to capture Antwerp. This strategic port city is the linchpin in Adolph Hitler's great gamble to defeat the Allies in the West, or at least to divide American and British forces and sue for peace. In his increasingly delusional state, Hitler believes that the Allies would join him in fighting the Russian forces approaching Germany on the eastern front.

In spite of the delays, German forces now rapidly approaching Bastogne from the east, southeast, and north, are determined to take the vital town and all the hard surface roads that are key to their rapid movement. Their chief concern is the intelligence report that indicates that crack American airborne troops are headed overland to the Bastogne area from France. However, with their momentum and superiority in both manpower and firepower, they feel confident they can brush aside any further resistance they might encounter and beat the paratroopers to the town.

Though the temperature continues to drop across the Ardennes, fog still clings tenaciously to the ground. The low skies continue to prevent Allied airpower from becoming a factor in the Battle of the Bulge. Without help from the flyboys, Allied generals must plot their next moves with just the ground forces at their disposal. They move divisions, regiments, and battalions here and there while thousands of ordinary foot soldiers, separated and lost in the rolling hills and forests of Luxembourg and Belgium, consider their next steps, next meal, and next place to sleep.

The Bourcy Crossroads

Near the small hamlet of Bourcy, northeast of Bastogne, light snow is falling on an abandoned farm. Inside a small shed, a whisper is heard.

"Will. Hey, Will."

Will is unresponsive, sound asleep in a produce bin, while Joey is awake and seated on the earthen floor of the structure. He is trying to calm himself by resorting to his tic of nervously pinching and kneading his collar. But it brings little comfort to the big man as he listens intently to the distinctive clatter of heavy, treaded vehicles on the move. Even though the sound is receding, Joey is frightened and cannot wait for Will to wake up. He whispers to his friend again, with rising urgency. Will stirs, then resumes the snoring and heavy slumber of a man so consumed by exhaustion he could nod off anywhere. This time, Joey pulls on his friend's arm as it hangs from the bin.

"Will, wake up!"

"What? Where am I? What the hell did I sleep on?"

"Turnips. Giant turnips."

Will pulls the most offensive turnip out from under him and examines the prize-winning root. He looks around in the darkness of the low-slung lean-to and focuses on Joey, who is huddled by the door under the tarp for warmth and the illusion of safety. Will doesn't see any reason to rise and shine.

"Ah, lemme sleep."

"Will, listen. I've been hearin' the tanks again."

The fear in Joey's voice is enough to rouse his friend. Will props himself up on his elbow and listens in the direction that Joey is looking. The moist, heavy air pressing down upon the farm muffles the world around them.

"I don't hear nothin'. Hey, I've been meaning to ask you. Whaddaya got in there?"

Caught in the act, Joey snaps his hand away from his collar.

"Nuthin', Will."

"Well, sure you do. Lemme see."

"You'll just make fun of me."

"Scout's honor. Lemme see."

As much as he trusts Will, Joey is afraid he will be ridiculed. Throughout his life people have picked on him. When they realized that the giant is meek, timid, and defenseless, they picked on him even more. But Will is different. He teases sometimes, but not in a mean way. Slowly, Joey finds his collar again and turns it inside out, revealing a little golden angel pinned there. It shines, even in the half-light, and Will takes an interest. Joey quickly explains.

"Mama pinned it on me at the train station. The fellas made fun of me somethin' awful. She said I gotta wear it. But she didn't say where! Do... do you like it?"

Will thought he had experienced the full gamut of Joey's quirks. A quip occurs to him, but he quickly discards it.

"Yeah, sure."

Will sees in Joey's blank expression that his response has fallen short of the mark, and he suddenly realizes how important the tiny golden angel is to his giant friend.

"It's nice, Joey. It's real nice."

When Joey lights up, Will feels the warmth and the awesome responsibility of being fully trusted.

Though there is nothing about their circumstances they would have chosen, they feel fortunate to have each other. Somehow, together, they are muddling through. The clucking of a chicken nearby breaks the stillness and brings a quick response from Joey with the rumbling of his cavernous belly. He looks up at Will, unsure of what to do. Fortunately, Will's survival instinct is enough for both of them.

"Ya hear that? C'mon."

Will and Joey duck out of the shed. They step through the snow and into a chicken coop, where just one bird is found. Will looks at the bird, at Joey, at the bird, and then spots a stack of wood scraps in the corner. He pulls loose a double handful.

"Here, take these and get a fire going."

Will takes a quick look around as things come into focus in the darkened structure.

"Fill that bucket with snow and get it boiling. And cut up a couple of turnips and toss them in."

Joey bends low out of the coop and drops the wood scraps to the ground with a clatter. As he scoops snow into the pail, he hears the aggravated squawking of the chicken, followed by a dull thud, then silence.

A short time later, in another outbuilding on the farm, there is a rustling of hay. An American soldier emerges from a pile of cattle fodder and sniffs the air around him. He reaches for another soldier dead asleep nearby and shakes him awake.

"Wilkinson. Wake up."

"Huh? What're you playin' at?"

Wilkinson brushes off the hay that warmed him during the night, sits up, and follows his friend's nose.

"I'll be damned. I thought I was dreaming."

At the far end of the barn, their lieutenant stirs, catches a whiff, and rises. Noting that Howard and Wilkinson are already up, he turns to stir Boyle, the fourth member of the ad hoc unit he formed during their pell-mell retreat. He pauses to take in the almost angelic face of the sleeping young man and reflects on how far Boyle has fallen. Fresh from the States, he was full of piss and vinegar before the Germans attacked. Now he is silent, rigid, fatigued by combat, and shocked by the shells that fell around him. Yet, as roughed-up, unshaven, and dirty as Boyle may be, he always appears to be at perfect peace when in repose. The lieutenant decides to let the sleeping dogface lie for just a little longer. He turns to his reliable foot soldiers, and they, with rifles in hand, stand ready to receive their first order of the day. He nods in the general direction of whatever is giving off the intoxicating aroma.

"Take a look."

Howard and Wilkinson slowly open the creaking barn door, step outside, and disappear into the mist.

Will tosses the plucked and chopped bird into the pot and joins Joey by the fire. Settled quite nicely on a couple of crates, they are warmed inside and out and feel pretty good about things in general. Will smiles as he takes in the scent of the bubbling broth.

"Hmm. Smells like what... onions?"

Joey is tickled and nods almost mechanically.

"Where'd you find them?"

"They wuz in the shed. And I found some potatoes too."

Behind them, Howard and Wilkinson materialize from the fog and approach Will and Joey with leveled rifles. Howard knows a couple of words of German.

"Hande hoche!"

Will and Joey obey, throw up their arms, and turn slowly to the menacing soldiers. Wilkinson visibly relaxes when he takes in their olive drab clothing.

"Hey, they look like grunts to me."

"Yeah, but I heard they caught some Krauts in our uniforms."

Howard zeroes in on Will, visibly the more alert of the two.

"Who won the World Series?"

"The Cards... beat the Browns."

"In how many games?"

"Lessee, four to two. Six! Six games!"

"Yeah, that's right."

Howard and Wilkinson lower their rifles. When the lieutenant steps out of the fog with sidearm drawn, the rifles rise again. The officer also ignores Joey and addresses Will, while waggling his pistol at him.

"Who are you boys?"

"28th Infantry, sir."

Unnerved by the lieutenant, Will seeks, and finds, a friendly face in Wilkinson.

"What unit are you guys with?"

"9th Armored... we..."

The lieutenant cuts Wilkinson off.

"I'll ask the questions, soldier!"

To Will's dismay, the lieutenant continues to brandish his handgun as he slowly walks around the seated soldiers. Having sized up Will, he studies the gentle giant beside him. Fancying himself a shrewd judge of character, the lieutenant is nonetheless unable to make heads or tails of Joey, whose expression is a combination of befuddlement and gnawing hunger. He abandons the effort and turns his attention back to Will, who has the misfortune of being covered with chicken feathers. The lieutenant peers into the boiling bucket full of broth and bobbing bits of meat and vegetable and continues to grill Will.

"What're ya boilin' there?"

"Onions and potatoes..."

"And giant turnips!"

The lieutenant finds Joey's sudden outburst of mirth totally out of order, tells him so, tightens his grip on his pistol, and drills Joey with angry eyes. Will almost blurts out a protest but stifles himself when he sees that his simple buddy does not take offence or even notice the lieutenant's exasperation. But Will has been teased all his life for being small, and he thinks bullies stink to high heaven. Oddly now, the tables have turned, and he finds himself protecting his oversized friend. Will resolves right then and there that nobody, not this son-of-a-bitch or anyone else, is going to pick on Joey. Piss on his pistol!

The officer pokes in the broth with a stick, wedges up a chicken leg against the inside of the bucket, and smells a fox. Satisfied that he has the goods on Will, he tightens the screws.

"Where'd you get the bird? You know the penalty for stealing."

Will feels his temperature rising once again but decides to confuse the mean-spirited officer with bullshit.

"Well, lieutenant... you see... it's like this. It was injured, see? So, I put it out of its misery, see? You mind giving it a taste?"

The lieutenant is torn between busting this insolent soldier or letting him off the hook as he surrenders to his own awakening hunger. He gives Will a long, stern look, a final reminder of his rank and authority. This time Will is not intimidated. In fact, he senses an opening.

"Can we put our arms down?"

The lieutenant nods to Wilkinson and Howard who lower their rifles as he holsters his sidearm. Joey ever so slowly drops his arms as Will scoops some steaming soup and hands the tin cup over. The lieutenant takes a sip, then blows on the surface and takes another sip. He nods approval and sends Howard off to fetch Boyle. They soon return. The lieutenant finds a crate, as do Howard and Wilkinson, and settles in by the fire. Only Boyle remains standing and looking into the smoke swirling above the fire. His mates ignore him. Will, still a bit on edge, studies Boyle with mild annoyance. Only Joey responds, fetching a crate and helping the distracted soldier take a seat.

Mesmerized by the fluttering flames of the fire, the men wordlessly share the stew, passing the tin cup from hand to hand. Joey drinks his fill, dips the cup in the bucket, and holds it out to Boyle. Though he is staring in Joey's general direction, Boyle does not reach for the cup. To everyone's surprise, he speaks.

"Where's the handle?"

Joey turns the handle of the cup toward Boyle.

"Here you go."

"No, on the bucket."

Boyle finally focuses on Joey's arm patch, the solid blood-red, bucket-shaped keystone that earned the Pennsylvania National Guard division its nickname. Somehow, in his agitated state, Will perceives Boyle's comment as an affront. The only fool he suffers lightly is Joey, and he gets ready to unload on this jackass. Joey's brotherly warmth toward Boyle gives him pause. To make matters worse, the lieutenant once again fixes Will with beady eyes.

Feeling cornered and overwrought, Will opts to talk his way out of it. Answering questions nobody asked, he expounds upon the 28th Division's reputation for hard fighting from the dawn of the Republic, through the Great War, all the way to the battle in the Hurtgen Forest just a month ago. Seeing he has piqued the lieutenant's interest, Will prattles on.

"Fellas, I was there when the 28th was honored to be the only American division to march through Paris for the liberation. You should've seen the gals linin' the street, cheerin' us on, but damned if they would've let us stop! We just kept marching all the way through and out of the city."

Attempting a Cockney accent, he adds.

"Bloody shame if you ask me."

Howard and Wilkinson are mildly amused.

"Will ya listen to me? Three months in England and I sound like a fookin' limey."

This gets a laugh from Howard and Wilkinson and a head shake from the lieutenant. All of this is lost on Boyle who finally turns away from Joey back to the fire and rocks back and forth on his crate muttering to himself.

"Red badge. Red badge. Red badge."

Will is struck dumb, but Joey continues to hold out the cup patiently waiting for Boyle to come to himself. All, save for Joey, share furtive looks as they cycle through guilt, relief, dread, and denial. They are glad they don't share Boyle's fate and have thus far survived the fighting with faculties intact. But as artillery sounds in the distance, a feeling of shame for distancing themselves from Boyle is quickly followed by foreboding that they could soon join him, or worse. As the others stare into the fire, Will takes a long look at Joey, who is still trying to feed Boyle. A blizzard of feelings blows through him, ranging from affection for the big ox to apprehension about Joey's fate and immediate future. He snaps out of it by promising himself that, one way or another, he is going to keep the big lummox alive.

Finally, Will takes the cup gently from Joey's hands.

"He ain't hungry."

To even his own surprise, Will has come all the way around to Joey's way of thinking, if you could call it that. Will pours the last of the broth into Boyle's canteen, to nods of appreciation from all the others.

As the fire slowly dies a hissing death in the steady snowfall, the last of the embers fade and wink farewell. The heat that enveloped them releases them as if from a trance, but no one can move, nor wants to, until the lieutenant feels the weight of his responsibility.

"OK, men, get your gear together. We're moving out."

The six men are soon trudging along a rutted farm country road in single file behind Wilkinson. They look up now and then toward the sound of small arms fire resounding from an indeterminate distance thanks to the disorienting effects of heavy forests and fog. There is nothing for it, but to keep walking. The heavy, wet snow turns the dirt to muck that pulls at their boots with a squishing sound that amuses Joey. Will shakes his head in wonderment at the smile on his buddy's face. They pass several abandoned farms before reaching a sign board that reads "Bourcy." The lieutenant signals for them to spread out as they move warily with rifles at the ready, save for Boyle, who is unarmed and oblivious. When they reach a paved road near the apparent center of the hamlet, the lieutenant calls a halt and waves the men over to the cover of a cut stone wall. He pulls out a tattered map of southern Belgium that he liberated from the abandoned farmhouse. Wilkinson steps back from the point.

"Where to from here, sir?"

"OK, let's see. Bourcy is too small to be on this map, but I make us right about here. This must be the road to Mageret, which is, I'd say, a couple of miles due south. And that would be the road to Noville."

Almost as one, they turn from the Mageret Road to look west into the fog in the direction of someplace called Noville.

"My orders are to get us to Bastogne."

Joey brightens at the name of the town, but Will nips him in the bud with a glaring roll of the eyes. After further examination of his map, the lieutenant looks to the southwest and points across the fields to a pine forest in the distance.

"The shortest route by a long shot is through those woods."

He looks skyward. The snow is intensifying and quickly accumulating in the fields.

"But we'd make better time on the road."

He opts to head south on the Mageret Road and moves the men out in that direction. After a mere twenty paces, there are heavy explosions down the road ahead, followed by the ripping sounds of high-caliber machine guns. Howard turns to the lieutenant.

"Sir, if we're supposed to get to Bastogne..."

The lieutenant follows Howard's shifting sightline from the hazards ahead to the hushed road to Noville.

"OK, right. Wilkinson, take the point."

They are not far down the Noville Road before Joey goes wide-eyed at the sight of deep tread marks still visible in the mud on the side of the paved road. He shares a worried look with Will, who nods in understanding. This must be the heavy armor Joey heard at dawn. But are they American or German?

Low Skies Over Noville

With sodden mist weighing upon Noville, it is difficult to see and be seen. Team Desobry arrived and deployed in the black of night, but, even after dawn's arrival, visibility is largely limited to forty yards. The CO gives a rare vent to exasperation.

"Goddamn fog."

However, during a quick tour of the village with an adjutant, the major is pleased to find his armor silent in defensive postures and his infantry dug in and communicating in low voices or with hand signals. He raises his binoculars to his eyes for what proves to be another frustrating attempt to get a fix on the heavy treaded vehicles he hears maneuvering across an arc from north to east. With low hills ringing farmland beyond the village, the sounds are echoed and distorted, making the enemy difficult to place.

"Goddamn fog!"

"Uh... yes, sir."

The adjutant's guarded response and nervously shifting feet underscore the tension in the air. For the good of his command, Desobry determines to moderate his attitude, to find a silver lining.

"Well, if we can't see them, they can't see us."

Inside an old stone tavern on the main road, Jack and his aides are converting the barroom into an emergency room. All of the chairs and tables are pushed to the walls, opening what will double as a triage and treatment space. Having cleared it of tavern supplies, Beagle loads a bulky, head-high wooden cabinet with boxes of sutures, gauze pads, medical tape, wraps, suction tubes, rubber straps, slings, and the like. Upon finishing, he joins Wallington behind the bar, where his friend is carefully packing shelves with hydrogen peroxide, ether, plasma, sulfa, and morphine. Finally, they lend a hand with Jack as he fills trays with alcohol to sterilize hypodermic needles, syringes, scalpels, hemostats, scissors, and other surgical instruments. Even as they prep the tavern for what promises to be a very busy day, the gravity of their situation somehow only hits home for Beagle when he watches the elderly tavern keepers decamp from their apartment above the bar and head down to their earthen basement for shelter. The old man lugs a jug of water and a bulky comforter and is followed by the old woman carrying a basket full of food. After the old man disappears into the cellar, his wife pauses at the landing, lifts a crucifix from the basket, and holds it forth while mouthing a prayer. Upon crossing herself, she gives Beagle a brave smile, then descends with the help of her husband.

Desobry swings the tavern door open and immediately gauges the apprehension of his medical staff. While his adjutant lingers in the doorway, the major steps over to Jack and observes several bottles of liquor and spirits behind the bar.

"Excellent choice for an aid station, Doctor. All the painkillers you'll need close at hand."

Desobry's gentle humor has the desired effect in lifting the fog of fear somewhat. But Jack is clearly feeling the weight of unpredictable expectations and struggles to match the major's surprising equanimity.

"Actually, a tavern is ideal with all this open space. But I don't know..."

"You'll be fine, Doctor."

"Thank you, sir."

Desobry steps outside and once again scans the socked-in farmland surrounding the village, hoping for rifts in the fog somewhere. There are none. But he notes a breeze beginning to blow and wonders if conditions are about to change. He takes a last cursory look around and is confident that they are as ready as they can be. But ready for what? He has no way of knowing the disposition or strength of his opponent. On the other hand, he is now fairly certain that his team has occupied the town in complete secrecy. He has the distinct advantage of surprise. He ponders the possibilities, trying to see several moves ahead. His adjutant sees only the ominous present.

"Can't we call in an air strike?"

"Not with this weather. We've got to sit tight."

Desobry's poise is impressive to Sarge, who is dug in nearby, and he remarks quietly to a nervous soldier beside him.

"Cool as a cucumber, that one."

To the amazement of all the Americans strung along a defensive line at the edge of town, the fog shifts enough to reveal a dozen panzers leading infantry toward the village a couple of hundred yards away. Sarge lets out a roar.

"Let 'em have it, boys!"

All hell breaks loose.

The shock waves from cannon fire and impact are felt on the Bourcy-Noville road where Will, Joey, and the others stop abruptly. They all take a knee accept Boyle who is standing still as a statue and looking away from the fighting. Joey gently helps Boyle to kneel as Howard calls back to the lieutenant.

"Whadda we do now?"

"I guess we need to go cross country."

He points south-southwest. Wilkinson takes the lead and disappears into the fog. As heavy explosions resound from the west and further away in the southeast, Joey cobbles together a version of his prayer for the poor guys who are under that shelling. Will hears the familiar sound of his mumbling friend and gives him a nod and a faint smile in spite of himself. On such a dismal, distressing day, this shared private moment is a comfort to them both. As the men tramp through the mushy field in a staggered single file, Wilkinson startles them by sprinting back from the point.

"Lieutenant. We've got railroad tracks up ahead."

The lieutenant pulls out his map and finds tracks intersecting the Noville road and angling toward Bastogne.

"OK men, onto the tracks and we'll make good time into town."

The 101st Arrives

Augusta Chiwy is stepping quickly along a Bastogne sidewalk, her face etched with concern at the growing thunder of conflict that surrounds her and resounds off the town's close-packed structures. It is the last straw for many who had hoped to ride out the conflict. A few more families head west out of town just as the first vehicles of a convoy of two-and-a-half ton American trucks pull into view. Chiwy joins several other bystanders to watch as the first elements of the 101st Airborne Division roll into Bastogne. A jeep pulls up to the curb and General Anthony McAuliffe steps out and surveys the area. He is quickly joined by several officers offering progress reports.

The day has not gone as planned. The division got off to a slow start with the bottleneck at the bridge over the Meuse River near Sedan. At one time during the day, the division was spread out up to 75 miles on the highway. Now finally at their destination, McAuliffe and his direct reports establish estimated times of arrival for each of the division's regiments. As pressure mounts from the east, McAuliffe weighs the disadvantages of deploying his forces piecemeal.

Another jeep rushes to the scene bringing Colonel Roberts, who exchanges hurried salutes with McAuliffe and pulls out a map which he has marked up for the general's use. He quickly describes the placement of his three armored teams and the possible scenarios that might unfold. As McAuliffe makes notations on the map accordingly, Roberts is interrupted by his radioman with an urgent call from one of his teams. Roberts listens to the call, gives quick and concise orders, and informs the general that he needs to get back to his command post. By this time, Colonel Ewell and several other key officers from the 501st Airborne Infantry Regiment arrive and huddle around McAuliffe for a briefing. And to the general's relief, an advance party from the 506th joins them. They all look on as McAuliffe spreads the map on the hood of his jeep and illustrates the situation.

"Gentlemen, we've got 10th Armored Division roadblocks in front of us with Team Desobry in Noville... up here, Team Cherry at Longvilly, and Team O'Hara at Bras... here and here. We need to establish a defensive perimeter behind them. OK, 501st, dig in south and east of Bastogne from Marvie, up through Neffe and Bizory, to this rail line, here. 506th, when your boys reach Mande St. Etienne I need them to get on up the Champs road to span the gap east of Longchamps, here, through Foy, to link up with the 501st at the rail line. Keep a sharp lookout so nothing slips through between you and Ewell's boys."

McAuliffe turns to thunderous explosions reaching Bastogne from the north.

"Sounds like our boys are catching hell up there."

When he looks from man to man, he sees that there is no need to impress upon them the gravity of the situation. The faces of his troopers are deeply etched with concern.

"OK, let's move out."

The officers salute as one and disperse toward their units. Upon remembering a passing comment Roberts made, McAuliffe calls out after them.

"And watch out for our stragglers!"

From her vantage point, Chiwy continues to watch in fascination as the trucks roll by. Half their number veers off toward the Longvilly road to the east, while the rest rumble out the Houffalize road toward Foy. She is unaware of a small crowd of citizens that has gathered behind her. Among them, one young woman brightens as she recognizes Chiwy.

"Augusta? Augusta Chiwy? It is Marguerite, from school."

"Oh, yes. Hello, Marguerite."

"So, you are home for Christmas? Where are you working now?"

"Saint Elizabeth Hospital. In Leuven."

"Ah, Leuven. So, you are close to Brussels. Renee is there. You know Renee, my sister. She is at Brugmann Hospital. Have you seen her?"

"Well, it's a very big city. And she would not remember me."

While the soldiers deploy, the two schoolmates share a few more pleasantries and vow to stay in touch before parting to go about their business. Meanwhile, McAuliffe determines that the Belgian Barracks at the north end of town are suitable for his CP and sets about making it so. When a jeep full of officers from the 502nd, the last of his paratroop regiments, stops at the barracks, they find McAuliffe inside studying the map of the Bastogne region.

"Five-oh-deuce, sir."

"I'm glad to see you boys."

"Sir, there is some confusion at the crossroads. Are we still headed to Werbomont?"

"Change of plans. The 82nd was sent there. Top brass gave us Bastogne."

"So where do you want us?"

"You fellas are gonna form up northwest of Bastogne with the 506th on your right flank. Make your strong points at Longchamps and Champs, here and here. We're going to mass our artillery at Senonchamps, here behind your left. Our field hospital will be just off the crossroads, here, at Sprimont."

McAuliffe looks from officer to officer to detect any questioning eyes but sees only grim determination. He points to an area and addresses the senior officer.

"When our glider boys get here, I'll place the 327th and the 401st off your left flank."

"Sir? Is that Allen's outfit? The 401st?"

McAuliffe's affirmative nod brightens a few faces. The 401st is a veteran bunch and their commander, Colonel Allen, is as tough as nails. The officers head back to their jeep to redirect their convoy. McAuliffe watches them depart as the sounds of battle intensify once again in the north. The general returns to the map, focuses on the straight, short road from Noville through Foy into Bastogne, and ponders the worst-case scenario.

"If Desobry's boys can't hold Noville, it's a straight shot into Bastogne. Jerry'll be on us before we're ready."

He makes a snap decision and turns to one of his officers.

"Let me know the minute the 506th is in place. We'll detach a battalion and reinforce Noville."

Then as the first officer moves out, he turns to another.

"Give Roberts a heads-up."

After an exchange of salutes, McAuliffe turns north toward the sounds of Noville being blasted to rubble.

"Hang on boys, we're coming."

The Defense of Noville

Choking dust fills Desobry's CP in Noville as the major huddles with his officers and radioman. As tank rounds land throughout the village, shaking ancient stones and mortar loose, small arms fire peppers walls and windows. Desobry shouts in frustration, to no one in particular.

"How the hell did they get through our landmines?"

"Sir, we had stragglers comin' in all night and this morning, so..."

His adjutant is subdued and almost inaudible.

"... we couldn't lay 'em, sir."

"OK, understood."

As worked up as he is, for Desobry there is no time for blame or recrimination. He is already planning his next moves and quickly illustrates his tactics on a rough map of the village that his staff has created.

"Pull back along the Houffalize and Bourcy roads. Hold here... and here. And get some recon on the Vaux road in case they try the back door."

His poise under fire is infectious, and his subordinates move in haste and confidence to execute his directives, saluting as they duck and run out of the building. Outside, they enter a maelstrom of dust and black smoke blown about in the concussion of heavy explosions, obscuring and revealing brightly burning vehicles. Knowing there is only so much he can do against overwhelming firepower, the major turns to his radioman.

"Get me Roberts."

The radioman raises Roberts' headquarters and gives the handset to the major, who waits for the familiar voice of his commanding officer.

"Desobry here. Sir, we're takin' heavy fire. It's a matter of time before they cut us off and reduce us. Request authority to withdraw, if necessary."

The major listens carefully. While he looks into the eyes of his youthful radioman, he takes great pains to convey calmness to the anxious soldier. His measured response to Roberts is encouraging as well.

"Yes, sir. What's that?... The 506th up the Foy road?... That's good news, sir. We'll hold."

As he listens further to Roberts, he nods at the radioman.

"Yeah, got it. I'll see what we can rustle up."

They both turn to an officer who is ducking back into the building and cursing the state of affairs in general. Desobry gives the handset back to the radioman and beckons the officer to come closer as tank rounds and heavy small arms fire rise to a deafening pitch. Although the man is only an arm's length away, the major must shout at him.

"Fill a truck with whatever arms we can spare and get down the Foy road! We've got reinforcements coming up fast! Troopers! Battalion strength! Many without rifles!"

Though the officer is wide-eyed with puzzlement, there is no time for Desobry to explain how the 101st had been resting and recuperating in Reims. With the prospect of a long respite after the hard fighting they endured in Holland, many were on leave in Paris and had to scramble back to base and board trucks for Bastogne unprepared for combat. But for all they lack, they are spoiling for a good scrap. Desobry lights a fire under his officer.

"Get goin'!"

"Yes, sir!"

Just then a half-track pulls up outside, and he shouts to his departing officer.

"And move that goddamn half-track! It'll draw fire!"

Stragglers on the Bourcy Rail Line

Will and Joey are walking alone again, unable to keep pace with the others. Even Boyle has outdistanced them, as Joey barely trudges along under his bulky load. To further dampen the mood, heavy explosions have been joined by a terrible new sound.

"Hey Joey, ya hear that? That's gotta be an MG42."

Will fancies himself an expert on German armaments.

"They say it can fire up to twelve hundred rounds per minute."

He turns to Joey, who is lagging behind him, and sees that his companion is inattentive. The machine gun rips again.

"It really does sound like someone tearin' a sheet."

Joey can only ponder the plight of soldiers on the receiving end of the devastating fire. With them in mind, he recites his prayer as he plods along and puts in another good word for Will. With the tempest of battle engulfing them, and Will a half-dozen steps ahead and unable to hear the prayer, Joey does not receive Will's customary affirmation. It adds to Joey's growing feeling of hopelessness. He is so exhausted and heavily loaded that he is damn near sleepwalking, but it is the disorientation of venturing through heavy fog that finally gets to him.

"Will!"

"What? What is it?"

"We're lost again."

"Look, Joey. We ain't lost. We just gotta follow the tracks."

Joey slowly shuffles up to Will, whose admonishing expression melts away. He searches for words to comfort his lumbering friend.

"C'mon, Joey. We're almost there."

He takes tentative steps forward, hoping to coax Joey along. It is not enough.

"Look, it's like I told ya before. When ya get like this, ya gotta think about somethin' else."

But his hulking companion appears to be frozen in place.

"I got it. Pretend you're walkin' to your girlfriend's house."

"OK, Will. I'll give it a try."

As Will moves forward slowly, Joey follows tentatively with a determined expression on his face. Still worried about his buddy, Will glances back from time to time. It appears that Joey is working out a puzzle in his head, but at least he's moving forward. After a spell, Joey stops dead on the tracks with a sagging, defeated posture. Will dearly wants to comfort his friend, but finds he can't stem his rising frustration, now verging on exasperation.

"Now what?"

"Will, it's not working."

"And why is that?"

"Well... because... I ain't got a girlfriend."

Noville Under Siege

Jack is on his hands and knees treating a soldier with a sucking chest wound, grimacing in sympathy with every shout of pain he hears in the tavern. He packs off the wound to stop the bubbling flow of blood and binds the man's chest tightly. Once satisfied the soldier can breathe, Jack looks quickly around the tavern. The air is thick with dust shaken loose by the impact of artillery and tank shells landing nearby. The floor is covered with casualties. The most severely wounded line the wall, the best shelter the structure offers. Sarge has a badly damaged arm in a sling but is feeling no pain thanks to a dose of morphine. As he slumps against the bar, he gives a running account of the battle. With few able to hear Sarge over the cacophony, a wounded soldier lying next to him makes up an audience of one. Sarge is especially impressed with the paratroopers.

"You shoulda seen 'em. Came through town on a dead run. Straight up the hill at those Nazi bastards."

"Whaddaya talkin' about?"

"Airborne! You know those crazy guys who jump outa airplanes!"

The door is shouldered open, and a medic from the 506th Parachute Infantry Regiment enters the pub weighed down by a sagging, wounded comrade. Once he situates the stricken soldier, he sets to work improving on his hasty field dressing. It is a particularly bloody wound, but the medic clearly has the temperament for the job. When he finishes, he takes a quick look around the room at casualties who are multiplying by the minute. While bullets drum the outside of the building and whine away in ricochet, the medic crawls over to Jack, who is taken aback by how cheerful the young man seems in the middle of complete chaos.

"Looks like you could use some help, Captain."

"Sure could. We have our hands full."

"I'm afraid there's gonna be a lot more. Our boys caught hell movin' up that hill. They're fallin' back now."

Shouting and commotion outside precede the arrival of more wounded troopers and Jack's aides somehow find spaces for all of them. Suddenly, shuttered windows at the back end of the building are struck and shattered, raining shards and splinters upon the wounded. It is an ominous development, indicating that the Germans are working their way around behind the village.

"Block that window!"

As though propelled by powerful springs, Wallington and Beagle jump to the task and shove the heavy cabinet in front of the window. An instant later, the cabinet is rocked by the jagged shrapnel of another near miss, shredding and blasting Jack's stores of medical supplies throughout the tavern. Thankful that the cabinet absorbed the blast, Jack is dismayed by yet another crisis. He will soon be short of wraps and bandages. Yet, as he watches the medic go from man to man, rendering the best care possible under the circumstances, and doing so in almost a cheerful manner, Jack finds his balance once again. He resolves to not convey discouragement and shouts to his aides.

"Salvage what you can!"

Wallington and Beagle find it tough going as they carefully work their way around the overcrowded room collecting any undamaged supplies. The corporal strikes upon a solution to the congestion.

"Doc, can we move some of these guys downstairs?"

"Negative. The dirt floors would play havoc with their wounds."

Beagle glances down the stairs into the basement and sees the old couple huddled together, silently praying with rosary beads in hand. The sound of a vehicle lurching up to the building signals the arrival of an ambulance. When the driver appears in the doorway with a pair of litters, Jack is relieved and quickly selects two of his wounded who require more intensive care than he can provide.

"OK, evacuate these two first."

The medic and Jack's aides join the driver as they heft the two men and carry them to the doorway. When Jack opens the door for them, the ambulance takes a direct hit and bursts into flames. Lost in the fire are a dozen litters stacked in the rear of the vehicle. As the tires begin to burn and belch black smoke, the men retreat into the tavern, and Jack slams the door shut to block the noxious fumes. The driver is in mourning. He's had that ambulance since the day the 10th Armored Division landed in France.

"What are we gonna do now, Captain? That's all the litters."

"I don't know, I don't know."

The catastrophes continue to stack up, when a soldier bursts into the room and quickly identifies Jack.

"Desobry's been hit! It looks real bad!"

"Heaven help us!"

With that plea, Jack is out the door in a flash with his medical bag. It is a short dash to Desobry's headquarters. Ducking under heavy fire, Jack is fortunate to arrive in one piece. He finds a section of the building collapsed in shambles, with the major's counterpart from the 101st dead under the rubble. It is a relief to discover Hank unscathed and holding a bloody towel to Desobry's head. Jack quickly cleans a deep gash and binds the wound tightly to slow the bleeding. But it is clear that intensive care is called for, and Jack brings the major's stunned adjutant back to his senses.

"Get a driver!"

Somehow, they manage to prop up Desobry in a jeep and send him south to Bastogne and the 101st field hospital beyond. Without the major, it is hard to imagine his team in a more desperate situation. But the layers of calamity only deepen.

At the north end of town, two troopers are sprinting into Noville along the main road. They are the last of the rearguard that covered their comrades' retreat after their assault ran head-on into a powerful German armored infantry attack. The first cover they find is among fellow troopers hidden in the ditch on the side of the road, and they dive in among them to a chorus of complaints and curses. But their looks and shouts of terror still all tongues.

"They're right behind us!"

"We're goners!"

One trooper peeks out of the ditch in curiosity. Emerging from behind a farm outbuilding, a panzer pivots onto the main road and rumbles into the village. The barrel of its cannon seems to be aimed right between his eyes, and he quickly joins his mates, who are hugging the bottom of the trench. He doesn't need to say a word as the clatter of the panzer moving unimpeded down the street is a telltale sound. One trooper manages just enough breath to speak for all of them.

"Where's our goddamn tanks?"

Well back behind the ditch, a Sherman tank lurches out from cover behind a barn and fires a round in haste, missing the panzer by a hair's breadth. When the panzer rotates to return fire, the Sherman reverses out of sight. The panzer hammers the barn, setting it afire. Without missing a beat, the Sherman pops out and fires again. The shell strikes the turret and breaches the barrel of the panzer's cannon, rendering it useless. After a quick assessment of the damage, the German tank slowly backs out of town. A trooper edges up to road level and watches in amazement as the panzer retires, then he turns to locate the source of the friendly fire and finds only a barn going up in smoke.

"What the hell?"

He drops back into the ditch and joins his mates as they count their blessings.

Just down the road, a dozen soldiers crouch behind a stone wall. Gunfire from German infantry who have advanced to the edge of town chips away at their cover. In spite of their peril, one young soldier among them, raised on a farm, is gripped by the bellowing terror of animals in the burning barn.

"You hear that? I gotta let 'em out!"

When he impulsively rises to their rescue, strong hands withhold and save him as machine gun fire digs up the ground he was about to tread upon. Now, above the tumult, the unmistakable sound of a squealing piglet is heard. It tears at the young trooper's heart, and he struggles to free himself. His comrade redoubles his grip.

"You wanna get yourself killed?"

To the astonishment of the concealed men, they hear soldiers cheering as though they are at a football game. A piglet that escaped the burning barn is dashing down the street, dodging and weaving with no awareness of the bullets stitching the road around it. An impromptu pig-calling contest breaks out among the beleaguered troopers lining both sides of the road as the piglet scampers past them.

"Here pig, here pig!"

"Let an Arkansan show you. Sooo-eee! Sooo-eee!"

"Minnesota to the rescue! Peega, peega, peega!"

"In Iowa I could make a pork chop jump off a plate. Kus! Kus! Kus!"

"Poig, poig, poig!"

When the piglet reaches the stone wall, the young trooper bellows out a call with all his might.

"Pig-hooo-eee!"

The piglet detours behind the wall and runs straight into his arms. He clutches the piglet to his chest as he would a rescued infant. His comrade is amazed, but already salivating as he reaches for the little porker.

"Whoo-ee! Tell the cook we're havin' fresh bacon in the morning!"

The ferocity of his young friend stuns him as his hands are slapped away.

"Get your dirty mitts off him! This here's a lucky pig!"

Dizzy Trout

As Will and Joey enter a densely forested area, the sounds of the engagement in Noville are muffled, but heavy fighting is heard clearly across the eastern horizon behind them. They take one step after another, the slush and slog of their boots in mud and snow beside the tracks becoming almost hypnotic. While Joey is just about asleep on his feet, Will is hypervigilant.

"Come on Joey. We gotta be just about there."

"I'm tired, Will. This tarp is heavy."

"I keep tellin' ya. You'll be glad we got it."

Shouts from the thicket ahead freeze them.

"Halt!"

"Dizzy!"

It takes Will a couple of beats to realize they are being tested.

"Dean!"

"Try again, Fritz!"

Will quickly scans his considerable knowledge of major league baseball.

"Uh, um, Trout?"

A wary trooper with the 506th steps out into view with his rifle leveled belt high. There is word up and down the line that Germans have been caught in American uniforms, so he is taking no chances. He steps forward to examine the two stragglers and sees the distinctive patch on Will's shoulder.

"28th? Where you boys comin' from?"

"Hosingen."

It doesn't ring a bell for the trooper.

"It's in Luxembourg."

The trooper is joined by a captain who steps forward for a closer look. He looks from Will to Joey, who seems oblivious to the situation, then back to Will.

"28th? I heard you guys got cut off. How the hell did you get out of there alive?"

"We walked."

"OK, wise guy. Hey, soldier!"

Amazingly, Joey nodded off, his chin on his chest, while standing. Will steps over to stir Joey and shakes him to a semi-alert state. Joey's drooping eyes smile at the sight of his buddy.

"Hi, Will."

The captain is through dealing with them and waves them through into the fog and trees beyond the checkpoint.

"Keep goin' a couple of miles and into Bastogne."

Joey looks beyond Will into the mist and darkening skies of day's end.

"I don't wanna get lost again."

Will shakes his head and prepares to rattle Joey's cage again. But as he studies the hunched hulk beside him, he entertains the thought that it would take a backhoe to dislodge Joey at this point. He considers his words as he weighs the captain's impatience.

"Look, we've been walkin' for three days now. It sure would be good to get a load off our feet. Even for just a little while. And..."

Indicating the gathering murk and imminence of nightfall.

"... and we won't be able to see our hands in front of our faces."

"Negative! The last thing I need is a couple of shell-shocked dogfaces hangin' around."

"Hell, we're OK."

"What about him? He looks dazed to me."

"Joey? That's how he always looks. Besides, he's with me."

At that moment, a patrol returns from the tree line south of the clearing and is challenged by the troopers. After he is satisfied the newcomers are friendlies, the captain huddles with them for a quick briefing.

"Any sign of the 501st?"

"No, sir. Nothing."

"I need a squad in those woods. Let me know the minute you catch sight of those boys."

As he deploys his men into the pine forest south of the rail line, the captain feels the vulnerability of their situation. The planned link-up with the 501st to close the gap between the two regiments has not yet taken place. With a German force of unknown size and strength approaching and his right flank dangling unprotected, he quickly scans a number of possible adverse scenarios. If the Germans manage to slip through, there is nothing to stop them from barging into Bastogne uninvited. And with the last of the day's light fading and snow beginning to fall through heavy mist, the possibility of mistaking troopers for the enemy rises exponentially. The prospect of spilling red American blood on new settled snow puts a knot in the captain's guts. One of his subordinates interrupts his troublesome train of thought.

"Sir, what about those two mugs?"

The captain looks over the sodden, unshaven, foul-smelling soldiers and concludes that Will and Joey are the saddest sacks he has ever seen, and a liability in any strategic scenario. But when he notes that it will soon be pitch dark and no time for these knuckleheads to be knocking about, he relents.

"OK, find some cover and take a break."

Relieved by the captain's unexpected, kind gesture, Will and Joey follow a trooper into the woods north of the clearing. While still in earshot, the captain barks out one last order for good measure.

"But get your asses into Bastogne at the crack of dawn!"

Chiwy and Jaquin

Discouraged by news of heavy German forces north and east of town, Jaquin struggles to stay focused as he takes inventory in his shop. He looks up when the bells on his pharmacy door jangle to see a sight for sore eyes. Chiwy, smiling, trim, and comely in her nurse's outfit, is like a bright light at the end of a dark and dismal day.

"Ah! Augusta Chiwy. You are home for Christmas?"

"Yes, Monsieur."

"Look at you! So big now, and a nurse! Your father must be very proud of you. We are all proud of you."

"Thank you, Monsieur."

"Oh, you just missed Renee. Renee Lemaire. She is helping me. You know her of course."

"I know her sister."

Chiwy takes all of the talk about Renee in stride. Everyone seems to know Gustave Lemaire's dark-eyed daughter. On the other hand, were it not for her mixed heritage, Chiwy is quite certain Renee couldn't pick her out of a crowd. Jaquin is perceptive enough to change the subject and to focus on the vibrant young woman before him.

"So, you are home."

Jaquin muses upon how far she has come. It seems like just yesterday she was a little girl, running and playing and laughing, and now she is a nurse. It is a wonder. The muffled sounds of battle from several points across a wide horizon intrude on his reverie and return him to the moment. He sees Chiwy holding a handwritten list, waiting patiently.

"So, my dear, is there something I can do for you?"

"Yes, Monsieur. I need a few things."

Jaquin takes the list, realizes that he needs his reading glasses, and searches his pockets. Once his glasses are in place, he shows surprise at the length of the list of items. Chiwy explains.

"I am treating people at the school."

"Yes, of course. They have nowhere else to go. You are an angel of mercy."

"I am a nurse. It is what I do."

Jaquin nods at Chiwy's firm resolve and begins to collect her supplies. Several sharp explosions from the north stop him. When he turns toward the sounds, he sees that Chiwy's good-natured expression is not immune to worry.

"It's so close, Monsieur."

"Yes, in Noville. But the Americans are there. And many more have come. You saw them?"

"Yes, but..."

"Don't worry, my dear. You will be safe in Bastogne."

Jaquin completes her order and places a full shopping bag on the counter. He checks the list once more then pauses to consider.

"You have hydrogen peroxide?"

"Yes, I have enough."

Then his eyes light up.

"Ah! We mustn't forget Felix Hoffman's little miracle. An analgesic, antipyretic, and anti-inflammatory all in one tablet."

As he nestles a bottle of aspirin in among the bandages and wraps, he grumbles something about it being one of the only good things to come out of Germany. That, and sauerbraten.

Chiwy produces her purse, but Jaquin is quick to thwart her.

"A Good Samaritan must never pay."

Chiwy indicates a willingness to protest.

"No, no, my dear. I insist."

Warmed by Jaquin's generosity, Chiwy manages a grateful smile and puts her purse away. Jaquin checks his timepiece and reads just shy of six o'clock.

"Oh! It's time."

He limps over to the large storefront windows and closes the blackout curtains. Then he accompanies Chiwy to the door and bids her to make haste ahead of the curfew. She steps out onto the landing and has a moment of playfulness as she forms little vapor clouds with her breath. Jaquin stands by patiently, thinking that no darkness can dent this delightful young woman's spirit. When she steps down into the deserted street, Jaquin wishes her a good evening and closes the door with a jangle of bells.

Lili of the Lamplight

Will and Joey are sharing the tarp again in a shallow hole lined with straw. Joey shows at both ends as his eyes peer down at his oversized boots. He wiggles his toes to no avail.

"Will, I'm cold. My feet are cold."

"Well, no wonder, those old boots are soaked through. We gotta get you some dry socks or you're gonna get trench foot."

Joey rearranges the tarp to cover his feet, exposing his friend to chill damp air. Will prepares to admonish him, but Joey cuts him short by reacting to the sudden sound of approaching foot treads.

"Babe?"

"Ruth! What are you, some kind of a nut? Even the Krauts know that one!"

Chastened by the disconnected voice in the trees, Joey hunkers down under the tarp and explains himself to Will.

"But he's my favorite ballplayer."

"Yeah, sure Joey."

Will is fired up on behalf of his humble friend and aims to turn the tables on the invisible intruder, who has wisely kept his distance. Will hisses a challenge.

"Lefty!"

"What?"

"You heard me. Lefty!"

"Grove!"

"Wrong. Lefty!"

"Shit... uhh... umm... Williams! The son-of-a-bitch tanked the world series."

"But he had a hell-of-a fastball."

"OK, chowhounds, get some grub. One man per hole."

"You go, Will."

"OK, Joey. But listen. You gotta keep movin' to stay warm. Shake your legs, flap your arms. You know, for your circulation. And whatever you do, keep your head down!"

"OK, Will."

After he watches his buddy slip out of the hole and disappear into the fog, snowflakes fall and tickle Joey's nose. He giggles to himself in spite of all the hardships he is enduring. For the moment, it is silent along the front, and he believes he can actually hear each flake gently landing.

Out of Joey's hearing, somewhere behind the perimeter established by the 506th and the 501st on the outskirts of Bastogne, a grizzled soldier brings a harmonica to his lips. Soon the melody of "Lili Marlene" carries through the woods and is ever so faintly heard by troopers dug in along the line. It summons the sentimental song that every soldier has heard at least a dozen times on the radio since they shipped out. Some hum along, some sing to themselves. It moves even the hardest characters and brings on the now too familiar ache of loneliness and homesickness.

"Underneath the lantern by the barrack gate
Darling I remember the way you used to wait
'Twas there that you whispered tenderly
That you loved me, you'd always be
My Lili of the lamplight, my own Lili Marlene

Time would come for roll call, time for us to part
Darling I'd caress you and press you to my heart
And there 'neath that far off lantern light
I'd hold you tight, we'd kiss goodnight
My Lili of the lamplight, my own Lili Marlene"

In the fields beyond the woods occupied by the troopers, visibility is measured in feet. Though there are no reports of German activity in front of them, minds are almost painfully concentrated for soldiers who imagine the slightest sound or shifting shadow to be hostile.

Several miles away Hitler Youth and older guardsmen of the Fatherland, all mustered to flesh out depleted divisions for the German counteroffensive, are settled in for the night. They are scattered across hills and woods beyond Noville in the north, across an arc to the east of Bastogne, all the way down to Marvie in the south. The replacements try their best to blend in with the hardened veterans, but they are unaccustomed to life in the field, to the mud that cakes their clothes, and the damp cold that penetrates to their bones. A large part of each is still at home with his mother or wife.

Even the veterans are not immune to feelings of longing and loss, but theirs are compounded by the drumbeat of death, having seen comrades torn and discarded by the thousands. With hollow eyes they search for an end to their misery as they peer in vain into the mist and falling snow.

With the evening meal served out, a cook in a shed well behind the ragged German line removes his greasy apron and carefully washes his hands. Satisfied they are as clean as they can be, he pulls out his beloved accordion that goes wherever he goes. He wiggles his fingers, rests his hands on the smooth keys, and locates the opening chord. Soon, the familiar melody drifts out of the shed and across the hills. For anyone within earshot, it brings back their last visit to a *biergarten* before the trek into the Ardennes, when they had raised their voices to sing "Lili Marlene" along with the recording by the Danish songbird, Lale Andersen.

> *"Unsere beiden Schatten sah'n wie einer aus*
> *Dass wir so lieb uns hatten, das sah man gleich daraus*
> *Und alle Leute soll'n es seh'n, wenn wir bei der Laterne steh'n*
> *Wie einst, Lili Marlene, wie einst, Lili Marleen"*

As they reminisce, they wish to be anywhere in the world other than this dark, desolate place. With no recourse, they sink deeper into their collars and hug themselves tighter inside their greatcoats.

Will finally reaches the head of the chow line with his and Joey's tin cups in hand. With mechanical motions, the cook slops lukewarm baked beans into the cups. As silent and somber as the line of troopers is, Will can't resist the urge.

"But waiter, I ordered steak and eggs."

"Move along, dogface. I got an army to feed."

On his way back toward the front line, Will passes a knot of troopers tipping the last of their beans into their mouths and talking quietly. He sure would enjoy shooting the breeze with them and catching up on the news. It would be a change of pace from his almost exclusive contact with his slow-witted friend. With a shake of his head, his thoughts return to the gentle giant.

"Hey, any of you guys got extra socks?"

"Good luck with that."

They turn away from Will and resume their quiet chatter, but one veteran trooper edges over to him.

"Hey buddy, you lookin' for dry socks?"

"Yeah, you got some?"

"I do and you can't have 'em..."

Though Will is taken aback by the stinging response, he watches with growing curiosity as the trooper opens his jacket collar to reveal a pair of socks wrapped around his neck.

"... but I'll give you a pearl. Hang your wet pair around your neck. By the time you need 'em, they'll be dry and you can switch 'em."

"Well, I'll be. Thanks."

The trooper turns back to his mates and rejoins their conversation. Smiling to himself, Will takes halting steps back toward the front, stepping carefully over roots and through brush. Suddenly, small arms fire erupts in the woods ahead, startling Will. He stumbles and falls, spilling the beans. Nearby, an angry voice calls out.

"What the hell ya shootin' at?"

Another responds, meekly.

"I saw something. I swear."

"Hold your fire!"

As the last echo of the gunfire rolls back from distant hills, a voice full of pain is heard.

"Medic!"

In desperation.

"Help me! Please!"

Despair.

"Mama!"

Weakly in defeat.

"Mama."

Joey? He sounds like Joey! By the faint light reflected from snow now accumulating, Will rushes through the woods toward the voice. Somehow, he goes directly to his hole and sees a dark form in the snow. It's a body. Will is breathless.

"Joey! I told you to keep your head down!"

Will paws at Joey's body trying to locate his wounds. But the giant simply lies there with his eyes closed and an enigmatic smile on his face. Then he turns to Will slowly and peacefully as if returning from a dream.

"Hi, Will."

"Joey, where are ya hit?"

"I'm not hit. I'm OK."

When Joey begins to sweep his arms and legs through the snow, Will is astonished.

"What the hell are you doin'?"

"What you told me to do."

Le Nut's Tavern 1994

"A snow angel? You gotta be shittin' me!"

"I told you he was slow!"

Seeing that Sarge immediately regrets his comment, Will softens as he continues to muse over his lunkheaded but loveable friend.

"I'm not sure he even knew where he was half the time."

Sarge studies a downcast Will and tries to make amends.

"Well, at least he had you to watch over him."

Will does not respond, while shaking his head repeatedly at the memory of some of Joey's stranger antics. Sarge wonders if there is something more that he can say, but for once refrains, sensing that Will's pain is deeply personal.

With a lull in the conversation that felt emotionally heated to him, Sergio ventures a melody from the stack of record albums he has been sorting through. Simpson gives the young man an enthusiastic thumbs up, encouraging Sergio to turn up the volume. Old men lost in a maze of memories bend their ears to listen to the song of eternal devotion and longing.

"Orders came for sailing somewhere over there
All confined to barracks was more than I could bear
I knew you were waiting in the street
I heard your feet but could not meet
My Lili of the lamplight, my own Lili Marlene

Resting in the billet just behind the line
Even though we're parted, your lips are close to mine
You wait where that lantern softly gleams
Your sweet face seems to haunt my dreams
My Lili of the lamplight, my own Lili Marlene"

When the song ends, there is almost a reverential stillness in the room. Such is the allure of the singer and the song, even fifty years on. At the bar, Sergio carefully lifts the record and returns it to its sleeve. Simpson breaks the silence.

"Marlene Dietrich! I can't tell you how many times she lifted my spirits."

Brown pounces.

"Yeah, but that wasn't her."

"The hell it wasn't!"

"It's that pretty English gal. Anne something..."

Before blood pressures can spike yet again, the Scot steps into the fray.

"Shelton. Anne Shelton. I'm afraid he has you there, old boy. And it was her version that played during the war."

Upon overhearing the Scot, Sergio turns the album cover to the veterans, revealing a smiling Anne Shelton in the full blush of youth. Though tempted to lord it over his companion, Brown is instead moved to admiration.

"She had the face and the voice of an angel."

The Scot steps in again to bring his new friends up to date.

"Aye, that she does. She is with us still."

Simpson looks to take back the ground he lost.

"OK, yeah. I remember her. What a dame!"

The Scot is tickled by the use of war-era slang.

"A Dame she is, having been named to the Most Excellent Order of the British Empire."

He expected no less than puzzled looks from a bunch of Yanks, so he continues.

"Shall we drink to Dame Anne Shelton?"

"To Dame Anne Shelton."

Glasses are raised and tipped for a swig all around, while Jack sips his red wine. The Scot takes his peacemaking a step further, nodding to Simpson.

"But let us not forget Marlene Dietrich. To Marlene Dietrich."

All respond again as good humor is restored to the gathering. Sergio takes a cue and searches until he finds a particular album. He pulls the vinyl disk from its jacket, wipes it with his sleeve and places it on the turntable. He cues up Marlene Dietrich in all her seductive glory and receives a raised glass and grateful eyes from Simpson.

> *"Falling in love again*
> *Never wanted to*
> *What am I to do?*
> *I can't help it*
>
> *Love's always been my game*
> *Play it how I may*
> *I was made that way*
> *I can't help it"*

Brown presses his luck.

"Excellent choice! From the movie 'The Lady of Shanghai,' I believe."

Now it's Simpson's turn to thrust the rapier.

"Ha! Wrong! It was the 'Blue Angel,' bonehead!"

"What's with you guys?"

Jaworski has finally decided to come between them. It is a task made all the more difficult since the two veterans are always sitting side by side, often glowering, but seemingly inseparable. Recognizing this, he takes another tack. He offers a story.

"You know, I had a buddy, actually a buddy of a buddy, who swears he shared a foxhole with Marlene Dietrich. After she became an American citizen in, let's see, 1937, she joined the USO and vowed to be the first to sing in a liberated Germany. She got her chance when we took Aachen."

Aachen, Germany

As artillery rumbles in the distance beyond the city, Marlene Dietrich is alone on the stage of a theater that was holed in several places during the Americans' successful, but bloody, campaign in November, 1944. She fills the space with her sultry come-hither voice.

"Falling in love again
Never wanted to
What am I to do?
I can't help it

Men cluster to me
Like moths around a flame
And if their wings burn
I know I'm not to blame

Falling in love again
Never wanted to
What am I to do?
I just can't help it"

A thousand American soldiers erupt in applause, drowning out the sound of explosions drawing nearer to Aachen. She bows to all the young men and ad-libs.

"My friends ask me, Marlene, why do you go so close to the fighting?"

She pauses for effect but betrays herself with an impish smile.

"I tell them, where else can I have a date with a thousand men all by myself?"

When the men rise to their feet, clapping and shouting in appreciation, they are astonished when she hikes up her skirt, removes a dozen garter belts from her thighs, and flings them one-by-one into the audience. Pandemonium ensues as the men surge to the front of the hall, scramble to secure the precious linen or, at the very least, to catch the scent of perfume on the lingerie. The military police ringing the auditorium have the unenviable task of maintaining crowd control and find their task further complicated when a shell detonates dangerously nearby. Two MPs closest to the stage rush to the singer's side and cover her with a heavy coat and helmet. While they whisk her off the stage in search of shelter, the crowd scatters in every direction.

Another artillery round shakes the ground. In the confusion outside, a young soldier is jostled and shoved into a crater. Stunned, and so angry he could spit nails, he curses the bums who dumped him into the hole. Suddenly, he realizes that he is not alone. A shadowy figure speaks to him seductively, playfully.

"So, handsome, do you come here often?"

At the sound of the sultry voice, the young man is battered by a different kind of bombshell and his jaw drops further than is humanly possible. But his instant fantasy evaporates as the artillery barrage continues. Reading the soldier's fear, his feminine companion almost purrs.

"I was very frightened. Now that you are here to protect me, I am no longer afraid."

When a lock of blonde hair slips from under Marlene Dietrich's helmet, the soldier bucks up and decides that he is the luckiest guy alive.

Le Nut's Tavern

After Jaworski finishes his tale and takes a well-earned quaff of ale, the veterans talk quietly around the table and agree that no one present can top that story.

An elderly gentleman of color enters the pub, closes his umbrella, and wipes his feet fastidiously. He zeroes in on the table of veterans, men who are clearly as long in the tooth as he is. He throws his shoulders back as far as they will go and strides proudly into the light of the lamp over the table. He is wearing the dress uniform and silver eagles of a full colonel, albeit retired.

"Mind if I join you fellas?"

"Pull up a chair. I believe you are the ranking officer here."

Encouraged by Jaworski's hospitality, Colonel Davenport slides a chair into place and settles in. He scans the gathering to find that all are saluting him with smiles on their faces. Breaking into a grin, he snaps a formal salute in return. The matron quickly comes to the table and takes the colonel's order. Jaworski takes a closer look at Davenport's nametag and nods in recognition.

"969th? Any others from your unit here?"

"Well, no. All the boys I knew left the service right after the war."

He sees that he has captured everyone's attention, and that they expect him to elaborate.

"Shoot. I don't want to spoil the party."

Veterans sure do love a story, particularly if they don't have to tell it. But Davenport is a man of many layers gained in a lifetime of challenge. Such depth serves to protect, but also impedes openness when it is warranted. He hesitates. Yet somehow, in the soft light of a tavern among this huddle of old soldiers in the heart of Bastogne, doubts and differences begin to fall away. They have, one and all, trodden the muddy roads of pain and regret and have reckoned with fifty years of memories, both good and bad. He opens his heart to them.

"Well... the sad truth is the army was hard on my people. Things only began to change in '48 when Truman integrated the military. Even then it was at the pace of a drunken snail."

This gets a laugh and lightens the mood, as the colonel hoped it would. He feels comfortable enough to divulge his misgivings.

"I have to admit, I had some doubts about returning to Bastogne."

"But you're here. You came back. You must have some good memories."

Jaworski's openness sets Davenport to thinking, and he slowly uncoils some remote recollections.

"Hmm. Well, we did make the best coffee. Every morning, no matter what! I can still smell it. And we never had to give a password to prove we weren't Germans."

It takes a beat or two before the men get the joke and share a good laugh as the matron arrives with Davenport's drink. After raising his glass to his new friends, he takes a generous drink. He licks the foam from his lips.

"Damn! There's just nothing like Belgian beer!"

All agree. Sarge edges his chair closer to the colonel to get a better look at his nametag. His searching expression reveals an effort to bridge the connection between this man and his own memories from the battlefield. Then it comes to him.

"Say, I remember you guys. Artillery. You really clobbered 'em!"

Davenport deflects the praise.

"That was thanks to McAuliffe's genius, an old gunner himself. He massed together all of our field pieces at Senonchamps and concentrated fire wherever the Germans tried to break through. The poor bastards obliged us by attacking from one direction at a time."

"I still say you did a hell-of-a job. Fellas, how about a toast to the 969th?"

"The 969th!"

The colonel is beaming as they all tip their glasses. He had some misgivings about returning to Bastogne for the reunion, a place awash with bittersweet memories. But as he scans the friendly faces around him, he realizes that there could not have been a warmer welcome.

"Thanks, fellas. But we can't forget McAuliffe. The Belgians sure didn't. They named the town square after him."

As each veteran revisits his own memories of the man, the Scot steps up to the wicket to do the honors.

"Gentlemen, shall we have three cheers for General Anthony McAuliffe? Hip, hip."

"Hooray!"

"Hip, hip."

"Hooray!"

Outside the rain has ceased and fog is rolling back in. The square is deserted, emptied of shoppers and passersby who were rung home to dinner by Saint Pierre. Staring serenely into the west, where some of the fiercest fighting took place, the bronze statue of McAuliffe stands apart in the town square that carries his name. But it does not stand alone, as the spirits of Americans, Germans, and Belgians who died in the battle for Bastogne swirl around the square in the mist. The last of the cheers from within the tavern sound like they are coming from fifty years away.

"Hip, hip."

"Hooray!"

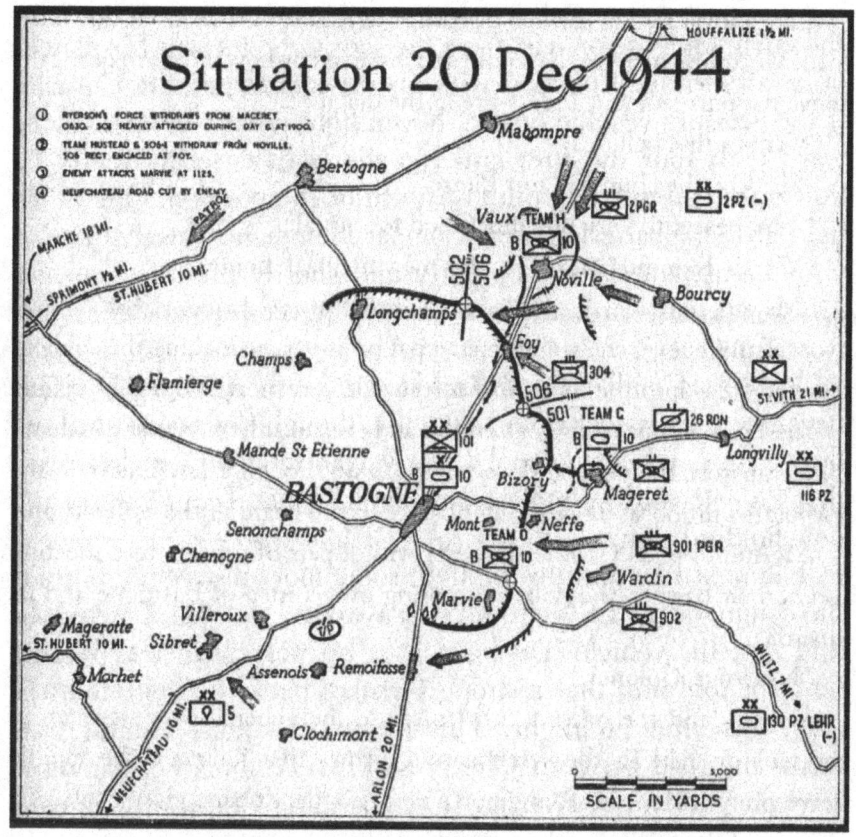

Situation 20 Dec 1944

HOUFFALIZE 1½ MI.

① RYERSON'S FORCE WITHDRAWS FROM MACERET
OBJO. 501 HEAVILY ATTACKED DURING DAY 6 AT 1900.
② TEAM HUSTEAD & 504 WITHDRAW FROM NOVILLE,
506 REGT ENGAGED AT FOY.
③ ENEMY ATTACKS MARVIE AT 1125.
④ NEUFCHATEAU ROAD CUT BY ENEMY.

Mabompre

Bertogne

MARCHE 18 MI.

SPRIMONT ½ MI.

ST. HUBERT 10 MI.

Vaux TEAM H

2 PGR

2 PZ (-)

502
506

B

10

Noville

Bourcy

Longchamps

Foy

ST. VITH 21 MI.

Champs

506

304

Flamierge

501 TEAM C

26 RCN

Longvilly

B

10

116 PZ

Mande St Etienne

101

Bizory

Mageret

BASTOGNE

Senonchamps

Mont

Neffe

901 PGR

Chenogne

TEAM D

B

10

Wardin

Magerotte

Villeroux

Marvie

902

ST. HUBERT 10 MI.

Sibret

Morhet

Assenois

Remoifosse

HOTEL 7 MI.

5

130 PZ LEHR
(-)

Clochimont

ARLON 20 MI.

NEUFCHATEAU 10 MI.

1,000

SCALE IN YARDS

20 December 1944

It is early morning in Bastogne. A jeep pulls up to the Hotel Lebrun. General McAuliffe steps out and notices a fair number of idle soldiers about. Will and Joey are among them, along with other stragglers from the 28th and several other units who survived the pell-mell retreat to reach Bastogne. When the general bounds up the steps, he startles a young sentry dozing in the doorway. The young man scrambles to his feet and collects himself, expecting to get chewed out.

"At ease, soldier."

Like a loyal friend, the bell of Saint Pierre rings the hour far down the road. McAuliffe turns to the sound and is moved by how it rises majestically above the bursts of small arms fire in the distance.

"What's that bell?"

"Sir? Oh, the church. Saint Pierre."

"Very peaceful. Very hopeful. Good for morale."

"Yes, sir. Reminds me of Sunday morning back home."

"Me too, son."

McAuliffe gives the young man a pat on the back, making the soldier's day, and steps into the lobby. Off to the side, a corporal, who goes strictly by-the-book, jumps to rigid attention and executes the smartest of salutes. Unfortunately, the general does not see him, though a few others in the corporal's unit do, as a scattering of snickers are heard in the coffee shop.

McAuliffe finds Colonel Roberts with a pair of officers in a meeting room, their back to the doorway, poring over a map of Bastogne and its environs.

"Nice digs, Colonel."

Roberts and the officers turn to salute the general, who steps up to the table to take in the symbols and arrows that illustrate the rapidly developing situations east and north of Bastogne. Roberts gives a sobering account of the reality on the ground.

"O'Hara has given way and reformed here, at Marvie. But I believe our worst fears have been realized with Team Cherry. They got bottled up and ambushed on the Longvilly Road. General, sir... we can no longer count on them as a cohesive fighting force."

As the two men contemplate the terror, confusion and bloodshed experienced by Cherry's shattered team, the silence is measured by the pendulum of a grandfather clock in the corner. Fortified by a deep breath, Roberts continues his briefing and draws McAuliffe's attention to a tiny village north of Bastogne.

"Desobry's team is holding fast in Noville, thanks to your boys. But they're surrounded, cut off here... between Foy and Noville. They're taking a hell-of-a beating."

"OK, let's get 'em out of there. We'll move in force through Foy and open that road."

McAuliffe consults his wristwatch.

"We'll jump off at noon."

Roberts steps aside with his officers to discuss the evacuation of Noville, while McAuliffe studies the map. The general is satisfied with his defensive posture to the east and north of Bastogne. His anxiety rises as he looks to the south and west, from Marvie all the way around and up to Champs, where he counts three main routes into Bastogne from those directions. Each of the three is a cause for great concern, where only patrols and hastily assembled roadblocks stand in the Germans' way. On closer examination, he locates yet another possible route directly into town from the south, a secondary back road through Assenois, which he files for future reference.

To date, ten different German divisions have been identified opposing the General's two divisions and change. Do the Krauts know the back door is open? When will they flow around Bastogne north and south of the town? How will he oppose them? When Roberts' officers depart, the colonel rejoins McAuliffe at the map, giving the general an opportunity to speak in confidence.

"Colonel, I think our combined forces are doing a hell-of-a job. They call your boys the Tiger Division for a damn good reason!"

"Thank you, sir."

"And I want to acknowledge the sacrifice you made in ceding overall command to me."

"With the pickle we're in, one head is better than two."

"Well, I don't know about that. We're in this thing together."

"You can count on us, General."

"I know I can. What you fellas have done here is beyond heroic."

McAuliffe pauses to consider his words.

"You know... it's a damn shame, all the news about the airborne coming to the rescue and not a word about 10th Armored. If I live through this, I'm going to make it my business to correct the record!"

"Thank you, General, for those kind words... and for understanding the role of armor."

"Let's see, maneuver and fire. Tanks are not artillery, not stationary. Have I got it right?"

"Yes, sir. Exactly right."

The two men share a smile and camaraderie that makes the enormous weight on their shoulders just a bit lighter. They head to the front door together and encounter Corporal By-the-Book, who has significantly improved his location and is determined not to be missed on this pass. He stands rigidly at attention saluting Roberts and McAuliffe, earning a two-for-one response. When the senior officers step out onto the landing and take in scores of idle soldiers strewn about, Roberts proposes a plan he has been formulating.

"Sir, all these men are stragglers from a dozen different outfits. I'd like to make a single, unified team out of them. We could use them to reinforce our perimeter where they're needed."

"Good idea. Can you give them some teeth?"

"Yes, sir. A couple of light tanks from 9th Armored, and more when our teams fall back. Wherever there's a fire…"

"… you'll have a fire brigade. That's fine, Colonel. Do what you can for these men. Give them a purpose."

McAuliffe and Roberts shake hands in a symbolic show of unanimity, while many more soldiers drift aimlessly into the area in front of the hotel. Unlike Will and Joey, most have the hollow expressions of men with harrowing tales to tell. They are a sullen bunch, and they wonder what the hell the brass has to smile about. As the general steps into his jeep to depart, he has one last question for Roberts.

"What do you want to call your new team?"

"I thought I'd let the men come up with a name."

"Good idea. Build up their pride, their *esprit de corps*. Let me know as soon as they are operational."

As McAuliffe's jeep pulls away, Roberts steps into the midst of the soldiers, followed by Corporal By-the-Book, who steps forward and seizes the moment.

"Attention for Colonel Roberts!"

The corporal is rewarded with a handful of grumbles and curses but is undeterred.

"You men! Fall in!"

Not one so much as budges, their sunken eyes moving from the flustered corporal to the fatherly colonel, who calls out warmly.

"Men, can you all hear me? General McAuliffe and I have decided to combine the lot of you into a single reserve force. You're from a number of different units, but from now on you will fight as a team."

Isolated murmurs and improved body language indicate he's on the right track.

"Now men, we need a name for this new team, and I am open to suggestions."

"Snafu."

"What's that, soldier?"

"SNAFU! Sir!"

Thinking that Roberts has either not heard, or does not understand the meaning of the term, a wag at the back of the gathering throws in his two cents.

"Situation normal, all fucked..."

"Fouled up!"

Corporal By-the-Book attempts to shout down the soldier.

"Situation normal all fouled up, sir!"

Roberts can only shake his head.

"What do you say, men?"

"It's poifect."

"Team SNAFU it is. Find shelter as close as possible to this location."

Roberts points to a machine shop across the road from the hotel.

"You will assemble here daily at oh-six-hundred."

Roberts turns and bumps into Corporal-By-the-Book, who is standing closer than a shadow, and proves you don't make colonel without learning patience. Or, for that matter, the importance of giving zealots something to do.

"Corporal, make a note of where these men are billeted and get 'em some dry socks and hot chow!"

"YESSIR!"

Noville on Fire

The village is choked with black smoke from burning oil and tires of wrecked vehicles. Here and there, flames brighten faces of men covered from head to toe with mud and soot. Their bodies hug the earth or stone walls for cover. Their hands hold rifles tightly. Their eyes strain as they stare into fog and the abyss of mortal conflict. For soldiers on the knife's edge of their nerves, every sound augurs another German assault.

A jeep skids to a stop behind the tavern, ejecting an officer into Jack's makeshift aid station. Jack quickly joins the breathless man at the doorway, while trucks and half-tracks begin to line up outside. Every conscious eye is turned to the doctor.

"Men! We've been ordered to evacuate!"

Jack's aides automatically go to the most grievously wounded.

"Hold those men! We're waiting for litters. Load the ambulatory first!"

Two dozen men are helped out the door, limping and groaning as they make their way. The ambulance driver sprints up to Jack after having taken a quick survey of any medical equipment that might still be in the trucks, or with the 101st.

Jack is hopeful.

"Any luck?"

"Sorry, Doc. Looked high and low. Couldn't find a one."

No litters. It is another blow in a day of crushing blows. Jack surrenders for the first time to a visceral feeling of powerlessness. It is all just too much. Reading Jack's pain and momentary paralysis, the medic ducks over to offer support and solidarity. The young man's bright face and positive presence are once again a shot in the arm. Jack takes a deep breath and claws his way back into control. He gathers his aides to give a sober assessment of the worst cases.

"Without litters, they can't be moved. The shock would kill them."

The medic nods in sad agreement while Jack sorts through his limited options. An explosion rocks the building and hastens Jack toward a decision.

"There's no good alternative for those men."

Jack indicates the prostrate men at the base of the far wall and weighs his next words very carefully.

"I'm staying behind with them and surrendering. I need someone to stay with me."

As he turns from the medic to the driver and his aides, Jack sees only blank expressions. Beagle finally pipes up, almost shouting over the clatter of gunfire outside.

"Doc, uh sir, we've heard they're shooting prisoners."

Jack considers using his authority to give an order, but quickly deduces that such a directive might be a death sentence.

"Then, I am asking for a volunteer."

With a lull in the gunfire, grim silence grips the room, save for the sounds of Sarge shuffling about and yanking on the storeroom door. It had been knocked almost clean off its hinges by the shockwaves of a blast. With his good arm, he manages to pull it free.

"Doc! Look! A door could be a litter. If we strap 'em down."

"He may be on to something, Captain."

The medic is quick to see the possibilities and joins Sarge in working doors free throughout the tavern. They soon have enough for all the men lying silently against the wall, but they lack enough strong arms to carry them. Quick thinking by the ambulance driver saves the day, as he calls out to troopers hustling back from the perimeter.

"Hey, you guys! Give us a hand!"

As quickly as Jack and the medic can manage it, the most gravely wounded are strapped down on the heavy wooden doors. Sarge lends his good arm to the troopers who have answered the call. Together, they hoist the doors carefully out of the tavern and onto several waiting vehicles. Meanwhile, Wallington and Beagle supervise the walking wounded as they are loaded into a variety of jeeps, trucks, and half-tracks. Jack quickly scans the tavern through the cloud of dust suspended in the air. Once he is certain that he is leaving no one behind, Jack pauses at the top of the stairs and invites the barkeepers to join him in flight. The old man shakes his head as they continue to finger their beads and pray.

On the Foy Road

Heavy fog has descended, mercifully covering the retreat of Team Desobry and their 101st comrades from the devastated village of Noville. Jack's truck is near the tail end of a long, slow-moving convoy as troopers slog south on both sides of the road. Heavy explosions far ahead bring all the vehicles lurching to a stop. Moments later, an officer bursts from the fog, sprinting back from the head of the column. Jack straps on his helmet and steps out of the truck to inquire.

"Why are we stopping?"

"Our lead tank's been hit! The road's blocked!"

In a flash the officer is gone, headed toward the tail end of the column. When small arms fire begins to peck at the convoy from the dark woods east of the road, soldiers and troopers follow their impulses and jump into the ditches on either side of the road. Though it is impossible to locate the enemy, they return fire blindly into the thicket and the dense forest beyond. The exposed wounded left behind cry out as gunfire strikes their vehicles, vaulting Jack and his medical staff into action. With some help, they manage to muscle all of the door-mounted men into the ditches, but not without injury. The last to descend is the ambulance driver who takes a round and cries out in alarm. Jack is quick to his side, tearing open a pant leg heavily spotted with blood. Jack is relieved when he finds the wound to be superficial.

"He winged ya. You'll be all right."

Higher caliber fire rakes the convoy, shattering the fence post above Jack's head and forcing him to lie flat in the ditch. When the heavy fire ranges further up the line, he looks up into the eyes of the medic who is face to face with him in the mud.

"Captain! The red cross on your helmet is a bullseye! Take it off!"

"Are you kidding me? I'm trying to squeeze my whole body into it!"

The sprinting officer appears out of the mist again, issuing orders left and right. He sees a heavy machine gun on a half-track unattended and spots Jack's aides in the weeds.

"You two! Get out of that ditch and put suppressing fire on those woods!"

Having rousted out the two men, the officer dashes into the mist toward the head of the column.

Neither has handled the weapon since basic training, but they clamber into the turret and quickly familiarize themselves with its operation. Within seconds, they are shredding pine trees with heavy 50-caliber rounds. As incoming fire from the tree line abates, others in the column join and decimate German foot soldiers whose last steps on earth are taken in the woods known as Bois Jacques.

Once again, the officer appears at a run, earning his pay many times over for the day. This time he is waving his arms toward the fields west of the road, where open ground shows no sign of hostile activity all the way to a collection of houses and barns in the distance.

"Mount up! We're going off-road around Foy! Let's go! Move it! Move it!"

Jack, Wallington, Beagle, the medic, and the limping-but-game ambulance driver are assisted by several soldiers as they strap the door-mounted wounded onto the vehicles once again. Descending carefully off the road and across a shallow ditch, the vehicles gun their way into frost-hardened fields and make slow headway south. When they reach Foy, troopers step out from cover and watch them warily in the failing light, weapons leveled against the slightest hint of treachery. The medic calls out to them from the back of Jack's truck.

"506th?"

With a guarded response in the affirmative, the medic is back with his unit. Jack stops the truck, and the medic trots up to his door.

"This is my stop, Captain."

"Thanks for your help."

Jack reaches for a shake of the hand and is rewarded handsomely.

"Any time."

There it is again. The medic manages a grin in even the grimmest of situations. How does he do it?

When the convoy reaches the road from Recogne, it takes a sharp left-hand turn into Foy and quickly reaches the Noville-Bastogne road. Standing in the middle of the intersection is the familiar MP who is silently waving the column onto the road headed south. Colleti is stunned by how little this bloodied, bedraggled group resembles the full armored combat team he directed north just two days before. He does a double take to recognize Jack's smart-aleck driver and is disarmed by the soldier's grimy face and haggard, bloodshot eyes. For his part, Wallington is clean out of wisecracks and can barely manage a grateful nod to the man whose white helmet indicates they are safely out of harm's way.

While his truck drones along, Jack uncoils from forty-eight hours under constant enemy fire and finds it difficult to keep his eyes open in the heated cab. With the evacuation came a sense of relief that so many of his patients made it out of Noville alive. But it is a fleeting sensation, as the lives he lost revisit and engulf him in waves of anguish. Almost as a survival instinct, his last waking image is the cheerful face of the young medic. It is like salve to an open wound, and Jack surrenders to sleep.

One by one, the vehicles disappear into thick fog and gathering darkness on the Bastogne road. The bell of Saint Pierre rings six o'clock, like a beacon from a safe harbor in the distance.

Curfew in Bastogne

As the sounds of heavy fighting abate in the east, light snow begins to fall in Bastogne. Here and there, townspeople are scurrying home to obey the curfew, tightly gripping their bags and bundles. Among the last is Dominique, a young mother herding her two small boys toward the bottom of Rue du Sablon, where the stout wooden spire of Saint Pierre is faintly outlined in the mist.

"Come on boys, hurry! Grandpapa will be worried!"

The older boy slips, stumbles, and falls very hard onto the sidewalk. Holding his arm, he screams in agony. Dropping her sack of groceries,

Dominique picks him up to carry him home. An older woman dashes to her side, takes the little brother's hand, hefts the groceries, and helps the distraught young mother all the way home. When they reach her father-in-law's house, Dominique turns to thank the older woman, but finds her already rushing up the street into the fog.

When the streets clear of pedestrians, a hush falls over Bastogne, broken only by the sound of a piano playing and a handful of Americans singing somewhere far up the street.

> *"Don't sit under the apple tree with anyone else but me*
> *Anyone else but me, anyone else but me. No! No! No!*
> *Don't sit under the apple tree with anyone else but me*
> *'Til I come marching home"*

Seated on the bench of her piano, Renee is working out the chords of the popular song as she goes along. Four soldiers, including Ruben, stand around the piano singing while discreetly passing a hip flask of hard drink. Ruben, unable to hold his liquor, is particularly lit up. As Renee's playing improves, his singing degrades in all but volume.

> *"Don't go walking down Lovers' Lane with anyone else but me*
> *Anyone else but me, anyone else but me. No! No! No!*
> *Don't go walking down Lovers' Lane with anyone else but me*
> *'Til I come marching home"*

Berta is in the adjoining kitchen putting together the evening meal. Marguerite and Gisele are sitting on chairs near the cellar door, with the younger woman sporting a heavy application of lipstick. The song ends to great cheers from the soldiers whose faces are flushed by the gullet-warming whiskey and proximity to pretty, young women. Ruben is ecstatic.

"What'd I tell you mugs? Ain't she terrific?"

While Ruben and two of his friends chat amiably with the sisters at the stairs, the fourth soldier only has eyes for Renee. Uncomfortable with his attention, she turns to her keyboard and begins halfheartedly to play "Air in G." As the tricky part approaches, she concentrates to get it right, does so, and then is lost in reverie as she continues the piece with great feeling.

She is startled when the attentive soldier pulls up a chair beside the piano bench, too close for comfort. He gets right to the point.

"Are you married, Renee?"

"Married? No. I am affianced. Is this the right word?"

Right word or wrong, the soldier's face brightens. Renee nervously goes to her pendant.

"I sure am sweet on you, Renee."

"Sweet? No, please."

"Don't you care for me some?"

"Care? Yes, of course. I care for all..."

The front door swings open suddenly. Lemaire steps in and stamps his feet, causing Renee to flinch involuntarily at the thudding sound. He swings his heavy sack to the floor and surveys the room with evident displeasure. All eyes are locked on him.

"What is this? Gisele, Marguerite go to the cellar!"

"Oh, Papa! We are not children!"

"Gustave, what is the harm?"

With Berta joining her two youngest daughters in alliance against him, he pauses to consider another path. A round of artillery lands in town, close enough to rattle the windowpanes. Somehow it calms him, and he continues evenly and firmly.

"Go down, girls. It is too dangerous."

He is right. When their mother signals support for Lemaire, Marguerite and Gisele slowly head down the stairs, with the latter griping as she goes. Berta soon follows them down with the evening meal in hand. Lemaire now has the three soldiers by the stairs in his crosshairs. Two of the men step forward, deferentially.

"Sir, begging your pardon. C'mon guys. It's curfew."

"Yeah, we don't want to get in Dutch with the MPs."

While the two head for the door, Ruben is slow to follow them as he struggles to get his jacket on. He manages to fill the sleeves but is dismayed to find he has back to front. He mutters to himself.

"Damned if I don't have it ass-backwards."

Renee stifles a laugh, but her father is not amused.

As his friends mock him, Ruben gives up, throws the jacket over his shoulder, and shuffles in the general direction of the front door. Having conquered three of the intruders, Lemaire turns his full attention to the handsome young man sitting close to Renee.

"Monsieur?"

"Slate. Robert Slate, sir."

Robert stands, steps forward, reaches for Lemaire's reluctant hand, shakes it and lowers his voice aside to Renee.

"My friends call me Bobby."

Renee repeats his name warmly, sending the soldier to seventh heaven.

"Boe-bee."

After Robert joins his comrades at the door, Renee's eyes go wide as Ruben reverses course back into the parlor and approaches her father. As he arrives face-to-face with the stern older man, Ruben is full of hail-fellow-well-met. He reaches out his hand.

"It's so nice to meet you, sir. My name... is Ruben."

No response from Lemaire. Has he not heard? Ruben tries again.

"That's Ruben... like the ssshhandwich."

Renee watches her father go from lukewarm to simmer. Once again, Ruben reaches for her father's hand and misses to the delight of his mates, who call out in unison.

"A swing and a miss! Strike one!"

Ruben tries and misses yet again. Lemaire begins to shake his head slowly as he heads toward his boiling point.

"Strike two!"

It is the last straw for Lemaire, whose face hardens considerably. Soldiers or no soldiers, he is the king of his castle! Fortunately, his princess reads the familiar look and ventures a voice as smooth as silk.

"Patience, Papa."

Ruben strikes out with one last swing and a miss, tipping his balance toward the door where his buddies help him find his sleeves, pull his jacket on, and bundle him out the door. Renee nods affectionately to her father, who takes a deep fortifying breath and firmly dismisses the soldiers.

"Messieurs, good night!"

Last to leave, Robert lingers in the doorway and catches Renee's eye with a hopeful look.

"Can I... I mean can we come again tomorrow night?"

With artillery sounding again in the distance, Lemaire goes to his default setting to protect his family.

"No! It is too dangerous!"

"I understand, sir. Sorry, sir. Good night, Renee."

When the door closes behind Robert, Renee goes to the window and parts the blackout curtains just wide enough to cast a sliver of light into the foggy night. She catches a glimpse of Robert's back as he jogs to join his three friends. Robert sees the faint light on his friends' faces and turns back toward the house. At the same instant, Lemaire shouts out.

"Renee! The blackout!"

Renee returns quickly to her senses and snaps the curtains shut. Hopeful, and yearning for a sign from Renee, Robert turns to see only darkness. An angel in a dream, extinguished.

A Field of Poppies

The little dark-eyed girl is walking with a large bouquet of poppies. She finds a place to sit and starts to weave the poppies into a wreath. Before long, she begins her song again.

*"Dans le ciel, les alouettes volent
Encore et encore bravement chantant"*

As she sings, a strong gust of wind blows through the field and scatters some of the blossoms she had picked. She patiently gathers the fallen flowers and returns to her weaving as she hums the melody of her song.

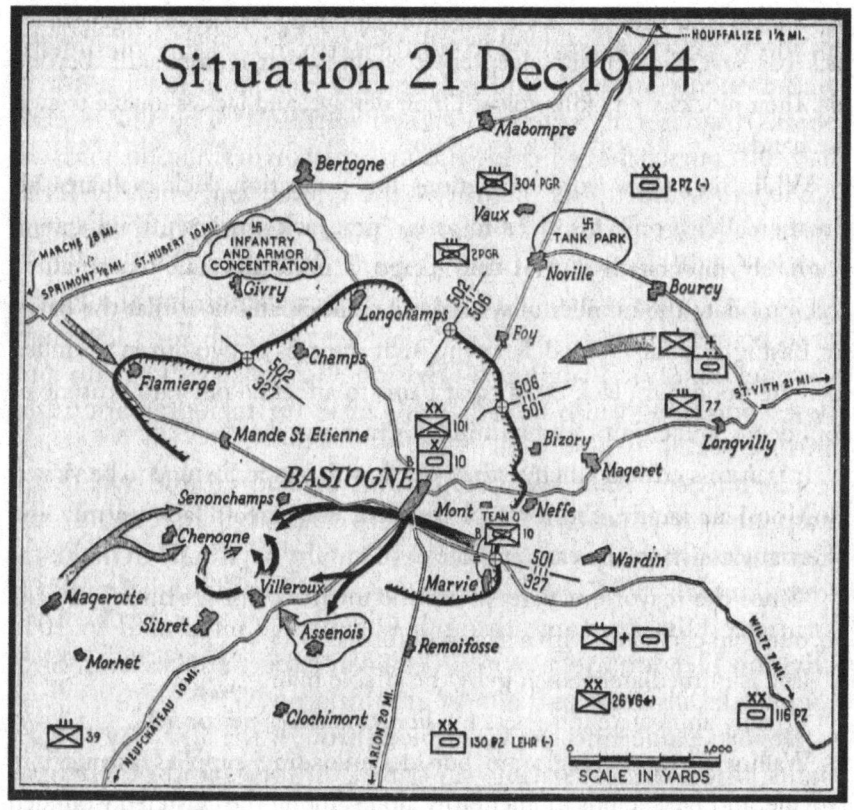

Situation 21 Dec 1944

····HOUFFALIZE 1½ MI.

Mabompre

Bertogne

304 PGR

XX 2PZ (-)

Vaux

INFANTRY AND ARMOR CONCENTRATION

MARCHE 18 MI.   SPRIMONT ½ MI.   ST. HUBERT 10 MI.

2PGR

TANK PARK

Givry

502 506

Noville

Bourcy

Longchamps

Foy

ST. VITH 21 MI.→

Champs

506 501

Flamierge

502 327

XX 101

77

Mande St Etienne

X 10

Bizory

Longvilly

BASTOGNE

Mageret

Senonchamps

Mont

TEAM O

Neffe

Chenogne

B   10

501 327

Wardin

Magerotte

Villeroux

Marvie

Sibret

Assenois

Morhet

Remoifosse

XX 26 VG(-)

XX 116 PZ

39

NEUFCHÂTEAU 10 MI.   ARLON 20 MI.→

Clochimont

XX 130 PZ LEHR (-)

1,000

SCALE IN YARDS

21 December 1944

As day dawns, all the remnants of the three 10th Armored combat teams have fallen back within the 101st Airborne defensive perimeter. With the stubborn armored roadblocks removed, German forces are now free to flow around to the north and south of Bastogne with the intent of encircling the town and cutting off all land routes for reinforcement and resupply.

Jack wakes up in the garage that sheltered his wounded overnight. When Hank stops by with the early news of the day, it is as bad as it can be. During the night, the Germans fired on and overran the 101st Airborne field hospital in Sprimont. In one stroke, American forces were shorn of their only surgical teams in the area when eleven physicians and

119 nurses and orderlies were killed or captured. Trained as a generalist, Jack has several men with deep chest wounds that require skills beyond his. Their clocks are ticking toward their demise, and Jack is unable to stop the hands.

While he awaits word on options for evacuation, Jack evaluates his situation. With only his aides to assist him, Jack's makeshift aid station is gravely understaffed. And the garage is unheated and too small to accommodate the number of wounded he anticipates now that the battle for Bastogne is fully joined. Knowing that the eyes of two dozen wounded men are upon him, Jack takes great pains to affect an outward attitude of confidence and control. But within he is in turmoil.

It is at this critical juncture that Jack has the good fortune to be visited by Monsieur Jaquin, the town pharmacist, who greets Jack warmly and offers any assistance he can render.

"Since the mayor evacuated, I am the town's senior remaining official. So, our help can come with a stamp of formality."

Jack is immediately taken in by the affable man.

"I really appreciate it. I guess my first concern is personnel."

Wallington and Beagle are outside unloading supplies salvaged in Noville, and Jack stands momentarily alone among the clustered wounded in the cold, dark garage. It paints a lonely picture for Jaquin, and the sympathetic older man offers to find Jack some professional medical help among the townspeople. Furthermore, he offers to assist in locating a more suitable location for the aid station.

Before Jack knows it, he is walking side by side down the street with Jaquin, checking his pace now and again to keep abreast of the pharmacist whose slow, irregular gait betrays a bum leg. They reach the town square then head down Rue de Neufchâteau. The older man shows Jack a large three-story building that he knows to be vacant. Though the upper floors are cluttered, the doctor finds the expansive basement more than suitable with its stone and mortar floor easy to mop clean. A coal-fired furnace with a bin full of fuel and an adjoining washroom clinch the deal for Jack.

They step back outside to find the sidewalk slippery with new-falling snow. Jack lends a hand, as Jaquin is now quite unsteady on his feet. It is tough sledding as they must carefully pick their way around army vehicles parked on the sidewalks of the narrow streets. When an artillery shell lands in town, Jack ducks and is amazed that Jaquin is unfazed. The older man smiles, indicating his defective limb.

"They had their chance in the last war."

The two men work their way through an alley to a side street, cross a road devoid of human activity, and arrive at a shuttered school building. Jaquin finds the front door open, and they step inside to hear a murmur of voices. With Jack lending a hand to the lame pharmacist, they follow the sounds slowly down a set of stairs. When they stop at the verge of a large open room, they see a young woman holding a small boy on her lap at the far end of the room. Standing by them is a nurse attending to an older boy whose face is wet with tears. Not wanting to disturb them, the two men stand patiently by. Jaquin, smiling with pride, whispers to Jack.

"This is Nurse Augusta Chiwy. She is quite young, but very capable."

Jaquin watches Jack out of the corner of his eye to gauge the doctor's reaction to the possibility of working with a woman of color. He is pleased to find no appreciable reaction.

The young woman, evidently the injured boy's mother, watches intently as Chiwy adjusts the sling over the boy's shoulder until it is comfortably supporting his splinted and heavily wrapped forearm. As the young mother rocks gently with agitation and worry, the little boy in her lap weeps in sympathy with his big brother.

"You have such strong boys, Dominique."

Another sidelong glance from Jaquin discovers Jack nodding and smiling almost imperceptibly at the nurse's bedside manner.

For the moment, Dominique stops beating herself up about her son's fall in the street the night before. It was not her fault, of course, but young mothers will always be young mothers. She discreetly wipes away a tear from her red, swollen eyes and manages a weak, exhausted smile.

"Yes, Grandpapa will be so proud."

A quarter hour past consuming a couple of aspirins, the older boy is now becoming himself again. He affects a brave demeanor for his little brother's benefit and follows it up by tousling the small boy's hair. Easing down off of his mother's lap, the little boy goes to his brother to admire his sling. Chiwy presses her advantage, engaging and further distracting Dominique.

"You are still at the farm? On Mardasson Hill?"

"No, we are here in Bastogne, with François' father."

Sensing that everything is going to be OK, the little one chimes in.

"Papa come home?"

"Tonight, perhaps. I don't know."

Dominique turns to Chiwy, away from the boys, with a furrow scarring her forehead. It is the pain of loneliness. And it needs to speak out, but only to someone trustworthy, like Chiwy.

"He is at the barracks all day, training. Then he goes to protect the farm at night... all night."

There are no pills to offer or perfect words to say. Instead, Chiwy takes Dominique's hand to steady her as she stands and conveys sympathy to the young mother through the simple act of touch. Last night was another long night for Dominique. With her injured son groaning and Grandpapa's coughing fits, she barely dozed off in her cold, empty bed. But this day is starting better. It turns out that Philippe's arm is not broken, only badly sprained. Moreover, Chiwy has conjured another kind of cure by producing a piece of hard candy for each of the boys. Soon, the brothers are roaming the room, exploring and chattering away. For Chiwy it is payment in full as she beams with the satisfaction of a job well done. She loves her work.

Jaquin takes the cue and ushers Jack forward, their cap and helmet in their hands. Chiwy receives them with a smile.

"Ah, Monsieur Jaquin."

"Good morning, Augusta. Hello, Dominique. This is Captain Prior of the 10th Armored Division medical staff. Doctor, this is Nurse Augusta Chiwy."

"Mademoiselle."

"Doctor."

Chiwy reaches for Jack's hand and shakes it formally. She seems to find something familiar in Jack's friendly face and features, though, of course, they have never met. It is an honest face, a face that emanates good will. It brings a twinkle to her eye. As Dominique circles the basement to collect her boys, Jaquin gets right to the point.

"Augusta, we are here to ask for your help."

"What can I do for you?"

Glancing about to find the children out of earshot, he continues in a low voice.

"It is most unfortunate, but the *Boche* destroyed the American hospital in Sprimont. Many doctors and nurses were killed. And so, Doctor Prior is setting up a hospital in the basement of a house on Neufchâteau, very near to the market square."

Jack is captivated by the obvious energy and enthusiasm of the young woman but feels a need to clarify the nature of his operation.

"Well, not a hospital."

Her attention is rapt, so Jack continues.

"It will be an aid station to stabilize the wounded for evacuation, strictly emergency medicine. I'm afraid it will be very bloody."

He pauses to read her reaction, finds her unperturbed, and continues.

"I need all the help I can get, but..."

Jack feels a sudden reluctance to ask for any kind of sacrifice from this bright-eyed young woman, but circumstances compel him to proceed.

"... I must warn you that if the Germans recapture Bastogne, you would be deemed a collaborator."

Chiwy turns to Jaquin with an unspoken question, to which the pharmacist responds.

"You would be shot."

Chiwy and Jaquin lock eyes and share a moment only people who have lived under the heel of the *Boche* could comprehend. It is each Belgian's duty to king, country, and conscience to do whatever it takes to defeat the enemy. She turns back to Jack and explores his face once again. What is it about him? It is a conundrum for Chiwy, a young woman with all the hopes and desires of her youthful age, but also a nurse with all the obligations that her profession entails.

"I am not afraid."

After commitments and arrangements are made for Chiwy to join Jack's team, the two men take their leave. Having overheard some of the conversation, Dominique comes to Chiwy's side to whisper a warning to her.

"Augusta, it is too dangerous."

"Yes, perhaps. But they need my help, so I will help."

Dominique wants to press her case, but Chiwy is having none of it.

"I am a nurse. It is what I do."

Chiwy is resolute as she holds Dominique with her eyes. This time it is Dominique who grasps her friend's hand firmly with both of hers. For the moment, theirs is a sisterhood of silence. As they watch Jack kindly help the older man negotiate his way up the stairs, Chiwy feels a sudden lifting of any concerns she might have had. She is completely at peace about her offer of allegiance to this good man.

"I trust the doctor. He has very kind eyes."

Once they step outside, Jack muses about the prospect of such highly capable assistance. Somehow his several dozen casualties and the inevitability of many, many more now seem more manageable. Even the plunging temperature feels like a cleansing blast of fresh air to Jack as he helps the hobbled pharmacist along the slippery, snow-covered sidewalks. Another round of artillery, much closer this time, both shocks and mocks Jack, pummeling his upbeat feeling.

Jaquin carries on as if out for a leisurely stroll with an old friend. Once again, he proves to be an indefatigable companion, able to shine a light into the darkest of places. He is brimming with pride about Augusta, a true daughter of Bastogne.

"Just as I told you, young Chiwy has a great spirit, and an excellent family. Her father is the town veterinarian."

"We're lucky to have her. But I believe you said there might be another."

"Yes, yes. The daughter of my good friend, Gustave Lemaire. He keeps the hardware store."

Stepping carefully once again through a tangle of parked vehicles during their long, slow slog up the road, they arrive at a checkpoint manned by MPs at the town square. The twosome stops behind a small group of townspeople waiting to be cleared to cross the road. It is a good excuse for

Jaquin to catch his breath as he brushes off a bench and sits for a spell. Jack remains standing, trying to hide his impatience with the delay. Mindful of the doctor's urgency, Jaquin points toward the far corner of the square.

"It's just there."

He must be indicating the storefront at the corner of Marche and Mathieu. Standing out from the dark and shuttered businesses around the square, it is brightly lit from within and beckoning to customers who are no longer in town.

Inside the hardware store, Lemaire is wearing his sunniest expression as he serves the only person to stop at his store all morning. To his chagrin, he is unable to find the machine part the gentleman needs and regretfully bids him good day. As the customer swings the door open to depart the muted sounds of small arms and mortar fire carry into the center of town from the vicinity of the Bourcy rail line, darkening Lemaire's mood. Have the Germans broken through?

"Damn the *Boche*."

He looks around at the well-stocked store now devoid of shoppers. In the stillness he hears Renee singing in the far reaches of the back room.

> *"Don't sit under the apple tree with anyone else but me*
> *Anyone else but me, anyone else but me. No! No! No!*
> *Don't sit under the apple tree with anyone else but me*
> *'Til I come marching home"*

The reminder of the previous, unpleasant evening with his parlor full of skirt-chasing American boys completes his eclipse from cheerful salesman to curmudgeon. Lemaire can't imagine how the day could get any worse.

"God damn the *Boche!*"

The shop door opens and Lemaire turns to see his old friend Jaquin step inside. Jack follows the pharmacist in, and the two men stamp their feet heavily upon oaken floorboards to clear the slush from their boots. With the sudden thudding sounds, the singing in the backroom stops abruptly and Lemaire miraculously recovers his good humor.

"Ah, Monsieur Jaquin."

"Good morning, Monsieur Lemaire. This is Captain Prior, a doctor with the American army."

Lemaire has conflicting feelings about the American forces that have occupied the town. Yes, they will defend us, but they will also bring fire down upon our heads. Bad for business! And yet, unlike the *Boche*, they always pay for what they need. All in all, he knows where his loyalties reside, but he reminds himself to keep his daughters under lock and key from here on in.

As he often does, Lemaire overthinks his challenges. He churns up a lot of energy, which he channels into a handshake that startles Jack with its vigor. Jaquin is quick to engage his old acquaintance.

"Do you have a moment, Gustave?"

"Yes, always for you, old friend."

"The doctor has a favor to ask of you. He is setting up... what did you call it, Doctor?"

"An aid station."

With a deep breath, Jack addresses the shopkeeper.

"Sir, we are short of medical staff and... and I understand your daughter is a nurse."

Lemaire stiffens with the mention of Renee. His protective impulses are impossible to hide. Again, Jaquin is quick to read the signs and chooses deferment as the correct path forward.

"Of course, it is your decision."

Lemaire seems relieved and visibly relaxes, yet he is not ready to give ground to the American.

"With all respect, Captain, I cannot give..."

He stops and turns to Renee's voice singing that abominable song again, coming closer as she approaches the front end of the storeroom.

> *"Don't go walking down Lover's Lane with anyone else but me*
> *Anyone else but me, anyone else but me. No! No! No!"*

She bumps the storeroom door open with her hip while lugging a large tin. She stops abruptly to take in the sight of three men staring at her, each for a very different reason. Jaquin glows with the warmth of a proud surrogate uncle. Her father's countenance is stern and defensive, but nothing she can't dismantle. But she puzzles over Jack, who clearly admires her, but there is something more. For his part, there can be no mistake. This must be the very same woman he saw in the doorway the night they rolled through town. Renee, suddenly self-conscious, flips back a lock of hair that has fallen astray.

"Hello, Monsieur Jaquin."

"Hello, my dear. This is Doctor Prior."

"Hello, Monsieur."

She hefts the large container onto the counter.

"Papa, this is the last of the cooking oil."

Apologizing for her soiled hands, she steps over to Jack and reaches for his hand. While they shake, Renee asks him questions with her eyes, her dark eyes. He has no answers and is momentarily struck dumb. Lemaire seizes the initiative.

"The doctor asks for your help with the wounded. But it is very dangerous, especially for you."

Lemaire turns to Jaquin for corroboration.

"I'm afraid he's right. If the *Boche* take back the town..."

Lemaire nods thoughtfully at Jaquin's words, as if there is nothing more to be said. The brutality of the Germans is well known to the people of Bastogne, who are painfully aware that even the perception of collaboration with the Allies is as good as a death sentence. Lemaire shifts into a stance of finality as he faces Jack. Renee turns to Jaquin.

"Where would we be?"

"Just off the square, on Neufchâteau."

When he observes his daughter weighing the request seriously, Lemaire deflates ever so slightly. Renee is quick to assuage him.

"Papa, I would be very close, if you need me."

Now it is Lemaire's turn to be speechless. After a lull in the fighting, they hear the battle intensify, now even closer in the northeast. Lemaire hopes that the danger speaks for itself, but Bastogne's peril has the opposite effect on Renee. She becomes quite firm.

"Papa, they are fighting for us, and dying. I must do what I can do."

Jack and Jaquin turn to Lemaire, whose resistance melts before the fire of Renee's determination, and he reaches for the counter to steady himself. While she may be his princess, she has inherited more than enough of his stubbornness, and it defeats him. But she tempers her resolve with empathy, going to her father's side and taking his arm. Jack looks on in wonder, while Jaquin considers the consequences of Renee's decision. Renee is perceptive.

"I am sorry, Monsieur. I am sure the days will be very long. I'll have no time to help you with the deliveries."

Alas, he has enjoyed her daily visits, but the pharmacist takes life as it comes.

"Don't worry, my dear. I need the exercise."

When an artillery strike shakes the building, Lemaire locks his worried eyes with Renee's. Her serene expression disarms him, and he keeps his peace. With the matter settled, Renee goes to the sink to wash up. She soaps her hands thoroughly, but the flow of water suddenly cuts off before she can rinse.

"Papa?"

Jaquin is quick to conjecture.

"Oh, my heavens! Have they hit the water station?"

Renee does what she can to clean her hands then turns her attention to her soiled clothes.

"I need to change."

As Renee puts on her coat, she catches a glimpse of her father's face in profile, downturned and wracked by worry. It is as though the weight of Renee's decision and several, perhaps, of his own now conspire to press down squarely, heavily, on his shoulders. As she passes her father on her way to the door, Renee stops and gives him a kiss on the cheek.

"Papa."

Suddenly, it is as if they are very much alone. She sees her doting father. He sees his little girl. She is in danger, but what can he do? He wants to protect her, but she is a grown woman now. She will always respect him, but there comes a time when their paths must diverge.

Renee turns to Jack and Jaquin, who are as still as garden statues, and bids them *adieu*.

"Messieurs."

Renee steps through the door and out into the falling snow. Lemaire goes to the window to watch her walk briskly across the square and out of sight. As Jack stands waiting for a cue from the pharmacist, Jaquin shuffles over to Lemaire's side and puts a brotherly hand on his shoulder,

"She is right, old friend. We all must do what we can do."

Jack's Aid Station

By midday, the new aid station is up and running with a fuller complement of medical staff since the two nurses reported for duty. Fortunately, the new casualty load is light and Renee and Chiwy quickly fit in. But a crisis of a different kind visits Rue de Neufchâteau when the electricity goes down along the length of the street. In the basement, a half dozen bulbs dangling at the end of wires flicker several times and die, along with the radio. Total darkness and silence bring out the groans of a dozen men. Fortunately, there are several lanterns close at hand, and they are promptly lit. Beagle fetches a spare battery from the truck and wires it to the radio. Once the music is restored, it is like medicine for the men, and they settle back into their low conversations.

Jack dispatches Wallington to learn what he can about the power outage, but he doesn't make it out the door before two corpsmen burst in carrying a wounded soldier on a stretcher.

The wounded man is crying out in excruciating pain and thrashing about. The corporal helps the beleaguered corpsmen navigate the stairs without dropping their man, while Beagle makes a space and lays a blanket on the floor of the basement. As the corpsmen transfer him to the floor, the wounded man desperately tears at his blood-soaked field bandages. Jack immediately locates the source of the man's agony and curses the evil minds that created white phosphorus artillery and mortar shells. When detonated, they scatter burning fragments that can burn through a man's skin clear to the bone. Once he cuts away the sizzling piece, Jack evaluates an even graver threat. The soldier's forearm is torn and bleeding profusely through field dressing. He calls out to Renee as he applies pressure to stanch the flow.

"Nurse! A tourniquet!"

Even with Jack trying to restrain the writhing soldier, Renee is unable to apply the tourniquet and is repulsed by the blood splattering everywhere. Chiwy observes her struggle and kneels by Renee's side.

"Let me help you!"

Chiwy methodically and efficiently completes the tourniquet, freeing Jack's hands to administer a syrette of morphine. Though Jack has noticed Renee's lapse, he does not give it weight, having learned after seventy-two consecutive hours under the gun that results are all that count. As the drug begins to have the desired effect, Chiwy wheels a hanger over and prepares an IV for the soldier. Though he is now moving and thinking in a slow-motion, morphine-induced haze, the soldier sees Chiwy as if for the first time. He sputters and spits out his hate.

"Hey! I don't want no... no darky treatin' me!"

When Chiwy recoils in surprise, it is enough to catapult Jack into a state of mind he rarely visits. Anger shouts out from a place deep within him.

"Without her help, soldier... you would die!"

The soldier's eyes roll back in his head and he faints away. When Jack confirms that the patient's pulse is steady and that he is breathing normally, he catches the eyes of the wounded soldiers lying around him.

"We're damned lucky to have her."

The malcontent's vitriol forces each of the men within earshot to contemplate his own prejudices. It is a silent, solemn moment, but it ends well when a few offer encouraging words to Chiwy.

"Don't mind what that jackass says."

"Yeah, you're one hell-of-a nurse!"

Chiwy's smile in return lights up the room as she hangs a plasma bag for the soldier. As Renee watches Chiwy work so well, a tear comes to her eye. She feels blindsided by all the suffering and frustrated by her inability to cope with it. She is brutal on herself and wonders how she can call herself a nurse. Though Renee was trained to fulfill the basic duties of her profession, she feels woefully unprepared for the physical and emotional trauma of an army at war.

Chiwy holds out the needle for Renee to complete the IV. Renee hesitates, then accepts Chiwy's offer. She disinfects the area, finds and pierces the vein, inserts the catheter, attaches the tube and gets the lifesaving plasma flowing. After Renee tapes the assemblage in place, she expresses her gratitude to Chiwy with watery eyes. It is one of those special moments when mutual trust is born.

Jack notices the corpsmen heading up the stairs and calls Wallington over to him.

"See if you can commandeer that stretcher."

The corporal picks his way through the wounded and bounds up the stairs to catch up to the corpsmen outside. Meanwhile, Renee wipes her eyes dry and continues to be productive. She cuts away the motionless soldier's bloody clothes, and cleans, disinfects, sutures and tightly binds his wounds. With Jack's go-ahead, she removes the tourniquet to complete the team's work of saving this soldier's arm and his life. Satisfied with her work, she does a thorough sweep of the area, bundles the ruined clothes and bloodied blankets, and makes her way to the back of the basement. On her way, a distressed, disoriented soldier calls out to her. She sets down her load and kneels beside him.

When Jack steps aside to clean his hands, Wallington appears on the landing with the coveted stretcher and a beam of satisfaction. Before Jack has a chance to express his pleasure, the corporal is knocked off balance when the radioman from next door throws the door open and searches the dim room for Jack.

"Captain! We got a call from the 506th up on Mardasson Hill! They've been shelled! Their medic is down!"

He stops, gasping for breath.

"And they can't raise the 101st. Can we respond, sir?"

"Tell 'em we're on our way!"

Jack calls out to Wallington.

"Pull the truck up!"

Jack sees that Chiwy is checking the IVs of several soldiers, but that Renee is idle, chatting with half a dozen men at the far end of the basement. He calls out to Renee as he quickly packs his medical bag. She does not hear him, but Chiwy has overheard everything. Having completed her rounds, she is quick to Jack's side.

"Doctor, I will go with you. Let Renee stay. She is helping their spirits. Do you see? It is her special gift."

Now Renee is laughing with the men, who clearly feel as close to heaven as they can get, given their situation. Even a blind man could see that Renee is in her element.

"OK, get your gear together."

Jack finishes packing his bag then steps over to brief Renee. When he rejoins Chiwy, he finds her stuffing plasma bags inside her coat, which she buttons tightly to hold them against her body. She answers his puzzled look.

"I am warming the plasma."

"Ha! Ingenious! OK, let's go."

Once outside, Jack and Wallington huddle over the day's situation map as Chiwy quickly points out the best route to Mardasson Hill. She declines the doctor's offer to replace him in the cab and sprints to the back of the truck, where she helps Beagle load the few stretchers that are available.

With all four aboard, the truck churns out of the snow and mud in front of the building and charges up the road to the town square. Colleti holds back traffic and waves them through and down Rue Houffalize. With Wallington laying on the horn, they make good time as other vehicles give way for the truck with the bright red cross. They pass Saint Pierre, take the right-hand fork toward Clervaux, and soon arrive at a roadblock manned by a handful of troopers. They are muffled from head to toe against the cold, but heavily armed, wary, and menacing. When an artillery shell lands nearby Jack flinches, but the troopers barely take notice. Jack rolls down his window and calls out to them.

"506th?"

"Nah, 501st."

The deadpan response is accompanied by a thumb over the shoulder indicating the left-hand turn just before the roadblock. As he rolls up his window, Jack files an unforgettable image of these hardened young men, whose eyes are sunken by battlefield stress and sleep deprivation. The corporal muscles the truck in reverse and then turns onto what amounts to a rough farm track, downshifts, and flogs the deuce-and-a-half ton vehicle up a long, gradual rise. More artillery rounds land in the woods ahead as the sound of small arms fire rattles down from the hill.

Mardasson Hill

Wallington skirts Mardasson Hill along the northern slope and pulls the truck up to a cluster of injured men lying in the snow. Jack and Chiwy are quick to examine and adjust field dressings and an improvised splint and sling. When they ask the men where the rest of the casualties are, they are told to cross the railroad tracks. As his aides load the wounded troopers onto the truck, Jack sprints into the woods, closely followed by Chiwy. When they reach the rail line, which lies on raised, open ground, they wait for gunfire to subside. When it does, they duck and dash across the tracks and down into the thicket beyond.

After clearing the scrub brush, Jack and Chiwy dodge through pine trees to a wounded man wailing in great pain in a spreading pool of blood. Jack grits his teeth, administers morphine, and pulls a blast-sharpened tree branch from the man's back. As the man slowly succumbs to the narcotic, Jack cleans and binds the gushing wound, while Chiwy works as quickly as she can to get an IV started. A shell explodes in a nearby treetop and Jack and Chiwy reflexively cover the soldier with their bodies as splinters of wood pepper the snow around them. Unmolested, they glance at each other and share a brief moment of relief. Jack's aides arrive with a stretcher, and a trooper breaks from cover and scrambles over to lend a hand. As the trooper and Wallington carry the wounded man to the rear, Beagle scurries alongside, carefully holding the plasma aloft, all the while marveling at how warm the bag is.

Jack and Chiwy split up and run crouching toward two soldiers lying in the snow some twenty yards apart. With strength well beyond her size, Chiwy strains and grunts as she drags a stunned trooper to the base of a sheltering tree. She cleans a glancing head wound and binds his head tightly. Like clockwork, Jack's aides are back and working their way over to her.

Before Jack can reach the second man, he attracts machine gun fire. Once again, he gets acquainted with muddy ground as bullets peck at the branches just over his head. A burst of friendly fire nearby startles Jack, as a well-concealed machine gun targets the German position. With incoming fire suppressed, Jack scrambles to a trooper lying on his side, rolls him onto his back, and gasps. It is the medic who was such a godsend in Noville. Jack finds no signs of life and is paralyzed with anguish and grief. Try as he might, he cannot square this silent body with the young trooper who was so full of life. Why take him? Why?

Suddenly, Chiwy is there beside Jack, shouting and pointing toward another body in the snow a horseshoe's throw away. Jack tears himself away and follows her. While Chiwy quickly searches for wounds on the man's torso, arms, and legs, Jack finds a strong pulse. He looks into the soldier's eyes and determines that the man is unconscious, likely concussed by a shell that blasted a crater nearby. As he digs in his bag for smelling salts, a German machine gun once again finds the range. He shouts to Chiwy.

"Get down!"

Fortunately, even though they are sitting ducks, neither stops a round. Playing possum with their faces in the snow and muck, they manage to persuade the German gunner to move on to livelier targets. Jack peeks over the trooper's body to see Chiwy's muddied face staring at him. When her eyes brighten, he assumes he looks the same. In spite of the gravity of the moment, she finds humor in their predicament.

"The *Boche* must be very bad with their shooting! They cannot see a black woman in the white snow!"

Jack can only manage a weak smile as he tries to revive the soldier.

"Or you're too small to see."

Jack's smelling salts do the trick as the trooper regains most of his senses. Jack and Chiwy take advantage of a lull in the fighting to help the unsteady man find cover behind a thicket of bushes. Two troopers join them and muscle their staggering comrade all the way back to the truck, where Jack's aides are assisting the last of the ambulatory wounded aboard. Jack and Chiwy split up to do a last search for wounded men in the woods. Finding none, they dash to the truck, jump into the back end together, and zero in on the most severely wounded. Wallington climbs into the cab and fires up the engine. With everyone aboard and safely stowed, Jack bangs on the cab.

"Let's go!"

Jack's Aid Station

It is a mad scramble to transfer all the wounded troopers from the truck to the basement. There, under the best light available, a closer search for tree-burst splinters, shrapnel, and other wounds is conducted. For those with tourniquets, it is a race against time, as circulation must be restored if limbs are to be saved. IVs are hung to replace precious fluids lost and to bring several stricken soldiers back from the precipice of oblivion.

Jack is propelled by adrenaline-fueled energy he did not know he possessed. As the wounded cry out in pain, he grits his teeth and goes from man to man. Chiwy is up to her elbows in blood once again, and Renee is changing field dressings and administering sulfadiazine tablets to fight infection.

Just when they appear to have a handle on the situation, the door is kicked open by a burly sergeant carrying a small, wounded soldier into the basement. Jack's aides clear a space and watch as the sergeant gently places the soldier on a blanket. The wounded man has a long, gaping laceration on his thigh and is crying out in agony, jangling Jack's nerves once again. While Chiwy does what she can to pinch the open wound, Jack searches his bag for morphine and finds none. It is the worst possible time to run out of the drug.

"Damn!"

Chiwy looks into Jack's eyes and sees only anguish. Yet the doctor does not miss a beat.

"Renee, get the ether!"

Renee drops everything and bustles off to the storage closet. Jack lends one hand to help Chiwy compress the wound and uses the other to bathe it with hydrogen peroxide. Renee returns with a can of ether, soaks a cloth and hands it to Jack who puts it to immediate use. The small soldier succumbs and appears lifeless, to the consternation of the husky sergeant. He watches while Jack rapidly pierces his patient's skin and closes the wound with a long, rough row of stitches. With the flow of blood slowed to a trickle, Chiwy binds the wound tightly and steps back while Renee wraps the little man in blankets. Jack catches the sergeant's eye and attention.

"He'll make it, but he'll be out for a while."

Stepping up to Jack, Renee's face is shadowed with concern as she gently shakes the half-empty can.

"Doctor, this is the last of the ether."

The previous half hour felt as if a typhoon had blown through the basement. Now there is stunned quietude, as if no one dares to speak, lest the tempest should return. Among the silent is the sergeant who has taken a knee beside his small friend and is watching over him. Renee and Chiwy clear away soiled linen and uniforms in an ongoing effort to maintain a modicum of sanitation. Jack watches them head to the rear of the basement and the washroom, then scans the room. There seems to be no end to the flood of damaged bodies, and he fights off a sense of doom. More than a few of these injured men have wounds that are inoperable without qualified surgeons. With a whiff of gangrene in the air, Jack realizes that some may need to lose either their limbs or their lives.

While he ponders the increasingly critical situation, Jack absentmindedly wipes blood off his hands and forearms. When Chiwy returns to the basement and asks what he would have her do next, Jack is amazed at how little her nursing outfit resembles human garb, spoiled as it is with mud and blood. It needs a thorough cleaning.

"Nurse, I want to draw you a new uniform. *Très petite.*"

Jack walks her over to Wallington and has a few words of instruction for him as he accompanies them up the steps to the landing overseeing the basement. Once they leave, Jack turns and scans the basement. He finds that he cannot shake the impression that he is standing on the shore of a sea of broken bodies. As he battles waves of physical and mental exhaustion, he has a fleeting sense of being not a part of the great drama unfolding around him, but rather an observer of it. His gaze falls upon the hefty sergeant bent unmoving over his small comrade. What is he thinking? What is he feeling? What will happen to him?

Unaware that the doctor is studying him, the sergeant finally realizes that there is nothing he can do. He rises to his feet and catches the attention of the man lying nearest his wounded friend. While indicating his sedated buddy, he speaks with soft authority.

"Keep an eye on him."

The soldier he addressed, who in profile appears to have no obvious wound, turns to the sergeant and reveals the other side of his face. It has been raked and disfigured by shrapnel and is covered by bloodstained bandages. The hapless fellow has but the one good eye left him, blinking randomly.

"Ye... ye... yes, sir."

Jack watches the sergeant trudge carefully between the bodies row on row and up the steps. With the lifelessness of a man beaten down by anguish, he slowly mounts the steps. He stops to thank the doctor for saving his buddy's life but is at a loss for words. Jack understands. In a war zone, the warrior and the healer are bound together by the blood of the wounded. No words are needed for each to show appreciation of the other. Finally, the sergeant raises a rigid hand to his forehead. Jack returns the salute and watches the sergeant head out into the cold.

When he steps back down to the basement floor, Renee comes up to him with a near empty case of bottles.

"Doctor, look. The hydrogen peroxide is almost finished."

"OK, thank you, Nurse. We should make it through the night. I'll get over to the 101st in the morning and see what they can spare."

Renee steps away just as Chiwy returns to the basement and strides proudly over to Jack.

"Nurse Chiwy, reporting for duty."

He turns to see Chiwy wearing a clean and starched, olive-drab US army uniform rolled up at the sleeves and ankles. Rescued by Chiwy's amazing spirit, bright eyes, and mischievous smile, Jack immediately feels easier. It is as if the horror of the previous few hours has been turned like a page in a book.

"As you were, Nurse."

"Now it is your turn, Doctor."

She indicates Jack's uniform. He looks down and is stunned by how filthy and unsanitary he is.

The pendulum is swinging wildly for Jack this day, from the adrenaline highs on the battlefield to the trenches of dejection in the aid station, where so much seems beyond his control. As if chiding Jack for having the luxury of introspection, the groans of the wounded and the stench of sweat, blood, and human waste from over a hundred men in a cramped, musty place return to him with a vengeance. He suddenly feels unsteady on his feet. He needs air.

Jack nods agreement to Chiwy and makes his way outside. There is a bite to the air as the temperature continues to fall. While he slogs through the snow to his office, Jack can't help but consider the dire health consequences of exposure and frostbite for the defenders of Bastogne out on the line.

Inside the office, he finds Hank huddling with the radioman.

"Any word on an evac route?"

Hank's slow steps over to Jack presage his answer.

"Doesn't look good, Jack. The Marche and Arlon roads are cut off now and there is hard fighting on the Neufchâteau road. But the road to Senonchamps might still be an option."

"Sir! I've got the 307th on the line."

As Hank steps over to the young man, Jack trudges over and falls heavily into his chair. He flattens the day's situation map on his desk and tries to make sense of the rapidly changing battlefield.

Pressing his headphones to his ears, the radioman listens carefully and relays to Hank what he is hearing.

"The Krauts have taken Chenogne and... and they're hittin' us hard at Senonchamps."

With this news, Jack realizes that the last of the contested hard-surfaced roads in and out of Bastogne is off limits. Absentmindedly, he drags his finger across the sector southwest of Bastogne until he arrives at the remote village of Assenois. He muses that there might be a back road there that may not be on the situation map and poses the possibility to Hank. Together, they conclude that if there is such a road, it is probably a morass of mud and no better than a cow path, impassable to anything but treaded vehicles. Hank wishes he could offer something hopeful, as all his thoughts are colored by empathy for the doctor's dilemma. Nevertheless, the evacuation continues to be on hold, and the lives of a dozen severely wounded men hang by a thread. Jack can ease their pain and prolong their lives, but he cannot work miracles. While he still hopes for one, the radioman is tuned to reality.

"I'm sorry, sirs. But it looks like no dice."

Hank acknowledges the radioman's report and follows up with a request.

"Put on some music. Something cheerful."

When Hank nods toward the doctor, the radioman gets his drift. While still listening intently to the headphones of his field radio, he switches on the shortwave set he lugged with him from the States.

"I sure am glad you brought that with you."

The young man smiles at Hank.

"Yes, sir. I couldn't ship out without it. It was a present from my Uncle Fenwick."

He adjusts the antennae, fiddles with the dial, and extends the conversation with the friendly officer.

"He was a static chaser over here in the last war. You know, family tradition, I guess."

Propelled by a pat on the back from Hank, the young man gives it his best shot. Unfortunately, he finds only chatter on the Armed Forces

Radio Service, the BBC, Radio France, and several other stations. He turns meekly to Hank, who has lingered nearby.

"Sorry, sir."

"Keep trying."

At the back of the room, Jack finally sets the map aside and hangs his muddy jacket on the chair behind him. After a moment of quiet reflection, he turns his attention to a handful of dog tags on his desk and gets to work updating his casualty records. To his dismay and disgust, he stains a page with blood under his forearm that he missed when he tried to clean up. He does his best to wipe the blood from the page but concludes that it is hopeless. He is soiled from head to toe and needs a shower in the worst way. Unaware that the officer who shares the quarters with Jack and Hank has come into the room behind him, Jack voices his thoughts to no one in particular.

"I need to wash up, but how?"

The officer steps up to Jack's desk.

"We may not have water, but... we have plenty of champagne."

"Ha! No drinking on duty!"

"Drinking? Hell no, Doctor. I shower with it."

Jack is beyond curious as he looks the officer over.

"Well, I'll be damned. You do clean up pretty well."

The officer heads over to his desk and returns with a bottle of champagne for Jack. He explains that he found a case of the stuff in the basement. Just then the radioman, who has continued to monitor several stations, spins back to the BBC in time to hear the first strains of Tommy Dorsey's band striking up a melody. With a burst of youthful exuberance, he calls out to Hank.

"Eureka!"

Frank Sinatra's voice soon fills the room.

> *"I'll be seeing you*
> *In all the old familiar places*
> *That this heart and mind embraces*
> *All day through*

In that small café
The park across the way
The children's carousel
The chestnut trees, the wishing well"

Jack looks up to see Hank studying him intently from afar and silently questioning after his well-being. Jack nods that he is OK. He pops the bottle, takes a whiff of the sweet nectar, and ponders the prospect of showering with champagne. On one hand he will greatly improve his sterility while, on the other, he will smell like a French whorehouse.

Noville 1994

Folded into a compact rental car, Jack heads north on the road to Noville for his first return to his baptism by fire. The sky is hung with heavy, threatening clouds, and the forests on both sides of the road are dark and brooding. It makes for a contemplative, melancholy mood, and he starts to feel the weight of a half century of history. When he switches on the radio and lands on Radio Luxembourg in the middle of a familiar song from World War II, any troubling thoughts he might have entertained dance gracefully away.

> *"I'll be seeing you*
> *In every lovely summer's day*
> *And everything that's light and gay*
> *I'll always think of you that way*
>
> *I'll find you in the morning sun*
> *And when the night is new*
> *I'll be looking at the moon*
> *But I'll be seeing you"*

Jack has no recollection of the first time he heard the song, in Bastogne, under siege, on a cold winter day. But its bittersweet message brings back his buddy, Hank. Though his friend is long gone, having perished in the war, Jack would wish him back to life if he could. When, for just the briefest of moments, he conjures Hank's friendly face, the song's true meaning is suddenly clear to him. Gone, but not forgotten.

Jack leaves the woods behind to find unlimited vistas across the fields on both sides of the road. The tiny hamlet of Foy goes by in the blink of an eye, and he soon enters the sleepy farming village of Noville. He eases off the road before the Bourcy turnoff and pulls up in front of a church that replaced the house of worship that was damaged irreparably during the battle for Noville. He steps out of the car into utter stillness, save for the sound of a tractor grinding across a field in the distance.

Jack looks up and down the main street, hoping for a familiar landmark or two to orient him. Finding none, he struggles to visualize his mad dash from the tavern to Desobry's command post, as neither building is where he remembers it. He is certain of one thing, however. That was the fastest he would ever run. Jack chuckles to himself, but the exercise of remembrance opens a floodgate for powerful impressions as the sights, sounds, and smells of that terrifying day rush back to him: the air dense with black, choking smoke; the machine gun fire ricocheting off buildings and stone walls around him; the roadside ditches lined with troopers desperately seeking cover; a wall of Desobry's headquarters caved in; and the major grievously wounded. But it was not all bad news. Finding Hank unharmed by the explosion in the CP that day was like discovering a golden nugget in a hillside of coal.

Somehow, Jack fights his way through waves of vivid, visceral sensations and stands alone once again on the quiet street.

"Hard to believe that any of us survived here."

Before he realizes it, he is walking in the grass and circling the church counterclockwise. His curiosity draws him to an enclosed area behind the structure, where he finds an elderly gentleman tending flowers by a stone monument.

"Hello, *bonjour.*"

When the old man looks up from his work to find a tall American peering at him over the wrought-iron fence surrounding the memorial garden, he returns Jack's greeting.

"*Bonjour, Monsieur.*"

"*Qu'est*... uh, what is this?"

"*Pardon. Je ne parles pas anglais.*"

The old man takes a break from his toil. He taps the monument with his trowel next to one of the names chiseled there, while placing his other hand over his heart.

"*Voici mon frère.*"

"*Frère*... Brother? Your brother?"

The faithful gardener waves his hand over the names on the marker.

"*Le sept du Noville.*"

"Seven? But there are eight. I see eight names."

As Jack ponders the contradiction, the Belgian resumes his work. Wishing not to intrude any further upon the man's solemn ritual, Jack offers his thanks and is rewarded with a respectful tip of the cap. The doctor feels energized by this chance meeting with a local fellow of about his age. Further, he feels linked to him through a unity of purpose in a place of remembrance. But the Belgian's memories are set in stone, while Jack's have been like mist, coming and going over fifty years. Perhaps this journey back in time will help Jack to finally wrestle his most persistent ghosts down to earth and put them to rest. He completes his walk around the church, then steps out onto the Bourcy road and strolls back toward the Bastogne-Houffalize thoroughfare.

At the intersection, he looks up the street once more to the area where he is fairly sure the tavern stood. The tiny town apparently no longer sustains such an establishment, but perhaps the building was repurposed. Or is it gone with only a vacant lot showing the contours of a foundation? Jack scans down the main road toward Bastogne and finds himself drawn to a nicely kept building that is kitty-corner from where he stands. He wracks his brain, muddled by the passage of five decades. It seems like the right place. Can it be Desobry's CP? It was badly damaged, but perhaps they rebuilt it. There is no one in sight to ask and he certainly doesn't want to disturb the old man tending his flowers. Even if the building still stood, it is likely that very few would know of its significance. But what of the man? Do they remember what Desobry accomplished here, outnumbered ten to one?

No sooner does he pose the question than it is answered by a large, colorful, commemorative street sign mounted on a stone wall: Rue du General Desobry. They renamed the Bourcy road in his honor! They also acknowledged the rank he achieved after he survived his wound and continued to render long and honorable service to his country. Well, how about that!

While he had hoped to take a different route back to Bastogne, perhaps get in a little sight-seeing, Jack notes the time and decides to simply reverse course. When he squeezes into the car, he suddenly feels stifled, compressed, even overheated, though he barely exerted himself during the day. Communing with apparitions is exhausting work. Once he rolls down the windows and gets underway, a deeply satisfying breath of pure Ardennes air restores his spirits. He switches the radio on and soon understands why the Luxembourg station is playing the old, wartime songs. Though it gets only passing notice in the states, the 50th anniversary of the battle is a big deal here in Belgium and in Luxembourg. The voice on the radio is mellifluous and friendly.

"Once again, welcome back to all the veterans from America. We are grateful forever and we remember all the fallen soldiers. And so, we meet again."

It can be the lead-in to only one song from the war. True to Jack's hunch, the sweet voice of Vera Lynn, daughter of an East London plumber and England's "gal next door," fills the car.

> *"We'll meet again*
> *Don't know where, don't know when*
> *But I know we'll meet again some sunny day*
>
> *Keep smiling through*
> *Just like you always do*
> *'Til the blue skies drive the dark clouds far away"*

As luck would have it, the sun breaks through the clouds and shines on bright red poppies lining the road and blowing about in a soft breeze. The effect is dazzling, mesmerizing, invigorating. Never one to sing in public, and for good reason, Jack can't help but join in on the familiar lyrics.

> *"So will you please say 'hello' to the folks that I know*
> *Tell them I won't be long*
> *They'll be happy to know that as you saw me go*
> *I was singing this song*
>
> *We'll meet again*
> *Don't know where, don't know when*
> *But I know we'll meet again some sunny day"*

While the brilliant blooms flash by, Jack realizes that he didn't notice the poppies under cloudy skies on the way up to Noville. Now they command his attention and stir a recollection of a poem written during the First World War. The poet was a physician who, in the absence of the unit's chaplain, presided over the funeral of a close comrade. That experience moved the doctor to take pen in hand and capture the essence of loss, sacrifice, and duty for all time, but Jack struggles to recall the first line.

"In Flanders field the poppies grow... no, the poppies... bloom?"

He falters and resolves to look into it as soon as he gets back to town. But his mind has wandered far in that direction, and he suddenly makes a crystal-clear connection between the blood-red poppies dotting the countryside and the blood of fallen soldiers during World War I.

The madness! Old men with medals lining their chests used obsolete tactics against modern weaponry and sent young men charging on foot into the withering fire of machine guns. They fell in waves, by the thousands. Their blood dotted the ground then, just as the poppies proliferate by the millions and bear silent witness today, and forever.

Approaching Foy now from the north, Jack slows to look for a place to pull off the road. Apparently, it is an unpopular maneuver, as several cars he hadn't noticed behind him zip by honking their horns. He pulls off quickly and checks carefully to be sure the road is clear. He steps out of the car and stares into the distance off the west side of the road. Without a soul in sight, Jack is startled by a boisterous voice behind him.

"Hallo!"

"Oh, hello."

Jack takes in the sight of a middle-aged man dressed in hiking clothes and a feather-topped fedora stepping through brush on the other side of the road. He feels a twinge of concern as the man steps into an uneven, overgrown ditch, wielding a walking stick with marginal success. When he lands safely on the hard surface road, the man is all red cheeks and smiles.

"You are American? Come to Bastogne? I am from Germany. My name is Kurt."

Kurt strides up to him and leans in to read Jack's nametag.

"Mister Jack?"

"Yes, but just Jack."

"Nice to be meeting you, Mister Just Jack!"

In a flash, he grasps and pumps Jack's hand vigorously. As Jack surrenders to Kurt's good humor, the German points with his cane to the fields that roll gently toward the scattered farm buildings of Foy.

"What do you see here?"

"Well, we came down from Noville through these fields somewhere along here. And you? What brings you here?"

"My father. I search for my father. His group reached here. The 26th *Volksgrenadiers.*"

"Is he buried at Recogne?"

"No, there was no body."

Jack feels a jolt of sympathy for Kurt, whose father was likely listed as missing in action and never found. So many young men died here. So many bodies were never recovered. Some were so shredded by explosions that their remains were scattered and consumed as they leached into the fields and forests around Bastogne. Jack ponders for a moment the painful yearning of loved ones who never learned what happened to their sons, brothers, husbands, or fathers. He is visibly moved.

Kurt, like many of his generation of Germans, came to terms long ago with the death of his father in the futile defense of Hitler's so-called

Thousand-Year Reich. Along with his personal loss, he carries the collective conscience of a nation responsible for the Holocaust. Such a background makes for an attentive and empathetic man. Hence, the last thing Kurt would ever want to do is cause discomfort for a complete stranger like Jack, clearly a very kind and considerate older man.

"Ah. Aha! Here is my father."

Kurt fishes a photo from his wallet and hands it to Jack. As he holds the picture, Jack sees a handsome young man with a distinctive, L-shaped scar on his chin in his full-dress *Werhmacht* uniform. As he handles the photo gingerly, Jack finds it worn about the edges and stained here and there with water, or perhaps tears. As if reading his mind, Kurt adds solemnly.

"My mother saved the photo on the day the shooting started in the Ardennes, and she never let it go. It was with her when she died."

Jack feels a surge of compassion for the young wife who must have repeatedly caressed the photo and pined away for the love of her life. He reverently hands the photo back to Kurt, who returns it to his wallet.

It is amazing how such a chance encounter could elicit from Jack such an emotional response. Nonetheless, he feels enriched and revived by the experience. Observing the American's brightening mood, Kurt smiles and continues his quest.

"So, was my father there in the Bois Jacques? Or did he reach to that village?"

Kurt makes a sweeping gesture from the thick pine forest east of the road all the way to the scattered farmhouses and barns of Foy in the southwest.

The two men stand side by side as still as sentinels, eyes fixed on the village a thousand yards away. Then Kurt remembers himself and turns to his new acquaintance.

"So, I don't know where. But it is not important..."

Jack turns to the shorter man.

"... because he is in here."

Kurt places his right hand over his heart.

Le Nut's Tavern

With no official reunion events scheduled for the day, each of the veterans spent time at a special place in or around Bastogne. Though so much can change in fifty years, some things never do. The sounds and smells of a battlefield are powerful impressions that give ground only grudgingly over time. While they walked in the fields, forests, and streets of Bastogne, each received visits from voices and faces of soldiers they knew but briefly while they were alive. Now they seem timeless and immortal in their memories. It has been a day of fullness for all.

Jack arrives at the pub flush with exhilaration from his visit to Noville, only to find Sarge alone at the table. Feeling a bit under the weather, Sarge chose not to venture far from the hotel, but he perks up considerably as Jack begins to recount the day's excursion. As the two quietly match their imperfect recollections of the battle in Noville, like pieces of a puzzle, most of the usual suspects trickle in.

It has been a good day and the weather has cooperated. To Jack's discerning eye, all of them have nice color in their skin thanks to a bit of exercise, improved circulation, and a hefty dose of vitamin D. While the matron brings their drinks to the table, Sergio looks on while toweling off his hands behind the counter. His tap work done for the moment, Sergio returns to sorting through a growing stack of long-playing records he has ferreted out of nooks and crannies around Bastogne. He is now fully attuned to the spirt of the gathering and gaining a new appreciation of the music of World War II.

Finally, the last of Jack's new circle of friends arrive.

McEvoy and Turner stop at the bar and have words with the matron before joining Jack, Sarge, and the others. Warmed by his camaraderie and shared experiences with the doctor, Sarge is almost back to his customary ebullient self as he welcomes the troopers to the table.

"How'd your day go?"

The two old men settle in and declare that there is not much to tell. They spent part of the afternoon in Foy, simply looking over the fields and furrows where they scrambled under heavy fire during the battle.

"There weren't many people about and..."

"... and they didn't speak much English, and we don't speak French, so..."

"... so, it was mostly just smiles and nods and such."

For a couple of guys with nothing special to share, they are tripping over each other to tell a story.

"Well, there was one thing."

All eyes turn to McEvoy.

"As we were fixing to leave, a young man called out to us."

"Yeah, he made us to understand that we should wait a minute."

"Then he dashed into a very old stone house, had to be hundreds of years old, and fetched out a tiny old lady."

"Warm as it was, she was all bundled up."

"With the young fellow's assistance, she managed to shuffle over to us and..."

"... and didn't she hand us each a fistful of poppies?"

On cue, the matron brings over their poppies in a vase she found in the storeroom and sets them in the center of the table. Jack is struck by the coincidence. It has certainly been a perfect day for the delicate red flowers to reach for the sky atop rigid green stems, and to cry out for attention.

"But the best part of it all was when she pulled us down to kiss us on both cheeks."

"What a grip she had!"

"Yeah. I don't know about you, but it made my day!"

The veterans are uniformly delighted by the story. Once the last of the drinks are ordered and delivered, they toast the ladies of Belgium.

In the quiet aftermath, Jack and Sarge take up their discussion once again. When they reach the part about the retreat from Noville and Jack describes how their column went off road to Foy, the old Screaming Eagles interject.

"Hey, Doc. When you got to Foy that was us, the 506th."

"You passed right through our lines!"

Something about the two old troopers triggers a memory for Sarge. When the remnants of Team Desobry staggered across the muddy, frosted fields of Foy, two grizzled troopers had stepped out from behind a haystack. Sarge remembers that as the moment when the heightened alert and frayed nerves of the forty-eight-hour siege in Noville melted away. It couldn't have been these same two fellas, could it? No. Not likely! But to Sarge it doesn't matter.

"Let me tell you, we were glad to see you guys. You saved our asses!"

"Yeah, sure. But what you guys did in Noville, you saved Bastogne."

Sergio takes the temperature of the room and, with a nod from the matron, gets things hopping with the Andrews Sisters. Sarge is delighted and sings along word-for-word.

> *"A buzzard took a monkey for a ride in the air*
> *The monkey thought that everything was on the square*
> *The buzzard tried to throw the monkey off of his back*
> *But the monkey grabbed his neck and said, 'Now listen Jack!'"*

With laughing eyes, Sarge repeats the last two words for Jack, who plays the straight man to Sarge's gagster.

"I'm listening, I'm listening."

Jack gives in to Sarge's enthusiasm and joins in with the singing, if you could call it that.

> *"Straighten up and fly right*
> *Straighten up and fly right*
> *Straighten up and fly right*
> *Cool down Papa, don't you blow your top*
>
> *Ain't no use in divin'*
> *What's the use of jivin'?*
> *Straighten up and fly right*
> *Cool down Papa, don't you blow your top"*

Sarge beckons for the others to join in as well. Normally, they would all scoff and laugh it off. But it has been a wonderful day and, to the delight of all gathered who are used to their grousing, the 82nd veterans lend their rusty voices to the merriment. The rest soon follow them.

"The buzzard told the monkey, 'You are chokin' me'
'Release your hold and I will set you free'
The monkey looked the buzzard right dead in the eye
And said 'Your story's so touching, it sounds just like a lie'"

Such is the general merriment that even a few bemused locals at a table in the far corner take a flying leap at the lyrics, landing on one out of three words, but acing the refrain.

"Straighten up and fly right
Straighten up and stay right
Straighten up and fly right
Cool down Papa, don't you blow your top"

All in all, this is the liveliest Le Nut's Tavern has been in a month of Sundays. Sarge is so excited that Jack fights off the urge to check his friend's blood pressure. When the song ends, Sarge raises a glass to the two Screaming Eagles and then wider to include Simpson and Brown, all of whom flew straight enough and right enough to survive the war.

"Whaddaya say we toast these crazy guys who jump out of airplanes."

Jack raises his wine glass as all the veterans hold their beers high. But something seems just slightly out of whack for Colleti.

"Hey, Jack! It's gotta be against some kind of regulation to toast the airborne with wine!"

Jack considers and turns to query the matron who has been standing by. Having heard the exchange, the wheels are already turning in her head and she smiles broadly to Jack.

"Why not the Airborne Beer?"

This gets everyone's attention.

"It is just new from Brasserie de Bouillon!"

Jack's nod of ascent sends the matron behind the bar where she sorts through the cooler. Quick as a wink, she returns with a bottle and a glass to Jack's side. She pops the top, pours half a serving and hands the bottle to Jack. He turns the label to see a cartoon of a soldier holding a helmet full of sloshing liquid. He is not sure what to make of it.

"Shall I tell you?"

Her question spurs their curiosity onward, and Jack turns the label to his table mates. They are all ears.

"So, the story goes that one of your paratroopers comes in from the fighting to see his friend in hospital. His friend is thirsty, so he walks in the town and finds a tavern. It is damaged from the bombs, but he finds a... What is the word?"

She calls out to Sergio.

"Comment dit-on un robinet de bière en anglais?"

"Beer tap."

"Ah, beer tap. The soldier finds a beer tap. Of course, he has to try it. It is working. He is very happy! But for his friend in hospital, it is sad. He looks around, but all of the glasses are broken. So, he has an idea. He fills his hat, his... how do you say?"

Sarge to the rescue.

"His helmet!"

It turns out she is more than a fair storyteller. She describes the trooper stepping through the rubble in the streets carefully to spill as little beer as possible while returning to his friend. Jack, enchanted by the story, guesses there must be an element of truth to it and follows the trooper in his mind's eye to what must have been the 101st aid station. As she continues, Jack imagines the trooper tipping the helmet to his friend's lips, causing a sensation as wounded troopers around him take notice.

"Hey! What is that? Beer?"

"Save some for me!"

Jack pictures Major Davidson, chief medical officer for the 101st Airborne Division storming over to them.

"What are you doing? I've got chest and stomach wounds here! If they drink, it could damn-well kill them! Get the hell out of here!"

The image of the normally placid major blowing his top brings a smile to Jack's face. As the matron continues her story, Jack visualizes the trooper with the helmet full of beer beating a hasty retreat. But he has not cleared the gauntlet and is challenged by a wounded officer who has overheard the dressing-down doled out by Davidson.

"Trooper! You are out of uniform. Get that helmet on!"

The trooper stops dead in his tracks. He is steps from the door where he could safely dump the beer. But, he thinks, this is Belgian beer! It would be a crime to pitch it. The poor fellow is paralyzed by indecision.

"That's an order, trooper!"

The matron happily concludes the story by posing the question.

"So, what we do not know. Did he waste the beer, or did he drink it?"

But Sarge is quick with a third alternative.

"Neither. I say he put his helmet on full and got his first shower in a month!"

Sarge illustrates his point by upturning an empty breadbasket on his head. The veterans respond by laughing with, and at, Sarge, who is thoroughly delighted with himself as he wipes breadcrumbs away. It all triggers a whimsical, pleasant memory for Jack, which he shares in an aside to Sarge.

"I prefer to shower with champagne."

"Yeah sure, Doc."

Sarge is only half listening to Jack as he soaks in the attention from the veterans. He is reminded of his original purpose when he observes beer glasses still in hand and expectant looks on their faces.

"Gentlemen. To the airborne."

"To the airborne!"

Situation 22 Dec 1944

22 December 1944

Bastogne is under siege. Random shells continue to land in town as German forces probe American defenses from all points of the compass. No air support for the battered American forces is possible due to low-lying clouds and fog hugging the landscape. With no sure evacuation route open, the conditions on the ground are critical for the wounded and the harried few caring for them.

Cautious hopes in hand, Jack arrives at the Belgian Barracks, the site of the 101st Airborne aid station and McAuliffe's HQ. As he steps up to the door he hears an authoritative order shouted from within.

"On the double, Private!"

"Yes, sir! Gangway!"

Before Jack can reach for the knob to enter, the door is yanked open, and a very youthful trooper rushes out with large packets stuffed full of documents. He passes the doctor, then doubles back and salutes.

"Oh, Captain! Here you go, sir."

He hands Jack a copy of the day's situation map, showing the disposition of American and German forces based on the best intelligence available at the time. In doing so, the private lightens his load by one map as he sets out to distribute a copy to every officer in Bastogne. He is already almost breathless.

"Hot off the press!"

"What's our situation?"

But the trooper is gone, having jumped into a waiting jeep and churned away in the mud and snow. Jack takes a moment to look the map over, noting the similarities to the previous day's map right off. There is a continuation of aggressive German probes from the east and southeast, a concentration of German armor in the Noville area, and a buildup of German infantry and armor northwest of Champs. It is in the southwest that the situation has shifted, and that the noose appears to have tightened. Roads that were hotly contested the day before now appear to be in German hands, though American forces are on the offensive nearby.

Jack folds the map and tucks it into his pocket. He is the picture of dejection as he enters the barracks and finds a beehive of activity. Officers are moving with haste in every direction, except for one man, apparently the mapmaker, who is standing in his office doorway wiping printer's ink from his hands. Peeking into doors as he makes his way down the hall, Jack locates Major Davidson. The major is seated at his desk looking through casualty records while calmly smoking his pipe. He looks up at Jack, who snaps a salute, and identifies himself.

"Captain Prior, MD. 10th Armored, sir."

Davidson returns Jack's salute and, in a glance, takes in the muddied red cross on Jack's helmet and the haggard appearance of a man who has been through the wringer. He indicates a chair with the stem of his pipe.

"Take a load off your feet, Doctor."

Jack does so as the major sets his papers aside and knocks out his pipe. Davidson emanates remarkable calmness for a chief medical officer responsible for an entire division under siege.

"10th Armored? Which team?"

"Desobry, sir."

"I hear his boys put up one hell-of-a fight. Stopped 'em cold."

"Yes, sir."

At the thought of his grievously injured commanding officer, Jack is flooded with a toxic mix of regret and shame.

"The major took a severe head wound. I did what I could and sent him down to your field hospital... only to get him killed."

"That was a tough night. But wait a minute. I've just been looking over the quartermaster's report on Sprimont."

The major quickly leafs through the pages.

"Desobry was not among the dead. In all likelihood he's in the care of a German physician as we speak."

Davidson interprets Jack's recovering breath as a grateful sigh of relief and a signal to move on. He settles back in his chair and refills and lights his pipe.

"So, Captain, what can I do for you?"

"Sir, we are down to the last of the hydrogen peroxide and out of ether and morphine. I'm using cognac for pain. All we have in abundance are sulfa pills and plasma."

"Which is prone to freezing. I understand your dilemma, Doctor. We're also short of all things medical. We lost everything when they hit Sprimont. Surgeons, nurses, tools, supplies. Everything."

"Understood, sir. And now with Senonchamps cut off, evacuation is impossible."

The major gives Jack a questioning look.

"I saw today's situation map. We're surrounded."

"Hey, chin up, Doctor. The airborne are here. We're used to being surrounded."

"Yes, sir. Is there any possibility of airlifting in surgical teams?"

"They'd have to come by glider, and that's not possible until the sky clears. Even then, they would be clay pigeons for Jerry. You've got to hang on and hope for the best."

"Yes, sir. Hope for the best."

Though he tries to put a brave face on it, Jack is discouraged by the course of the conversation thus far. Exhaustion of the spirit adds to exhaustion of the body, and Jack slumps ever so slightly in his chair. As the major puffs away on his pipe and searches for additional words to encourage Jack, a typewriter rattles to life in the adjoining office. Jack turns to see one of Davidson's staff attacking the daily reports, and he involuntarily fixates on the machine as the young trooper's fingertips dance over the keys. Without realizing it, Jack begins to think out loud.

"Boy, I could sure use one of those."

"Private Morgan? He's a crackerjack all right."

"Oh! Well... no... uh."

With a sudden jolt of self-awareness, Jack sits erect and banishes everything but his primary concern from his thoughts.

"Sir, I've got one hundred and thirty men just about lying on top of each other, and more wounded coming every day. Can you take any?"

Davidson studies Jack for a moment, then knocks out his pipe, stands, and steps out from behind his desk.

"Come with me."

The major leads Jack out of his office, down the bustling hallway, and through a pair of swinging doors to the riding arena where Belgian cavalry trained for generations. Jack's eyes widen in amazement as he takes in the expansive ground completely covered with more than 600 wounded troopers. It is a stunning revelation for Jack.

Davidson follows the younger man's gaze as Jack looks from man to man. It is an exercise the major knows all too well. This trooper is alert. That one is sedated. Here is a head wound, and there a broken arm. For Jack, the sheer volume of injury and incapacitation is mesmerizing, but when a man cries out in pain, he reacts. The sympathetic major is working overtime to look on the bright side.

"It's not ideal from the standpoint of sterility. But at least they're in from the elements and out of the line of fire."

Jack can only nod in acknowledgment, as the major continues.

"We're looking for small victories here, Captain."

Jack continues to survey the room and is deeply moved. He lights upon an area clearly set aside for the mortally wounded, where a chaplain is kneeling beside a motionless trooper administering last rites. The tableau brings vividly to mind the bodies lying silently on the periphery of Jack's aid station. With watering eyes, he turns to the major and struggles to find his voice.

"It... it's gotten to the point... where I am setting aside the worst cases... to do what I can for the boys who have a chance."

"And that, Doctor, is the hardest thing you'll ever have to do."

When it is apparent that his words have sunken in, the older man rests a fatherly hand on Jack's shoulder and guides him out of the arena. On the way, Davidson debates whether to share advice he was given in his youth, when darkness and fear tormented him. He never forgot it, has lived by it, but has never shared it, until now.

"Don't know if this will help, but it helps me. If..."

As they pause before the major's office, Jack turns to the man as an apprentice would to a master craftsman.

"... if you find yourself in a dark room, light a candle."

"Yes, sir. Light a candle. Thank you, sir."

Even though the comforting words do not really register, the sentiment does, and Jack feels decidedly calmer. When he shows signs of preparing to take his leave, the major has one other design as he spots Morgan brewing a pot of coffee. He makes an offer, but Jack demurs. The major insists.

"One cup of coffee. And that's an order."

Jack turns to the smell of fresh coffee and surrenders to the therapy of aroma. The major sweetens the pot further.

"I'll see what we can rustle up for you. No point in your going back empty-handed."

As Jack steps over to the coffee pot, Major Davidson instructs Morgan to collect for Jack whatever medical supplies can be spared. Morgan steps out of the door, but ducks quickly back inside again as an officer barges down the hall under a full head of steam. When Morgan ventures forth again, he sees the officer talking animatedly with Colonel Kinnard outside General McAuliffe's office. Morgan watches the two disappear together into the room, pulling the door closed behind them and muffling their voices. But Morgan has heard bits and pieces, just enough to start a rumor if he so chooses.

The Ultimatum

Kinnard ushers the officer to the threshold of McAuliffe's private quarters, where the general is stirred from a catnap he earned after consecutive days with next to no sleep. What Kinnard has to say quickly sweeps away the cobwebs.

"General, sir. Two German officers came through our lines under a white flag."

"They want to surrender?"

"No, sir. They want us to surrender."

"Us, surrender? Aw, NUTS!"

"Sir, they were ordered to deliver a message to you."

McAuliffe turns to the officer.

"Read it."

The officer does so, while Kinnard consults a map to locate the towns mentioned in the message.

"To the USA commander of the encircled town of Bastogne: The fortunes of war are changing. This time the USA forces in and near Bastogne have been encircled by strong German armored units. More German armored units have crossed the river Ourth near Ortheuville, have taken Marche and reached St. Hubert by passing through Hompre-Sibret-Tiller. Libramont is in German hands. There is only one possibility to save the encircled USA troops from total annihilation. That is the honorable surrender of the encircled town. In order to think it over, a term of two hours will be granted, beginning with the presentation of this note. If this proposal should be rejected, one German artillery corps and six heavy A.A.

battalions are ready to annihilate the USA troops in and near Bastogne. The order for firing will be given immediately after this two-hour term. All the serious civilian losses caused by this artillery fire would not correspond with the well-known American humanity."

The officer looks up into the eyes of General McAuliffe, the very picture of grit and determination, and adds the signatory almost sheepishly.

"The German Commander."

The son-of-a-bitch didn't even have the balls to sign his name! McAuliffe slowly shakes his head but keeps his thoughts to himself. The general's driver appears at the door and catches Kinnard's eye.

"Sir, your driver is here. You wanted to congratulate the unit that took out a German roadblock."

McAuliffe nods, puts on his jacket and helmet, and follows the driver out the door. During the short drive to the location where the unit to be recognized is standing down, he engages in an internal debate on how to respond to the German ultimatum.

"We're running low on everything. Food, medicine, ammunition. We are outnumbered and outgunned. But, with blood already shed to hold Bastogne, this is sacred ground. I'll be damned if we're going to give it up!"

As if in retort, he approaches troopers jogging in place and slapping their arms as they battle the plummeting temperature. He continues listing items on the negative side of the ledger.

"Without winter gear, our boys are freezing."

Somehow, the troopers manage to smile as they wave to the popular general. His driver slows and yields the road when an ambulance spins and slides by on the way to the barracks with yet more seriously wounded men aboard. The general's musings march on.

"Our aid stations are overcrowded... and many of those boys will die if they're not evacuated."

Heavy claps of thunder signal the concentrated fire of the American long guns he collected just southwest of the town.

"Those boys have been doing a hell-of-a-job."

American artillery has broken up many a German heavy patrol or assault. McAuliffe chuckles as he recalls the routine of his favorite artillery battalion, the all-black 969th. One officer keeps his crew on task, loading and firing their powerful M1 155mm Howitzers, by leading the popular call-and-response marching song.

> *"You had a good home but you left!"*
> *"You're right!"*
> *"You had a good home but you left!"*
> *"You're right!"*
> *"Jody was there when you left!"*
> *"You're right!"*
> *"Your baby was there when you left!"*
> *"You're right!"*
> *"Sound off!"*

At this command, the howitzer shakes the ground and splits the air with a lethal projectile that arches quickly toward its intended target. With the sound of the shell's devastating impact in the distance, the officer shouts a postmortem.

"Hitler! Count your children!"

Then he calls out, with a tinge of regret.

"OK! Knock off boys! That's our ten."

Once the echoing sound of the artillery is swallowed up in the snow-covered hills, McAuliffe rearranges the priorities in his list of nagging concerns.

"Hell, we're even rationing artillery shells!"

With his task accomplished, and the young troopers he congratulated flush with their small victory, McAuliffe heads back to the barracks. He returns salutes from Jack and Morgan in the hallway, as they go over the medical supplies assembled for Jack's use. The general finds his office full of men anxiously awaiting his return and decision. Kinnard steps forward.

"Sir, the Germans are standing by for a response."

"Well, I don't know what to tell them."

"What you said initially would be hard to beat."

Jack's Aid Station

"Nuts? He said nuts?"

Hank is incredulous. He has heard that just one word can make a big difference, but this one is a doozy! A smile creeps onto Jack's lips as he elaborates.

"They gave McAuliffe an ultimatum, and he felt a need for brevity."

Having met curbside on Jack's return from the 101st, the two men marvel at the general's audacity. When an artillery round lands down the street, Hank ducks into the office and Jack steps into the aid station toting a box of medical supplies. Beagle hustles out to help unload the jeep, and Wallington is not far behind. When the corporal steps inside with the last of the boxes, he finds Jack taking a quick inventory.

"Any luck, Doc?"

"They had extra sutures, bandages, tape, and the like. They're short of everything else."

"No, I mean... can they take some of our boys?"

"They're packed full like we are, but with six-fold our number."

"Six? Six hundred wounded?"

"Or more. And they're laid out on the dirt of a riding arena exposed to all manner of pathogens."

The corporal's brow is knitted by a question. Jack elaborates.

"Bacteria. They'll lose a lot of boys to infection if they don't get the medicines they need. That we all need."

Wallington knows the score.

"Which will happen when the sun breaks through."

Jack adds another option.

"Or Patton does."

While his aides get busy clearing the supplies stacked inside the door, Jack spots Chiwy changing a young soldier's dressing. She responds to Jack with a hopeful expression on her face. He shakes his head. The tireless nurse takes a quick look around the overcrowded basement, pulls a deep breath, and gets right back to work. The corporal returns to Jack's side and follows his eyes around the room.

"It's been pretty quiet, Doc. Nothing we couldn't handle."

"Where's Renee?"

Wallington is first to locate her, kneeling down beside one of the most severely wounded men lying silently at the back of the room. Jack recognizes him, the one they call Smitty. Though the soldier is unresponsive, Renee is whispering to him as she changes his dressing. Listening in while Frank is dozing, Sal and Slim observe Renee with growing admiration.

Wallington is apparently unimpressed.

"What's the point? Poor guy doesn't even know she's there."

"We can't know that for sure."

With Jack's comment, the corporal is uncharacteristically subdued. He shuffles away to join Beagle in packing the supplies into the cupboards by the washroom. When they finish, Beagle heads outside for a smoke.

For the moment, Jack stands alone in the midst of the wounded, mesmerized by Renee as she continues to whisper to Smitty and stroke his forehead with a damp cloth. It is almost as though the war has retreated and simple human kindness has stepped into the breach. His reverie is rudely interrupted when Beagle bursts through the door. The young man appears to be on the verge of shock.

"Captain, sir! We got a coupla' locals at the door!"

"What's their situation?"

"Well, I can't say for sure, but I think the woman is havin' a baby!"

Stepping quickly outside, Jack finds a distraught man shouting and pointing at the red cross over the door as his pregnant wife lies in a barrow. When the man tries to help his wife out of the cart, Jack rushes to assist him and calls on his orderly, who is overawed by the whole affair. Beagle is used to the bloodshed of battle, but this is different. He imagines her dropping the baby right then and there. Wallington is quick as a flea to locate the stretcher, rush to the woman's side, and yank the orderly back to his senses. Together, they carry the woman up the steps and set her down inside on the landing, where the corporal turns to Jack.

"Should we take her upstairs?"

Jack quickly sorts through his options. Without heat or light, the upper floors would be unsuitable, yet the basement is packed to the gills. Mother Nature intervenes, forcing Jack's hand.

"No time for that! Her water has broken!"

"Oh, my God! Here it comes!"

Traumatized by the vision, Beagle feels faint and unstable on his feet, to his buddy's consternation.

"Get ahold of yourself! That's an order!"

All conscious heads turn toward the commotion as Wallington and the chastened orderly carefully negotiate the steps down into the basement. A half-dozen soldiers shift their aching bodies while Jack manages to clear a space. His aides carefully transfer the woman to a blanket that Chiwy has spread for her. At the nurse's request, they hustle away to get warm water and clean linen. When Jack kneels to examine the woman, Chiwy beats him to it.

"Let me help. This is my training."

The basement goes silent as Chiwy calmly guides the woman to breathe and push, breathe and push. Renee is attentive from afar as she works on another of the worst cases, a prostrate soldier whose eyes are covered by bloody bandages in need of changing. As she delicately peels the dressing away, Renee and a hundred men listen to Chiwy's coaching and the hard breathing of her patient. Meanwhile, Sal is taking bets.

"OK, genius. Which is it, a boy or a girl?"

"Two bucks sez it's a boy."

"And I say it's a girl."

They both produce two dollars and lay the bills on the blanket. Frank stirs nearby, and Sal looks to enlarge the pot.

"Frank. Hey, Frank! Wanna get in on this?"

Frank grumbles and turns over.

While Chiwy toils to bring new life into the world, Renee suddenly finds herself in a duel with death when the soldier's breathing becomes irregular, culminates in a sharp intake, then stops altogether. Renee feels for the artery in his neck and finds no pulse. She responds vigorously with chest compressions and rescue breaths, checks for signs of life, then resumes her attempts at resuscitation. She bends all her strength and thoughts toward the soldier, as though willing him to live.

But the young man is gone. There is nothing that can be done. Resigned, she absentmindedly works the chain holding his dog tag free from behind his neck to find a Star of David medallion attached. She looks upon the soldier's face fully for the first time and is struck by the young man's resemblance to Josef. Her eyes moisten and she fights back tears.

When the baby cries out for the first time, shrill and sharp in the silent room, Renee's tears flow freely down her cheeks.

Frank stirs again.

"Whaaa... what the hell?"

Sal and Slim are quick to make sport of him.

"Hey, Frank. Didn't know you had it in ya. Congratulations."

"Give the man a cigar!"

The baby is now crying continuously as Jack clamps and cuts the umbilical cord and sterilizes the stump. As Chiwy washes and swaddles the baby, the mother picks up her head with the help of her spouse and calls out weakly to the nurse from the depths of exhaustion.

"My baby. Is my baby all right?"

"Yes, yes. She is a perfect angel!"

"A girl?"

"A beautiful baby girl."

The woman smiles and succumbs to the strain. Her husband lays her head down and turns worried eyes to the doctor. Jack tries to assure the new father that his wife will be fine, while Chiwy stands and rocks the baby in her arms. As she turns, Chiwy catches Renee's lifeless eyes looking on from across the room. Chiwy pulls back the wrap and tilts the baby's face to Renee, who in turn wipes away her tears, nods, and manages a weak, brave smile in gratitude to Chiwy.

With budding maternal instincts, Chiwy revels in the moment.

"Doctor! Come smell how sweet. She has the breath of heaven on her!"

"Yes, of course. The scent is one of the many attributes of a newborn that strengthens the mother's attachment to the baby."

"Yes, Doctor. But... smell her."

Chiwy rocks the baby close to Jack, who bends to inhale deeply. He comes away from the restorative experience all smiles. When the woman shows signs of life, Jack directs Chiwy's attention to her. The nurse kneels and carefully places the baby in the mother's waiting arms, as the relieved husband strokes his wife's sweat-soaked hair away from her forehead. Slowly, the basement returns to normal. Several men discuss, in their unvarnished way, the miracle of life.

Sal folds four bucks into his pocket.

A Field of Poppies

The little dark-eyed girl has lost track of time as the sun completes its daily sojourn and sinks out of sight. She finishes the last of the wreaths and admires her work. The melody returns.

"Nous sommes les mortes
Il y a peu de jours nous vivions
Nous voyions le coucher du soleil"

The little girl sings without much thought about the meaning of the words. Belgian girls memorize the song early on and follow in the footsteps of their big sisters, mothers, and grandmothers. Gathering poppies and making wreaths of remembrance are rites of passage from girlhood to womanhood.

Situation 23 Dec 1944

23 December 1944

The defenders of Bastogne wake to find that the German encirclement of the town is complete. Relief, reinforcement, resupply, and evacuation of the wounded by land are all off the table. Yet, far from feeling daunted, one wit in a foxhole simply declares that they are just the hole in a doughnut, and all he needs is a cup of coffee to make like Clark Gable and dunk it.

Heavy pressure is being exerted on American forces along an arc from Wardin in the southeast, through Marvie and Assenois in the south, up to Mande St. Etienne in the west. But, on the bright side, the skies have cleared of clouds, raising hopes that American flyboys will soon get in on the act.

With the sun brilliant above the horizon, its powerful rays work their way through the blackout curtains hanging in the basement windows of the Lemaire residence. The dust dances in the slim streak of sunlight as it creeps across the floor and onto Renee's bed.

She is on the verge of waking but has found a subconscious place of utter peace. She is unwilling to let it go as Josef's voice comes to her like a gentle breeze.

"*Ani met alaih*', Renee. I love you."

The corners of her mouth twitch up into a smile, but suddenly drop as another voice enters her dream.

"I sure am sweet on you, Renee."

As if sensing competition, Josef asserts himself.

"I love you, Renee!"

At this moment, her father bounds down the stairs in his heavy boots, playing wooden steps like kettle drums once again. Now, Josef is calling out in anguish.

"Renee? Renee! RENEE!"

Her father's bellowing voice fills the basement and rattles Renee awake.

"Renee! Time to get up!"

Lemaire steps over to the window and parts the blackout curtain, flooding the basement with dazzling sunlight. When he pounds back up the stairs, Renee sits up in bed. Stunned, looking blankly around her, she instinctively reaches for her pendant and is comforted to find it flush against her warm breast.

"Oh! The sun!"

She quickly doffs her nightgown and dons her nursing outfit. It is only a matter of minutes before she scurries up the stairs toward the prospect of a brighter day.

Across town, Hank pulls the blackout curtains open in the office and finds Jack asleep at his desk, his head weighing heavily on his forearms. Slowly, Jack lifts his eyes and focuses on the casualty records and dog tags before him, then higher to see Hank standing before him with two steaming cups of coffee.

"What? What'd you say?"

"I said, coffee's up."

"Damn, I fell asleep."

"You must've needed it, Jack."

Jack takes the cup carefully, fearing he might spill its contents and ruin his records. He sips the jolting elixir.

"Whoa! That's strong stuff. Thanks, Hank."

While the caffeine goes to work on his senses, Jack works the kinks out of his neck. Every muscle in his body aches from the previous day's eighteen-hour shift, but duty calls. Hank smiles and shakes his head as he watches his friend depart and slam the door behind him. In the short walk over to the aid station, Jack is further awakened by the morning chill. He greets Beagle, who is outside the aid station in a cloud of tobacco smoke, and steps into the basement. From the vantage point on the landing, his eyes adjust with difficulty to darkness stabbed by streaks of bright sunlight from east-facing, uncovered basement windows. Wallington steps up to him and discreetly hands him a pair of dog tags.

"Lost two during the night. The graves registration boys have already been here."

Jack nods solemnly as he ponders the work of the Quartermaster Corpsmen who have the thankless job of retrieving, identifying, and burying the dead. As he studies the tags he tries to match the names to faces, but fails. There have been so many. In a momentary lapse, Jack surrenders to the futility of his efforts. For some of these young men, he is not the healer they need. He is not saving their lives. The best he can do for them is to hold the inevitable at bay for a matter of days, or even hours.

Jack picks out Chiwy at the back of the room checking a soldier's vital signs. She sees Jack and gives him a smile. Hell, her whole nature is a smile. She loves what she does and is damned good at it. She is a powerful shot of adrenaline for the soul.

As Jack and the corporal make their way across the room toward her, Chiwy continues to work along the back wall and finally reaches Smitty. Her voice fairly blooms with hope.

"Doctor! The pulse is stronger!"

Wallington tries to make amends.

"Huh! And I thought he was a goner. Maybe Renee is on to something."

Slim has overheard everything and turns to Sal to pass on the encouraging news.

"D'ya hear that? Smitty's still kickin'!"

"That Renee. She's gotta be some kinda angel!"

Frank, being Frank, is typically unfiltered.

"C'mon, live, you son-of-a-bitch! You owe me poker money!"

Then, showing a side of himself he rarely reveals, Frank softly adds a whisper of encouragement.

"Hang on, Smitty."

The Pathfinder

Renee is striding briskly through the frigid morning air on her way to the aid station.

Across the street a half-dozen soldiers are warming themselves around a fire in a 55-gallon drum. Among them, Ruben is the first to notice her.

"Hello, Renee. Hello!"

"Oh, hello Roo-been."

At the sound of her voice, Robert turns from the fire and jogs over to her. He is trailed by the taunts and teases of the others as they razz the Romeo that he fancies himself to be.

"Hey, Renee. Where ya been?"

"I am working... in the aid station."

At this most inopportune moment for Robert, his commanding officer arrives and barks loudly from across the street to him.

"Hey, Slate! Fall in on the double!"

"I gotta go."

Robert retreats but stops in the middle of the road and calls back to Renee.

"Can I see you tonight?"

Torn by fealty to Josef and sympathy for this lonely soldier, Renee tries to work up a response. When she finally finds the words to say, they are drowned out when an American cargo plane, a ponderous C-47, roars by low overhead, trailing smoke. Everyone on the street ducks instinctively. Several more planes pass over and bank away from the town. The men are as surprised as Renee is, but quick to debate a variety of theories. Is it a harbinger of good things to come?

When Slate and the other soldiers are quickly mustered and jog away, Renee resumes her route to the aid station, picking up her pace. Her progress is once again arrested when a dozen voices raised in celebration reach her from the fields at the western edge of town. Several more planes thunder by overhead, as Renee dashes down a side street. She breaks into the open and immediately spots a soldier perched on the top of a brick pile. He appears to be manipulating a device of some kind.

"Pardon me, what do you do here?"

"I'm a pathfinder, Ma'am."

"Pathfinder? I don't understand."

"This here's a radio beacon for the C-47s."

She follows his eyes to see another string of the cargo planes homing in on Bastogne. They are under heavy fire from German forces in the distant woods but hewing a straight line, nevertheless. It is a testament to each crew's training, but also to the lack of maneuverability of the stout workhorse aircraft. The roar of the planes and the staccato of anti-aircraft bursts chasing them are sensory overload for Renee. What is happening? The pathfinder takes advantage of her attention.

"You see the parachutes?"

"Ah! The parachutes!"

Renee suddenly understands the purpose of the whole expedition and is clearly delighted as multicolored parachutes drift into view dangling large canisters. Her unexpected joy brings out her beauty, and the pathfinder is in clover. Wow, what a dame!

"Yeah, that's right. Now look, the red chutes are ammo. The greens are rations. And you see that white one?"

"Yes!"

"That'll be medical supplies."

He turns back to see how impressed Renee must be with him but finds, to his mild disappointment, that she is gone. She is off as fast as her feet can carry her through the snow and mud, making a beeline for the white parachute. She slips and slides to the spot where it fell only to find the chute being wadded up by a soldier, while another cuts the canister free. Her sudden presence is a surprise to Will and Joey working nearby, and to the rest of the SNAFU detachment sent to collect the airdropped supplies and chutes.

Disappointed, she slogs over to sit on a tree stump. An officer tenders an apology.

"Sorry, Mademoiselle. I have orders to collect all of these provisions."

Several soldiers have stopped to take in the sight of the dark-eyed beauty suddenly and incongruously appearing among them. They only see her skin deep, evidenced by the whistles of a few would-be wolves among them. But Joey is studying her more carefully.

"Hey, Will, isn't that... ?"

"Yeah, the nurse. She's at the 10th. She sure is a looker."

"Yeah, she looks... she looks... sad."

"C'mon Joey, don't worry about her."

But Joey is genuinely worried about her. While all others present see Renee as a dish, she reaches Joey on a different level. In his simpleminded way, he thinks she is acting out her feelings for an audience of one, him. He observes her carefully as she watches the C-47s throb across the sky over Bastogne. When she draws a sudden breath, he turns to see what she sees. A C-47 has taken a direct hit and is spinning out of control. When it crashes and burns Renee is devastated. No one could have possibly survived. She is startled when an officer hollers out nearby.

"Look lively SNAFU! Get those canisters over to the warehouse. And you two! Get those chutes over to the aid station double quick!"

When Renee turns to watch Will and Joey load the parachutes into a trailer behind a jeep, Joey's mood is lifted by the sudden hopefulness in Renee's eyes. Will seeks clarification of their orders.

"Sir, which one?"

"The 101st. Doc Davidson wants 'em."

Just as swiftly as she brightened, Renee is crestfallen to hear this. Joey rolls up a white parachute, but baulks at tossing it into the trailer when he sees Renee looking on as if in mourning. Joey struggles to make sense of it all. *What is she saying to me?* Without a word uttered, Renee gets up and looks across the field to see that all the chutes have been gathered. She brushes off her uniform and heads back to town. Joey watches her every step as he tries to divine the deeper meaning of Renee's disappointment.

"C'mon Joey."

Will's call is unheeded as Joey remains riveted to the spot by indecision. Will is accustomed to Joey's quirky behavior, but the driver who has jumped into the jeep and is revving the engine is not.

"Hey! Let's go!"

Finally, Joey's delay draws the ire of the officer in charge.

"Get the lead out, soldier!"

Spurred to impulsive action, Joey wads up the chute and stuffs it under his jacket. He looks meekly around and concludes that he was not observed. But when he jumps into the back seat, Will looks him up and down suspiciously. *What the hell is Joey up to now? The last thing they need is to get into hot water.* Will prepares to challenge his friend, but Joey's facial features are so contorted by concentration it is almost laughable. He reconsiders and whispers to his buddy.

"Geez, Joey. It looks like you're putting on some weight."

"Um, it must be the pancakes."

The driver bursts forth.

"Pancakes! I'm sick of pancakes! Every fuckin' day! They taste like goddamn cardboard!"

The driver glances at Joey over his shoulder and does a double take. Joey looks from the driver, to Will, back to the driver.

"What? I love pancakes."

As soon as the words are out of his mouth, American dive bombers suddenly spiral out of the clouds to hammer German positions in the distant woods. A great sound of cheering is heard near and far across the American defensive perimeter.

Jack's Aid Station

The fortunes of war are changing yet again. So is the weather. After a sunny morning, dark clouds once again smother the sun. Late in the afternoon, snow is now falling and quickly accumulating in the street in front of Jack's aid station.

While Beagle is outside for a break, Wallington is assisting Chiwy. Together, they check and switch plasma bags at the front end of the basement. Jack is methodically inspecting wounds for infection at the back end. Renee is nowhere to be seen. When he hears Beagle call to him, the corporal looks up to see his buddy standing on the landing, pointing his thumb over his shoulder.

"We got a couple of doggies at the door. They got something for Renee."

"Tell 'em to get in line!"

Wallington's quip draws laughter from a dozen men, all of whom are hoping that when they get back on their feet they'll be at the front of that line. Beagle is persistent, and the corporal excuses himself from Chiwy and climbs the steps to join the orderly at the door. Though she doesn't miss a beat with her work, Chiwy is curious and cocks one ear toward the doorway. After the corporal takes a quick peek outside and quickly shuts out the blowing snow, he turns to the orderly.

"Who are those mugs?"

"Couple of SNAFUS, I'd say. Ya know what I mean?"

Beagle rolls his eyes comically and points to his head. This gets a guffaw or two from a couple of wounded soldiers leaning against the basement wall by the door. Wallington cracks the door for another look.

"Geez, I dunno. They look OK to me. At least the little guy does."

He steps outside, and after a brief conversation with the visitors Wallington reenters with a rolled-up parachute in his hands and a surprised look on his face. Beagle speaks for all of them.

"What the hell?"

"You got me. The big guy sez it's a present for Renee, for Christmas."

Puzzled, Chiwy makes her way over to the door to get a closer look. When Renee enters the basement from the washroom in the far corner, Chiwy makes a snap decision.

"Here, I'll keep it for her."

As Renee locates Jack and begins to step carefully toward him, Chiwy lets in a light dusting of snow as she makes a hasty retreat out the door. Renee is soon at Jack's side.

"What can I do now?"

"I guess we'd better sterilize all these."

Jack points out a pile of soiled sheets in the corner, thinking that there will always be a need for long strips and wraps even with the ample quantity of supplies and medicines now in hand. Unfortunately, the need for medical personnel was badly underestimated. Just one surgical team came in by glider and was quickly whisked over to the 101st.

Jack scans the back of the room, where his most critically wounded are languishing. If only they could be carefully moved over to the 101st, they might have a chance. But the surgeons will have their hands full with Davidson's boys for several days. As Jack tries to beat back waves of foreboding, he watches blankly as Renee bundles the linen in her arms and retraces her steps back to the washroom.

Hank is next to let in snow and stands at the landing until his eyesight adjusts. He picks out his friend in the dimly lit room.

"Hey, Jack. You gotta minute?"

All ears turn to Hank, hungry for news, any news. But he awaits his friend before elaborating and speaks to Jack in a very low voice at the top of the stairs. For those who can see him clearly, Jack's evident disappointment at what he hears speaks volumes. When Chiwy returns, Jack scans the basement and sees that everything is under control. He has a quick word with Chiwy and leaves the building with Hank.

Down the street, Will and Joey are walking and talking quietly, until Will stops on a dime and turns to his giant companion.

"You want what? A Christmas tree?"

"Well sure, Will. We always have a Christmas tree."

"Jeez, Joey, don't you know where we are?"

The big fellow brightens. He knows this one.

"Yeah, 'course I do. It's Bos..."

Will rushes to close the gate before the goose gets loose.

"Wait! Don't answer that!"

"... ton."

"Ya lummox!"

The Washroom

Renee drops her bundle and takes a long, deep breath. It has been another day of whipsawing emotions, of fullness and emptiness, hope and despair, and lives saved or lost. Though surrounded by people, she finds herself utterly alone with her thoughts.

She turns up the lantern and stokes the fire in a large cast iron stove. When she absentmindedly opens the spigot, she is reminded that the water is cut off. Renee steps outside to fill a bucket with snow and looks up into grey swirling clouds in the darkening skies. To her surprise a white parachute appears swinging to earth high above the rooftops of Bastogne. She feels a jolt of energy and takes halting steps toward the chute. She stops, regards the bucket by the door, sighs and returns to her task. Once the pail is full, she looks up for one more glimpse. There is no trace of the parachute and she experiences a moment of disorientation. Was it ever there? Perhaps it was only a wisp of a cloud, or snow blown about making and unmaking suggestive shapes in the sky.

She steps back into the washroom and suddenly feels dizzy, unsteady. The effort to keep up appearances, to be cheerful in the face of so much suffering, so many young men's lives cut short, and so much blood, has taken a toll on Renee. Moreover, she is weary and footsore and would love nothing more than to put her feet up, and perhaps savor a hot cup of her mother's tea. But what would her father say of her lassitude? She collects herself and dumps the snow into a large cast iron pot on the stove. As she fetches more snow, the distinctive voice of Billie Holiday filters faintly into the washroom from the radio in the basement. It is a recording that Josef played for her once while accompanying the languid song of longing on the piano.

"Someday he'll come along, the man I love"

Her emotions become a tangle as she blinks back tears. After the melted snow starts to boil, she feeds the sheets into the pot and stirs them with some considerable exertion.

"And he'll be big and strong, the man I love"

After a spell, she steps over to the clotheslines where laundered sheets are hung to dry. She takes several down and folds them onto the counter. Without thinking, she wraps the last one around herself like a gown as the song continues like a cherished memory.

"And when he comes my way, I'll do my best to make him stay"

As she stands in the glow cast by the lantern, she closes her eyes and drifts along the narrow path between delirium and dream. She falls out of light into darkness. She opens her mouth to speak, but no words pass her lips.

"He'll look at me and smile; I'll understand"

When Renee opens her eyes, Josef steps out of deep shadows and turns darkness to light. He stands before her, smiling and reaching down to her.

"Then in a little while, he'll take my hand"

"May I have this dance?"

"Yes, my husband."

When Josef takes her hand, Renee rises from the shadows to join him on a spot-lit dance floor, where her sheet becomes a beautiful white, silken gown. It is their wedding reception, and a twelve-piece orchestra takes up the romantic Gershwin melody. Josef and Renee step and sway slowly in a warm embrace. All else is indistinct, a blur, until a lithe, little man steps into the limelight and strikes up a wedding polka on his clarinet. He is joined by three others playing an accordion, a violin, and a mandolin. All are in black, their clothes, their hats, and their beards.

Lemaire is none too pleased since he brought the orchestra all the way from Paris. Nothing is too good for his princess. Somehow, he manages to contain his aggravation, and soon musicians from the orchestra surrender to the infectious dance music and play along. Josef begins to spin and swirl his bride, and she throws her head back in laughter. In their spreading glow of love, smiling faces of family, friends, and well-wishers appear and fill the banquet hall. When the beautiful couple passes Renee's family, all her kin rise up from their chairs, with glasses held high, and offer their blessings to the newlyweds.

"À votre santé."

Then they pass Josef's family, who call out in unison.

"L'chaim."

Another half-turn brings Renee's family forward, her father foremost, now shouting.

"Santé!"

Then Josef's family steps assertively onto the dance floor as one. Even Josef's father miraculously comes to his feet. With the vigor of a much younger man, he takes a beautiful woman in his arms to join in the dance. Could it be Josef's mother? She's alive!

"L'chaim!"

As the polka approaches its climax, Renee and Josef, to their shared consternation, behold their families competing, even jostling for primacy. It is the worst of possible outcomes for Renee. The couple dances and twirls almost frantically and passes Chiwy, resplendent in a luminous green gown.

"Renee."

The music stops and all the people disappear into the shadows. The strength and warmth of Josef's hand in hers slip away as their fingertips gently part.

"Renee. Renee!"

She opens her eyes to find herself on the floor of the washroom with Chiwy kneeling before her in olive drab. She struggles to rise and Chiwy is quick to brace and help her friend to a chair. Instinctively, Chiwy examines her and concludes that Renee must have fainted.

Renee's head slowly clears.

"I... I could feel..."

"What could you feel?"

"I was dancing..."

Renee looks up into Chiwy's eyes, which are full of concern. She has alarmed her petite friend, and it troubles her to do so. She wills herself to her feet, unwinds the sheet she wore as a gown in her fever dream, and folds it onto the counter. She turns to Chiwy and offers a weak smile.

"How silly I am."

Renee collects herself, focuses once again on the work at hand, and muscles several sodden sheets out of the cauldron and into the sink. Chiwy pitches in, gingerly wringing the steaming hot sheets out while continuing to puzzle over Renee's behavior. When she hangs the sheets on the clothesline, she hears Renee weeping softly, trying not to be heard. Chiwy crosses the washroom to stand by her friend's side. She follows Renee's vacant gaze to the new bundle of badly bloodstained sheets and blankets Chiwy had carried in.

"Renee, what is it?"

As Renee continues to stare blankly at the bundle of soiled linens, Chiwy searches for a chink in Renee's emotional armor, an opening to Renee's heart. Though they have only shared a short time together, Chiwy has seen many sides and surfaces of Renee. But what is in her depths? She is hesitant to query Renee for her private thoughts, wondering if the answers might be too complex for her friend to express.

Chiwy opts for low-hanging fruit, their day-to-day experiences since they were thrown together, to try to understand what is happening to her friend. After all, Renee is a nurse in an aid station surrounded by a raging battle. It is no place for the faint of heart. Could it be a simple matter of revulsion?

"Is it the blood?"

No response.

"Is it the pain? The suffering? The death?"

Renee reacts viscerally, as it calls to mind the handsome soldier who took his last breath just a day ago, while she knelt by his side.

"They are so young... and..."

She can't shake the resemblance of the young man to her Josef.

"… and so lonely."

Chiwy sees a change in Renee's countenance with this comment. There! It is unmistakable! A chord has been struck and color returns to Renee's cheeks as she revisits the warmth and wonder of her vision.

"Augusta, it was as if I was there. At my wedding."

Ah! There is joy in Renee's life. Chiwy is relieved.

"So, you are married. How very nice for you. Where is your husband now?"

"I don't know. I don't know."

Then Renee catches herself.

"Oh! No, we're not married."

Just as quickly as the sun came out, the clouds return and darken Renee's visage.

"Someday soon… I hope."

Chiwy realizes that there is more hidden than shown, but she thinks it best to let the moment pass. Renee will offer more when she is ready. Yet Chiwy is still captivated as she watches Renee's hand drift to her bosom where it lingers and probes. What does this mean? As if in answer to her friend's curiosity, Renee offers a brave smile and fishes out her pendant, to Chiwy's delight.

"Oh, my!"

"It's a gift… from Josef."

"Josef?"

"My fiancé."

"It is beautiful."

"It's Raphael, the angel of healing."

"It is perfect. Especially for you."

Over Renee's shoulder, Chiwy spies Jack in the hallway studying the contents of the cupboards, wondering where his aides stored the sutures. He turns to query the nurses but decides against it when, to his credit, he perceives in their postures and attitudes a heart-to-heart conversation. He carries on digging through the boxes.

Renee sees only Chiwy, whose face glows golden in the lantern light.

"Can I tell you something?"

Somehow the washroom feels like a sanctuary to Renee, where her hopes and dreams are safe. Still unaware of Jack nearby, Renee wonders just how much more she can share of the weight she carries with this open and trusting young woman. She opts instead to share a secret wish.

"When I was dancing with Josef, I wore a silken gown... that I made from a parachute. I know it seems silly, but I have tried to get one, but..."

Renee opens her hands to show that they are empty. Chiwy is struck by the coincidence. Can it be? She quickly makes sense of the gift from the two soldiers and can barely hide her mirth. Her response is intended for Jack to overhear.

"Well, it's almost Christmas. Perhaps there will be a parachute for you!"

Chiwy sees that Jack has indeed heard and is questioning her with his eyes. Was it she who put the parachute on his desk? Chiwy nods and smiles, forcing a smile from Jack. He finds the sutures and heads back to work, tickled by the idea of playing Santa Claus.

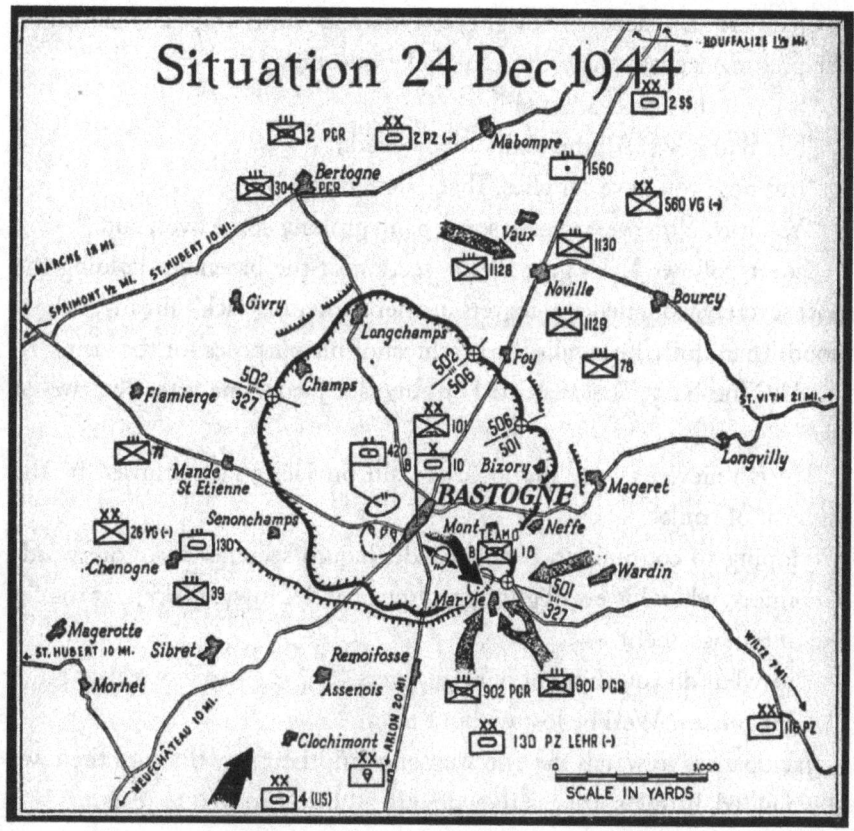

Situation 24 Dec 1944

24 December 1944

Though radio traffic and rumors point to an eventual breakthrough to Bastogne by Patton's forces, the town remains under German guns. The cold and snow are intensifying and stifling the town with the harshest winter weather of the century. Even so, on this day before Christmas, the citizens who remain and the soldiers among them continue to hope and pray for a silent night.

Monsieur Jaquin takes it upon himself to look in now and again on the wounded and his new friend, Jack Prior, at the aid station, hoping to bring a bit of cheer. Jack meets Jaquin on the landing where they stand together looking over wounded men in various attitudes of resignation and repose, spotted here and there with bright red blood on white wraps and bandages. The pharmacist asks the sixty-four-dollar question.

"So, will they be evacuated?"

"No. Bad news. All the roads are blocked."

"But now you have supplies. That's something."

"Yes, it is. Now we can ease some pain, prolong some lives, but..."

Jaquin follows Jack's gaze to the section of the basement holding the most severely wounded and regrets further darkening Jack's already somber mood. Thankfully, he recalls the brightest of his purposes for the visit.

"Ah! The baby. They named her Augusta Jacqueline after the two of you."

He is relieved to see the look of pain on Jack's face eclipsed by the slightest of smiles.

Hoping to continue to turn the tide, Jaquin searches for more words of comfort, when his eyes light upon Renee and Chiwy working at the far end of the basement.

"So, what do you think of our daughters?"

"The nurses? We'd be lost without them."

Jack pauses to watch the two women work their way through the rows of wounded, lifting spirits as they do. He is almost moved to tears.

"They're heaven sent."

"Yes, heaven sent."

The satchel full of prescriptions hung over his shoulder reminds Jaquin that his day is far from done. There are so many people to see, the sick and the elderly who are shut-in and alone. With his bum leg, he will be lucky to finish his deliveries before the curfew.

"Well, I must go... my son."

As Jaquin rests a fatherly hand upon Jack's shoulder, the two men scan the room full of broken bodies, many barely out of boyhood. When he finally continues, Jaquin's voice is choked with emotion.

"You are all our sons now. Sons of Bastogne."

With his batteries recharged by the pharmacist's abundance of good will, Jack gets back to work. As Jaquin departs he has warm words for

Wallington at the doorway and for Beagle outside on yet another smoking break.

While the orderly watches the older man hobble up the street through the swirling snow, a jeep crests the rise from the town square and heads directly down to the aid station. Corporal By-the-Book leaps out from behind the wheel, barges past Beagle, flings open the door, and shouts from the landing.

"Attention for Colonel Roberts!"

No one moves a muscle.

Roberts is quick to follow his brown-nose corporal in. He finds his subordinate inside standing rigidly at attention and orders him to take his ease. The colonel strains to adjust his eyesight in the darkened room. After a moment, he makes out the figure of Jack Prior, who is looking up at Roberts while kneeling beside a wounded man.

"Carry on, Doctor."

Now better adjusted to the low light, the colonel looks from face to upturned face as he unfolds a piece of paper.

"Men, I have a Christmas message from General McAuliffe. Can you all hear me?"

Frank is awake for once and calls out from the back of the room.

"Loud and clear!"

Roberts raises his voice, nonetheless.

"Merry Christmas."

Muted grumbles and groans greet the first two words of McAuliffe's message. Roberts is undeterred.

"What's merry about all this, you ask? We're fighting. It's cold. We aren't home. All true. But what has the proud Eagle Division accomplished with its worthy comrades of the 10th Armored Division, the 705th Tank Destroyer Battalion, and all the rest? Just this: we have stopped cold everything that has been thrown at us from the North, East, South and West. We have identifications from four German panzer divisions, two German infantry divisions, and one German parachute division. These units spearheading the last desperate German lunge were headed straight west for key points when the Eagle Division was hurriedly ordered to stem the advance. How effectively this was done will be written in history."

Slim beams with pride.

"Say, imagine a bunch of mugs like us going down in history."

Roberts is hitting his stride.

"We are giving our country and our loved ones at home a worthy Christmas present, being privileged to take part in this gallant feat of arms and truly making for ourselves a Merry Christmas."

After Roberts departs and the buzzing of conversation among the men dies down, Frank pipes up.

"Speaking of gallant feet..."

To their great surprise, Slim and Sal behold their buddy uncharacteristically grinning, almost unable to contain himself.

"... you guys oughta pal around after the war. You'd make a hell-of-a pair."

So unused to Frank approaching anything like levity, Sal and Slim simply share a look of incredulity. Frank is still grinning like the cat that ate the canary as he continues.

"Hell, don't you see? If worse comes to worse and you lose those lovely gams, I figure you could save a lot on shoes."

Though the cognac has dulled their pain they are both aware that their wounds are severe. Unless they are evacuated to a surgical hospital, they could each lose a leg. Frank's one and only attempt at wit finally dawns on them. They hold out their good feet, side by side, and make a left foot, right foot pair of comparably sized feet.

"Ha! Good one, Frank."

Frank is mighty pleased with himself. However, when a wounded soldier props himself up with considerable effort and turns on the radio, Frank quickly recovers his sour mood at the sound of Axis Sally introducing a song.

"Hey buddy! Shut that bitch up, will ya?"

Without a countermanding request, the soldier props himself up again and reaches for the radio, but he holds back as the next melody spreads a hush over the basement. Even Frank is cowed into silence by the angelic voices of The Vienna Boys Choir as they sing "Silent Night" in their native tongue.

> *"Stille Nacht! Heilige Nacht!*
> *Alles schläft, einsam wacht*
> *Nur das traute hochheilige Paar*
> *Holder Knabe im lockigen Haar*
> *Schlaf in himmlischer Ruh!*
> *Schlaf in himmlischer Ruh!"*

The Washroom

Day fades to dusk.

The blackout curtains are closed.

The lantern is lit.

Chiwy muscles a large basket of dirty linen into the room and drops it heavily. For one so small, she has remarkable strength, but even she is beginning to wear down after four long days of hard labor. She takes a couple of sharp breaths and chides herself as she evaluates the amount of work yet to be done. For a moment, she regrets not being home with her father for Christmas Eve, but there is no rest for nurses in a combat zone. They are the weariest of the weary, on this or any other night.

Renee enters the washroom wearing the face that she keeps for the wounded soldiers. She is warmed by the attention of the men whose spirits she lifts. But once she is out of their sight Renee cannot sustain the feeling, and the shine is swept from her dark eyes. Recalling their unfinished conversation from the evening before, Chiwy wonders if there is more that Renee wants to reveal to her, or anything she could do to comfort her friend. Chiwy regards her friend silently, patiently, pondering how best to prime the pump.

"Well... tomorrow is Christmas. Wouldn't some fresh linen be a nice present? Then we could close our little laundry business."

The door to dialogue is open, but Renee does not step through. She is impassive, barely nodding acknowledgment. Perhaps she will perk up if she gets busy.

"Let's get these things boiling right away."

Chiwy indicates the full basket on the floor as she steps over to check the blankets hanging on the lines. Having stoked the fire in the stove earlier and left the cast iron doors open to the laundry area, she is pleased to find them dried enough for their purposes.

"And these can go back."

Leading by example, Chiwy disappears behind the hanging blankets. She takes down half a dozen, folds them onto a chair, and turns to find that Renee has not moved from her spot. Nor has she made a sound. Chiwy can't help but wonder if Renee has ventured beyond exhaustion. Has she passed her breaking point? Chiwy clears the last line and completes her stack of blankets, then steps over to Renee and looks up into the dull eyes of her taller friend. She rests a gentle hand on Renee's forearm. Her touch has an immediate effect, and Renee comes alive.

"I'm all right. It's nothing."

Chiwy is doubtful. Something tells her that tonight, of all nights, Renee might open up with a bit of coaxing.

"Renee, we have been working together for four days."

"It seems like much longer."

"Yes. So, we are sisters now. You can talk to me."

"Thank you, Augusta. But I am all right, really."

Nevertheless, even as Renee takes a deep breath and gets to work, she appears to be reconsidering Chiwy's offer. Renee dumps the dirty linen out of the basket and loads the clean blankets for the return trip back to the basement. When she reaches the doorway, she hesitates and sets the basket down. Several seconds pass before Renee makes eye contact with Chiwy. When her words finally come, they are just above a whisper.

"Well, there is something."

"Yes?"

"It is about Josef."

She sits and Chiwy pulls up a chair in anticipation. Renee's story, which she has kept buried for several months, comes tumbling out.

Brussels, Belgium

It is a crisp autumn Sunday morning on the 3rd of September 1944; the kind of weather that puts an extra spring in one's step. Renee hardly needs the boost as she strides toward Josef's flat, conveniently located along the route she always walks from the tram stop to her church. Though she usually stops by his apartment after the service, on this day she has a special reason for looking in first thing in the morning. The bakery next to the station made a batch of *cramique*, the traditional raisin bread that Josef and his father so enjoy. It is a rarity in these days, with shortages in everything. And very expensive. But she doesn't care. It will be worth it to see the looks on their faces.

Even as the splendid morning and the intoxicating aroma from the fresh loaf in her shoulder bag propel her along, she is puzzled by the eerie silence in the city. Why are there no bells announcing morning services? Why are the streets deserted? An old man appears just ahead, carefully making his way out of doors and down steps to the sidewalk. He stumbles. Renee rushes to support him. With Renee's help, he finds a bench worn smooth by decades of sitting. Renee sits down beside him, ready to assist him further as he recovers his equilibrium.

"Are you all right, Monsieur?"

"Yes. Thank you, my dear."

As he speaks, he looks toward her and past her, and she realizes he is blind.

"Listen."

At the old man's prompting, Renee turns to the faint sound of a church bell ringing somewhere in the city. Another bell chimes in, nearer. Here and there, people trickle out of their homes into the street, taking in the air and sunlight tentatively, as if they had been living in caves. Still more bells begin to ring and soon the streets are filling up with people chattering vigorously. The old man cocks his well-practiced ear, gathering bits of information from a dozen colliding conversations, while Renee tries to read the hopeful expression dawning on his face. Soon, church bells are ringing all over Brussels. Renee is almost laughing as she revels in the joyous cacophony but is flummoxed when she tries to make sense of it.

"What is it?"

"The British have come. Their tanks are on the Ghent road."

Somehow, after years under the heel of the Hun, the words don't quite compute for Renee.

"What? What did you say?"

The old man is listening intently to a conversation two doors down.

"The *Boche* are gone!"

"Can it be?"

The old man turns his full attention to Renee.

"I heard everything last night. They filled their trucks with what they could steal. And the Gestapo..."

He falters, unable to hide his disgust.

"... the Gestapo did their dirty business in the dark. Like rats!"

It was a night of terror for dozens of citizens who were beaten and dragged from their homes. The old man is shaking with anger as he recalls it.

"The filth! The stench!"

Renee instinctively reaches out and takes his gnarled hands. He is soothed by Renee's touch, scent, and soft voice. Finally, he manages a deep cleansing breath in and out, as if to expel the choking pollution of German occupation. Next door, a man climbs a ladder and rips down a Nazi flag. Others quickly cluster below him to tear it apart. Renee sees it, but still can't believe it.

"Can it truly be?"

The old man is certain. His misty eyes blink and search for her.

"Yes, my dear. It is the liberation!"

As Renee gathers herself to stand, he gives her hands a gentle squeeze and then releases them as though bidding her to take flight. She rises and takes halting steps. Before she is aware of it, she is running down the street. She arrives at Josef's building and pivots on the stair post knob. Four flights fall away under her flying feet. As she races down a hall, a door cracks, and Renee catches a glimpse of a very old woman as she passes.

"Good morning, Madame! Isn't it wonderful?"

The old woman crosses herself and quietly closes her door. Ecstatic and nearly oblivious with joy, Renee reaches Josef's door and knocks loudly. To her surprise, the door gives way. She is blind to the damaged door frame and hardware as she steps inside the dimly lit room and calls out cheerfully.

"Josef. Josef! It is the liberation!"

As she awaits an answer she glances around the room and begins to register things out of order. The piano bench is tipped over and Josef's sheet music is scattered on the floor. She picks up his handwritten transcription for "Air in G."

"Josef?"

The rooms are as silent as a tomb. She steps behind Josef's piano to find his father's armchair on its back amid blankets strewn about. She can almost hear her heart pounding as she puts the pieces together and imagines the heavy tread of hobnailed boots, the explosive break-in, the banging of furniture against the walls, the thud of bodies thrown to the floor, the thunder of violent abduction.

The sounds of celebration rise in the street outside, as church bells are joined by car horns, shouting, singing, and even musical instruments that have been stowed away and silent for four long years. The Bach transcription drops from her hand as Renee sinks to her knees. Her eyes fall upon the broken vase, with the last of the season's poppies strewn about on the floor. There they lay like so many casualties on a battlefield.

The Washroom

Renee wipes away a tear and turns to fully face Chiwy.

"He was gone, and his father too. From that day, I have heard nothing."

"Dear God, Renee! How terrible for you! But perhaps they are..."

Chiwy is silenced as Renee slowly casts her eyes to the floor and pitches forward in her chair, her elbows to her knees. When she does so, the pendant slips free of her blouse. Before Chiwy can reach out to comfort her, Renee rights herself and takes the healing angel gently in her hand. Still with her gaze averted, she softly intones.

"When I look in the mirror... I no longer know myself. It's like I became a different person on that day."

There are no words to say as the women find stillness in their shared sanctuary, giving Chiwy time to mull over the deeper meaning of the pendant as Renee caresses it.

"You've taken a hard blow to your heart, but you're still standing, still giving... like Raphael. It is a reason for living and..."

Renee meets Chiwy's eyes, as though encouraging her to continue. Chiwy nods toward the gift from Josef.

"... and you still have hope."

Somehow, Chiwy has touched the place where the deep breath of loss and longing is held captive. Renee releases it with a sigh. Certainly, Josef's father could not survive the relocation to a labor camp. But Josef? He is young and strong. Yes, perhaps.

Telling the story that has been her secret burden allows a shaft of light to enter Renee's darkness. Finding someone she could fully trust made it possible. Given all they have been through together, Renee and Chiwy can bare their souls to each other. It is a rare moment of peace for Renee.

Renee works herself up to the hint of a brave smile. As always, Chiwy is amazed at her friend's resilience, her ability to maintain an upbeat front in the face of so much pain and loss, day in and day out. It is baffling!

"But... you are so cheerful with the soldiers. How do you do it?"

"I have no choice. They could be dead tomorrow..."

Renee sets her jaw, and soft resignation yields to firm resolve, as she continues.

"... but they are alive today!"

"Yes, they are alive today."

All the pieces of the puzzle seem to fall into place for Chiwy. She knows what gets Renee out of bed in the morning, propels her over to the aid station, and drives her onward through the day. She is a nurse. It is what nurses do. But it is Josef, the missing lover, who is the last clue to the riddle that is Renee. With his loss, it is as if the only thing Renee can do with her shattered heart is to give all the pieces away. With so many young men suffering and dying, her days have been overfull with giving.

The two healers arrive at a place of shared solace after the offering and receiving of confidence. It is unlikely that any two people in Bastogne are any closer than they are at this moment. Chiwy strikes a lighter note and begins to smile with her eyes.

"Renee, I must confess. When we first started together, I thought you were flirting with all the boys. Then I watched you. I saw how much you care for them."

"Of course, it is my profession."

"No, it is more than that. To them you are the mother, the wife. Or the sweetheart. Like tonight, with the boy who wants to write a letter home."

That isolated incident in the aid station was a revelation for Chiwy. It summed up everything she now knows about her Renee, about her friend's extraordinary compassion. She had been watching Renee comfort Pearson as he began to drift off. Then something had pulled him back, something fleeting. A touch... a scent... a voice.

"Caroline?"

When Renee had bent close to whisper in his ear, Chiwy had read the unmistakable words on her lips.

"I am here."

Chiwy had watched Pearson take a deep breath, smile wanly, and close his eyes.

As she recounts the moment for Renee, so vivid in her mind, Chiwy is full of admiration. Renee simply, honestly, gives every indication that she believes herself to be unworthy of Chiwy's esteem.

"I must do what I can do."

But Chiwy has seen it all in just the few days they have been working together. She presses on.

"Even if they cannot be saved, if they are dying, they believe you are an angel... come to carry them home."

"I'm no angel."

"You are to them. They call you the Angel of Bastogne."

Renee slowly shakes her head as she looks down at her hands. They are red and chapped from the hot water and bleach, yet the fingers are long and sensitive enough to play the piano with delicate touch and feeling.

While she ponders them impassively, Renee turns over in her mind all she has witnessed in this tireless, selfless young woman standing before her.

"No. No, it is you. I watch you stop the blood and fix their broken bones."

Renee manages a weak smile as she continues.

"I wish I could be more like you."

This surprises Chiwy, who quickly recovers.

"And I wish I could be more like you! You fix their broken spirits."

Renee still discounts what she is doing, bringing the focus back to Chiwy.

"You have saved so many lives."

"As have you! You give them hope. It is a very powerful medicine."

Chiwy's insistence slowly softens Renee. As she basks in Chiwy's bright eyes, Renee suddenly has an insight.

"We are so different. But... together..."

Chiwy immediately grasps Renee's hands, and her meaning.

"Yes. Together, we give everything."

Renee is revived by Chiwy's irrepressible spirit, and she cannot resist hugging her new friend. Soon enough, they get back to work sterilizing sheets and blankets. After a spell, Renee ventures, hesitantly, even further into Chiwy's confidence.

"Augusta, may I share something else with you?"

She has seen many different emotions at play on Renee's face, but this expression is entirely new.

"Some soldiers came to my home. I played piano for them, and we sang together. In those moments, I was very happy."

Renee pauses to fortify herself.

"But there was one soldier who said he is sweet on me and..."

It is almost too much for her, and Renee can only add meekly with downcast eyes.

"... and I did not discourage him."

"I'm sure he is just another lonely soldier."

Despite Chiwy making light of the whole affair, Renee is still subdued. Chiwy tries to bridge her to a better place.

"But Renee, this is how you are. You are kind. You didn't want to hurt his feelings."

Renee is not convinced. She turns to Chiwy with a look of dismay, hoping for an answer, but fearing there is none.

"Then... then why did he come to me in my dreams?"

Chiwy stops her work and considers her next words carefully.

"So, this is troubling you. But... you love Josef?"

Renee's hand goes automatically to her pendant. Somehow, Josef feels more alive to her now than he has for months.

"Yes."

"And you are true to Josef?"

"Yes! Of course!"

Renee defends their love vigorously. But as her hand falls away from the pendant, Josef seems to slip away again, out of her reach.

"I feel that... in a way... I have been unfaithful to him."

"Love is stronger than that."

"Yes, but I guess... I guess I am lonely too."

Chiwy is suddenly emphatic.

"But you are not alone!"

Renee's uplifted eyes signal for Chiwy to continue, to help her heal the deepest wound of all.

"We all want someone to hold us, to keep us safe, to take away our pain. It is normal."

With an ear to a bell pealing and anti-aircraft fire crackling in the distance, Chiwy gets back to work and almost admonishes Renee.

"Come now, it's best to stay busy."

As Chiwy heaves the soiled linen onto the counter, Renee moves slowly, thoughtfully, to the basket of clean blankets by the interior door. Once there, she pauses to reflect before returning to the basement and her mission of mercy. It has taken a conscious effort to put on a cheerful mask every day. With each cry of pain and each young man's life extinguished, it has become harder and harder to do so. To top it all off, she feels that she has betrayed the love of her life! When his life must be in danger. The guilt has been unbearable. To face it all alone has been devastating.

But now it is all out in the open, and Renee has a confidante, someone to turn to, someone at her side who is more, much more, than a sister. She seeks out her friend's eyes in the soft light of the lantern's glow. For all the support she has given her friend, Chiwy concludes that Renee remains tormented by her tangled affairs of the heart. She rewards Renee with a smile of encouragement, a smile of affirmation and absolution.

"Cheer up, Renee..."

The two nurses turn as one to the sound of heavy explosions marching toward them across Bastogne, accompanied by the droning of aircraft now overhead. Chiwy dims the lantern and opens the back door to take a look. Anti-aircraft bursts reflect off fuselages of German bombers gliding by in the moonlit sky. When the ground begins to shake, it is at once a terrifying and an exhilarating moment for Chiwy. As she looks evil dead in the eye, she experiences a surge of triumph over the deafening tumult and shouts to her friend.

"... temptation is not a sin. Lightning will not strike you!"

Suddenly, a light as bright as a welding torch turns night into day. The unmistakable sound of a descending bomb is followed by a crash as the bomb pierces the wood-framed building all the way to the basement floor, where it detonates. The explosion cripples the structure and blasts dust and debris into the washroom and out through the window and door, obscuring all.

A Field of Poppies

The little dark-eyed girl stands by the side of the road with a basket full of poppy wreaths. A horse-drawn cart pulls up with two much older girls riding in the back. Each has a basket of wreaths as well. The little girl climbs aboard and feels like a big girl in their company. While they ignore her and chatter away about this and that, the little girl returns to her song.

> *"Aimions et etions aimes*
> *Et maintenant nous sommes allongès*
> *Dans les champs de Flandre"*

Rue de Neufchâteau

While bombs continue to fall elsewhere in Bastogne, there is great turmoil in front of the aid station. Much of the building has collapsed and smoke from fires ignited by kerosene lanterns is beginning to seep out of the wreckage. Driven by the cries of survivors inside, Jack and a half-dozen soldiers work frantically to clear away sections of wall, floorboards, and roofing. Quick progress is made in pulling debris away from the front door, opening the way up the basement steps for many wounded men to be helped out to safety. Those who can walk are guided to the office next door. Others are so weak and stunned by the blast they collapse in the snow, unable to take even one step further.

When flames begin to lick out of the wreckage, a cruel winter wind fans the fires and blows glowing embers chaotically about. Screams of terrorized men within pierce the night and torment Jack and the soldiers desperately trying to reach them. Several vehicles pull up, and the number of hands digging in the rubble quickly multiplies. Jack shifts his attention to the growing mass of humanity in front of the aid station. As he tends to the survivors of the blast, his eyes dart back and forth, searching in vain for any sign of the nurses.

Beagle emerges from the shadows looking bruised and bewildered. Jack tries to examine him but is waved away.

"I'm all right, Doc. Just a little scuffed up."

The orderly takes his place beside Jack, helping to stabilize the patients lying in the snow. Their efforts are mocked when the last of the German raiders drops down to strafe the concentration of men and vehicles illuminated by the growing blaze. While the soldiers scatter, Jack pulls Beagle to safety under a parked vehicle. As high-caliber rounds tear up the ground outside, Jack turns to the young man.

"Where is... ?"

"Inside, sir... I..."

Beagle chokes on his words and continues with tears in his eyes.

"... I went out for a smoke. I should've been in there with him!"

The words wound Jack. If not for Pearson's letter and a glass of champagne, he too would have been at his post in the basement. But he is quick to comfort the heartbroken young man.

"It's not your fault."

Once the strafing stops, Jack and Beagle crawl out from under the truck. Colleti arrives from the town square and helps to organize the rescue effort in the building's rubble. A couple of guys from the motor pool arrive with heavy pry bars, which are immediately put to good use dislodging heavy joists and beams. It is an extraordinary team effort. Even Hank shows up with his head heavily wrapped.

"Hank, you need to..."

"Hell, Jack, I'm OK. I taped it up pretty good."

The last thing Hank needs is strenuous exertion, with the gash in his forehead and a probable concussion. But he quickly proves indispensable during the relocation of dozens of wounded men out of the bitter cold and into the shelter of the office building next door. Grateful for the support, Jack stays with the most grievously wounded still sprawled in the snow. Any attempt to move them further is agony for them, and for Jack. Once again, he is desperate for litters. With little more than his healing hands at his disposal, he does what he can to make them as comfortable as possible.

Above the racket of men shouting and hammering away at the wreckage, a soldier is heard crying out for assistance with as much energy and urgency as a human voice can muster. On the far side of the building that still stands, albeit precariously, the soldier has forced open a cellar window to find hands reaching up to him. He is quickly reinforced by several men, another window is kicked in, and a steady stream of wounded are lifted out of the basement. Eventually, even this avenue of salvation is closed, as the section of the building above the cellar windows teeters and shifts. One man, who climbed down to help, is pulled out at the last second. With the sickening sound of cracking timbers, the last of the structure comes down, blowing a blizzard of sparks into the night.

Jack is scrambling to triage men now suffering from burns, blunt trauma, and lacerations that complicate their already dire prognoses. Meanwhile, Hank continues to orchestrate the passage of any who can walk, alone or assisted, over to the office, where they spill into adjoining hallways and storerooms. Among the men lending Hank a hand with the stunned survivors is Sarge, who wears a sling on his bum arm, the arm that could easily have been lost without Jack's intervention in Noville. The doctor calls out in concern.

"Easy, Sergeant!"

"Look, Doc. I've still got one good arm!"

Jack shakes his head in wonder and turns to behold one of the most welcome sights of all. A medic jumps out of a jeep that skids to a stop in front of the aid station and offloads a stack of litters. In short order, the prostrate men shivering in the snow are carefully hefted and carried to the relative safety of the office. Once they are taken care of, Jack works his way through the tangle of vehicles and building scraps heaped here and there, checking for survivors on the ground, behind snowbanks, in the shadows of buildings, everywhere. Until others are recovered from the building, he has done what he can in front of the aid station.

Before heading next door, he estimates the sheer volume of the wreckage and evaluates the efforts of the able-bodied men working to clear it. They are really putting their backs into it, but is it enough? With time of the essence for any men still alive inside, Jack concludes it is not. What other manpower is available? From out of left field, the idea of using German prisoners occurs to him. He gets Sarge's attention.

"We need more help! Get over to Roberts' CP and see if we can use the POWs!"

"Yes, sir!"

Having delivered the medic and the litters, the jeep begins to pull away. Sarge flags the driver down.

"Hey! Hold your horses!"

Using his good arm, he vaults into the front seat.

"Roberts' CP, and step on it!"

Le Nut's Tavern 1994

Somber faces are turned to Jack, who has picked up the thread of the story of that terrible night before Christmas. But he is losing steam as the memories become progressively more painful. Once again, Sarge is sensitive to Jack's situation and takes advantage of Davenport's late arrival to the gathering.

"Hey, Colonel! We missed you at the parade today!"

"Yeah, sorry fellas. I had to look into something that's been doggin' me for years."

Sarge's ploy succeeds, and all eyes turn from the doctor to the colonel, who is not sure he wants the attention.

"It's a really sad story, from a long time ago."

It only redoubles their interest, but Davenport won't budge.

"I can't ask you to hear it."

"But... that's why we're all here."

Several veterans nod in agreement with Sarge. When Sergio brings the colonel a beer, he is grateful for the interlude to quench his thirst. Finally, surrounded by friendly eyes, he relents.

"Well, OK. It's about the 333rd, another black artillery unit. They were behind the 106th and got overrun that first day. A few of them made it to Bastogne and joined up with us at the 969th. The rest never made it."

Several veterans murmur in condolence.

"There was something else. A rumor, I guess, about what happened to some of our boys who got captured. I had to check it out for myself in a little place called Wereth, up near the German border. Sure enough, I found a cross above a ditch outside of town and met the farmer who put it up, Hermann Langer. He was a child during the war, you understand, but he remembers that some of our boys were hiding in the barn and his parents took 'em in and fed 'em. And he remembers our boys gave him Chiclets."

This brings smiles and nods of remembrance of the chewing gum that was standard issue in their army rations and a sensation in Europe.

"Well, I guess somebody ratted on 'em, and the SS came and took our boys away."

Like Jack before him, now it is clearly the colonel's turn to try to surmount the most painful part of his story. It is as though a deep shadow has covered the old veteran, and the room goes silent in anticipation.

"They found our boys when the snow melted in the spring, eleven of them. Those Nazi bastards cut our boys, hurt 'em real bad. And shot 'em and... and threw 'em in the ditch."

A life of discipline and self-control has served Davenport well, but he fails to stop the rising anger within. It catches him off guard with an intensity that ignores the fifty years that have marched past since the incident. But when he looks from face to sympathetic face, his anger crests, crashes, and dissipates on the soft sands of empathy. Nonetheless, the recounting of the horrific atrocity has drained strength from his voice, which continues just above a whisper.

"I told you it was a sad story."

He takes a sip of beer while several veterans shake their heads, turn to each other, and offer colorful oaths against the evil of the Nazis. Davenport surprises them when he continues in a much lighter tone.

"But it's not the whole story."

All eyes turn to him again.

"I went to the Henri-Chappelle American Cemetery, where a few of the boys from the 333rd are buried."

The colonel paints a vivid picture for the veterans of walking under the bronze Angel of Peace that bestows the laurel branch on the thousands of noble dead interred at the cemetery, and of looking out over row upon row of white crosses. It is as though his new friends are experiencing those profound moments with him as they ring the table at Le Nut's. They can just about picture him, with plot map in hand, stopping at the end of a row, checking his map again, and making his way along the crosses while noting the names of the deceased as he walks.

"I found one of our boys, James Stewart of West Virginia. And wouldn't you know it? There was a girl there with flowers."

It was at that moment that Davenport realized that there was a wreath of red flowers laid before each of the crosses in the row beyond the girl. In her basket were enough wreaths to finish the row, and she worked her way along toward the colonel while humming a simple melody. When she joined him in front of Stewart's cross, he asked in his broken French what she was doing. She responded in perfect, schoolgirl English.

"The flowers are to remember the Americans who gave their blood for Belgium."

She swept her hand along a row of perhaps fifty headstones.

"All these soldiers are for my village."

While she stooped to lay a wreath before Stewart's cross, the colonel stood silently by contemplating the brief life that Stewart lived. What kind of guy was he? Who were his buddies? Did they laugh together? Cry together? What about at home? Who loved him and was loved by him?

Davenport invited the girl to stand by the stone for a photograph, and he made a permanent image of the unexpected, magical moment. Yet he wondered about the coincidence.

"Is it just for the fifty-year anniversary?"

"No, Monsieur. I come here every year. We all do."

He turned with her to see other young ladies laying wreaths. When the girl took up her task once again, Davenport offered to help and received a wreath reverently into his hands. Before bending to place it before the next gravestone in line, he touched the delicate pedals with wonderment.

"What is the name of this beautiful flower?"

"We call it *coquelicot rouge*."

"Cocali what?"

But the girl's attention had been captured by a friend calling to her from across the cemetery. And the colonel turned away from his vision to offer a puzzled visage to his new friends in the pub. Colleti is quick to make sense of what the girl said.

"*Rouge*. Red! That must be the red poppy."

Jack is quick to follow, having done a bit of research.

"Symbol of the fallen soldier."

Colleti has apparently boned up on the topic as well.

"And the national flower of Belgium..."

For Colleti, as is true for Jack, it has been a revelation to discover the dazzling beauty of the red poppy and to truly internalize the symbolism of the blood-hued flower.

"... where so many have fallen."

As Sarge ponders the MP's final thought, a light bulb flickers on in his head.

"Hey, wasn't there a poem?"

The Scot clears his throat.

"Right you are. Lieutenant Colonel John McCrae, a Canadian physician in the First World War."

Jack checks his pockets, pulls out a paper, and unfolds it. Then he digs for his reading glasses as the Scot begins to recite the poem from memory.

"In Flanders fields the poppies blow"

With glasses in place, Jack reads the poem along with the Scot's rendition.

"Between the crosses, row on row,
That mark our place; and in the sky
The larks, still bravely singing, fly
Scarce heard amid the guns below.

We are the Dead. Short days ago
We lived, felt dawn, saw sunset glow,
Loved and were loved, and now we lie,
In Flanders fields."

The Highlander pauses after the first stanza to look into the doctor's glistening eyes. It is a cue for Jack to lament the loss of life.

"So many young men."

"Dulce et decorum est..."

Jack perks up at the presence of another classicist and completes the line.

"... pro patria mori."

The Scot's next utterance almost catches in his throat.

"The old Lie."

Respectful of the solemnity embracing the veterans, the matron has been standing by. Once they restart their various low conversations, she steps in to clean up the table a bit, humming a simple melody. Though he is not an especially musical man, Davenport could swear it is the same tune the girl was humming at the cemetery. He asks her about it, and she stops abruptly.

"Oh! We learned it when we were little girls. We called it the poppy song. It is the same poem, the Flanders poem."

Others join the colonel in asking her for a rendition. She is reluctant, but buoyed by their positive spirits, she gives it a go.

"Dans le champs de Flandre
Les coquelicots en coup de vent
Entres les croix, rang par rang
Qui marquent notre place"

She pauses, self-consciously, and looks into the encouraging eyes of old men who have come from so far away and from so long ago. Among them, Davenport is deeply moved by the song. He folds his hands and closes his eyes as he did while standing before Stewart's grave in deep contemplation of what the young soldier and all the others sacrificed. A deep breath vanquishes the matron's skittish nerves, and she sings full-throated. The entire pub goes silent.

> *"Dans le ciel, les alousettes volent*
> *Encore et encore bravement chantant"*

For the colonel, her soaring voice becomes one with the plaintive pleas of larks singing high in the sky above the cemetery.

> *"Nous sommes les mortes*
> *Il y a peu de jours nous vivions,*
> *Nous voyions le coucher du soleil*
> *Aimions et etions aimes*
> *Et maintenant nous sommes allongès*
> *Dans les champs de Flandre"*

Lost in reverie, Davenport finds himself in the midst of the field of white crosses once again. He watches the girl finish her row and then make her way over to her friend, who has emptied her basket as well. He calls out to her.

"Wait! What is your name?"

The girl walks back to the colonel arm-in-arm with her friend.

"I am Gabrielle. And here is Veronique."

"Thank you, girls... for remembering."

As the young ladies respond warmly to Davenport's gratitude, a little dark-eyed girl, who the veteran hadn't noticed working nearby, approaches cautiously and stands shyly behind the much older girls.

"And who is this little angel?"

But Gabrielle and Veronique have turned to call out to other friends arriving at the cemetery. The colonel kneels before the little girl, who continues to avert her gaze toward the ground.

"What is your name?"

The response, barely above a whisper.

"Renee."

It has been a day of surging emotions for him, as he shuttled from sorrow to simple joy, and from his solitary mission to the companionship of new friends. For the colonel, the whole week has been altogether exhilarating and exhausting.

Yet now, as though stepping out of shadows into bright sunshine, he repeats the little girl's name under his breath. Like poetry.

"What was that?"

Davenport takes in Sarge's wide eyes.

"A little girl at the cemetery. Her name is Renee."

The uncanny coincidence causes Sarge to turn to Jack with a question written all over his face. By this time and station in his lifelong journey, Jack has come to accept the ever-present hand of fate and happenstance, and simply takes it all in stride.

"Huh! Renee. A popular name."

But he looks up to the matron for verification, who smiles in return.

"Yes, especially in Bastogne."

Situation 25 Dec 1944

25 December 1944

Though the threatened obliteration of the town has still not come to pass, a night of aerial bombardment has left many dead or severely wounded among the populace. The toll on American soldiers is high as well, but, as Christmas day dawns, the defenders of Bastogne remain in place, well dug in and as alert as a hair trigger. Their vigilance is warranted. German forces that have been heard maneuvering along the western perimeter are preparing a massive, concerted strike with heavy armor and infantry. Well concealed in a stand of trees, the commander of a battery of German artillery checks his timepiece. Ready at their posts, the eyes of a half-dozen gunnery crews are on him, ready to respond to his signal to open fire. They picked Christmas day for what they hope will be a final thrust into the heart of Bastogne.

There is no awareness of this new threat in basements throughout the town, where those who remained in Bastogne are hunkered down. As Dominique keeps a semblance of ritual in her morning duties, she moves through dust suspended in the air from the shaking of the frame and foundation of the old man's house during the night. She scurries about and sets a table, after a fashion, and spoons watery gruel into bowls for her boys. When she wakes them, they drag their blankets across the basement floor, wrap themselves tightly, and sit listlessly at the table. Remembering how they went to bed with groaning, empty stomachs, Dominique knows the food will not be enough for her boys. Tears edge her sleep-deprived eyes as she turns away from them and recriminates herself under her breath.

"What kind of mother am I? I can't even feed my children."

When Grandpapa awakens from heavy sleep, he slowly focuses on his daughter-in-law, whose face is riven with pain and anxiety.

"What is it, my child?"

Craving adult company and conversation, Dominique quickly goes to his bedside.

"François never came."

"Oh, well. Perhaps with the bombing he couldn't get through."

"Or... he..."

She catches herself with the darkest of thoughts, then tries to hide her distress from the boys. She fails. When Philippe drains his bowl and turns to ask her for more, he can see that something is very wrong with Mama. Grandpapa deflects his attention.

"So, boys, do you see? I told you we would be safe."

Their eyes follow his wiry hand as he gently pats the heavy stones in the foundation. Their gaze drifts back to their mother, who unsuccessfully tries to stifle a sob. Grandpapa lands on yet another diversion.

"Philippe! Please look for me. Is Saint Pierre still standing?"

The older boy steps over to the cellar window and, standing on his toes, parts the blackout curtain and looks out into heavy smoke pouring from a burning building nearby. Little Adrien spies a box, pulls it over, and climbs up to be nearly cheek to cheek with his brother. A switch in the wind blows the smoke away, yielding a clear view of the ancient church.

"Yes! Yes, it is there!"

"Thank you, boys. You have given me a wonderful Christmas present."

In spite of the deprivation brought on by the siege, the absence of François, Philippe's injury, and other misfortunes, the old man believes they have much to be thankful for. They are safe, thus far, and they have each other. Having raised the boys' spirits and teased out a half-hearted smile from his daughter-in-law, the old man settles back into bed and Dominique pulls the blanket up to his chin. She wipes her eyes clear and watches Philippe and Adrien fondly as they stare in wide-eyed fascination at enormous snowflakes beginning to fall outside. Alone in the perfect world of their private snow globe, the boys do not notice the commencement of heavy cannonade west of Bastogne. In a matter of minutes, the bell of Saint Pierre begins to ring.

At the other end of town, on Rue de Neufchâteau, the bell is barely audible at Jack's wrecked aid station while the crash of colliding armies echoes down the streets and alleys of the town. Undeterred, Americans and German POWs continue to work side by side in the rubble to recover bodies, with the thinnest of hopes that some may still be alive. Not one of them has slept, having worked on the site through the night, and their movements are almost mechanical.

Jack steps gingerly through the wreckage in response to a shout from the medic. He passes Beagle, who is digging forlornly in the general area he thinks his friend may have been when the bomb detonated. When Jack reaches an area cleared down to the basement floor, the POWs join their American counterparts in doffing their caps in a show of respect. Kneeling by the body, the medic checks for vital signs and finds none. He removes the unfortunate soldier's dog tag and hands it up to Jack. Beagle stops digging and looks over to Jack with hollow eyes. All Jack can offer the young man is a despondent shake of the head. It is not Wallington.

Heavy return fire from nearby American positions doubles the concussion of battle shaking the town, and Jack looks out toward the western horizon. He speaks softly, as if to himself.

"When will it end?"

"What's that, sir?"

The medic is at his side as Jack watches the POWs carefully bag and lift the body from the hole. Suffering from his own brand of battle fatigue, Jack is numb and seeing things as if through clouded glass, hearing things as though underwater. He turns to the medic slowly, as if just now registering his presence and his query.

"The agony."

When Jack turns back toward the increasingly fierce fighting in the west, the medic follows his gaze to see plumes of black smoke beginning to rise from vehicles on fire. He ponders Jack's response and can think of no better way to describe the whole situation.

The Western Perimeter

A lonely farmhouse stands at the center-point of the line held by the 401st Glider Infantry Battalion, off the left flank of the troopers of the 502nd. It has been a relatively quiet sector thus far, but today's action is more than making up for it as the Germans rain artillery, tank, and mortar fire down on the glider men. Inside the farmhouse, Colonel Allen's aide hands him the field radio.

"General McAuliffe? Colonel Allen of the 401st... They're hitting us pretty hard, sir."

He pauses to listen to the general's queries and gives his anxious aide a wink of reassurance.

"Their armor? Off road. The ground is frozen... Yes, sir, with infantry. Request permission to fall back."

This time Allen's eyes widen just a bit, as he is taken off guard by the general's response.

"What's that?... Stay put?... Let their tanks through?"

Now his aide is alarmed.

"And zero in on their infantry?... Yes, sir. We'll stop 'em one way or another."

One of his officers is at the window, calling to Allen with a tremulous voice.

"Colonel! You'd better take a look!"

Allen goes to the window and sees a German tank bearing down on his command post. He orders his men to collect all of the maps and documents and points to the back door.

"Hightail it, boys!"

No sooner have they spilled out of the farmhouse than the stone building is rocked by an 88-millimeter shell, sending debris and shrapnel into the trees. All his staff reach the woods safely and disappear into the thicket. They may never stop running. Allen finds cover and calls out to his men to shelter in place, and for his radioman to get his keister forward! The young aide picks his way through the undergrowth to hug the biggest tree he can find near his commander and calls out meekly.

"Here, sir."

Allen edges forward into a clearing to get a good vantage point, to the chagrin of his aide, who hears random small arms fire nicking the tree limbs around Allen. As he scans the battlefield with his binoculars, the colonel observes a favorable turn of events.

"Well, I'll be damned. They're turning north, away from Bastogne. I count ten, no, eleven panzers headed toward Champs. That puts them directly in front of our Hellcats."

Allen scans the tree line north of his position but sees no sign of the American tank destroyers. Suddenly, the Hellcats let loose with a thunderous volley. Their high-velocity, armor-piercing projectiles impact and immobilize several panzers. They keep up a vicious and relentless hellfire, and seven German tanks are soon crippled and aflame. Tank crewmembers fortunate enough to survive squeeze out and fall to the ground, wounded, terrified, or both.

"Bingo! Fish in a barrel."

Allen is forgivably jubilant, then troubled, as the four remaining tanks move out of range of the Hellcats. As they disappear into the mist and falling snow on the road to Champs, he shouts to his radioman, still hunkered down behind an ancient tree.

"Raise Swanson's CP in Champs! Tell him he's got four panzers comin' up the Hemroulle road!"

While the radioman tries to make the connection, the colonel continues to survey the battlefield. The weather shifts enough to give him a view of Champs just over a mile distant. The sights and sounds of heavy fighting there are unmistakable to Allen.

"Damn! The Five-oh-deuce are really catchin' hell up there."

A Schoolhouse in Champs

A trooper bursts into an empty one-room schoolhouse and quickly scans the space with his M1 Thompson machine gun. To his relief, the building is abandoned. He shouts to his mates outside.

"Clear!"

A lieutenant and several other troopers spill into the room and plaster themselves against the walls. The officer assigns lookouts and, once he is satisfied with their deployment, gives his men a break.

"We'll hold here for now."

As they look vacantly around the room at desks and chairs overturned and scattered, one trooper lays eyes on the blackboard and is not happy with what he sees written there. He finds a rag and sets out to erase it.

"Look at this! Some Nazi son-of-a-bitch wrote his propaganda on the board."

"Wait a minute, Jonesy. I took German in school. It's about Christmas, see?"

The lieutenant points to the word *Weihnachtsnacht* and proceeds to translate the message.

"Let the world see, uh... no, let the world never see such a Christmas again! To die far from one's children, one's wife and mother, under the fire of guns, there is no great... no greater cruelty. To take away a son from his mother, a husband from his wife, a father from his children, is this worth... uh, worthy of a human being? Life can only be given and... let's see... accepted, so we can love and respect each other. It is from the ruins, blood and death that universal brothers... uh... brotherhood will be born."

"Well, I'll be damned. A Kraut wrote that?"

Jonesy looks from eye to eye to eye, while each trooper contemplates the surprising depth of emotion he is feeling. A startling burst of friendly machine gun fire nearby is followed by a cry of pain from a German soldier, followed by a plea for help.

"Doktor! Helf mir! Bitte!"

Each of the troopers recognizes the youthfulness of the voice. He could be just a boy, somebody's kid brother. With more gunfire, the urgency in the voice pierces even the most hardened hearts.

"Mutter!"

Then faintly.

"Mutter."

Jack's Office

The office floor is crowded with bodies. It is very cold within, as snow blows through damaged windows and shutters haphazardly repaired. But the men are under shelter and, for the time being, not under fire. For Jack it is a small victory, but it pales as a counterweight to the loss of so many men and two angelic nurses.

A quick visit from Hank, who is now working out of Roberts' command post, gives Jack his first pick-me-up in twenty-four hours. This time he comes bearing gifts in the form of a jerry can of hot coffee and a dozen tin cups. The mugs are filled and passed around. The men respond to the restorative brew with smiles on their gaunt, pallid faces. Those whose wounds prevent them from drinking savor the aroma, a welcome change from the stench of war. Satisfied he has done all he can for the moment, Hank quizzes Jack on any additional needs he might have. With just the one woodstove in the office, the temperature in a large, drafty side room is hovering just above freezing. Jack is quick to respond.

"We need blankets, and more heat."

"I'll see what I can do."

When Hank muscles the broken door open, Beagle and another soldier enter carrying yet one more survivor of the bombing. As they do, smoke from the smoldering wreckage blows into the room, followed by the medic, who forces the door closed again. Jack quickly scans the room for space.

"Put him over there!"

When Jack steps carefully through the room and reaches the battered young man, the medic reports in a low voice.

"Still no sign of your nurses, sir."

Already in the depths of discouragement, Jack reaches for as much stoicism as he can muster while he works with the medic to clean and bind the injured man's wounds. Unaware of Beagle's special friendship, the medic matter-of-factly continues his report to the doctor.

"But we found your corporal."

Jack feels a fleeting hope against hope. It is quickly dashed as the medic continues.

"He was gone."

Jack seeks out his aide for corroboration, but Beagle can only nod to Jack while fighting back tears. The world stops turning for the two of them, as they share a few moments of contemplation and sorrow. What are they going to do without the corporal?

Wallington had been the vital cog in the machine since the three men landed together in France. Since their arrival in Noville, they had been to hell and back together. Now, for Jack and Beagle, a hole has been blown through their lives. Slowly, the pressing realities of the wounded and the fury of war return. The orderly heads back to the excavation of the aid station, and the doctor picks his way carefully to yet another man calling out in pain. It seems that it will never end. The agony.

No sooner does Beagle leave than reinforcements arrive. One soldier lugs several dozen blankets into the office, while another begins to cobble together a little pot belly stove in the back room. He works quickly and soon feeds a chimney pipe out through a window. As he shreds an old "Stars and Stripes" newspaper to get the fire started, a soldier lying nearby asks him to save Bill Mauldin's cartoon. He locates the comic strip, which quickly goes from hand to hand around the room. When he adds kindling and scraps of wood, the fire rises quickly, bringing light and warmth. Jack watches from the doorway with relief as cold, sick and damaged men shift their positions to face the fire's radiance, bringing a glow to their eyes.

Light a candle.

Jack reflects on how often the comforting words of wisdom from Major Davidson keep popping up. The front door is forced open again to the loud complaints of men blasted by frigid air. Smoke sweeps into the room and swirls around the silhouette of a very small, helmeted soldier. As is the case every time the door opens, Jack cannot suppress a rush of hope and anticipation.

One fellow by the door calls attention to the diminutive visitor, his voice as bleary as his eyes.

"Look at that tiny soldier."

The tiny soldier becomes a petite woman in uniform, as she steps into light cast by a lantern burning brightly near the door. Jack takes several halting steps forward, stops, and stares wide-eyed in wonderment.

"Nurse Chiwy?"

Jack makes his way quickly to the front of the building. He reaches out to hug Chiwy but refrains at the last moment due to an excess of modesty.

"But how... ?"

Chiwy is all smiles.

"I flew. I flew from the washroom. Is this the word?"

The wounded man who spoke up first responds, attempting to rise to Chiwy's cheerful manner.

"Well, shore. If you wuz a bird... or an angel."

The medic puts his two cents in.

"Blew. You blew out of the building."

"Yes, yes. I blew out of the building, and the bomb was the wind."

Standing with hands on hips in amazement before Chiwy, Jack sees the edge of a bandage under Chiwy's helmet. At his request she removes her headgear, revealing a head wrapped in dressing, spotted here and there with blood. Jack races through the possibilities. Was she knocked unconscious? Who found her? Who cared for her? With a delicate touch, Jack lifts the bandage to get a look at her wounds, but she brushes him away and recovers her head with the helmet.

"Stop! I am fine now. You need my help!"

She scans the room, evaluating the situation, then she catches Jack's eye with a worried look.

"But where is... ?"

Jack shakes his head. Without another word, the two healers get to work.

The Rogue Panzer

As Colonel Allen continues to survey the battlefield from as close as he can get to a catbird seat, his radioman scrambles up to him.

"Colonel, sir. I've got Swanson on the line from Champs."

Allen puts the handset to his ear.

"Gimme the scoop, Swannie."

"Thanks for the heads-up, Colonel. We picked off all three of them."

"Three? But there were four, four panzers headed your way! Are you sure you only stopped three? Swannie?... Captain?"

Several miles away and well behind the front line, a couple of troopers are shooting the breeze in a foxhole. A buddy calls out from a hole nearby.

"Hey, Brasner, did you ever see that pretty nurse in town?"

"Yeah, what a dish! Renee... Renee something. What about her?"

"The Krauts bombed her aid station last night. And they ain't found her yet."

With this bad news, the chatter among all within earshot stops abruptly. What a shame! What a goddamn shame! Young men, including those who have not yet known a woman, cannot fathom how something like this can happen. Where's the justice? Whoever did this has got to pay! Angry thoughts along these lines are slowly displaced as several heads turn to the grind and rattle of an approaching heavy, treaded vehicle. Brasner's mate hoists up to the edge of the hole and watches a tank materialize through the mist. Something about the whole picture seems out of whack.

"Braz, there's a tank comin' straight at our hole."

Brasner is unfazed and unarmed as his bazooka and bag of rockets sit on the edge of the hole next to his helmet. He continues shoveling out the muck at the bottom of the foxhole.

"Relax will ya? We're way behind the line."

Machine gun fire kicks up mud and snow. The trooper slides back down into the hole, while his helmet rolls to Brasner's feet.

"What the hell?"

Brasner picks up his buddy's helmet to hand it back and sees that high-caliber bullets have pierced it. He is momentarily stunned and speechless until the tank rolls directly over his foxhole, blasting him with choking exhaust.

"Arghh! You Kraut Nazi bastards."

When the tank rolls on, he reaches for his helmet and finds it crushed. But his bazooka is intact. Brasner leaps out of his hole with rage-fueled force, grabs the tube and rocket bag, and tears off after the panzer. He makes up ground, then skids to a stop when he sees a young trooper hunkered down under cover.

"Can you load this baby?"

The young man looks up to see a man possessed, eyes the bazooka and nods. Brasner hands him the bag and yanks him up and along behind him as they pursue the tank, which seems to have a mind of its own as it crashes through brush and saplings. When the two troopers close to within 30 yards, the effective range of the bazooka, the tank stops abruptly on a rise overlooking Bastogne in the distance. Heated debate can be heard from within the tank.

"Nein, nein. Das radio ist kaputt!"

Brasner picks up on a few words and gets the drift. These guys must be unable to contact their unit. Their sudden appearance behind American lines starts to make sense.

"Ha! The bastards are lost."

As Brasner kneels and lines up his shot, his companion fumbles with the bag.

"C'mon, c'mon! Let's send 'em to hell."

When the hatch pops open and the tank commander emerges to take a quick look around, the troopers duck into the brush. With powerful binoculars, the German officer scans Bastogne and, in the shifting mist and smoke, sees an assemblage of troops. He calls down instructions to his crew and watches the cannon rotate toward the target. He adjusts his field glasses to take a closer look and realizes with a start that many of the soldiers he sees are Germans. They are shorn of their white camouflage and their coal-scuttle helmets, no doubt thanks to souvenir-hunting GIs. But their grey greatcoats give them away as they stand tall among Americans in olive drab amid wreckage of what must have been a sizeable wood-framed building.

An American with a red cross on his helmet joins the soldiers standing by as a stretcher bearing a battered, bloodied body is handed slowly, carefully up from below.

As the commander witnesses the solemn scene from afar, a voice is heard from within his tank.

"*Kanone abfeuern?*"

"*Nein.*"

The commander takes a quick look around and drops back into the tank. When he swings the hatch closed with a resounding clang, Brasner scrambles out from cover to kneel in the open behind the tank. He finds himself alone and turns to the young trooper still hiding in the bushes.

"Get your ass over here. Load me up!"

But the tank quickly pivots and reverses course.

"He's coming back to get us!"

The terrified trooper is certain they've been spotted and heads even further into the woods. Brasner catches up to him and wrestles him to the ground behind a thicket. The tank rumbles by, and Brasner once again hustles out into the clearing, pulling the young trooper with him. He yells to the trooper to load him up, and the young man finally does so. When the trooper taps his helmet, Brasner fires and hits the tank in its engine compartment, one of the few vulnerable spots on the well-armored panzer. The engine stalls. Brasner turns to see his comrade wide-eyed with the realization that they just might slay this beast. The young man is quick to load the bazooka this time, and Brasner's second strike sets the panzer ablaze.

From a dozen well-concealed positions nearby, troopers rise as one with shouts of "hurrah!"

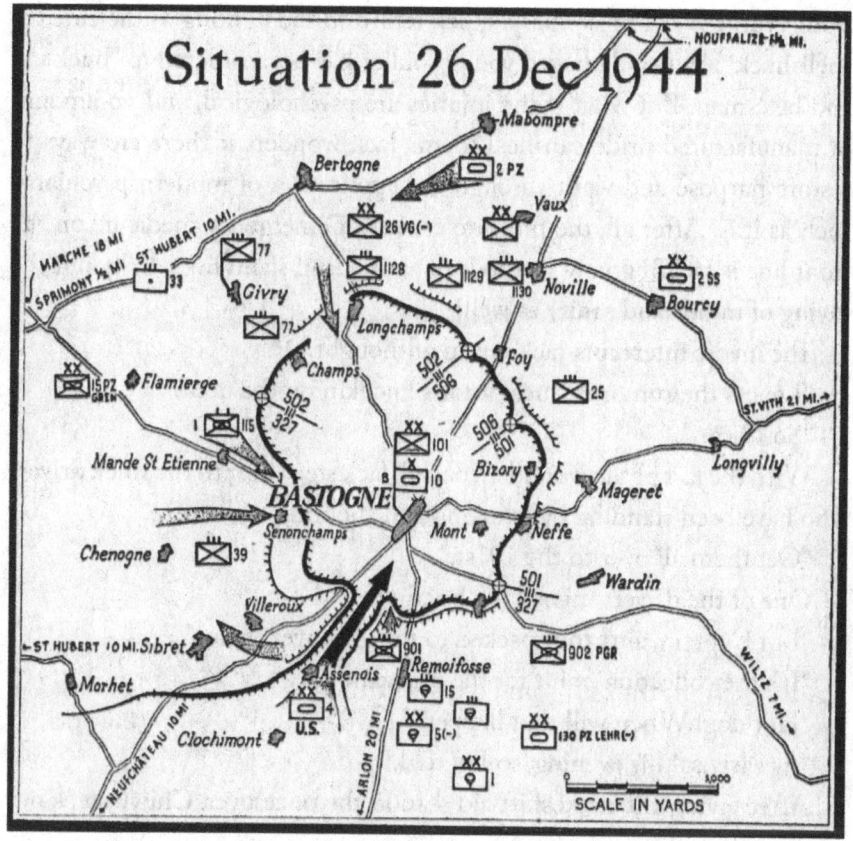

Situation 26 Dec 1944

26 December 1944

The morning wears on while Patton's relief forces approach Bastogne from the south. The imminent breakthrough dominates the scuttlebutt among the wounded being loaded into trucks in front of Jack's aid station. Once they are all aboard, they will be transported to the Belgian Barracks, the assembly point for the long-awaited evacuation.

As Jack watches Beagle go through the motions, he ponders the young man's pain. Though he is physically unscathed, Beagle is clearly damaged. What can be done?

With few protocols in place for handling combat stress, Jack and his fellow healers are largely on their own. One school of thought left over from World War I prescribes a quick return to the fighting as the cure for shellshock. Many a damaged young soldier has been ordered to "buck up" and be a man. But what if the injuries are psychological, and no amount of manufactured pride can heal them? Jack wonders if there are ways to restore purpose and vigor through the application of modern psychiatry, such as it is. After all, the pressure cooker of emergency medicine on the front line is yielding new methods of saving limbs and lives. Why not the saving of minds and sanity as well?

The medic interrupts Jack's train of thought.

"I guess the rumor is true. Patton's knockin' on the door."

"So I hear."

With the last of the wounded loaded, Jack steps over to the truck drivers who have been standing by, smoking and shooting the breeze.

"Get them all over to the 101st."

One of the drivers missed the briefing.

"But Captain, ain't they packed to the gills over there?"

"It's the collection point for the evacuation."

"Hot dog! When will that happen?"

"As early as this evening, so I'm told."

After giving the makeshift aid station the once over, Chiwy steps out to report to Jack.

"That's everyone, Doctor. I will go with them?"

"You have done enough, more than enough."

But Chiwy is determined.

"There is so much more to do."

"Well, you could report to Major Davidson."

Even the irrepressible Chiwy, with all the advantages of youth and enthusiasm, looks the worse for wear, yet she manages a smile. Jack is amazed at her perseverance, but still concerned.

"But I strongly recommend that you get some rest first."

"I will soon. I promise."

Chiwy is crestfallen when the last truck heads over to the 101st before she can get on board. But, as luck would have it, a jeep pulls up with a familiar figure at the wheel.

"Well, howdy-do nurse!"

"Oh, hello Virgil. Can you give me a ride?"

Virgil clears shotgun for her. As she steps into the jeep, Chiwy turns back to Jack. Her smile has returned.

"Doctor! This is the best driver in all of the army!"

"Aw shucks, Ma'am. You're just plain kind-hearted."

Virgil guns the engine but grinds the gears badly. Virgil and Chiwy share an amused look. Here we go again. The jeep leaps forward, and they head up the road. Before they move out of earshot, Jack hears Chiwy offer Virgil a song.

"Mairzy doats and dozy doats... "

Virgil joins in.

"... and liddle lamzy divey
A kiddley divey too, wouldn't you?"

Their laughter is swallowed up as the jeep crests the rise at the town square and disappears from sight. Jack shakes his head and turns to the medic beside him.

"Think she'll take a break?"

"No, sir. That little lady is the hardest worker I've ever seen!"

"That she is, and so much more."

Suddenly alone on the street, the two men stand as if rooted to the spot, too fatigued to venture even another step. Finally, the medic breaks the spell.

"What the hell were they singing?"

"Damned if I know."

Eventually, the two men step over to watch soldiers of two nations digging together in the rubble of the aid station. Sadly, their hard work is going unrewarded as they are finding only lifeless bodies now. No translations are needed among the excavators as they mumble and mourn together.

The medic takes his leave with a salute, which Jack returns. In one continuous motion, Jack reaches out and grasps the medic's hand. Though they only worked closely together for a matter of hours, they are forever bound by an experience they will never be able to forget. That makes two medics forever taking up residence in Jack's heart.

Alone again, Jack finds Colleti looking his way from the middle of the wreckage. They offer each other a nod and a look packed with as much meaning and acknowledgment as a firm handshake. When the MP turns back to his work, Jack skirts the wreckage on his way to the office.

Once inside, Jack steps through the blankets, sheets, and towels left behind after the exodus of the wounded. He sets his helmet on the desk, pulls a handful of dog tags from his pocket, and sits down heavily to go through them. As he records the names in his casualty records, he comes across Pearson's tag and gently kneads it as he stares into space. Hank is sorting through documents and files nearby.

"You OK, Jack?"

"Yeah. He saved my life."

Hank can't make the connection.

"How's that?"

As Jack holds up Pearson's dog tag, ready to offer an explanation, Colleti works the door open. He spots Jack and calls over to him.

"Captain, we found your nurse."

When Jack's face brightens ever so slightly, the MP shakes his head grimly and steps back outside. Even though he has prepared himself for the worst, Jack is still staggered by the news. He rises slowly, painfully, and heads toward the door, then stops for a moment of reflection and returns to his desk. He hefts the gift-wrapped parachute under his arm and heads outside.

Colleti is back up on the pile with a handful of POWs standing in a semi-circle around an opening in the debris. As he passes somber men with pry bars at ease and hats and helmets in hand, Jack picks his way to where he can see the body clearly. Softly, he confirms.

"Yes, it is Renee."

Directed by Colleti, two very young POWs throw a blanket over Renee's body and carry her respectfully on a stretcher through the wreckage. They follow Jack's careful steps down to ground level and gently lay her down in the snow. Beagle is there, his eyes blinking back tears. Jack understands completely.

"It's OK. I want to cry too."

Once they set Renee down, the POWs stand dutifully by to see if further assistance is required in any way. Jack kneels beside the body and sees Renee's face in what strikes him as peaceful repose. He sets the package down beside her, revealing words he wrote on the paper: "Merry Christmas Renee." He sets the wrapper aside, covers Renee with the parachute, and carefully tucks it under her body until she is completely bound and concealed. A call from a POW in the wreckage breaks the funereal mood.

"Ah! Aha! *Kamerad*!"

Jack turns to see an older soldier, who could be a grandfather, holding forth a pendant on a broken chain. He passes it to Colleti, who walks it down to Jack. Without taking a close look at the piece, he stands and absentmindedly puts it into his pocket. Time stands still for the moment as he looks into the tearful eyes of the two young POWs, soldiers whose faces have not yet been touched by razor blades. A flash of rage jolts him as he curses Hitler for sending boys and old men to the front. He nods his appreciation to the young men.

"*Danke*. I'll take her from here."

As Jack hefts Renee's body, he nearly loses his balance. He takes a couple of wayward steps back into the road just as a convoy rushes past on the way to the western perimeter. Colleti's response is quick and powerful, pulling Jack to safety and pressing Renee's body to Jack's chest, lest she fall.

"That was close, Doctor!"

Colleti vigorously waves the following truck out further around the wreckage.

"Watch out, you son-of-a-bitch!"

"Put a sock in it, Colleti!"

At this point in the siege and after the relentless pounding that Bastogne has endured, Colleti is used to disrespect from frazzled soldiers and shrugs it off, eventually offering encouragement to the troops as they pass.

"Go get those bastards!"

Roberts' fire brigade is off to plug a gap in the line near the Senonchamps road. Will and Joey are seated in the back of the last truck with a dozen grim-faced soldiers. As they pass the aid station, only Joey takes notice of the man with the red cross on his helmet holding what looks to be a body wrapped tightly in a white parachute. He alone makes the connection to the nurse, the dark-eyed beauty whose eyes were edged with sadness. Joey screws up his features to lock in his sorrow, determined to guard his feelings from the scrutiny of the hardened men around him. But no one on board is the wiser. Each is alone with his thoughts as they head into battle.

A dozen columns of raven-black smoke from burning vehicles now stain the horizon ahead of the convoy. This does not portend well for the cold, tired foot soldiers in the trucks as they bounce roughly over bricks dealt randomly in the street from shattered buildings.

Lemaire Residence

Gisele has been watching at the window and rushes to open the door when she sees Jack approaching. As she opens the door, she calls back into the house.

"Papa! Mama! It is the doctor."

Jack steps across the threshold cradling Renee's body in his arms, still tightly wrapped in the parachute. Gisele leads him to the back room where Lemaire is seated at a table, flanked by his wife and Marguerite. He is haggard, having kept vigil since the moment he heard of the disaster at the aid station. Slowly, painfully, he rises to receive Renee's body. Unburdened, Jack's words come spilling out.

"I'm sorry. I failed... I failed to protect her."

"No, Doctor. It falls on me."

Marguerite is quick to refute him.

"No, Papa. No."

But he is adamant. Anger, guilt, and pain combine in his confession as he cradles his princess in his arms.

"It was my decision to stay in Bastogne."

Then, as if completely drained of energy and emotion, the devastated father confesses.

"I'm an old fool."

Berta clears the sofa for Lemaire who gently places Renee's body there and immediately collapses onto his knees beside her. Gisele and Marguerite rush to kneel beside their father and wrap comforting arms around him.

It is an extraordinarily tender moment, but Jack is distressed to see Renee's mother excluded, standing rigidly by the couch with her emotions in check. For several minutes, no one stirs. No sound of battle intrudes. Only the ticking of the grandfather clock can be heard. Finally, Lemaire rises and hugs Gisele and Marguerite close to him while Berta searches for the correct thing to do at times like this.

"Doctor, would you like some tea?"

Before Jack can respond, she directs Gisele to the kitchen to heat some water.

As closely as Jack and Renee worked together, and as much as he learned about her and admired her, it has only been for a matter of days out of Renee's nearly thirty years on this earth. It pales next to the fullness of her family life.

"Thank you, but... I need to get back. This is your time."

Lemaire rises stiffly to his feet, reaches out for Jack's hand, and shakes it firmly with both of his.

"Thank you, Doctor, for bringing my daughter home. Thank you."

"I am so very, very sorry."

Try as he might, Jack cannot suppress a surge of guilt. He should have been in the aid station with her. He left his post.

A conscience can be a brutal thing.

Somehow, he makes it to the door, turns, and looks into the eyes of the mourning family one more time. No blame or recrimination is written on their faces.

When Jack steps outside he finds that the temperature has continued to plummet in Bastogne. But cold air is like shock treatment for a troubled mind. It reminds us that our primary function is survival. Jack steps down to the street and stuffs his hands into his pockets, where he finds Renee's pendant.

He pulls it out and studies the exquisite miniature portrait of an angel holding an infant. He retraces his steps and knocks at the door. Marguerite answers.

"Doctor?"

No words come to him as he hands her the pendant.

"Ah! From Renee! Thank you, Doctor. Thank you."

Marguerite stands patiently before Jack, awaiting words he seems on the verge of uttering. But what can he say? This young woman shivering in the doorway has lost her sister, her confidante, her friend. Her family has made the ultimate sacrifice and will never be whole again. Finally, he simply nods, and, when she responds, he drinks in her kind words, gratefully.

"Please come to see us again. You are always welcome here."

As the door clicks into place behind him, he turns to face the cold with just enough fortitude to get through another day.

Unaware of Jack's presence, Sarge passes by across the street waving his good arm about while regaling a private with one or another of his slightly exaggerated tales. Jack stops to listen to their chatter as they recede. The private finally gets a word in edgewise.

"So Sarge, did ya hear Patton's comin' to rescue us?"

"Yeah, yeah, I heard the news. Get out the ticker tape. The son-of-a-bitch will want a parade!"

McAuliffe's Headquarters

Roberts enters and salutes. McAuliffe returns the salute and briefs the colonel while holding the handset of a field radio out to him.

"We've got four Shermans in front of our roadblock on the Assenois Road. We need verification."

Roberts nods and takes the handset.

"This is Colonel Roberts. What's your situation?"

Roberts listens to the trooper on the line.

"I understand your caution... That's right. The Krauts captured some of our tanks. Get me unit info from the lead tank."

Roberts listens carefully while the trooper calls out to the tank, and he faintly hears someone shouting back to the trooper. The trooper relays the information, and Roberts repeats it as he listens carefully.

"Third Army... Fourth Armored Division... 37th Tank Battalion... Company C."

As the trooper calls out to the tanker again, Roberts gives a hopeful nod to the general. Then he overhears a new voice.

"What's that?... Is that their First Louie?... Put him on."

As Roberts awaits the officer, McAuliffe interjects.

"Get his name. That young man deserves a medal."

Roberts has him on the line.

"Colonel Roberts, here... That's right, Lieutenant, 10th Armored Division. I'm here with General McAuliffe of the 101st Airborne. He wants to thank you personally... What's that?... What're you called?... King? Say it again... Cobra King, right."

Roberts takes it in stride, but McAuliffe is puzzled.

"Cobra King? The man?"

"No, sir. It's the name of their tank. They use the company letter in the name. Company C, so C for Cobra."

Roberts' hint of a smile betrays more than just a measure of pride for the armored forces as he elaborates for the general's edification.

"They don't want to be thanked as individuals, but as a team!"

The general breaks into the widest grin possible under the circumstances.

27 December 1944

Dawn breaks and the Germans awaken to their error in leaving a back country road through Assenois lightly guarded. In spite of German infantry and armored pressure from east and west of the road, U.S. Army traffic through Assenois is increasing. Reinforcements are arriving in Bastogne, and the evacuation of the wounded can finally take place. Among the units that shot the gap during the night is the 64th Medical Group, an all-black outfit. Their seventy ambulances form the core of the evacuation convoy now idling in front of the Belgian Barracks. Once they are all fully loaded with injured men, they'll form a convoy and run the same gauntlet out through Assenois to field hospitals in Neufchateau.

Jack, Chiwy, Beagle, and the 101st medical team are nearing the end of a backbreaking shift that started when the ambulances began to arrive after midnight. Working tirelessly, they carefully lifted scores of litter cases into the ambulances and loaded several hundred ambulatory wounded onto deuce-and-a-half trucks. At reveille, Will and Joey and various other SNAFU irregulars were called upon to load duffle bags belonging to the evacuees into a half-dozen trucks.

Once Major Davidson gives them the "green light," and the ambulances begin to snake out of the compound, one more vehicle pulls up at the tail end. Behind the wheel is the driver whose ambulance was blasted in Noville. He quickly picks Jack Prior out of the crowd.

"Hey, Captain! Whaddaya know?"

Jack is surprised, almost delighted to see him still in one piece, even if his vehicle doesn't appear to be.

"Well, I'll be damned! Don't they know your driving record?"

"Yes, sir. I mean no, sir. I mean, ain't she a beauty? I knocked together a couple of wrecks. Didn't want to miss this parade. And look, I got me a Caddy!"

A little levity turns out to be pretty good medicine for Jack as he takes in the collection of odd-fitting parts with "Cadillac" hand-painted on the side. When the driver limps out to bang proudly on the hood, Jack is reminded of the man's wound.

"How's the leg? Any pain?"

"Only when I drive. Goddamn clutch."

"Ha! Well, good luck. See if you can keep the wheels on this one."

"Yes, sir."

As Jack steps away to consult with Beagle, several SNAFU soldiers take an unscheduled break and attract the attention of their CO. Scowling, the officer steps over to give the idlers a proverbial kick in the pants. With a shrug at the sight of Frankenstein's ambulance, he barks at Will and Joey to load the odd-looking vehicle with the last of the duffle bags. Their work quickly dispatched, Will wipes his brow and trudges away, but Joey appears agitated, immovable, unable to square what he sees.

"Hey! That's not a Cadillac!"

Jack has been a bemused observer of their little drama from a distance but is moved to correct the oafish soldier.

"Believe me, soldier, he has more than earned the illusion."

As the Cadillac rattles forward to append itself to the end of the column, Davidson joins Jack to watch the procession and offers the final word.

"That's all of 'em."

"What about the field stations?"

"They're all in. I'd say we evacuated near a thousand. Everyone who can handle a long, hard ride has a one-way ticket out of here."

"And the rest?"

"We're down to fewer than a hundred. Our boys are setting up a sterile location that will accommodate the lot as we speak. Thanks to Jerry leaving the back door open, we'll have several surgical teams up and running in no time."

"I guess I'd better head over there to see if they need a hand."

"Doctor, you've done enough for today, and maybe for a lifetime, just keeping your boys alive."

"I had a lot of help."

Jack retrieves indelible images of Chiwy and Renee working around the clock. Together, the three of them kept several dozen men with complex head, chest, or stomach wounds breathing long enough for the surgeons that came in with Patton's relief column to get right to work on them. He makes a mental note to visit with them while they rest in the Barracks and await their turns on the operating tables.

As Chiwy approaches the two men she seems, to her remarkable credit, fresh, ready, and eager for her next task. She joins Jack and the major as they watch the last of the vehicles turn the corner onto Rue de la Maison Forte and disappear from view. The momentary stillness that comes over the compound corresponds with a sudden ratcheting down of Jack's energy. He has been operating on caffeine and adrenaline for days, and now it all comes crashing down like withdrawal from a powerful drug. He turns to see Chiwy's eyes glistening with sorrow, or joy, or perhaps both. He gives a penny for her thoughts.

"Well, what do you think?"

"Oh, I am thinking how happy Renee would be to see them all going home."

Renee was full of life. Then she was gone. It is a void that is difficult to contemplate. But as time passes, and painful memories soften, Jack and Chiwy will remember her much as the soldiers will who were touched by her during some of the most critical hours of their wartime experiences. Renee, the one the men called the Angel of Bastogne, was gentle and compassionate. The world can ill afford to lose so much goodness at one time and all in one person.

As if to take up the slack left by Renee's absence, Chiwy is ready to get back to work. She catches Davidson's attention.

"Ready for my next duty."

"We are done here, Nurse, unless the captain needs your services."

Chiwy looks from Davidson to Jack, who shakes his head.

"You can stand down."

"But there must be something I can do."

Now Jack is smiling as he draws himself to attention.

"Nurse Chiwy, you are relieved."

Her smile in return lights up the compound. When Davidson heads in to his office, Jack and Chiwy remain, together, relieved that their ordeal has ended, but regretting their inevitable separation. They were a hell-of-a team. Chiwy looks up to the doctor.

"Do you hear that?"

"What?"

"Nothing. Silence."

With the Germans scrambling to pinch off Patton's relief column well south of Bastogne, the thunder of pitched battle is stifled by the heavily forested hills of the Ardennes. There have been no artillery strikes in Bastogne all morning, no small arms fire echoing in from the fields ringing the town. Even the bell at Saint Pierre is standing down. Gradually, a sound seldom heard of late is rising. Here and there, women step out into the streets to greet their neighbors and talk about where meat, cheese, and their beloved baguettes might be procured.

Faced with the prospect of downtime, Chiwy is torn between family and duty. She neglected her father during the siege, even gently chided him for not leaving town. But she glowed in her father's love when he declared he would not leave Bastogne while his daughter was under the guns of the goddamn *Boche*! Perhaps now she could take a few hours to prepare a belated Christmas dinner for him. It would be like the olden days, happy golden days of yore. But even as she recalls the warmth of her father's hearth and home, she knows that it could be just a matter of hours before a new wave of casualties washes into town, and Major Davidson will need help. She knows that she could never decline a call to service.

Then there is this tall American, this man of healing standing beside her. Though the days of the siege have been fraught with peril, for Chiwy they have also been packed with meaning, and more than just a little bit of magic. Beyond her family, she has never been closer to anyone than Renee and Jack. The nurse will always be her sister. But Jack? He has touched her in a special way. Even her father, ever perceptive, offered to "will" her to the doctor so that they might continue working together. She laughed it off then and does so again now, in her secret self. But when she catches yet another glimpse of Jack's sympathetic eyes, her inner laughter stops. Is there more to their working relationship than she lets herself believe?

Perhaps as a safe haven from a looming tangle of emotions, she invites Renee back into her thoughts. As she scans the silent compound, Chiwy conjures her friend's downcast expression and last words in the washroom, and her own emphatic response.

"I am lonely."

"But you are not alone!"

As soon as that exchange was made, the world came crashing down on the nurses. Now that Renee is gone, how can Chiwy follow through and fulfill her promise to Renee? After some thought, she decides to dedicate her work to Renee and pledges, right then and there, to keep the memory of her friend alive in her heart for as long as she lives.

Renee will never be alone.

It is the kind of resolution that is good for the soul.

At this moment, Davidson's jeep pulls up, with Private Morgan at the wheel. The private salutes Davidson as the major steps out of his office. After a few quick words with his clerk and a hand-off of keys, the major heads over to the jeep. Morgan salutes Jack and Chiwy, the tiniest soldier he ever did see! She returns the salute smartly, and they both get a kick out of it. He reports that he has finished Jack's casualty records and heads into the office to fetch the papers. Davidson steps into his jeep, prepares to leave, and offers an afterthought.

"Nurse, do you need a lift?"

"A lift? Oh! Yes, please. Thank you very much."

While Jack watches Chiwy join the major in the jeep, he reflects on the fact that he is seeing her off yet again, saying goodbye for the second time. Or is it the third?

On the night of the bombing, when cries of distress coming from within the aid station ceased, did he say goodbye? If he did, why did he keep seeking Renee and Chiwy in the shapes and shadows shifting in the light of the burning building? Even though the nurses failed to materialize when dawn exiled that terrible night, he can't recall ever giving up hope. Perhaps a part of him said goodbye. But in a war zone, goodbyes are really wishes that you'll meet again. Even if you don't know where, don't know when.

As if receiving his thoughts, Chiwy turns round in her seat as the jeep pulls away and gives Jack a look that speaks volumes of the story they wrote together during the past week. At the aid station and in the field, they were stretched well beyond their limits. Up to their elbows in blood, they cheated death themselves and for dozens of young soldiers. Through the saving of lives, they are united in ways that can never be broken. Chiwy smiles and Jack understands. No words or gestures are necessary.

After the jeep pulls away, Morgan returns from the office and calls Jack back to the moment.

"Here you go, Captain. Typed and carbon-copied in triplicate..."

Beagle, who has been hunched in a heap on an empty crate while staring at the ground, looks up and pays attention to their exchange. Morgan has completed a task that would have been Wallington's to fulfill, had he survived. It is all too much for the orderly.

"... one each for battalion, division, and Third Army, and the original for your files, sir."

While Morgan, of course, is none the wiser, Jack cannot mistake the jumbled emotions that dance over Beagle's face. It is as if the young man would cry out to the heavens for his lost friend, if he had the energy to do so. Morgan fishes Jack's handwritten records out of a large manila envelope and hands them over.

"And here are your notes, sir, if you want to check my work."

Jack thumbs through the pages, pausing to contemplate the blood-stained page with several entries partially obscured.

"I had a little trouble with that one, but I think I worked it out OK."

But Jack is already on to the next page, and the next. He tries to match names with faces contorted with pain, with cries of agony, with lives shortened but, to his great discouragement, fails repeatedly. Morgan misreads Jack's tortured expression as displeasure.

"Here, I'll deep-six those for you, sir."

Jack simply slides the handwritten notes into the envelope and tucks the package under his arm.

"While you got me, sir, is there anything else I can do?"

"No, that'll do it."

Several dozen more townspeople have now stepped out of their darkened dwellings and into the streets, including children called upon to help lug food and firewood home. The faces of the adults are drawn from lost sleep and worry, and the children appear joyless. Morgan has a bright idea, excuses himself from Jack, and disappears into the barracks. He quickly returns with two sizeable cardboard boxes and sets them down in the snow.

"Captain, I managed to get my hands on more chocolate bars than we know what do to with. Permission to... ?"

When Morgan nods toward the children, Jack quickly takes his meaning and automatically includes Beagle in the equation of his thoughts. He catches Morgan's eyes and nods toward his aide. Morgan's puzzled look is quickly replaced by comprehension once he studies the dejected soldier. The private squishes through the slushy snow and mud over to the orderly.

"Captain says to distribute these."

Beagle looks up with lifeless eyes from the boxes of chocolate bars to Morgan, and then to Jack who nods confirmation and points toward the children. The orderly surveys a scattering of children whose sunken eyes mirror his own. He cracks open a box and shows the exposed bars to the children. Though their parents give permission, the shy children hesitate. Beagle trudges over to the nearest cluster of boys and girls, who reach hesitantly into the box. Soon others join to quickly empty the carton.

Word quickly spreads in the neighborhood and Beagle is soon surrounded by children as he cracks open the second box. While the little ones shout and cheer, the orderly takes a deep cleansing breath and turns sparkling eyes to Jack.

Among the children approaching Jack's aide is Philippe, who is helping his mother restock their food stores during the lull in the fighting. A sack filled with whatever Dominique could find so far hangs from his good shoulder. Beagle puts a chocolate bar in the bag and, after the boy makes a request in broken English, adds another bar for his little brother. When his mother beckons to him, Philippe heads back to rejoin her, but stops when he recognizes the doctor from Chiwy's clinic. Unaware, Dominique is now impatient.

"Come, Philippe!"

Then she recognizes the object of his attention.

"Oh! Good morning, Doctor!"

Jack recognizes her but cannot recall her name.

"Madame... ?"

"Dumonde, Dominique Dumonde. And this is Philippe."

"Hello, Philippe."

The boy has been watching the soldiers, the "GI Joes," and is eager to imitate them. To his mother's chagrin, he drops his sack to the ground. It frees his good arm to give Jack a spirited salute. Jack returns the salute, giving Dominique an unexpected swelling of pride. If only François was here today to see his big boy. But no, he is away training for the day when the Belgians can take up arms again. So much is bittersweet in her life right now. Despite all the hardship that has been inflicted on her family and her people, the Americans have held Bastogne. Everyone in town is saying that better days are coming.

"Thank you, Doctor."

Early January 1945

On a rare a day off from work at Davidson's aid station, Chiwy heads down a deserted street on her way to the Lemaire residence. As she walks, Chiwy summons visions of Renee pressing cold packs on the foreheads of feverish soldiers, and feeding and bathing those unable to care for themselves. Step by careful step through the rubble of collapsed buildings, Chiwy recalls Renee's many other tasks, all delivered with the bravest of smiles. Here was Renee changing dressings and giving medications, and there was Renee sanitizing linen, spreading cheer, and shedding tears. By the time she reaches her destination, Chiwy is flooded with fond feelings and memories of her friend.

Yet as she steps up to the landing, she has an unexpected surge of dread. Will her visit with Renee's family just be a stinging reminder of all that they have lost? Try as she might, Chiwy can't recover her customary high spirits and wonders whether there might be a better time to call on the family.

Chiwy knocks, just once. Perhaps no one is at home. Not realizing she had held her breath, she exhales a not entirely unwelcome sigh of relief. Then the door opens to reveal Renee's mother. Having known no sleep for many days, the older woman's eyes are careworn and cavernous, yet they flicker with recognition.

"Mademoiselle Chiwy?"

"Yes. Madame Lemaire, I have come to pay my respects."

"Please, come in."

Berta has never met Chiwy, but the young nurse's open face and trusting eyes somehow match Renee's effusive praise of Chiwy's character perfectly. In any event, there could be no mistake. There is but one Augusta Chiwy. She is known on sight to most everyone in town, and all are beguiled by her energy and positivity. Regardless, Chiwy does not know what to expect from Renee's family at this extraordinary time. As she follows the bereaved woman slowly into the dining area, no further words pass between them. Yet, it is not an uncomfortable silence, which Chiwy finally breaks.

"Madame, I am so sorry for your loss."

"Thank you, Mademoiselle."

"Is Monsieur at home?"

"No, they are all down at the store. Let me take your coat."

Madame lays Chiwy's coat over the arm of a couch.

"Please, sit down. I'll make some tea."

Berta puts a kettle of water on the stove and stokes the fire below. Meanwhile, Chiwy's attention is drawn to framed photographs on a hutch. There is one of the Lemaire couple in wedding garb. The bride is stone-faced, but the groom betrays the hint of a smile, as if in anticipation of three daughters yet to descend from heaven. There are formal portraits of Gisele and Marguerite, but apparently none of Renee, though there is a picture of the young father with a little girl standing before him. Perhaps it is Renee.

Berta joins Chiwy on the couch, with two cups of aromatic tea.

"Thank you, Madame."

They sip their tea in silence. Chiwy wants to say more, but senses that simply being there for Madame is enough for the moment. It is certainly enough for Chiwy, whose mood and level of comfort slowly rise like the steam escaping her teacup. But she detects Madame drifting away.

"Is there a better time?"

"No, please. Will you stay a while with me?"

"Of course, Madame."

Berta has been very adept at suppressing her sentiments. She has been a quiet stabilizer for a family with a domineering, demonstrative husband who doted on his three precocious daughters, his beautiful flowers. In turn, the girls tried to live up to Papa's expectations by showing him their strengths and joys, reserving their woes and weaknesses for Mama.

It has been a mother's burden to bear, but she has carried it with dignity and kept the family sailing along on an even keel. But now the ground has shifted beneath Berta's feet. As has often been the case over the years, she takes refuge in formality.

"How is your family?"

"Everyone is fine. Thank you, Madame."

As the two women sip their tea, the world is thankfully subdued, with only the grandfather clock in the side bedroom sounding the slow passage of time. When Chiwy finishes her tea, she takes her cup and saucer to the kitchen and returns to the room by way of the hutch. There she pauses and turns to Renee's mother.

"May I?"

With a nod of permission from Berta, Chiwy gently lifts the photograph of Lemaire and the little girl. It must be Renee, his little princess and a dark-eyed beauty, standing proudly with a bouquet of flowers in her hand. Chiwy turns to see a weak, forced smile on the older woman's face and eyes brimming with tears. Something has tipped the balance. Is it the photograph? Chiwy carries the picture over to Madame, who cradles it in her hands. After several moments of study, she looks up from the photograph to Chiwy, asking a question with her own dark eyes.

"Will you let me in? My heart is breaking."

Chiwy answers by taking the older woman's hand, and any remaining distance between them falls away.

"When Renee was a little girl, she loved... to pick... the red flowers."

The dam that Madame so carefully erected to contain her feelings begins to crack as she chokes on her words.

"I called her... Little Poppy."

A fleeting memory of Renee running and playing, gaily laughing on a summer day, is the final straw for Berta. She teeters and falls against the young nurse, weeping for her baby girl. Is there anything as soul-shaking as a mother's grief? With Chiwy gently squeezing her hand, Berta slowly regains her balance and her composure.

The front door swings open, and Marguerite calls out.

"Hello, Mama?"

Madame wipes her eyes dry and offers Chiwy a grateful smile. Then she takes a deep breath and puts on a cheerful face. Perhaps it is just this mannerism, and certainly the dark eyes, but Chiwy is suddenly struck by her resemblance to Renee. Marguerite bustles into the room.

"Ah! Hello, Augusta."

Her little sister is close behind.

"Gisele, this is Augusta Chiwy."

Once again there is no need for an introduction. Chiwy is a true daughter of Bastogne, and Gisele is bubbling with excitement.

"Renee told us all about you! She called you an angel of mercy! Didn't she, Mama?"

Madame nods and turns to Chiwy, who is quick to deflect the praise.

"Ah, no. It was Renee. She was... no, she is the angel. For me, she will always be an angel of healing... an angel of hope."

"You are so kind, Mademoiselle."

With Berta's warm words, Chiwy rekindles the private moments she just shared with Renee's mother. Yet, she is struck by the distance between the woman's despair and the ebullience of her daughters. Then it occurs to her that they are wiser than their years, certainly Marguerite is, and are doing whatever they can to lift their mother's spirits nearly a week on from the tragedy. A knowing look from the elder sister seems to confirm Chiwy's suspicion. And she suddenly realizes that she has become a part of their effort and feels a sisterly affection growing among the three of them.

Since Chiwy had only visited to express sympathy, she could not have hoped for more. She has discovered what almost feels like a second family, bound together by memories of Renee.

Nevertheless, Renee was their loving daughter and sister, their family's loss. Not hers. It should be their time together.

"I must go now. My father is expecting me. Thank you for the tea, Madame."

Soon the four are standing together, Chiwy holding her topcoat. The girls are momentarily at a loss for what to say as they turn and defer to their mother. To their surprise and delight, Berta embraces Chiwy with all the tenderness a mother feels for a daughter. Gisele and Marguerite quickly wrap their arms around the two, and *très petite* Chiwy disappears in the folds of a familial embrace. Finally, they separate, revealing a glowing Chiwy.

As the sisters follow behind, Madame takes Chiwy's arm and walks her toward the front door. They pass a large, darkened room where a single candle stands atop a piano, softly illuminating a formal portrait of Renee. Unable to look away, Chiwy asks for leave to enter. With permission granted and encouraged, Chiwy steps reverently into the room, as if entering a holy shrine. After a moment adjusting to the low light, Chiwy notices a parachute rolled up in a corner of the room. It is a mystical moment, the portrait, the single candle, the parachute, and Chiwy finds herself on one knee caressing the smooth fabric.

"With your permission, Madame. May I cut a piece? To remember Renee?"

"Yes, of course. Please do."

Madame finds her pinking shears in the drawer of a small dresser and hands them to Chiwy, who looks the parachute over and then cuts a square with a dark stain in the middle. She reflects on its significance, cuts it in two and puts the pieces into her pocket. She hands the shears to Berta.

"Thank you, Madame."

When they reach the door, Berta helps Chiwy into her topcoat. They turn to face each other one more time. Renee's mother is first to speak.

"Please come see us again."

She takes Chiwy's hands tenderly, and Chiwy reciprocates in kind.

"Yes, Madame. Please express my sorrow to Monsieur."

"I will. Thank you…"

She gives Chiwy's hands a knowing squeeze, holding tight the small, strong hands of the young woman.

"... Augusta."

As they stand before the open door, Berta offers the bravest smile she can muster, a smile that says "thank you" to Chiwy for being there with her, for letting her show her feelings, for letting her cry.

When the door clicks gently into place behind her, Chiwy steps down into the street and stands rooted to the spot for a moment, as if not knowing where to turn, or how to process all that just happened. The somberness and the weight of the family's loss were more than offset by the exuberance of the sisters, the grateful tears in Berta's eyes, the warmth of their arms wrapped around her.

Somehow it all helps Chiwy to feel validated and loved, and she suddenly feels light on her feet as she walks along the sidewalk. But in the shadows cast by the late afternoon sun, Chiwy soon feels the bite of bitter cold. She bundles up and makes haste down the street. At the corner, she steps clear of the buildings and into dazzling rays of the setting sun. Just above the horizon, the sun is as red as the poppies that blow throughout the Ardennes, where so many young men have fallen, and she finds that she can look directly into its beating heart without discomfort. She suddenly feels an ethereal presence, but it is a youthful, playful spirit.

"Ha! Little Poppy!"

Hotel Lebrun 1994

It is late morning, and Jack and Sarge are nursing cups of coffee in a little café just off the lobby. Their conversation wanes as Jack looks away every time someone enters the hotel. Each time he finds it is no one he knows and nods almost apologetically to Sarge, who reads just a hint of disappointment.

"Expecting someone?"

"Well, hoping, hoping for someone. Augusta Chiwy. Last I heard she was planning to be here."

Sarge remembers Chiwy well but wonders how Jack stayed connected with her for fifty years. Jack anticipates Sarge's next question.

"We've exchanged Christmas cards over the years."

Sarge waits for more, and Jack obliges him.

"Not sure we'll recognize each other."

"Look 'em in the eyes, I always say. Only part of you that never changes."

Sarge studies his old comrade, whose mind seems to be wandering away, perhaps in search of a pair of eyes with just a hint of mischief. Jack slowly works his way back to his companion and casts around for something to say.

"Let's have another cup of coffee."

"And let's have another piece of pie"

"What's that?"

"Well, sure, you remember. It's a song from the depression."

Tickled that he has reached his distracted friend, Sarge gives it a shot.

"Just around the corner
There's a rainbow in the sky
So let's have another cup of coffee
And let's have another piece of pie"

A smile creases Jack's lips almost imperceptibly. For Sarge, it is a small victory. He never fails to amuse himself, but it is all aces when Sarge enlivens someone else. He feels like Jack is now finally, fully present with him.

"So, remind me, Doc. What time is the ceremony?"

"Ten-thirty."

Jack glances at his wristwatch.

"Oh, my gosh! We'd better get going."

Jack grips the shoulder bag hanging heavily from his chair and squeezes it to confirm its contents. Sarge is a keen observer, detecting Jack's satisfaction at finding everything in order in his satchel. He knows the feeling of being certain something is there, but checking anyway, often more than once. Now Sarge's curiosity is piqued. What does Jack have in that bag?

Having flagged down the waitress and paid the bill, Jack gets up and walks away from the table without his shoulder bag! He suddenly remembers, scolds himself, and retrieves it. Sarge gets a chuckle out of this and concludes that he should stick close to Jack. It is going to be one of those days! But he does so at his peril, when Jack suddenly stops in the middle of the lobby, causing a minor collision between the two aging veterans.

"It was right here. On this spot."

Sarge glances around the lobby and then back at Jack, who is apparently flush with a pleasant memory.

"The last time I saw her was right here."

Much has changed in the hotel over fifty years, but the ghosts remain.

Hotel Lebrun 1945

It is mid-January, and the fortunes of war have changed yet again. A dozen officers file out of a staff meeting in Roberts' command post, Jack and Hank among them. They form animated knots in the lobby to discuss the rapidly shifting situation in the Ardennes.

After the breakthrough to Bastogne from the south, Patton's forces continued to repulse German attacks east and west of the Assenois Road and to widen the relief corridor between Neufchâteau and Bastogne. As a result, US Army traffic is moving largely unmolested, bringing in reinforcements and supplies. Though the Germans continue to hammer away at Bastogne's defenders from several directions, the town has not fallen, thanks to the combined efforts and grit of the 101st Airborne Division, the 10th Armored Division, the 705th Tank Destroyer Battalion, and Team SNAFU. Now, with American and British forces pressuring the enemy from the north, any German forces west of Bastogne and Houffalize face the threat of being cut off and systematically reduced. While ground forces hack away at German positions, the dreaded American fighter-bombers known to the Germans as *Jabos* rule the skies over the Ardennes. The heady first days of the counteroffensive are a distant memory for the *Werhmacht*.

Based on Roberts' briefing, Hank is confident that the defenders of Bastogne will soon go on the offensive. As he listens to his friend, Jack ponders how this portends a new surge of casualties. At least this time around there is an abundance of medicine and surgical talent. The nightmare of holding gravely wounded men without hope of evacuation is over. But the anguish he felt, and the cries of pain he heard, will haunt Jack for the rest of his life.

Chiwy steps into the hotel lobby and drapes her topcoat over her arm, revealing her St. Elizabeth nursing uniform. It has been thoroughly cleaned and brushed and fits her trim physique like a glove. She has done her hair and applied makeup, but it is her smile that lights up the lobby. She approaches Jack.

"Hello, Doctor."

It has been some time since Jack has seen her, with Chiwy hard at work at the 101st aid station and Jack assisting surgical teams in town. At the sound of Chiwy's voice, Jack turns and takes in a sight for sore eyes.

"Nurse Chiwy. Wow! You look terrific!"

He sweeps his hand through the air along the length of her body, but is suddenly self-conscious, almost blushing.

"I mean... uh... your outfit."

Chiwy responds with a full measure of mischief in her eyes.

"Thank you, Doctor."

Jack recovers.

"I thought you already left for Leuven."

"I leave today."

"Which way will you go?"

She sees concern creeping into Jack's expression. There is still a great deal of fighting in the Ardennes. Fortunately, the Germans never crossed the River Meuse, and some trains are running again west of that strategic river.

"I will go the long way... Neufchâteau, Dinant, Namur. Don't worry, I will be safe. When will you leave Bastogne?"

"Hard to say. But it could be any day now."

"So, I want to give you something from Renee."

Chiwy stands on her toes and leans in, while Jack instinctively bends to her. She gives him a light peck on the cheek. He catches the scent of her perfume. After living with so much stench and waste and death, he breathes it in gratefully. A few officers offer low whistles for what appears to them to be a gesture of affection.

Chiwy is single-minded in her purpose and pays them no mind.

"And this is from me."

Now Chiwy's eyes are dancing, full of life, and the mischief has migrated to her smile. She gives his other cheek a more prolonged kiss.

"Ooh la la, Captain."

As Jack's face reddens, this is enough for Hank, who steps in to educate the officers who know little to nothing about Chiwy and her tireless efforts to save American lives. Sure, they knew about Renee, everyone did. And yeah, sure, there was another nurse at the aid station. But for most of them, Chiwy would forever stand in Renee's long shadow. Nevertheless, they mean no disrespect.

Chiwy turns her attention to her handbag, which she opens and sorts through while Jack turns to the men with a shrug of the shoulders. Finding what she sought, Chiwy reaches to Jack's left chest pocket.

"And this is so you will never forget."

Jack turns back to Chiwy and finds her flattening the flap of the pocket. When she looks up to him, he meets a gaze full of depth and meaning and concentrates on her words.

"It's a gift."

Jack responds with a puzzled smile as Chiwy fusses over his uniform a bit more. When she stands back to appreciate just how good Jack looks showered, shaved, and laundered, Hank cannot resist a gentle tease of his friend.

"Hey, Nurse Chiwy. Bet you didn't think he could clean up so well."

She turns to Hank with laughing eyes and a smile that thanks him for all the support and friendship he has given the doctor. When she turns back to Jack, she catches his eyes once again and offers softly, just above a whisper.

"Remember."

Hotel Lebrun 1994

Jack is lost in thought, looking around a lobby overcrowded with apparitions, as faces and gestures recall men he once knew. In such an otherworldly atmosphere, movement is slowed and sound is muted, save for an old clock that methodically measures the mortality of mankind and questions what matters. What is wheat and what is chaff? What is wheat and what is chaff?

Then, the voice. Her voice.

"Remember."

Jack experiences a moment of absolute clarity as all the tumblers locked away in his memories click into place. His inner voice speaks aloud.

"I remember."

"Yeah, sure, Doc. Remember..."

Since reuniting, Sarge has marveled at Jack's ability to transport himself back and forth through time, to bring the dark days of Bastogne back to life, while shedding light and meaning upon them. Most men would be whipsawed by the experience! Now, as Jack lingers, Sarge is keeping an eye on the hour.

"... but do it at the ceremony."

Thanks to a morning of warm hospitality and darn good coffee, the two men are in high spirits as they cross the street to Place Général McAuliffe, where they enter thin, low-lying fog. While several people are about, Jack takes special notice of a very elderly man bundled against the damp being wheeled slowly across the square by a youthful health aide. The old man is tightly gripping a bit of newspaper in his knobby, arthritic hand as he stares into the mist ahead of him.

Jack's gaze lights upon a restaurant at the far corner of the square and, seeing that there is time enough, leads Sarge across the open plaza. By way of Jack's expression, Sarge knows the telltale signs of another ghost hunt in progress. Stopping in front of the Giorgi Restaurant, a popular eatery, Jack is certain.

"This has got to be it. The hardware store was here."

"Oh, you mean Lemaire's place."

Peering through the glass, Jack sees beyond the tables being set in expectation of lunchtime diners, and through the veil of time. Lemaire and Jaquin are there. And Renee can be faintly heard singing in the storeroom. Then she appears, a dark-eyed beauty! The sense of relief and reinforcement he felt when the nurse volunteered is as fresh as if it happened yesterday. It all slips away when Renee turns out to be a comely young waitress smiling and waving "hello" to Jack.

Nonetheless, Jack has a surge of energy as he walks away from the restaurant, causing Sarge to double-quick step a couple of times to keep up. They reach the bronze statue of General McAuliffe midway in the square and entertain their private thoughts and impressions of the man who steered the defense of Bastogne with a very steady hand. They linger too long there, however, and Sarge begins to sense reluctance in Jack. Something seems to be sapping his friend's strength and resolve.

With some prodding from Sarge, they make their way to the Sherman tank parked at the top of Rue de Neufchâteau, where Sarge ponders the fate of the crew of a tank holed by a German antitank shell. He locates the commemorative plaque and reads it aloud.

"This tank, knocked out in December 44, recalls the sacrifice of all the fighters for the liberation of Bastogne and Belgium."

Sarge is moved by the sentiment. He turns to express his appreciation, but finds Jack enthralled by a small crowd gathering down Rue de

Neufchâteau, where the aid station once stood. Sarge knows the score by now and waits patiently by. As he does so, Sarge turns his attention to the old man being carefully wheeled down the hill toward the gathering. His aide seems hardly more than a girl.

"Hang on tight there, little lady."

Jack's mind is elsewhere. The small crowd disappears in the mist, and the hollers of desperation from men trapped in the burning building echo up the street. They seem to be everywhere, faces disembodied, swirling about in the fog. Jack has tussled with dark thoughts throughout the years since that fateful night, but this time he feels completely surrounded. They are too powerful here. He turns to Sarge as if in a confessional. Sarge is fully aware of the significance of this day's event, and of the tug-of-war Jack must be feeling, and intuitively gives Jack a brotherly pat on the shoulder.

"Doc, you couldn't save them all."

No discernable reaction from Jack.

"And for heaven's sake, you couldn't stop the bomb!"

Sarge is making every effort to join Jack's team, even to pinch-hit for him in battling the faces and voices in the mist. Jack finally stirs.

"No, I guess not. But I should have been with them. I left my post."

Sarge is unable to find the words to express how unfair Jack is being to himself. But words are unnecessary among old comrades. By his presence beside Jack, he exerts a powerful, positive force that helps Jack work his way back completely to the moment.

"You know, I've waited a long time for this day. Now... I don't feel equal to it."

"Well, sure you are, Doc."

"She should be here for this."

"Chiwy?"

"Yeah, I guess I need her here."

A middle-aged man wearing his Sunday-best separates from the crowd and calls out to Jack.

"Hello, Doctor Prior!"

Striding up the street with great purpose, the mayor of Bastogne is quickly upon them. He shakes hands with Sarge and Jack vigorously, takes their arms in his own, and proudly walks them down the street and into the modest gathering. With the exception of the veterans from the pub who have assembled at the rear of the crowd, Jack is among strangers. But, thanks to the town newspaper, they know all about him and the aging Americans, sons of Bastogne one and all, who have returned to their second home after fifty long years.

A hush falls over the crowd. The mayor offers a few words of introduction, then invites Jack to share what he has in his shoulder bag. Jack pulls out a bronze plaque he commissioned before departing for the reunion. He clears his throat, finds his voice, and reads the inscription.

"In memoriam. Site of the AID Station of the 20th AIB 10th Armored Division where over thirty US wounded and one volunteer, Belgian nurse Renee Lemaire, were instantly killed by a German bomb. December 24, 1944."

There is polite applause from the townspeople, nods of appreciation from the veterans, and a discreet thumbs-up from Sarge. After an assistant to the mayor produces a hammer and tacks the plaque to the building, the mayor steps forward.

"Now, Doctor, if you will permit me to read your words in French."

As the mayor translates the plaque, Jack scans the crowd, looking from face to face. The people give him many smiles in return. There is no sign of Chiwy, but the old man in a wheelchair is there, gripping his newspaper and studying Jack's face with watery eyes.

The mayor finishes his reading to louder applause and chatter among the townspeople. As he shakes Jack's hand, the mayor takes his leave.

"Thank you, Doctor. I am sorry, but I have another duty to attend to."

Jack watches the young politician work through the crowd as it slowly disperses, among them the health aide who has turned the old man in the wheelchair around. No one notices the frailest of signs in the old man's body language, the newspaper raised in his shaking hand, or the eyelids blinking with frustration. As the wheelchair rolls away up the street and back into the light fog, Jack joins the veterans, who are effusive with praise.

"That was really something, Doc, remembering those boys after all these years."

"And the nurse, Renee Lemaire."

"The Angel of Bastogne."

Sarge feels a need to interject.

"Yeah. But remember. There were two angels of Bastogne."

Jack listens as though from a distance, feeling a bit faint. Ever the healer, he wonders. Is it dehydration? The toasts did go on and on last night. Perhaps he'd better stick to red wine. He scans other medical possibilities for his lightheadedness and rejects them all. In a toss of whimsy, he notes that his shoulder bag is light one plaque. Is his burden lighter as well? Now that he has fixed that fateful Christmas Eve forever in bronze, will the stubborn spirits call it all square and let him be? Somehow, while on this strange path of conjecture, Jack manages to stumble on the curb and into the street. Colleti shouts in alarm.

"Watch it, Doc!"

Colleti is surprisingly agile and strong for all his years as he pulls Jack from the path of a purple-haired, punk-rock teenager zipping by on a moped. Suddenly, the old MP is wide-eyed at the coincidence. This is their second dance on this very spot!

"Wow, you couldn't make this stuff up. It's like Yogi Berra says... it's *déjà vu* all over again."

Jack is apologetic.

"Sorry, I forgot myself for a moment."

"No problem, Doc. I forget myself all the time. It's the other stuff I can't forget..."

Colleti pauses as he looks around at nothing in particular.

"... the sounds... the smells..."

Jack takes up the thread.

"The faces and the voices. I still hear them."

Jack and Colleti share a special bond and a solemn memory. It was here that each was tested on that cold, dark Christmas Eve. They were tasked with keeping order and saving lives that night when it seemed humanly impossible to do either. Somehow, they muddled through. During the painful days that followed, the wreckage yielded the remains of Jack's nurse and several dozen young men. For all the broken bodies recovered, one stayed with Colleti long after the others turned into the dust of buried memories. He can see him now, Jack's driver, a wise guy who needled him and managed to elude discipline. An artful dodger if he ever saw one. He also remembers the grudging respect he gave the corporal after the escape from Noville and how Beagle cried when his buddy's body was found. He can still see the young soldier holding his lifeless friend tight until the graves registration boys gently separated the two.

As Colleti wipes a tear from his eye, Jack produces a handkerchief from his shoulder bag for him.

When they rejoin their group, Jack and Colleti find that the veterans have huddled for some reason. They surround a young Asian woman in a bright white smock holding a tray of food samples. It is at this moment that Jack realizes that the building now adorned with his plaque is a Chinese restaurant and that the enterprising proprietor is taking full advantage of the event. Sarge is particularly impressed with the Szechuan chicken.

"Mmm, very tasty."

Having whetted their appetites, the veterans make plans to retreat to the tavern for lunch. As Jack takes one last look around, he hears a voice calling out.

"Doctor! Doctor Prior!"

He turns to see a lively woman of a certain age stepping through the dwindling crowd, but he does not recognize her. She gives him a hand.

"It is Maggie."

"Maggie?"

Then he spies the pendant of the angel Raphael holding an infant around her neck. There must be only one like it in the world. Jack is whisked back in time once again.

"Marguerite?"

Marguerite follows his eyes to the pendant.

"Yes, yes, from Renee. You remember."

"Yes, I remember."

"Look who is staying with me."

Marguerite's half turn opens the way for a tiny woman shuffling toward Jack, clutching a cane. Marguerite tries to assist her, but Chiwy shoos her away. She will make this journey of five meters and fifty years to reunite with Doctor Prior without any help. Jack thought so then, and he is no less certain now. There is only one Augusta Chiwy!

"Nurse Chiwy."

"Doctor Prior."

As they step closer, Chiwy wobbles a bit. Jack responds automatically to her infirmity, and Chiwy waves him off as well. She regains her balance and approaches Jack. He bends down to her and they share kisses on each other's cheeks, and doesn't he get a whiff of her perfume once again? He breathes it in and breaks out in a smile. She wobbles once more, and he takes her free hand to steady her. This time she accepts the support. He searches for something to say, then finally offers.

"It's so nice you recognize me. I've changed so much."

"No, for me, you are the same."

It occurs to Jack that Sarge is right on the money. He said that eyes never change, and Jack is struck by how Chiwy's still dance, full of life, with a hint of mischief. The years are swept away as they explore the windows to each other's souls for a moment. It is a most welcome sojourn.

Jack suddenly feels remiss and calls out to the veterans standing by.

"Fellas! Meet Marguerite, Renee Lemaire's sister. And this is Nurse Augusta Chiwy."

Marguerite is quick to add.

"An angel of mercy!"

And Sarge is even quicker.

"The unsung heroine of Bastogne!"

"Shush! Stop it, both of you."

In spite of her modesty, Chiwy is beaming with pride. The veterans speak almost as one.

"It's an honor to meet you, Madame."

"Doc Prior told us all about you."

"You saved so many of our boys."

Chiwy insists that she was only doing her job.

"I am a nurse. It is what I do."

But there is no stopping the old boys as they line up to shake her hand. Several ask to have photographs taken with her, and she acquiesces. Then several veterans hand their cameras to Marguerite, and they assemble for a group shot with Chiwy. She beckons for Jack to join them and he completes the picture. It makes the veterans' day. When they break up and begin to head back up to the square, Sarge catches Jack's attention.

"Doc, we're gonna grab a bite at the pub, before the shuttle."

"OK, I'll meet you there."

Meanwhile Marguerite and Chiwy have stepped over to Jack's plaque. Marguerite caresses the raised letters spelling Renee's name and dabs at her eyes. As she observes Jack from a distance, she expresses what is in her heart.

"He's such a good man."

Chiwy agrees.

"Yes, and... he has kind eyes."

Jack has not overheard, but when he returns to them he can surmise what sentiments have passed between the ladies by the affection expressed in their eyes.

"Thank you, Doctor, for remembering my sister."

This time it is Marguerite who steps up to give Jack a fond embrace. She steps back to wipe her teary eyes, leaving Jack deeply moved by her gesture. So much has passed among the three of them during just a few minutes that words cannot do justice to what they feel as they stand together in comfortable silence. Finally, they exchange information on their plans for the week and resolve to meet later in the evening for dinner at Hotel Lebrun.

But there is just one last thing, one puzzle that remains unsolved. Jack digs into his pocket and produces a rectangle of white silk. It is cut by pinking shears with a dark stain on its edge. He lays it on his palm and holds it out to Chiwy with questioning eyes. Chiwy smiles and, with Marguerite's hand to steady her, digs in her purse. She produces and unfolds an almost identical piece of silk and pairs it with Jack's, reuniting the dark stains of Renee's blood.

The Nuts Festival

The three of them part company at the top of the street, as Chiwy and Marguerite head home and Jack angles toward the tavern. The fog has dissipated, and a freshening breeze breathes life into the countless American and Belgian flags hanging around the square. Uplifted by his encounter with the ladies and feeling years younger, it seems to Jack that everything is right with the world.

As he fairly strides along, he becomes aware of an assemblage of animated townspeople just down Rue Houffalize. On seeing that the shuttle has yet to arrive at Le Nut's, he decides to investigate. When Jack steps in among them, he is intrigued by the growing anticipation in their uniformly upturned faces. Suddenly, the crowd starts to scramble as walnuts in the shell begin to rain from the sky. Jack looks up to the balcony of the town hall, where the mayor is flanked by a young couple who are tossing handfuls into the crowd.

"What the hell?"

"Excuse me, Monsieur?"

Jack turns round to find a stout gentleman near his own age grinning widely at him, amused by Jack's puzzlement at the unexpected turn of events. Jack receives his outstretched hand.

"I am François Dumonde."

"Jack Prior."

They shake while the walnuts continue to fall like hailstones amid shouts, cheers, and laughter. François takes a close look at Jack's nametag.

"10th Armored Division? I was with the 5th Belgian Fusiliers."

When the Belgian turns his attention to the falling nuts, Jack joins in the merriment. But his reflexes are not what they used to be, not by a long shot. After several failed attempts to catch a nut, he gives up and turns to query François.

"What is all this?"

François laughs.

"So, I will tell you. From the very olden days, the people came in from the farms to celebrate the, how do you say, *la moisson*, uh... the harvest of the tree nuts. It is the Nuts Festival!"

"Ha! A Nuts Festival in Bastogne. What a coincidence."

François ponders the meaning of the word, then he brightens.

"Oh, yes, *une coïncidence*. Bastogne is also famous for "Nuts!" thanks to your General McAuliffe."

François turns his attention to the falling nuts, continuing his story as he catches a walnut and hands it to Jack.

"It was always in *l'automme*, when the young men and women came into town from their farms to... you know... to make a match. It still is, but this year we also have a special ceremony today, for all of our visitors."

François indicates other veterans amongst the townspeople. Jack recognizes several from the parade and exchanges nods and smiles with them, as François continues.

"My grandfather, even my father, grew many nuts here. But now..."

François catches another walnut and holds it out as "Exhibit A."

"... they come from California!"

Jack shares a laugh with François and surrenders completely to the great spirit of the ancient ritual. Momentarily as joyful as a child, Jack lunges several more times and finally snags a walnut. He turns a beaming face to François, who offers one more nugget of information while pointing up at the balcony.

"Oh, and you see this young man and woman? They are *les nouveaux mariés*."

Jack processes the French words.

"New... hmm... married. Oh, they are newlyweds."

"*Exactement*. It is the tradition."

Just as suddenly as they started, the nuts stop falling. The young couple blows kisses from the balcony while the crowd slowly disperses, abuzz with expressions of joy and good will. Delighted by the whole affair, Jack lingers, taking it all in. When he finally gets underway back up toward the square, François falls in step with him and looks up at the tall American.

"You were here in Bastogne?"

"That's right, and in Noville."

"Ah, Noville. *Très triste*... a very sad story."

François' mood darkens considerably, but with Jack's expression of keen interest he feels compelled to continue.

"When the *Boche* left, we found many of our people murdered. Just citizens, do you see? No collaborators."

When François goes silent, consulting with his ghosts perhaps, Jack keeps his peace. But he pipes up when the vacant eyes of the old couple huddled in the basement come to him.

"Wait! What about the tavern keepers? Were they killed?"

"Well, they executed the priest and the teacher... but..."

François digs deep.

"... no, I am sure of it. The old man and woman lived for many more years."

Jack is clearly comforted by this news, to François' relief.

"You will go to Noville?"

"I was there yesterday."

"Did you see the monument behind the church? The names of the murdered ones are on the stone. *Le Sept du Noville*."

"Yes, I was there. Wait... did you say seven? I counted eight names."

"Yes, eight. Seven from Noville, and a boy from Luxembourg."

As the two men stroll along, one would be excused for assuming them to be lifelong friends with countless shared reminiscences, so fully engaged are they. François continues.

"The *Boche* would force the boy to fight with them. But, no, he would not. So, he ran away to Belgium. He was hiding in Noville."

When they crest the rise, they shuffle to a stop and take in the flag-festooned square. Several doors down, a shuttle bus pulls up to Le Nut's. Jack is ready to shift gears, but an impression from his visit to Noville asserts itself.

"I saw an old man planting flowers around the stone."

"Ah, yes, the old man. He is there, *toujours*. Always."

Before Jack can quiz François further, Sarge calls out from the queue of veterans who are trickling out of the tavern and boarding the bus.

"There you are, Doc. I thought you were gonna miss it."

Jack is so thoroughly captivated by his new friend, that he rightly believes the other veterans would enjoy François as well. He extends an invitation to the amiable Belgian veteran.

"We're going up to the American memorial on Mardasson Hill. Would you care to join us?"

"Yes, yes. I am happy to join. My farm is very near to there."

"Fellas, say hello to François Dumonde of the 5th Belgian Fusiliers."

Several veterans shake François' hand and usher him aboard with them, leaving Jack at the tail end of the line. On the verge of boarding, he hears the voice of a young woman calling out.

"Sir? Your pardon?"

It is the teenaged health aide from the plaque ceremony pushing the old man, whose eyes are wide as he points his rolled-up newspaper at Jack. The girl is very agitated, almost on the verge of tears.

"I am sorry, sir. But I think he tries to see you. He is always stopping the wheel with his hand and making me to turn!"

Jack slowly lowers himself to one knee beside the old man and examines his wiry hand. The palm has been rubbed raw and it seems to Jack that the young woman is certain she will be blamed for his injury.

"Why would he want to see me?"

The old man tries to speak but cannot. Instead, he proffers his newspaper to Jack, who finds his name circled in a notice about the plaque dedication in the Bastogne weekly. He looks up from the paper into eyes that are beginning to sparkle, within an ancient body that becomes as energized as it possibly can, despite severe limitations. Jack tries to read the tea leaves.

"Perhaps he just remembers the war. What is his name?"

"He is Monsieur Jaquin."

"Jaquin? Can it be?"

The old man has yet another surge of energy and, to his aide's great dismay, rocks with excitement in his chair. Jack carefully wraps Jaquin's withered body in his arms. It is a tender moment witnessed by the veterans on the bus who are seated on that side. Sergio bounds out of the tavern, onto the bus, and into the driver's seat. Time to go, but Jack and Jaquin continue to embrace as Jack searches for words to say. He finds that there is no way he can express how vital the pharmacist was to his sanity during the siege.

Sarge taps on the window. Jack waves in acknowledgment and stands. He questions the aide.

"Where is Monsieur staying?"

She tries to respond but is still at sixes and sevens. Instead, she reaches into her pocket and pulls out the business card of a senior home in Bastogne. She hands it to Jack, who in turn addresses Jaquin.

"May I come to visit tomorrow?"

Jaquin's eyes, eyes that have seen nearly a century of horror and hope, fill with tears of joy.

The First Six Notes

It is slow going through town for the shuttle as the narrow two-lane road is further squeezed by parked cars lining both sides. The business district of Bastogne is hopping, having rolled out the red carpet for the reunion. It has turned into a beautiful day, and the sidewalks are crowded with visitors, shoppers, and lunch-breakers. Jack watches from the bus as friends meet and exchange pleasantries or catch up on family news. Now and again, someone recognizes the veterans inching by, having seen the parade or witnessed them walking about for several days in Bastogne. Tending toward youthfulness, they watch and wave. Here and there are elders who lived through the war. They are unaware of the passing bus and happy just to navigate the sidewalk without losing their balance.

The day has been full to the brim already for Jack. Marguerite and Chiwy at the dedication. A chance encounter with an affable Belgian veteran. And then Jaquin! He is suffused with warmth and well-being, and gradually realizes that the music playing on a cassette that Sergio plugged in is reinforcing his feelings. Sarge is closest to the driver and leans in to comment on the music.

"Hey, Sergio..."

His first impulse is to request the oldies. But he changes his tune upon observing the young man's evident enchantment with the piece.

"... what's that music?"

"Oh, yes, sir. It is Chopin, Opus 9, E-flat Nocturne."

Apparently, the piece has been a bone of contention between Simpson and Brown seated behind Sarge, and an opportunity for one to gloat.

"Ha! Chopin! What'd I tell ya?"

Sergio catches Sarge's eye in the rear-view mirror.

"Shall I change it?"

"No, please. Let it play."

When the traffic comes to a complete standstill, Sergio turns to Sarge.

"I listen to this music when I am driving... to be peaceful."

Sarge gets a kick out of this, even as he observes growing signs of impatience from the young man stuck in bumper-to-bumper traffic. To compensate, Sergio slides into the role of a tour conductor, one of several part-time jobs he pieces together for a decent income. In this role he is a veritable font of information and anecdotes.

"It is interesting to know that Chopin dedicated the piece to Marie Pleyel, a famous Belgian concert pianist of the last century."

As he listens to Sergio, Sarge is impressed with the young man's command of English. Heck, he has been continually amazed at how many languages most Belgians speak, and speak well. There is no question now that Sarge is a convert. If Sergio has a fan club, he wants to be a member.

"You sure know your classical music."

Sarge settles back and reflects on how well the day is turning out. To grapple with his personal demons in Bastogne, he has employed a variety of stratagems, his good humor foremost. Now, several days into the reunion, Sarge is finding that he needs this ploy less and less. The apparitions have nearly faded away, replaced by the smiles of the townspeople and the camaraderie of the veterans. As he loses himself in the lilting Chopin melody, the whole world seems to be in perfect harmony, and Sarge is blissfully silent, for once. Jaworski takes advantage of a lull in the action to offer Jack a compliment.

"That was really something today, what you did for those soldiers and that nurse. What an awesome experience you had here."

"What about you? You were at McAuliffe's HQ. That must've been memorable."

"Nah, I was just the mapmaker."

"Mapmaker? The daily situation maps?"

"Just during the siege, then Patton's boys took over."

"I relied on those maps. They brought order to the chaos. They still do." Jaworski feigns a scolding tone as he wags his finger.

"You weren't supposed to hang on to them."

"Yeah, I know. If I got captured, the Germans would know the disposition of our forces. But I figured if they reached where I was, our goose was cooked anyway."

"Ha! Can't argue with that."

The shuttle finally begins to move forward. Animated conversations between François and several veterans seated around him capture Jack's attention momentarily. But as the sidewalks of Bastogne roll slowly by, Jack becomes lost once again in the faces he sees and the stories they tell. Ever the close observer of the human condition, he wonders who they are, if they are healthy, whether they have loved and lost, and if they are lonely. What does the future hold for them?

Wordlessly, sadness and joy, faith and despair, fullness and solitude, and the full spectrum of human emotions rise up to Jack in response. The heightened sensitivity of a lifelong healer is a blessing and a curse. Life is a gift. But it can be taken away. You can't save them all.

Knowing how forgetful he can be, Jack moves his shoulder bag from the seat beside him to his lap. He examines the contents within and is satisfied with what he finds. But a powerful scent from the bag is a trigger. He closes his eyes and they are there once again, the voices, the faces, the shouts of agony. Jack opens his eyes and they are gone, though he continues to be surprised by the intensity of his feelings here, in Bastogne. In a well-practiced manner, he shakes it all off. Yet he hugs his shoulder bag all the more tightly to his chest.

Jack turns to Jaworski and finally picks up the dangling thread of their conversation.

"Yeah, the maps. I confess that for a long time I put them away with everything else and tried to forget the whole thing."

"You had it rough, no question about it. But I'm glad to see you stuck to doctoring."

"Well, no, I switched to pathology."

"How's that?"

"Research. I heard enough cries of pain to last me a lifetime."

The shuttle stops abruptly and draws closer attention from several pedestrians, including a young mother who kneels to point out and explain who the veterans are to her son. The little boy gives a rudimentary salute, and Jack returns it in kind. It is another surprising intersection of past and present for Jack, and he wonders if any other veterans saw the boy.

"Hey, did you see...?"

Will, seated alone several seats back, is looking out that way but seems to be in his own world again. The rest of the veterans are engrossed in conversation, including Simpson and Brown, who seem to be engaged in another one of their mutual snits. Jack turns back to the window to prolong the heart-warming experience but finds no trace of the woman or the boy on the crowded sidewalk.

Sarge has apparently been simmering on a stove and finally blurts out a question for the two antagonists that has nagged him for a couple of days.

"You know, I just gotta ask you guys. For all the pissin' and moanin' you do, why are you always together... joined at the hip?"

Brown is emphatic.

"Believe me, if I could get away from the son-of-a-bitch, I would."

"Likewise."

They are clearly not birds of a feather, and Sarge is now groping to make sense of it.

"OK, I just don't get it. How'd you guys meet up anyway?"

"Thought you'd never ask."

Here we go again! Simpson rolls his eyes as his erstwhile comrade and verbal pugilist launches into a story Simpson has suffered through many, many times.

"It was D-Day. We jumped around 2:00 in the morning and the flak was bursting all around us. It was like jumping into fireworks, you know, like the grand finale. You could see the tracers coming up right at you. They had me zeroed in! I was flapping my arms so hard to get clear, I swear I flew to safety!"

"What a crock of shit! The wind blew us all over creation!"

"I'm tellin' you I flew! Like I had wings."

All are listening to Brown now and join in guffawing away the nonsense, but unwittingly encouraging him to continue since he now has a captive audience.

"Anyway, after all that, don't I land in a lake? The bastards flooded the fields to drown us, carrying seventy pounds of gear like we did. But I grabbed a root and pulled myself out. Then I froze! There was something in the bushes, so I pulled out my cricket."

Simpson adds his two cents in a bored, matter-of-fact manner.

"You clicked once, I clicked twice."

"You're getting ahead of me. Anyway, that cricket saved a lot of lives. Happen to still have mine!"

He reaches into his blazer pocket. Has he kept the cricket there all along waiting for the right moment? Brown's exuberance falters when he finds his pocket empty.

"Oh, hell! What did I do with... ah!"

His other pocket yields the little metal clicker that was issued to all the D-Day airborne troops to help them identify their comrades in the darkness. Anticipating interest among the veterans, he hands the cricket to Simpson, who starts the clicker on its journey, hand-to-hand, around the bus. Brown is beaming.

"It was the sweetest sound I ever heard!"

"We agree on that! But that was the last time we agreed on anything!"

"Stop interrupting me! So out of the bushes steps this knucklehead right here."

Simpson ignores him and continues along his line.

"Case in point? Our objective was the bridgehead on the Merderet River. So, I sez let's go, and I move out. And this bonehead sez I'm going the wrong way!"

"Well, you were!"

Sarge jumps in.

"I get it now. You were all turned around in the drop and didn't know where the hell you were! You guys met on a blind date!"

He scores with this one and then doubles down.

"What'd ya have, a shotgun wedding?"

Polite laughter subsides, making space for McEvoy, who has also been trying to puzzle out what ties this odd couple of old troopers together. He decides he has been digging too deeply.

"Look, I get it. You're both airborne. It's as simple as that."

Brown shoots him down.

"Nah, that ain't it. I just can't get away from him."

In spite of themselves, several of the veterans are lured into Brown's web, to the sheer delight of the weaver. His grudging seatmate is forced to play along. The veterans take turns venturing explanations.

"Seems pretty clear to me. A couple of boys, lost and scared to death, find each other."

"And live to tell the story."

"They shared a baptism of fire."

"An unforgettable experience."

"An unbreakable bond."

"Blood brothers for life."

Simpson and Brown bat down all the speculations with shrugs and head shakes. Having been silent the long while, the Scot finally antes up.

"Which puts me in mind of Shakespeare."

He seems to have an inexhaustible store of famous quotations.

"From this day forward to the ending of the world,
But we in it shall be remembered—
We few, we happy few, we band of brothers;
For he today that sheds his blood with me
Shall be my brother."

Simpson throws cold water.

"Yeah, but nah. That ain't exactly it."

Now patience is wearing thin, especially with the Scot, who expected a better reception for his recitation of the bard's wisdom. Realizing that the string is running out, Brown offers a deadpan explanation.

"Look, I literally can't get away from this jackass. He lives next door."

Sarge takes the bait.

"How the hell did that happen?"

"We married sisters."

Simpson, who always gives the final punchline, however reluctantly, proclaims from the only stage he'll ever stand on.

"Twins."

A chorus of guffaws is followed by Sarge's commiseration.

"You poor bastards!"

Taunts and laughter soon give way to an interlude of reflection as the traffic thins and the bus picks up speed.

In the ensuing calm, Jack finds himself studying the side streets for landmarks. Was this the side street to Chiwy's clinic? He remembers walking down the road with Jaquin. Was it about here that they turned? It was one of the most important days of his life. First, they sought out Chiwy, then Renee. What would he have done without them? He shudders even now to think of the alternatives, all bad. His train of thought is interrupted when Sergio says to no one in particular.

"We are coming to Saint Pierre. The Gothic hall was built in the 15th century, but the tower dates to the 11th and 12th centuries."

François takes his cue and offers his thoughts about the significance of the church.

"During all the fighting, the church bell was ringing for the people of Bastogne. And now..."

Studying his wristwatch closely as the hands tick toward noon, François is joined in anticipation by the veterans. Their patience is rewarded when the new bells of Saint Pierre ring six distinctive, familiar notes.

"... now they ring for you."

Sarge identifies the first six notes of The Star-Spangled Banner.

"Well, I'll be damned. Oh–oh say can you see? Belgium sure knows how to say thank you! Is it just for the reunion?"

François reassures him.

"No, we will always remember."

Mardasson Hill

The veterans ponder the surprising tribute as the bus follows the right-hand turn beyond the church and onto Rue du Clervaux. Their meditative silence persists for so long that François is almost reluctant to interrupt their reverie.

"Ah, here is *le tournant*."

François indicates a left-hand fork onto a secondary road. Sergio makes the turn, downshifts, and begins a long, slow ascent toward a hilltop that is completely obscured by trees. It is the first time up the hill for all of the veterans aboard, except for Jack.

It was fifty years ago, that mad dash up the hill with Chiwy and his aides. But it takes no effort whatsoever for Jack to recall the wrecked vehicles; the concussion of artillery shells landing nearby; the hollow eyes of troopers who were living, eating, sleeping, and fighting outside in the cold for days on end; and the gut-wrenching discovery of the Noville medic lifeless on the ground.

Just as quickly as it obscured his vision, the veil of reminiscence lifts, and the drab, snowbound battleground Jack remembers so well yields an early-summer world of bright colors. The fields and the forests are lush and green. Red poppies line the road, waving in a gentle breeze at the end of their blooming cycle in one more plea for all who pass to remember.

Bastogne Remembers

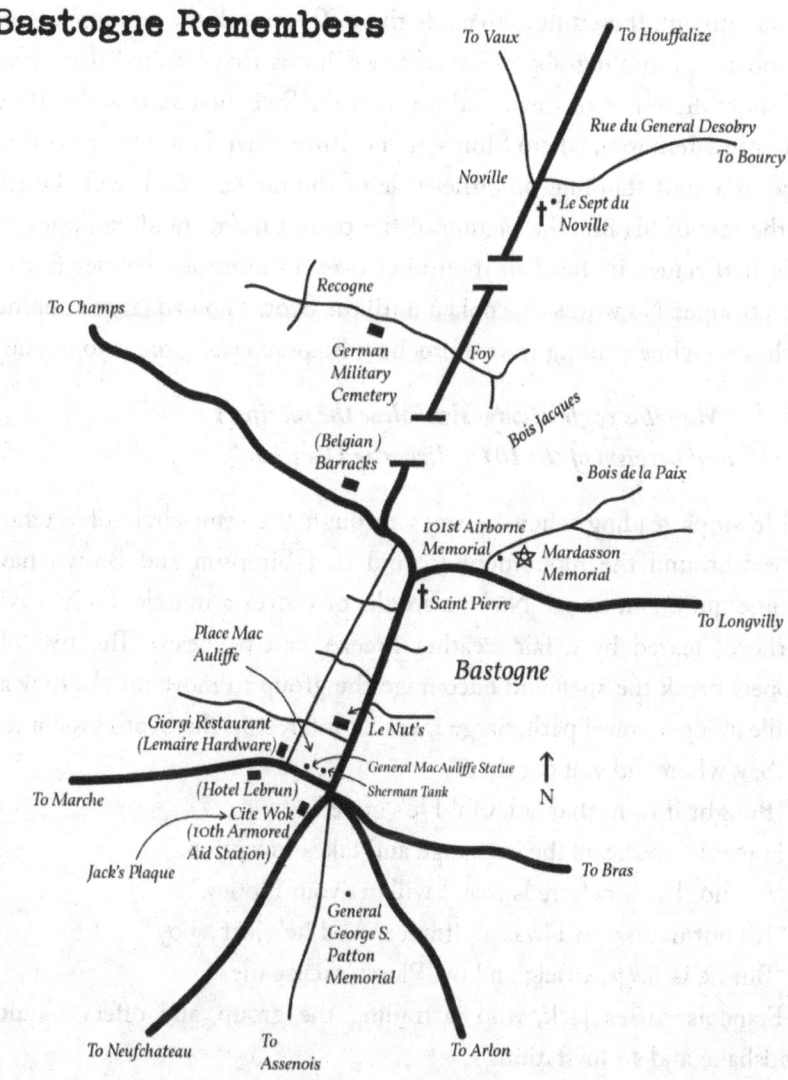

To Vaux

To Houffalize

Rue du General Desobry

To Bourcy

Noville

† Le Sept du
Noville

Recogne

To Champs

German
Military
Cemetery

Foy

Bois Jacques

(Belgian)
Barracks

Bois de la Paix

101st Airborne
Memorial

Mardasson
Memorial

† Saint Pierre

To Longvilly

Place Mac
Auliffe

Bastogne

Giorgi Restaurant
(Lemaire Hardware)

Le Nut's

General MacAuliffe Statue

To Marche

(Hotel Lebrun)

Sherman Tank

N

Cite Wok
(10th Armored
Aid Station)

Jack's Plaque

To Bras

General
George S.
Patton
Memorial

To Neufchateau

To
Assenois

To Arlon

As they crest the hill, Sergio begins his spiel on the monument for the benefit of his new American friends.

"The construction began in 1946. When they were excavating, soil from the site was sent to your President Truman."

When he glances in the mirror, the young man sees that he lost his audience, as the veterans try to see through the trees and catch a glimpse of the monument. It continues to elude them. They reach the parking lot and disembark, grumbling about the stiffened limbs that resulted from even this short drive out of town and up the hill. Their first stop is the 101st Airborne Memorial, where Simpson and Brown hand over their cameras to be in a shot standing on either side of the marker. Each will cherish, for the rest of his life, the picture of the two of them standing beside an eagle that hangs its head in mourning over an upturned helmet from a fallen trooper. No words are spoken until the Scot, who had lagged behind, catches up while reading from a brochure he purchased from a young boy.

> *"May this eagle always symbolize the sacrifices*
> *and heroism of the 101st Airborne Division."*

He stops reading when he steps through the semi-circle of veterans arrayed around the monument to find that Simpson and Brown have become quite emotional. No one speaks or moves a muscle. Only leaves overhead, teased by a fair-weather breeze, can be heard. The two old troopers break the spell and encourage the group to move on. As they all shuffle along a gravel path, Sarge takes an interest in the Scot's brochure.

"Say, where did you get that?"

"Bought it from that lad. Oh! He's gone."

François overhears the exchange and takes exception.

"Ah, no. The brochure is free. I will get your money."

"It's not necessary. T'was a pittance. And he's just a boy."

"But he is *Belge*, a Belgian boy! Please excuse me."

François passes Jack, who is trailing the group, and offers a quick handshake and an invitation.

"Doctor, you must come to my home for a dinner. Dominique is *la meilleure cuisinière*, um, the best cook in Bastogne!"

"Dominique? Wait, do you have a boy... damn... what was his name?"

But François is gone in hot pursuit of the transgressing youth. As he marches down the path, François passes Will, who is far behind, detached from the veterans, plodding slowly up the path. Jack feels a twinge of concern and slows his steps so that Will might walk beside him. When the two reach the other veterans at the head of the path, they find the group stopped as one. Jack follows their line of sight to take in the massive, awe-inspiring monument on Mardasson Hill. Up on the open hilltop, the breeze has stiffened and begun to flutter and snap American flags hanging all around the grounds. After a spell, several veterans find benches that are placed for optimal views. As they settle in together, each keeps his thoughts to himself while taking in the magnificent, columned wings of a structure that, from overhead, takes the shape of a five-pointed American battle star. Finally, Sarge pipes up.

"Like I said, Belgium sure knows how to say thank you."

The Scot continues reading passages from the brochure.

> *"Dedicated 4 July 1946 to the memory of 76,890 soldiers in the Battle of the Bulge who were killed, wounded, or missing."*

He adds for no one in particular.

"And some, perhaps... are missing to this day."

Each veteran can picture friends they lost during the war. Even one or two who were never found. They can still hear their voices and see their faces as clearly as if they were sitting beside them. A fine picture they would make, boys barely out of their teens sitting next to old men in the twilight of their lives. Could they reach each other through time? If they could, how would they communicate? Would there be touch? Would there be feeling? Perhaps this is the kind of magical hilltop where they might converse, where they might indeed meet again. Eyes become misty with the effort. Then, ever so grudgingly, voices and visions evaporate, and the monument once again towers over them. The Scot looks up from his brochure and reads the expressions on the faces of his new friends.

"Sorry, mates. I've soured the mood."

Davenport has been silent for the most part all day, but he is quick to reassure the Scot.

"It's OK. It's why I'm here. To honor... "

He stumbles when he fails to drive away dark thoughts of eleven young men tortured and slain on a cold winter night so long ago. The doctor picks him up, determined to reduce the colonel's solitary burden.

"... and to remember."

Acting on his own advice, Jack summons the spirit of the closest friend he had in the service. Hank made it all the way to Bavaria only to become one of the last American casualties during the 10th Armored Division's campaign in 1945. Hank had every hope of surviving the war as German resistance crumbled before the Tiger Division's drive across southern Germany, but a sniper's bullet claimed him. He went to his maker haunted by what he witnessed the day before when the 10th Armored Division liberated a concentration camp near Landsberg.

Jack only hopes that the anguish Hank experienced, when he saw walking skeletons and dead bodies stacked like firewood, was mitigated by the fact that the Nazis were on the verge of utter collapse and defeat. By that point, they were scheduled to check into their permanent home in hell, compelling the ghosts of their victims to wander the earth forever, bearing witness and weeping wherever man's inhumanity to fellow man persists.

Will has just the one ghost. While Joey has never been far from his thoughts, once Will decided to go to the reunion his buddy became a daily presence. Now that Will is in Bastogne, each day has brought vivid memories ranging from frightening to absurd. Time and time again, Will catches himself shaking his head at something Joey said or did. He doesn't know whether to laugh or cry.

With all the other benches full, Will sits alone apart from the others. As the leaves chatter in the breeze above his head, Will contemplates the significance and purpose of the monument. It stirs him to slide a slim packet of letters out of his pocket. They are all from Joey's mother. He selects one.

> *"April 3, 1945. Dear Will. Thank you for your letter of March 17th and for your inquiry after my boy Joey's health. He is much the same as when he was shipped home last month. Though I pester them, the doctors won't say whether he will regain his faculties. They just say it's a miracle he's still alive with such a severe head wound."*

Will drops his hand holding the letter to his lap. As he looks up at the monument honoring Joey and 76,889 other American casualties during the Battle of the Bulge, an inner dialogue begun in 1945 unspools once again.

"I tried to protect him. I told him, over and over, Joey..."

He startles the veterans by shouting out.

"...Joey! Keep your head down!"

The anguish in his voice throws a series of flashes across Jack's radar of compassion.

"Are you OK?"

Will steadies himself, nods to Jack gratefully, and finds the tenuous path from guilt to absolution. It gives him just enough strength to continue reading the letter.

> *"The good news, if there is any, is that a very nice young*
> *nurse seems to have taken Joey under her wing. She often sits*
> *with him during her time off. A mother can only hope!"*

Will smiles in spite of himself. He just can't picture it. Joey? With a nurse? Ha! Breaking into Will's whimsical woolgathering, the Scot is back at it with his brochure.

"This is interesting. There is a chamber beneath the monument with an altar for each of three faiths, Roman Catholic, Protestant and Jewish. It is decorated with mosaics by the French artist Fernand Leger."

The Scot turns to the veterans to gauge their level of interest and catches only Will's eye from across the way.

"No doubt a peaceful place for reflection and remembrance."

As Will ponders the Scot's words, Sarge looks from the monument to the veterans, then back to the monument, and levels a challenge to his compatriots.

"It's gotta be a hell-of-a view from the top. What do you say we head up?"

Fortunately, the breeze freshens and breathes life and vigor into the old men, lending considerable assistance to Sarge's infectious enthusiasm. Defying their sore backs and creaking limbs, the veterans slowly stand and assemble. When they get underway, only Will lingers behind. This time Jack offers just a questioning look. Will reassures the doctor with what can only be read as steadfastness and resolve.

"I'll meet you up there."

With that, Will trudges off on his own private mission. As he skirts the monument, he finds a stretch of the walkway where the forest has been cleared, affording a view of farmers' fields in the foreground and the Bastogne townscape a couple of miles distant. In the stillness, the packet of letters calls to him again. He seeks and finds one postmarked, April 11th, a turning point in his life.

> *"Dear Will. I am sorry to inform you that my Joey*
> *passed during the night. I wanted you to know as*
> *soon as possible because you were like a big brother*
> *watching over him. He admired and needed you so."*

Will's response is a gentle whisper within.

"I needed him too."

That day in February 1945, when Joey was severely wounded, had been the worst day of Will's life. Then word came of Joey's death in April of that year and blew a hole in his heart. Now, half a century later, he wipes a tear from his eye, stands, and steps back onto the path.

Will soon arrives at a long set of descending stairs and realizes he has located the underground cavity. On his way down he passes several men of all ages standing idly by but does not think much of it. As he nears the bottom of the stairs and his eyes adjust to the darkness of the sheltered space, he sees three separate altars topped by colorful mosaics that depict only women. Of the dozen or so people visiting the altars, all are women.

One places a child's music box on the Catholic altar, while another balances a time-faded portrait of a smiling young soldier in dress uniform on the Protestant altar. And one very elderly woman holds a bouquet of flowers in her hand as she moves in slow motion to lay them on the Jewish altar. Will wonders about the long journey through life she endured to be here at this moment.

"Gee, I never really thought about what it was like for the women."

It is a stunning revelation to think of the wives who saw their husbands off to war and never saw them again, of the daughters who lost their fathers, and of mothers who mourned silently for sons they had suckled at their breasts and rocked to sleep in their arms just scant years before. Will leans heavily against the fieldstone wall that lines the steps down and reflects on his own journey through war and peace, love and loss, pain and joy and sorrow. All along the way, Joey has been a constant companion, a ghost that haunts him like no other.

But mind you, he is a friendly ghost, the big lug nut.

Over the years, from time to time, Will couldn't help laughing at the memory of Joey. But here in Bastogne his recollections are bittersweet, leaning toward bitter. Fortunately, he has the letters from Joey's mother to comfort him. He carefully extracts the last letter he received from her before she passed away and skips to the closing paragraph.

> *"Joey was the last of my kin. When I am gone, you will be the only one left to remember him. I hope the enclosed will help you to do so."*

He tips and gently shakes the packet until a small, shiny object drops into his open hand. It is Joey's lapel angel. At that moment, two women pass him on their way up, and it occurs to him that the objects and mementos left every day at the altars must be gathered, catalogued, and stored in a warehouse. He gets to thinking he would like to make a more permanent addition to the memorial, like what Doctor Prior did with his plaque. He glances around his immediate area, considers the stones in the wall, and makes his selection. Without a second thought he wedges the little angel deep in the gap between two stones.

"I remember you, Joey."

Light a Candle

Up on the monument, the veterans have all made their way to the railing facing Bastogne and are mesmerized by the view. Had they eagles' eyes they would see farmers in their fields, children playing in the playgrounds, shopkeepers happily ringing up their sales, a populace at peace. Perhaps it is historical justice for a town brutalized three times during the century. Of course, there are scars and reminders, but it seems that, in this corner of the world, the good life is lived in harmony with everyone, everything, everywhere. Is this not what American blood was shed for, so that the bells of freedom will ring here and around the world? For those who fought in Bastogne and all who remember them, this place is and will remain, in perpetuity, sacred ground. Sarge breaks the spell.

"Heaven on earth."

Jack happens to glance down to see a Belgian boy fast-walking away from the monument, now and again looking over his shoulder. Well behind, François is pursuing the boy as fast as his paunch can propel him. It brings a smile to Jack's lips.

"Such delightful people."

"And so grateful."

Sarge measures the grand expanse of the monument with a wave of his good arm, to emphasize his point about Belgian thankfulness yet again. Davenport expands on the sentiment as he peers into the distance.

"And tolerant. They don't seem to have an ounce of prejudice. Same was true in '44."

"Too bad that wasn't the case back home, or in the army."

Colleti is a student of history, who knows that black soldiers faced a two-front war, against fascism abroad and racism at home. Back then the army was segregated. Hell, even the blood supply was segregated.

Davenport appreciates the old MP's support.

"Yeah, you're right there. My people served and protected, but they never got respected. Anyhow, Truman got the ball rolling and the army got it together, eventually. It became a place where I felt I could make a difference. So, I stuck with it."

"And made colonel!"

Sarge is the picture of affability, and Davenport can only smile at his comment and nod his head proudly. As all the veterans add affirmations, the goodwill that the colonel feels from these men is soul-warming.

"Anyhow, I'm glad I came to the reunion. This place, these people, you fellas..."

He produces a handkerchief to dab his eyes.

"... it's like medicine."

When they signed up for the reunion, they couldn't have known what it would be like. All have been travelers and seekers on the long path of life, yet each carried unanswered questions with him to Bastogne. Fortunately, their solitary journeys of discovery and remembrance have been fruitful and therapeutic. They found, learned, experienced most if not all of what they sought. However, it is any man's guess whether they would have been near as successful without the camaraderie and support shared by this double handful of veterans. Together they formed a brotherhood, with each man receiving the assurance and support needed to fully commune with his ghosts, to hold close those who are dear, and have a fighting chance against those who are hostile.

Something about witnessing the emotional end of Davenport's quest stirs Sarge to soliloquy.

"It's been a shot in the arm for me too... being here with you guys... but..."

The veterans take notice of a new tone from the genial man.

"... it took me a lot of dead ends and detours to get here."

Murmurs of encouragement all around.

"I tried to put suppressing fire on them, you know what I mean? I drank scotch..."

He nods to the Scot.

"... a lot of scotch!"

Only other veterans of combat can know of Sarge's unnamed "them." They are the darkest memories, the ones that are dug in deep and stubborn as hell. And all too many of the men know about the bottle and the blackout curtain it draws in your life.

While Sarge and several others swap stories about duels with their demons, Jack's sixth sense picks up Will's quiet return at the far end of their formation along the railing. The doctor steps back, observes a bit of healthful glow about the quiet man, and is rewarded with Will's first smile in a dog's age. Jack can only conclude it is a sign of healing. A fragment of a memory flickers back to Jack, and he speaks with what he thinks is his inner voice.

"Light a candle."

Colleti overhears him.

"What's that?"

"Oh... it's just something I was told..."

Jack turns from Colleti to the Screaming Eagles.

"... by one of your doctors, Major Davidson. He simply said, if you find yourself in a dark room, light a candle."

Jack leans against the rail and takes in a peaceful view that is so much at odds with the thoughts he is dredging up.

"I tried like hell to forget. The bomb, the fire... the agony."

Sarge is at his side, as he has been much of the week.

"Painful memories."

"Yeah, very painful, very dark."

No sooner does Jack utter these words, when something scares a large flock of jet-black crows from a tree. Their cacophonic calls of distress to each other offer Jack a brief reprieve, as the birds give voice to solidarity that is impossible to ignore. As Jack watches the crows trace wide circles in the sky, he ponders the circuitous path he has taken.

"I tried to ignore 'em, deny 'em, bury 'em. But they always came back... especially on Christmas Eve."

Somehow, Jack's last comment draws Will back fully into the fold, and he expresses what all the veterans are thinking.

"How unfair is that?"

But, of course, there is no answer. War knows no holiday, clock, or calendar. Nor any human yearnings or aspirations. The fortunes of war are fickle, rarely forgiving, and most often cruel. War swings its scythe indiscriminately, and often cripples with guilt those who survive it.

"I was trained to fix broken bodies, not broken spirits. We've got to heal the invisible wounds too... mine included."

Jack looks around to sees long faces and realizes he has struck a raw nerve.

"Sorry, fellas. Now I've fouled the mood."

Sarge is having none of it and is joined by others in encouraging Jack to continue. Jack obliges them, while brightening considerably.

"Well, but then the children came along. As they got older, they asked me what was the most exciting thing that ever happened to me? It could only be one thing. I was reluctant at first. But if I have learned anything, it is to never turn away an inquisitive child. To my surprise, the more I talked about it, the more I remembered. The more I remembered, the better I felt. Eventually, I even wrote my story down."

"Light a candle."

Jack turns to Davenport, who has apparently internalized Major Davidson's simple words, having lit more than his share of candles over the years. Jack is appreciative.

"That's right. To shed light into my own darkness and heal my wounds, I had to remember."

Jack reaches into his shoulder bag and pulls out a large manila envelope. As the veterans look on with growing interest, he pulls out his handwritten casualty records.

"That's why I brought these along, my documentation of all the men who were in my care during the siege. Not sure why I kept it. I suppose I thought it was a souvenir from the war."

Jack hopes to continue elevating the mood.

"I've got a trunk full of the stuff."

Several chuckle and voice agreement as they picture their own trunks and duffle bags full of memorabilia from the war tucked away in a storeroom or attic.

"I guess I had a notion that I would read out the names when I got here, up on this hill."

He becomes a bit self-conscious when he realizes he is doing all the talking again. Yet no one else steps in to fill the void, save for the crows still circling and complaining above the trees as they contemplate returning to their roosting place.

Jack leafs through his records until he reaches the one with the dark stain. He wonders whose blood it is. Someone near the top of that page perhaps? Jack strains to attach faces to the names.

"It's getting harder and harder to picture any of them, just boys most of them. Though I guess I will always hear the screams of pain. But now... when I do... I try to remember them as more than just men who were horribly wounded, men who were dying..."

Jack falters. The Scot interprets his hesitancy as a plea for assistance.

"Short days ago, they lived, felt dawn, saw sunset glow."

The man from the Highlands has seen the look on Jack's face in pubs all over Scotland, when old men put down their pints and stare into the distance. Jack is grateful for the hand-up.

"Yes, they lived."

"They loved and were loved."

With the Scot step for step with him on the well-worn path of reminiscence, Jack feels reinforced. Nevertheless, he slides the casualty records into the envelope and back into his shoulder bag.

"In hindsight, it seems like such a simple thing. Remember."

Jack has come a long way. Now that the finish line is in reach, his affability is infectious.

"It's impossible to forget, so remember! I highly recommend it. I find it to be quite restorative, almost energizing."

Davenport agrees.

"Like medicine."

Sarge, who is happily back to his old self, is quick with a quip.

"Can I get it over the counter?"

Unbeknown to Jack, Will has made his way up close to his side. Will's own act of remembering Joey has so lightened his own load that he feels that he has sympathy to spare and can help to heal the healer.

"Still, it's too bad it all comes back to you on Christmas Eve."

"Not at all. It's a gift."

Will readies a response while the crows settle and a hush falls over the men, the monument, and the fields, forests, and hills of the Ardennes.

"I'd like to hear the names."

A Field of Poppies

Wild poppies thrive across a wide swath of Central Europe. Their ubiquity calls to mind the thousands upon thousands of fallen soldiers in World War I who had the fatal misfortune of being ordered to charge into machine gun fire, cannonade, and poison gas. The red petals evoke the blood shed by so many young men as they lay dying in fields of battle far from home, leading a world in mourning to conclude that the blossoms are nature's method of remembrance.

Lieutenant Colonel John McCrae's poem continues:

> *"Take up our quarrel with the foe:*
> *To you from failing hands we throw*
> *The torch; be yours to hold it high.*
> *If ye break faith with us who die*
> *We shall not sleep, though poppies grow*
> *In Flanders fields."*

As the last of the men and women who served during World War II slip ever so gently away, each to his or her Flanders field, there is only one thing we must do. Remember. We cannot break the faith, but, as time passes, it is ever more difficult. Each generation has its heroes and villains, making history a crowded place. Soon, only dusty books will keep alive the memory of those who served, except for those who inherit a special obligation. And so, another dark-eyed girl lays poppy wreaths on graves of American soldiers in a faraway place.

And she sings.

Afterword

Doctor John T. "Jack" Prior was a friend and mentor who gave me a copy of his World War II memoir and accepted my offer to produce a documentary film of him revisiting Bastogne. Sadly, he passed away before we got the project off the ground. I wrote a screenplay instead, which I eventually converted to this work of narrative nonfiction, wherein I add depth and dialogue to a story of real people and events.

His daughter, Anne Prior Stringer, and his nephew, Reverend Richard Prior, read my manuscript and provided encouragement and support. While visiting with Augusta Chiwy in Belgium in 2015, Anne gave Ms. Chiwy a letter from me and secured her blessing for my effort, finding her "very clear about being happy that her story was being told." Anne also gave her a photograph of Doctor Prior posing with my three sons, to which Ms. Chiwy responded, fifty years on from when she first said it, "he has kind eyes."

Glenn H. Ivers

www.ingramcontent.com/pod-product-compliance
Lightning Source LLC
Chambersburg PA
CBHW012204030726

47494CB00022B/2248

* 9 7 8 1 9 5 0 4 4 4 3 9 7 *